BRIDES of LEHIGH CANAL

Trilogy

WANDA E. BRUNSTETTER

BRIDES of LEHIGH CANAL

❦

Trilogy

BARBOUR
PUBLISHING

For more information about Wanda E. Brunstetter, please access the author's
website at the following Internet address: www.wandabrunstetter.com

Published by Barbour Publishing, Inc., P.O. Box 719, Uhrichsville, Ohio
44683, www.barbourbooks.com

*Our mission is to publish and distribute inspirational products offering
exceptional value and biblical encouragement to the masses.*

 Member of the
Evangelical Christian
Publishers Association

Printed in the United States of America.

Kelly's
CHANCE

BRIDES *of* LEHIGH CANAL

BOOK ONE

DEDICATION/ACKNOWLEDGMENTS

To my husband, Richard,
born and raised in Easton, Pennsylvania, near the Lehigh Canal.
Thanks for your love, support, and research help.

To Char and Mim,
my brother-in-law and sister-in-law.
Thanks for your warm hospitality as we researched this book.

Chapter 1

Lehigh Valley, Pennsylvania—Spring 1891

*K*elly McGregor trudged wearily along the towpath, kicking up a cloud of dust with the tips of her worn work boots. A size too small and pinching her toes, they were still preferable to walking barefoot. Besides the fact that the path was dirty, water moccasins from the canal sometimes slithered across the trail. Kelly had been bitten once when she was twelve years old. She shuddered at the memory... Papa cutting her foot with a knife, then sucking the venom out. Mama following that up with a poultice of comfrey leaves to take the swelling down, then giving Kelly some willow bark tea for the pain. Ever since that day, Kelly had worn boots while she worked, and even though she could swim quite well, she rarely did so anymore.

As Kelly continued her walk, she glanced over her shoulder and smiled. Sure enough, Herman and Hector were dutifully following, and the rope connected to their harnesses still held taut.

"Good boys," she called to the mules. "Keep on comin'."

Kelly knew most mule drivers walked behind their animals in order to keep them going, but Papa's mules were usually dependable and didn't need much prodding. Herman, the lead mule, was especially obedient and docile. So Kelly walked in front, or sometimes alongside the team, and they followed with rarely a problem.

Herman and Hector had been pulling Papa's canal boat since Kelly was eight years old, and she'd been leading them for the last nine years. Six days a week, nine months of the year, sometimes eighteen hours a day, they trudged up and down the towpath that ran alongside the Lehigh Navigation System. The waterway, which included the Lehigh Canal and parts of the Lehigh River, was owned by a Quaker named Josiah White. Due to his religious views, he would not allow anyone working for him to labor on the Sabbath. That was fine with Kelly. She needed at least one day of rest.

"If it weren't for the boatmen's children, the canal wouldn't run a day," she mumbled. "Little ones who can't wait to grow up so they can make their own way."

Until two years ago, Kelly's older sister, Sarah, had helped with the mules. Then she ran off with Sam Turner, one of the lock tender's boys who lived along their route. Sarah and Sam had been making eyes at each other for some time, and one day shortly after Sarah's eighteenth birthday, they ran away together. Several weeks later, Sarah sent the family a letter saying she and Sam were married and living in Phillipsburg, New Jersey. Sam had gotten a job at Warren Soapstone, and Sarah was still looking for work. Kelly and her folks hadn't seen or heard a word from the couple since. Such a shame! She sure did miss that sister of hers.

Kelly moaned as she glanced down at her long, gray cotton skirt, covered with a thick layer of dust. She supposed the sifting dirt was preferable to globs of gritty, slippery mud, which she often encountered in early spring. "Long skirts are such a bother. Sure wish Mama would allow me to wear pants like all the mule boys do."

In the past when the wind was blowing real hard, Kelly's skirt billowed, and she hated that. She'd solved the problem by sewing several small stones into the hemline, weighing her skirt down so the wind couldn't lift it anymore.

Kelly looked over her shoulder again, past the mules. Her gaze came to rest on her father's flat-roofed, nearly square, wooden boat. They were hauling another load of dark, dirty anthracite coal from the town of Mauch Chunk, the pickup spot, on down to Easton, where it would be delivered.

Kelly's thoughts returned to her sister, and a knot rose in her throat. She missed Sarah for more than just her help. Sometimes when they'd walked the mules together, Kelly and Sarah had shared their deepest desires and secret thoughts. Sarah admitted how much she hated life on the canal. She'd made it clear that she would do about anything to get away from Papa and his harsh, stingy ways.

Kelly groaned inwardly. She understood why Sarah had taken off and was sure her older sister had married Sam just so she could get away from the mundane, difficult life on the Lehigh Navigation System. It didn't help any that Kelly and Sarah had been forced to work as mule drivers without earning one penny

9

of their own. Some mule drivers earned as much as a dollar per day, but not Kelly and her sister. All the money they should have made went straight into Papa's pocket, even if Mama and the girls had done more than their share of the work.

In all fairness, Kelly had to admit that, even though he yelled a lot, Papa did take pretty good care of them. He wasn't like some of the canal boatmen, who drank and gambled whenever they had the chance, wasting away their earnings before the month was half over.

Kelly was nearing her eighteenth birthday, and even though she was forced to work without pay, nothing on earth would make her marry someone simply so she could get away. The idea of marriage was like vinegar in her mouth. From what she'd seen in her own folks' lives, getting hitched wasn't so great, anyway. All Mama ever did was work, and all Papa did was take charge of the boat and yell at his family.

Tears burned in Kelly's eyes, but she held them in check. "Sure wish I could make enough money to support myself. And I don't give a hoot nor a holler 'bout findin' no man to call husband, neither."

Kelly lifted her chin and began to sing softly, "Hunks-a-go pudding and pieces of pie; my mother gave me when I was knee-high. . . . And if you don't believe it, just drop in and see—the hunks-a-go pudding my mother gave me."

The tension in Kelly's neck muscles eased as she began to relax. Singing the silly canaler's tune always made her feel a bit better—especially when she was getting hungry and could have eaten at least three helpings of Mama's hunks-a-go pudding. The fried batter, made with eggs, milk, and flour, went right well with a slab of roast beef. Just thinking about how good it tasted made Kelly's mouth water.

Mama would serve supper when they stopped for the night, but that wouldn't be 'til sundown, several hours from now. When Papa hollered, "Hold up there, girl!" and secured the boat to a tree or near one of the locks, Kelly would have to care for the mules. They always needed to be curried and cleaned, in particular around Herman and Hector's collars where their sweaty hair often came loose. Kelly never took any chances with the mules, for she didn't want either of them to get sores or infections that needed to be treated with medicine.

After the grooming was finished each night, Kelly fed the animals and bedded them down in fresh straw spread along the floor in one of the lock stables or in their special compartment on the boat. Only when all that was done could Kelly wash up and sit down to Mama's hot meal of salt pork and beans or potato and onion soup. Roast beef and hunks-a-go pudding were reserved for a special Sunday dinner when there was more time for cooking.

After supper when all the dishes had been washed, dried, and put away, Kelly read, drew, and sometimes played a game. Mama and Papa amused themselves with an occasional game of checkers, and sometimes they lined up a row of dominoes and competed to see who could acquire the most points. That was fine with Kelly. She much preferred to retire to her bunk in the deck below and draw by candlelight until her eyes became too heavy to focus. Most often she'd sketch something she'd seen along the canal, but many times her charcoal pictures were of things she'd never seen before. Things she'd read about and could only dream of seeing.

On days like today, when Kelly was dog-eared tired and covered from head to toe with dust, she wished for a couple of strong brothers to take her place as mule driver. It was unfortunate for both Kelly and her folks, but Mama wasn't capable of having more children. She'd prayed for it; Kelly had heard her do so many times. The good Lord must have thought two daughters were all Amos and Dorrie McGregor needed. God must have decided Kelly could do the work of two sons. Maybe the Lord believed she should learn to be content with being poor, too.

Contentment. Kelly didn't think she could ever manage to achieve that. Not until she had money in her pockets. She couldn't help but wonder if God cared about her needs at all.

Herman nuzzled the back of Kelly's neck, interrupting her musings and nearly knocking her wide-brimmed straw hat to the ground. She shivered and giggled. "What do ya want, ol' boy? You think I have some carrots for you today? Is that what you're thinkin'?"

The mule answered with a loud bray, and Hector followed suit.

"All right, you two," Kelly said, reaching into her roomy apron pocket. "I'll give ya both a carrot, but you must show your appreciation by pullin' real good for a few more hours." She shook her finger. "And I want ya to do it without one word of complaint."

Another nuzzle with his wet nose, and Kelly knew Herman had agreed to her terms. Now she needed confirmation from Hector.

Mike Cooper didn't have much use for some of the new fangled things he was being encouraged to sell in his general store, but this pure white soap that actually floated might be a real good seller—especially to the boatmen, who seemed to have a way of losing bars of soap over the side of their vessels. If Mike offered them a product for cleaning that could easily be seen and would bob like a cork instead of sinking to the bottom of the murky canal, he could have a bestseller that would keep his customers coming back and placing orders for "the incredible soap that floats."

Becoming a successful businessman might help him pursue his goal of finding a suitable wife. Ever since Pa had died, leaving him to run the store by himself, Mike had felt a terrible ache in his heart. Ma had gone to heaven a few years before Pa, and his two brothers, Alvin and John, had relocated a short time later, planning to start a fishing business off the coast of New Jersey. That left Mike to keep the store going, but it also left him alone, wishing for a helpmate and a brood of children. Mike prayed for this every day. He felt he was perfectly within God's will to make such a request. After all, in the book of Genesis, God said it wasn't good for a man to be alone, so He created Eve to be a helper and to keep Adam company. At twenty-four years old, Mike thought it was past time he settled down with a mate.

Mike's biggest concern was the fact that there weren't too many unattached ladies living along the canal. Most of the women who shopped at his store were either married or adolescent girls. One young woman—Sarah McGregor—was the exception, but word had it she'd up and run off with the son of a lock tender from up the canal a ways. Sarah had a younger sister, but the last time Mike saw Kelly, she was only a freckle-faced kid in pigtails.

Then there was Betsy Nelson, daughter of the minister who lived in nearby Walnutport and regularly traveled along the canal in hopes of winning folks to the Lord. Betsy wasn't beautiful, but she wasn't as ugly as the muddy waters in Lehigh Canal, either. Of course, Mike wasn't nearly as concerned about a woman's looks as he was with her temperament. Betsy should have been sweet as apple pie, her being a pastor's daughter and all, but she could cut a body right in two with that sharp tongue of hers. Why, he'd never forget the day Betsy raked old Ross Spivey up one side and down the other for spitting out a wad of tobacco in the middle of one of her daddy's sermons. By the time she'd finished with Ross, the poor man was down on his knees, begging forgiveness for being so rude.

Mike grabbed a broom from the storage closet, shook his head, and muttered, "A fellow would have to be hard of hearing or just plain dumb-witted to put up with the likes of Miss Betsy Nelson. It's no wonder she's not married yet."

He pushed the straw broom across the wooden floor, visualizing with each stroke a beautiful, sweet-spirited woman who'd be more than happy to become his wife. After a few seconds, Mike shook his head and murmured, "I'll have to wait, that's all. Wait and keep on praying."

Mike quoted Genesis 2:18, a Bible verse that had become

one of his favorites since he'd decided he wanted a wife: " 'And the Lord God said, It is not good that the man should be alone; I will make him an help meet for him.'

"I know the perfect woman is out there somewhere, Lord," he whispered. "All I need is for You to send her my way, and I can take it from there."

Chapter 2

Kelly awoke feeling tired and out of sorts. She'd stayed up late the night before, working on another charcoal drawing of an ocean scene with lots of fishing boats on the water. Not that Kelly had ever seen the ocean. Her only experience with water involved the Lehigh, Morris, and Delaware rivers and canals. She'd only seen the ocean in her mind from stories she'd read in books or from the tales of those who had personally been to the coast.

If she could ever figure out a way to earn enough money of her own, Kelly might like to take a trip to the shore. Maybe she would open an art gallery there, to show and sell some of her work. She had seen such a place in the town of Easton, although Papa would never let her go inside. Kelly wondered if her drawings were good enough to sell. If only she could afford to buy a store-bought tablet, along with some oil paints, watercolors, or sticks of charcoal. She was getting tired of making her own pieces of charcoal, using hunks left over in the cooking stove or from campfires along the canal. Kelly let the chunks cool and then whittled them down to the proper size. It wasn't what she would have liked, but at least it allowed her to draw.

Kelly swung her legs over the edge of the bunk and stretched her aching limbs. If a young woman of seventeen could hurt this much from long hours of walking and caring for mules, she could only imagine how older folks must feel. Papa worked plenty hard steering the boat and helping load and unload the coal they hauled, which might account for his crabby attitude. Mama labored from sunup to sunset as well. Besides cooking and cleaning, she always had laundry and mending to do. At times, Mama even steered the boat while Papa rested or took care of chores only he could do. Kelly's mother also helped by watching up ahead and letting Papa know where to direct the boat.

Stifling a yawn, Kelly reached for a plain brown skirt and white, long-sleeved blouse lying on a straight-backed chair near the bed. She glanced around the small cabin and studied her meager furnishings. The room wasn't much bigger than a storage closet, and it was several steps below the main deck. Her only pieces of furniture were the bunk, a small desk, a chair, and the trunk she kept at the foot of her bed.

I wonder what it would be like to have a roomy bedroom in a real house, Kelly mused. The canal boat had been her primary home as far back as she could remember. The only time they lived elsewhere was in the winter, when the canal was drained due to freezing temperatures and couldn't be navigated. Then Kelly's dad worked at one of the factories in Easton. Leaving the few pieces of furniture they owned on their boat, the McGregor family settled into Flannigan's Boardinghouse until the spring thaw came and Papa could resume work on the canal. During the winter months, Kelly and her sister had gone to school when they were younger, but the rest of the year, Mama taught them reading and sums whenever they had a free moment.

Kelly's nose twitched and her stomach rumbled as the distinctive aroma of cooked oatmeal and cinnamon wafted down the stairs, calling her to breakfast. A new day was about to begin, and she would need a hearty meal to help get started.

"We'll be stoppin' by Cooper's General Store this afternoon 'cause we need some supplies," Papa announced when Kelly arrived at the breakfast table. He glanced over at Mama, then at Kelly, his green eyes looking ever so serious. "Don't know when we'll take time out for another supply stop, so if either of you needs anything, you'd better plan on gettin' it today." He slid his fingers across his auburn, handlebar mustache.

"I could use a few more bars of that newfangled soap I bought last time we came through," Mama spoke up. "It's a wonder to me the way that stuff floats!"

Kelly smiled at her mother's enthusiasm over something as simple as a bar of white soap that floated. *I guess things like that are important to a woman with a family. Mama doesn't have much else to get excited about.*

Kelly ate a spoonful of oatmeal as she studied her mother, a large-boned woman of Italian descent. She had dark brown hair like Kelly's; only Mama didn't wear hers hanging down. She pulled it up into a tight bun at the back of her head. Mama's eyes, the color of chestnuts, were her best feature.

Mama could be real pretty if she was able to have nice, new clothes and keep herself fixed up. Instead, she's growing old before her time—slavin' over a hot stove and scrubbin' clothes in canal water, with only a washboard and a bar of soap that bobs like a cork. Poor Mama!

Papa's chair scraped across the wooden planks as he pulled his wiry frame away from the table. "It's time to get rollin'." He nodded toward Kelly. "Better get them mules ready, girl."

Kelly finished the rest of her breakfast and jumped up. When Papa said it was time to roll, he meant business. For that matter, when Papa said anything at all, she knew she'd better listen.

At noon, the McGregors tied their boat to a tree not far from the town of Walnutport and stopped for lunch. Normally they would have eaten a quick bite, then started back up the canal, but today they were heading to Cooper's General Store. After a bowl of vegetable soup and some of Mama's sweet cornbread, they would shop for needed supplies and more food staples.

Kelly welcomed the stop not only because she was hungry, but also because Papa had promised to buy her a new pair of boots. She'd been wearing the same ones for more than a year, and they were much too tight. Besides, the laces were missing, and the soles were worn nearly clear through. Kelly had thought by the time she turned sixteen her feet would have quit growing. But here she was only ten months from her eighteenth birthday, and her long toes were still stretching the boots she wore. At this rate, she feared she'd be wearing a size 9 when her feet finally stopped growing.

Kelly ate hurriedly, anxious to head over to the general store. She hadn't been inside Cooper's in well over a year because she usually chose to wait outside while her folks did the shopping. Today, Kelly planned to check the mules and offer them a bit of feed, then hurry into the store. If she found new boots in short order, there might be enough time to sit on a log and draw awhile. She always found interesting things along the canal— other boats, people fishing, and plenty of waterfowl.

Too bad I can't buy some oil paints or a set of watercolors, Kelly thought as she hooked the mules to a post and began to check them for harness sores, fly bites, or hornet stings. *Guess I should be happy Papa has agreed to buy me new boots, but I'd sure like to have somethin' just for fun once in a while.*

Kelly scratched Hector behind his ear. "If I ever make any money of my own, I might just buy you a big, juicy apple." She patted Herman's neck. "You, too, old boy."

Mike whistled a hymn as he dusted off the candy counter, always a favorite with the children who stopped by. He was running low on horehound drops but still had plenty of licorice, lemon drops, and taffy chews. He knew he'd have to order more of everything soon, since summer was not far off and a lot more little ones would be coming by in hopes of finding something to satisfy their sweet tooth.

Many boats were being pulled up the Lehigh Navigation

System already, and it was still early spring. Mike figured by this time next month his store would have even more customers. Last winter, when he'd had plenty of time on his hands, Mike had decided to order some Bibles to either sell or give away. If someone showed an interest and didn't have the money to buy one, he'd gladly offer it to them for free. Anything to see that folks learned about Jesus. Too many of the boatmen were uneducated in spiritual matters, and Mike wanted to do his part to teach them God's ways.

Mike leaned on the glass counter and let his mind wander back to when he was a boy of ten and had first heard about the Lord. Grandma Cooper, a proper Englishwoman, had told him about Jesus. Mike's family had lived with her and Grandpa for several years when Mike's pa was helping out on the farm in upstate New York, where Mike had been born. Ellis Cooper had no mind to stay on the farm, though, and as soon as he had enough money, he moved his wife and three sons to Pennsylvania, where he'd opened the general store along the Lehigh Canal.

Mike's father didn't hold much to religious things. He used to say the Bible was a bunch of stories made up to help folks get through life with some measure of hope.

"There's hope, all right," Mike whispered as he brought his mind back to the present. "And thanks to Grandma's teachings, I'd like to help prove that hope never has to die."

When he heard a familiar creak, Mike glanced at the front door. Enough daydreaming and reflecting on the past. He had customers to satisfy.

As he moved toward the front of the store, Mike's heart

slammed into his chest. Coming through the doorway was the most beautiful young woman he'd ever laid eyes on. *Don't reckon I've seen her before. She must be new. . .just passing through. Maybe she's a passenger on one of the packet boats that hauls tourists. Maybe. . .*

Mike blinked a couple of times. He recognized the man and woman entering the store behind the young woman: Amos and Dorrie McGregor. It wasn't until Amos called her by name that Mike realized the beauty was none other than the McGregors' younger daughter, Kelly.

Mike shook his head. It couldn't be. Kelly had pigtails, freckles, and was all arms and legs. This stunning creature had long brown hair that reached clear down to her waist, and from where he stood, not one freckle was visible on her lovely face. She looked his way, and he gasped at the intensity of her dark brown eyes. *A man could lose himself in those eyes. A man could—*

"Howdy, Mike Cooper," Amos said, extending his hand. "How's business these days?"

Mike forced himself to breathe, and with even more resolve, he kept his focus on Amos and not the man's appealing daughter. "Business is fine, sir." He shook the man's hand. "How are you and the family doing?"

Amos shrugged. "Fair to middlin'. I'd be a sight better if I hadn't hit one of the locks and put a hole in my boat the first week back to work." He gave his handlebar mustache a tug. "In order to get my repairs done, I had to use most of what I made this winter workin' at a shoe factory in Easton."

"Sorry to hear that," Mike said sincerely. He glanced back at Kelly, offering her what he hoped was a friendly smile. "Can this be the same Kelly McGregor who used to come runnin' in here, begging her pa to buy a few lemon drops?"

Kelly's face turned slightly pink as she nodded. "Guess I've grown a bit since you last saw me."

"I'll say!" Mike felt a trickle of sweat roll down his forehead, and he quickly pulled a handkerchief out of his pant's pocket and wiped it away. Kelly McGregor was certainly no child. She was a desirable woman, even if she did have a few layers of dirt on her cotton skirt and wore a tattered straw hat and a pair of boots that looked like they were ready for burial. *Could she be the one I've been waiting for, Lord?*

Mike cleared his throat. "So what can I help you good folks with today?"

Amos nudged his wife. "Now don't be shy, Dorrie. Tell the man what you're needin'. I'll just poke around the store and see what I can find, while you and Kelly stock up on food items and the like."

Kelly cast her father a pleading look. "I'm still gettin' new boots, right, Papa?"

Her dad nodded. "Yeah, sure. See if Mike has somethin' that'll fit your big feet."

Mike felt sorry for Kelly, whose face was now red as a tomato. She shifted from one foot to the other and never once did she look Mike in the eye.

"I got a new shipment of boots in not long ago," he said quickly, hoping to help her feel a bit more at ease. "They're right over there." He pointed to a shelf across the room. "Would you like me to see if I have any your size?"

Dorrie McGregor spoke up for the first time. "Why don't

you help my husband find what he's needin'? Me and Kelly can manage fine on our own."

Mike shrugged. "Whatever you think best." He offered Kelly the briefest of smiles and then headed across the room to help her pa.

Kelly didn't know why, but she felt as jittery as one of the mules when they were being forced to walk through standing water. Was it her imagination, or was Mike Cooper staring at her? Ever since they'd entered the store, he'd seemed to be watching her, and now, while she stooped down on the floor trying on a pair of size 9 boots, the man was actually gawking.

Maybe he's never seen a woman with such big feet. Probably thinks I should have been born a boy. Kelly swallowed hard and forced the threatening tears to stay put. *Truth be told, Papa probably wishes I was a boy.* Most boys were able to work longer and harder than she could. And a boy wasn't as apt to run off with the first person who offered him freedom from canal work, the way Sarah had.

Kelly glanced around the room, feeling an urgency to escape. She stood on shaky legs and forced herself to march around the store a few times in order to see if the boots were going to work out okay. When she was sure they were acceptable, she pulled the price tag off the laces and handed it to Mama. "If ya don't mind, I'd like to wait outside. It's kinda stuffy in here, and since it's such a nice day, maybe I can get in a bit of sketchin' while you and Papa finish your shopping."

Mama nodded, and Kelly scooted quickly out the front door. The sooner she got away from Mike Cooper and those funny looks he kept giving her, the better it would be!

Chapter 3

Kelly's heart was pounding like a hammer as she exited the store, but it nearly stopped beating altogether when Mike Cooper opened the door behind her and called, "Hey, Kelly, don't you want a bag of lemon drops?"

She skidded to a stop on the bottom step, heat flooding her face. She turned slowly to face him. *Why does he have to be so handsome?* Mike's medium-brown hair, parted on the side and cut just below his ears, curled around his neck like kitten fur. His neatly trimmed mustache jiggled up and down as though he might be hiding a grin. The man's hazel eyes seemed to bore right through her, and Kelly was forced to swallow several times before she could answer his question.

"I. . .uh. . .don't have money to spend on candy just now. New boots are more important than satisfyin' my sweet tooth." She turned away, withdrawing her homemade tablet and a piece of charcoal from the extra-large pocket of her apron.

Kelly was almost to the boat when she felt Mike's hand touch her shoulder. "Hold up there. What's your hurry?" His voice was deep, yet mellow and kind of soothing. Kelly thought she could find pleasure in listening to him talk awhile—if she had a mind to.

"I was plannin' to do a bit of drawing." She stared at the ground, her fingers kneading the folds in her skirt.

Mike moved so he was standing beside her. "You're an artist?"

She felt her face flush even more. "I like to draw, but that don't make me an artist."

"It does if you're any good. Can you draw something for me right now?"

She shrugged. "I suppose I could, but don't ya have customers to wait on?"

Mike chuckled. "You've got me there. How about if you draw something while I see what your folks might need? When they're done, I'll come back outside, and you can show me what you've made. How's that sound?"

It sounded fair enough. There was only one problem. Kelly was feeling so flustered, she wasn't sure she could write her own name, much less draw any kind of picture worthy to be shown.

"Guess I can try," she mumbled.

Unexpectedly, he reached out and patted her arm, and she felt a warm tingle shoot all the way up to her neck. Except for Papa's infrequent hugs, no man had ever touched her before. It felt kind of nice, in a funny sort of way. *Could this be why Sarah ran off with Sam Turner? Did Sam look at my sister in a manner that made her mouth go dry and her hands feel all sweaty? If that's* what happened to Sarah, then Kelly knew she had better run as far away from Mike Cooper as she possibly could, for he sure enough was making her feel giddy. She couldn't have that.

She took a few steps back, hoping the distance between them might get her thinking straight again. "See you later," she mumbled.

"Sure thing!" he called as he headed back to the store.

Kelly drew in a deep breath and flopped down on a nearby log. The few minutes she'd spent alone with Mike had rattled her so much she wondered if she still knew how to draw.

In all the times they'd stopped by Cooper's General Store, never once had Mike looked at her the way he had today—like she was someone special, maybe even pretty. *Of course,* she reminded herself, *I usually wait outside, so he hasn't seen me in a while.* The time it took for her folks to shop was a good chance for Kelly to sketch, feed and water the mules, or simply rest her weary bones.

Forcing her thoughts off the handsome storekeeper, Kelly focused her attention on a pair of mallard ducks floating in the canal. The whisper of the wind sang softly as it played with the ends of Kelly's hair. A fat bullfrog posed on the bank nearby. It seemed to be studying a dragonfly hovering above the water. The peaceful scene made Kelly feel one with her surroundings. In no time, she'd filled several pages of her simple drawing pad.

Kelly was pulled from her reverie when Papa and Mama walked up, each carrying a wooden box. She rolled up her artwork and slipped it, along with the hunk of charcoal, inside her pocket. Then she wiped her messy hands on her dusty skirt and jumped to her feet. "Need some help?"

"I could probably use another pair of hands puttin' stuff away in the kitchen," Mama replied.

"Will we be leavin' soon?" Kelly asked, glancing at Cooper's General Store and wondering if Mike would come back to see her drawings as he'd promised.

"Soon as we get everything loaded," Papa mumbled. "Sure would help if we had a few more hands. Got things done a whole lot quicker when Sarah was here."

Kelly watched her dad climb on board his boat. He'd been traveling the canal ever since he was a small boy. Except for winter when he worked in town, running the boat was Papa's whole life. Though he had a fiery Irish temper, once in a while she caught him whistling, singing some silly tune, or blowing on his mouth harp. Kelly figured he must really enjoy his life on the canal. Too bad he was so cheap and wouldn't hire another person to help out. Most of the canalers had a hired hand to steer the boat while the captain stood at the front and shouted directions.

I wish God had blessed Papa and Mama with a whole passel of boys. Sarah's gone, and I'm hoping to leave someday. Then what will Papa do? Kelly shrugged. *Guess he'll have to break down and hire a mule driver, 'cause Mama sure can't do everything she does now and drive the mules, too.*

As Kelly followed her mother into the cabin, she set her thoughts aside. They had a long day ahead of them.

Mike hoisted a box to his shoulders and started out the door. He had offered to help Amos McGregor haul his supplies on board the boat. It was the least he could do, considering that Amos had no boys to help. Besides, it would give him a good excuse to talk to Kelly again and see what she'd drawn.

Mike met Amos as the older man was stepping off the boat. "Didn't realize you'd be bringing a box clean out here," Amos commented, tipping his head and offering Mike something akin to a smile.

"I said I'd help, and I thought it would save you a few steps." Mike nodded toward the boat. "Where shall I put this one?"

Amos extended his arms. "Just give it to me."

Taken aback by the man's abruptness, Mike shrugged and handed over the box. Amos turned, mumbled his thanks, and stepped onto the boat.

"Is Kelly on board?" Mike called, surprising himself at his sudden boldness. "I'd like to speak with her a moment."

Kelly's dad whirled around. "What business would ya have with my daughter?"

"She was planning to show me some of her artwork."

Amos shook his head. "Her and them stupid drawings! She's a hard enough worker when it comes to drivin' the mules, but for the life of me, I can't see why she wastes any time scratchin' away on a piece of paper with a stick of dirty, black charcoal."

"We all need an escape from our work, Mr. McGregor," Mike asserted. "Some read, fish, or hunt. Others, like me, choose to whittle." He smiled. "Some, such as your daughter, enjoy drawing."

"Humph! Makes no sense a'tall!" Amos spun around. "I'll tell Kelly you're out here waitin'. Don't take up too much of her time, though. We're about ready to shove off."

Mike smiled to himself. Maybe Amos wasn't such a tough fellow, after all. He could have said Kelly wasn't receiving any visitors. Or he could have told Mike to take a leap into the canal.

A few minutes later, Kelly showed up. She looked kind of flustered, and he hoped it wasn't on account of him. It could be that her pa had given her a lecture about wasting time sketching. Or maybe he'd made it clear he wanted no one calling on the only daughter he had left. Amos might be afraid his younger child would run off with some fellow the way his older daughter had.

He needn't worry. While I'm clearly attracted to Kelly McGregor, I don't think she's given me more than a second thought today.

Kelly's legs shook as she lifted one foot over the side of the boat and stepped onto dry ground. She could hardly believe Mike Cooper had really come looking for her. Papa was none too happy about it and had told her she wasn't to take much time talking to the young owner of the general store. Kelly figured it was probably because Papa was anxious to be on his way, but from the way her father had said Mike's name, she had to wonder if there might be more to his reason for telling her to hurry. Maybe Papa thought she had eyes for Mike Cooper. Maybe he was afraid she would run off and get married. Well, he needn't worry about that happening!

Mike smiled as Kelly moved toward him. "Did you bring your drawings?"

She averted her gaze. "I only have a few with me, and they're done up on scraps of paper sack so they're probably not so good." She blinked a couple of times. "I got some free newsprint from the *Sunday Call* while we were livin' in Easton, and those pictures have a white background. They're on the boat and might be some better."

"Why not let me be the judge of how good your pictures are? Can I take a peek at what you've got with you?"

Kelly reached inside her ample apron pocket and retrieved the tablet she'd put together from cut-up pieces of paper sack the size of her Bible. She handed it to Mike and waited for his response.

He studied the drawings, flipping back and forth through the pages and murmuring an occasional "ah. . .so. . .hmm. . ."

She shifted her weight from one foot to the other, wondering what he thought. Did Mike like the sketches? Was he surprised to see her crude tablet? The papers were held in place by strings she'd pushed through with one of Mama's darning needles. Then she'd tied the strings in a knot to hold everything in place. Did Mike's opinion of her artwork and tablet matter? After all, he was nothing to her—just a man who ran a general store along the Lehigh Navigation System.

"These are very good," Mike said. "I especially like the one of the bullfrog ready to pounce on the green dragonfly." He chuckled. "Who won, anyway?"

Kelly blinked. "What?"

"Did the bullfrog get his lunch, or did the dragonfly lure the old toad into the water, then flit away before the croaker knew what happened?"

She grinned. "The dragonfly won."

"That's what I expected."

Kelly pressed a hand to her chest, hoping to still a heart that was beating much too fast. If only Papa or Mama would call her back to the boat. As much as she was enjoying this little chat with Mike, she felt jittery and unsure of herself.

"Have you ever sold any of your work?" Mike asked.

She shook her head. "I doubt anyone would buy a plain old charcoal drawing."

He touched her arm. "There's nothing plain about these, Kelly. I have an inkling some of the folks who travel our canal or live in nearby communities might be willing to pay a fair price for one of your pictures."

Her face heated with embarrassment. "You. . .you really think so?"

He nodded. "The other day, a packet boat came through, transporting a group of people up to Allentown. Two of the men were authors, and they seemed real interested in the landscape and natural beauty growing along our canal."

Kelly sucked in her lower lip as she thought about the prospect. This might be the chance she'd been hoping for. If she could make some money selling a few of her charcoal drawings, maybe she'd have enough to purchase a store-bought drawing table, a good set of watercolors, or perchance some oil paints. Then she could do up some *real* pictures, and if she could sell those. . .

"How about I take two or three of these sketches and see if I can sell them in my store?" Mike asked. "I would keep ten percent and give you the rest. How's that sound?"

Ten percent of the profits for him? Had she heard Mike right? That meant she'd get ninety percent. The offer was more than generous, and it seemed too good to be true.

"Sounds fair, but since I've never sold anything before, I don't know what price to put on the drawings," Kelly said.

"Why not leave that up to me?" Mike winked at her, and she felt like his gentle gaze had caught and held her in a trap. "I've been selling things for several years now, so I think I can figure out a fair price," he said with the voice of assurance.

She nodded. "All right, we have us a deal, but since these pictures aren't really my best, I'll have to go back on the boat and get ya three other pictures."

"That's fine," Mike said as he handed her the drawings.

"The next time we come by your store, I'll ask Papa to stop; then I can check and see if you've sold anything."

Mike reached out his hand. "Partners?"

They shook on it. "Partners."

Chapter 4

Shaking hands with Mike Cooper had almost been Kelly's undoing. When Mike released her hand, she was trembling and had to clench her fists at her sides in order to keep him from seeing how much his touch affected her.

Mike opened his mouth as if to say something, but he was cut off by a woman's shrill voice.

"Yoo-hoo! Mr. Cooper, I need you!"

Kelly and Mike both turned. Betsy Nelson, the local preacher's daughter, was heading their way, her long, green skirt swishing this way and that.

Kelly cringed, remembering how overbearing Betsy could be. She didn't simply share the Good News, the way Reverend Nelson did. No, Betsy tried to cram it down folks' throats by insisting they come to Sunday school at the little church in Walnutport, where her father served as pastor.

One time, when Kelly was about seven years old, Betsy had

actually told Kelly and her sister, Sarah, that they were going to the devil if they didn't come to Sunday school and learn about Jesus. Papa overheard the conversation and blew up, telling sixteen-year-old Betsy what he thought of her pushy ways. He'd sent her home in tears and told Kelly and Sarah there was no need for either of them to go to church. He said he'd gotten along fine all these years without God, so he didn't think his daughters needed religion.

Mama thought otherwise, and while the girls were young, she often read them a Bible story before going to bed. When Kelly turned twelve, Mama gave her an old Bible that had belonged to Grandma Minnotti, who'd died and gone to heaven. It was during the reading of the Bible story about Jesus' death on the cross that Kelly had confessed her sins in the quiet of her room one night. She'd felt a sense of hope, realizing Jesus was her personal Savior and would walk with her wherever she went—even up and down the dirty towpath.

What had happened to her childlike faith since then? Had she become discouraged after Sarah ran away with Sam, leaving her with the responsibility of leading the mules? Or had her faith in God slipped because Papa was so mean and wouldn't give Kelly any money for the hard work she did every day?

Kelly's thoughts came to a halt when Betsy Nelson stepped between her and Mike and announced, "I need to buy material for some new kitchen curtains I plan to make."

"Go on up to the store and choose what you want. I'll be there in a minute," Mike answered with a nod.

Betsy stood grounded to her spot, and Mike motioned

toward Kelly. "Betsy, in case you didn't recognize her, this is Kelly McGregor, all grown up."

Kelly felt her face flame, and she opened her mouth to offer a greeting, but Betsy interrupted.

"Sure, I remember you—the skinny little girl in pigtails who refused to go to Sunday school."

Kelly knew that wasn't entirely true, as it had been Papa's decision, not hers. She figured it would be best not to say anything, however.

Betsy squinted her gray blue eyes and reached up to pat the tight bun she wore at the back of her head. Kelly wondered if the young woman ever allowed her dingy blond hair to hang down her back. Or did the prim and proper preacher's daughter even sleep with her hair pulled back so tightly her cheeks looked drawn?

"I was hoping you would help me choose the material," Betsy said, offering Mike a pinched-looking smile.

Mike fingered his mustache and rocked back on his heels. Kelly thought he looked uncomfortable. "I'm kind of busy right now," he said, nodding at Kelly.

"It's all right," she was quick to say. "Papa's about ready to go, and I think we've finished with our business."

"But you haven't given me any pictures," Mike reminded her.

"Oh. . .oh, you're right." Kelly's voice wavered when she spoke. She was feeling more flustered by the minute.

"Kelly, you got them mules ready yet?" Papa shouted from the bow of the boat.

Kelly turned to her father and called, "In a minute, Papa." She faced Mike again. "I'll be right back with the drawings."

She whirled around, sprinted toward the boat, and leaped over the side, nearly catching her long skirt in the process.

A few minutes later, Kelly came back, carrying three drawings done on newsprint and neatly pressed between two pieces of cardboard. Two were of children fishing along the canal, and the third was a picture of Hector and Herman standing in the middle of the towpath. She handed them to Mike. "I'll have more to show you the next time we stop by."

Mike lifted the top piece of cardboard and studied the drawings. "Nicely done, Kelly. Very nice."

Heat rushed to Kelly's face. "Thanks. I hope the others will be as good."

"I don't see why they wouldn't be." Mike held up the picture of Kelly's mules. "Look, Betsy. See what Kelly's drawn."

"Uh-huh. Nice." Betsy barely took notice as she grabbed hold of Mike's arm. "Can we go see about that material now?"

"I guess so." Mike turned to Kelly. "See you in a few days."

She nodded. "If Papa decides to stop. If not, then soon, I hope."

"Kelly McGregor!" Papa's voice had grown even louder, and Kelly knew he was running out of patience.

"Ready in a minute," she hollered back. "See you, Mike. See you, Betsy." Kelly grabbed hold of the towline and hurried off toward the mules waiting patiently under a maple tree. A few minutes later, she was trudging up the towpath, wishing she could have visited with Mike a bit longer.

Kelly glanced over her shoulder and saw Betsy hanging onto Mike's arm. A pang of jealousy stabbed her heart, but she couldn't explain it. She had no claims on Mike Cooper, nor did she wish to have any. Betsy Nelson was more than welcome to the storekeeper.

Mike headed for the store, wishing it were Kelly and not Betsy clinging to his arm. As he reached the front door, he glanced over his shoulder and saw the McGregors' canal boat disappear around the bend. He'd wanted to spend more time with Kelly, but Betsy's interruption had stolen what precious moments they might have had.

As he stepped into the store, Mike shot a quick prayer heavenward. *Is Kelly the one, Lord? Might she make me a good wife?*

"Mr. Cooper, are you listening to me?" Betsy gave his shirtsleeve a good tug.

Mike refocused his thoughts and turned to look at Betsy, still clinging to his arm.

"The material's on that shelf, and please feel free to call me Mike." He pulled his arm free and pointed to the wall along the left side of his store. "Give me a minute to put Kelly's drawings in a safe place, and I'll join you over there."

Mike could see by the pucker of Betsy's lips that she wasn't happy, but she headed in the direction he had pointed.

Did Betsy think he would drop everything just because she wanted his opinion on the material she wished to buy? Mike doubted his advice counted for much. He knew little about kitchen curtains. His mother had decorated the house he lived in, which was connected to the back of the store. Since Ma's death, he hadn't given much thought to her choice of colors, fabric, or even furniture. If it had been good enough for Ma and Pa, then it was good enough for him.

Mike placed Kelly's drawings on a shelf under the counter and headed across the room to where Betsy stood holding a bolt of yellow and white calico material.

She smiled at him. "What do you think of this color?"

He shrugged. "Guess it would work fine."

For the next half hour, Mike looked at bolts of material, nodded his head, and tried to show an interest in Betsy's curtain-making project. He felt relieved when another customer entered the store, but much to his disappointment, Betsy was still looking at material when he finished up with Hank Summers' order.

"Have you made a decision yet?" Mike called to Betsy from where he stood behind the counter.

"I suppose the yellow and white calico will work best." Betsy marched across the room and plunked the bolt of material on the wooden counter. "I'll take ten yards."

Ten yards? Mike thought Betsy was only making curtains for the kitchen, not every window in the house. *Guess women are prone to changing their minds.*

Betsy grinned at him and fluttered her pale eyelashes. "I'm thinking of making a dress from the leftover material, and I want to be sure I have plenty. Do you think this color will look good on me?"

Mike groaned inwardly. He didn't want to offend the preacher's daughter, so he merely smiled and nodded in response.

Kelly's CHANCE

As soon as Betsy left the store, Mike pulled Kelly's pictures from under the counter, took a seat on his wooden stool, and studied the charcoal drawings.

Kelly McGregor had talent; there was no doubt about it. The question was, would he be able to sell her artwork?

Chapter 5

Over the next couple of days, Kelly daydreamed a lot while she walked the towpath. Was it possible that Mike Cooper might be able to sell some of her drawings? Were they as good as he'd said, or had Mike been trying to be polite when he told Kelly she had talent?

"Sure wish he wasn't so handsome," Kelly muttered as she neared the changing bridge where she and the mules would cross to the other side of the canal. A vision of Mike's face crept into her mind, and she began to sing her favorite canal song, hoping to block out all thoughts of the storekeeper.

"Hunks-a-go pudding and pieces of pie; my mother gave me when I was knee-high. . . . And if you don't believe it, just drop in and see—the hunks-a-go pudding my mother gave me."

Kelly found herself thinking about food and how good supper would taste when they stopped for the night. Mama had bought a hunk of dried beef at Mike Cooper's store, so they would be having savory stew later on.

It was time to get the mules ready to cross over to the towpath on the other side of the canal. Soon they were going up and over the changing bridge, as Kelly lifted the towrope over the railing. Obediently, Hector and Herman followed. In no time, they were on the other side, and Papa was able to steer his boat farther down the canal.

Kelly was relieved the towline hadn't become snagged. Whenever that happened, they were held up while Papa fixed things. Then he was angry the rest of the day because they'd lost precious time. Every load of anthracite coal was important, and payment was made only when it was delivered to the city of Easton, where it was weighed and unloaded. The trip back up the navigation system to Mauch Chunk was with an empty boat, and Papa never wanted to waste a single moment.

Today they were heading to Easton and would arrive by late afternoon if all went well. Kelly knew there was no way Papa would agree to stop by Cooper's General Store on the way to deliver their coal, but coming back again, he might.

Maybe we'll get there early enough so I'll have time to get some drawing done, Kelly told herself. If there was any possibility of Mike selling her artwork, she needed to have more pictures ready to give him.

Kelly didn't realize she'd stopped walking until she felt Hector's wet nose nudge the back of her neck. She whirled around. "Hey there, boy. Are ya that anxious to get to Easton?"

The mule snorted in response, and she laughed and reached out to stroke him behind the ear. Not to be left out, Herman bumped her hand.

"All right, Herman the Determined, I'll give you some attention, too." Kelly stroked the other mule's ear for a few seconds, and then she clicked her tongue. "Now giddy-up, you two. There's no more time to dawdle. Papa will be worse than a snappin' turtle if we make him late tonight."

The day wore on, and every few miles the boat came to another lock where they would wait while it filled with water to match the level of the canal. Then they entered the lock, and the gates enclosed the boat in a damp, wooden receptacle. Right ahead, the water came sizzling and streaming down from above, and gradually the boat would rise again, finally coming to a respectable elevation. The gates swung open, Kelly hooked the mules back to the towrope, and they resumed their voyage.

Ahead was another lock, and Papa blew on his conch shell, letting the lock tender know he was coming. When they approached the lock, Kelly saw another boat ahead of them. They would have to wait their turn.

Suddenly, a third boat came alongside Papa's. "Move outta my way!" the captain shouted. "I'm runnin' behind schedule and should've had this load delivered by now."

"I was here first," Papa hollered in response. "You'll have to wait your turn."

"Oh, yeah? Who's gonna make me?" The burly looking man with a long, full beard shook his fist at Papa.

Standing on the bank next to the mules, Kelly watched as Mama stepped up beside Papa. She touched his arm and leaned close to Papa's ear. Kelly was sure Mama was trying to get Papa calmed down, like she always did whenever he got riled.

Kelly took a few steps closer to the canal and strained to

hear what Mama was saying.

"Don't tell me what to do, woman!" Papa yelled as he leaned over the side of his boat. The other craft was right alongside him, and the driver of the mules pulling that boat stood next to Kelly.

The young boy, not much more than twelve or thirteen years old, gave Kelly a wide grin. His teeth were yellow and stained. Probably from smoking or chewing tobacco, Kelly figured. "Looks like my pa is gonna beat the stuffin's outa your old man," he taunted.

Kelly glanced back at the two boat captains. They were face-to-face, each leaning as far over the rails as possible. She sent up a quick prayer. *Not this time, Lord. Please help Papa calm down.*

"Move aside, or I'm comin' over there to clean your clock," the burly man bellowed.

"Amos, please!" Mama begged as she gripped Papa's arm again. "Just let the man pass through the lock first. This ain't worth gettin' into a skirmish over."

Papa shot the man a look of contempt and grabbed hold of the tiller in order to steer the boat. "I'll let it go this time, but you'd better never try to ace me out again."

Kelly breathed a sigh of relief as Papa steered the boat aside and the other vessel passed through the lock. She'd seen her hot-tempered father use his fists to settle many disagreements in the past. It was always humiliating, and what did it prove—that Papa was tougher, meaner, or more aggressive than someone else? As far as Kelly could tell, nothing good had ever come from any of Papa's fistfights. He was a hotheaded Irishman who'd grown up on the water. His dad had been one of the men who'd helped dig the Lehigh Canal, and Papa had said many times that he'd seen or been part of a good many fights throughout his growing-up days. If only he would give his heart to Jesus and confess his sins, the way Kelly and Mama had done.

Herman nuzzled Kelly's shoulder, and she turned to face her mule friends. *If God really loves me, then why doesn't He change Papa's heart?*

Mike had been busier than usual the last couple days, and that was good. It kept him from thinking too much about Kelly McGregor. How soon would she and her family stop at his store again? Could he manage to sell any of her drawings before they came? Was Kelly the least bit interested in him? All these thoughts tumbled around in Mike's head whenever he had a free moment to look at Kelly's artwork, which he'd displayed on one wall of the store. The young woman had been gifted with a talent so great that even a simple, homemade charcoal drawing looked like an intricate work of art. At least Mike thought it did. He just hoped some of his customers would agree and decide to buy one of Kelly's pictures.

As Mike wiped off the glass on the candy counter, where little children had left fingerprint smudges, a vision of Kelly came to mind. With her long, dark hair hanging freely down her back, and those huge brown eyes reminding him of a baby deer, she was sure easy to look at. Nothing like Betsy Nelson, the preacher's daughter, who had a birdlike nose, squinty gray blue eyes, and a prim-and-proper bun for her dingy blond hair.

Kelly's personality seemed different, too. She wasn't pushy and opinionated, the way Betsy was. Kelly, though a bit shy, seemed to have a zest for life that showed itself in her drawings. She was a hard worker, too—trudging up and down the towpath six days a week, from sunup to sunset. Mike was well aware of the way the canal boatmen pushed to get their loads picked up and delivered. The responsibility put upon the mule drivers was heavy, yet it was often delegated to women and children.

I wonder if Amos McGregor appreciates his daughter and pays her well enough. Mike doubted it, seeing the way the man barked orders at Kelly. And why, if she was paid a decent wage, would Kelly be using crude sticks of charcoal instead of store-bought paints or pencils, not to mention her homemade tablet?

Mike's thoughts were halted when the front door of his store opened and banged shut.

"Good morning, Mike Cooper," Preacher Nelson said as he sauntered into the room.

"Mornin'," Mike answered with a smile and a nod.

"How's business?"

"Been kind of busy the last couple of days. Now that the weather's warmed and the canal is full of water again, the boatmen are back in full swing."

The preacher raked his long fingers through the ends of his curly, dark hair. His gray blue eyes were small and beady, like his daughter's. "You still keeping the same hours?" the man questioned.

Mike nodded. "Yep. . .Monday to Saturday, nine o'clock in

the morning till six at night."

Hiram Nelson smiled, revealing a prominent dimple in his clean-shaven chin. "Sure glad to hear you're still closing the store on Sundays."

Mike moved over to the wooden counter where he waited on customers. "Sunday's a day of rest."

"That's how God wants it, but there's sure a lot of folks who think otherwise."

Not knowing what else to say, Mike merely shrugged. "Anything I can help you with, Reverend Nelson?"

The older man leaned on the edge of the counter. "Actually, there is."

"What are you in need of?"

"You."

"Me?"

The preacher's head bobbed up and down. "This Friday's my daughter's twenty-sixth birthday, and I thought it would be nice for Betsy if someone her age joined us for supper." He chuckled. "She sees enough of her old papa, and since her mama died a few years ago, Betsy's been kind of lonely."

Mike was tempted to remind the preacher that his daughter was two years older than he but decided not to mention their age difference—or the fact that most women Betsy's age were already married and raising a family. "Isn't there someone from your church you could invite?" he asked.

Pastor Nelson's face turned slightly red. "It's you Betsy thought of when she said she'd like to have a guest on her birthday." He tapped the edge of the counter.

Mike wasn't sure how to respond. Was it possible that Betsy

Nelson was romantically interested in him? If so, he had to figure out a way to discourage her.

"So, what do you say, son? Will you come to supper on Friday evening?"

Remembering that the Nelsons' home was next to the church and several miles away, Mike knew he would have to close the store early in order to make it in time for supper. This would be the excuse he needed to decline the invitation. Besides, what if the McGregors came by while he was gone? He didn't want to miss an opportunity to see Kelly again.

"I–I'm afraid I can't make it," Mike said.

The preacher pursed his lips. "Why not? You got other plans?"

Mike shook his head. "Not exactly, but I'd have to close the store early."

Reverend Nelson held up his hand. "No need for that, son. We'll have a late supper. How's seven o'clock sound?"

"Well, I—"

"I won't take no for an answer, so you may as well say you'll come. Betsy would be impossible to live with if I came home and told her you'd turned down my invitation."

Mike didn't want to hurt Betsy's feelings, and the thought of eating someone else's cooking did have some appeal. "Okay," he finally conceded. "Tell Betsy I'll be there."

Chapter 6

*K*elly hummed to herself as she kicked the stones beneath her feet. They had made it to Easton by six o'clock last night, and after they dropped off their load of coal and ate supper, she'd had a few hours to spend in her room, working on her drawings.

Now they were heading back to Mauch Chunk for another load. By five or six o'clock they should be passing Mike Cooper's store. Kelly hoped she could talk Papa into stopping, for she had three more drawings she wanted to give Mike. One was of a canal boat going through the locks, another of an elderly boatman standing at the bow of his boat playing a fiddle, and the third was of the skyline of Easton, with its many tall buildings.

Kelly was pretty sure her pictures were well done, although she knew they could have been better if they'd been drawn on better paper, in color instead of black and white.

She stopped humming. *Someday I hope to have enough money to buy all kinds of paints and fancy paper.* Even as the words popped into her mind, Kelly wondered if they could ever come true. Unless Papa changed his mind about paying her wages, she might never earn any money of her own. Maybe her dream of owning an art gallery wasn't possible.

"At least I can keep on drawing," she mumbled. "Nobody can take that away from me."

Kelly's stomach rumbled, reminding her it was almost noon. Since they had no load, they would be stopping to eat soon. If Papa was hurrying to get to Easton with a boatload of coal, Kelly might be forced to eat a hunk of bread or some fruit and keep on walking. Today, Mama was fixing a pot of vegetable and bean soup. Kelly could smell the delicious aroma as it wafted across the space between the boat and towpath.

A short while later, Kelly was on board the boat, sitting at the small wooden table. A bowl of steaming soup had been placed in front of her, a chunk of rye bread to her left, and her drawing pad was on the right. She'd decided to sketch a bit while her soup cooled.

Kelly had just picked up her piece of charcoal to begin drawing when Papa sat down across from her. "You ain't got time to dawdle. Get your lunch eaten and go tend to the mules."

Tears stung Kelly's eyes. She should be used to the way her dad shot orders, but his harsh tone and angry scowl always upset her.

"My soup's too hot to eat yet," she said. "I thought I might get some drawin' done while I wait for it to cool."

Papa snorted. "Humph! Fiddlin' with a dirty stick of

charcoal is a waste of time!" He grabbed the loaf of bread from the wooden bowl in the center of the table and tore off a piece. Then he dipped the bread into his bowl of soup and popped it into his mouth.

Kelly wasn't sure how she should respond to his grumbling, so she leaned over and blew on her soup instead of saying anything.

Mama, who was dishing up her own bowl of soup at the stove, spoke up. "I don't see what harm there'd be in the girl drawin' while her soup cools, Amos."

Papa slammed his fist down on the table so hard Kelly's piece of bread flew up and landed on the floor. "If I want your opinion, Dorrie, I'll ask for it!"

Kelly gulped. She hated it when Papa yelled at Mama. It wasn't right, but she didn't know what she could do about it. Only God could change Papa's heart, and she was growing weary of praying for such.

"Well, what are ya sittin' there lollygaggin' for?" Papa bellowed. "Start eatin', or I'm gonna pitch your writing tablet into the stove."

Kelly grabbed her spoon. No way could she let her dad carry through with his threat. She'd eat all her soup in a hurry, even if she burned her tongue in the process.

Awhile later, she was back on the towpath. She'd given the mules some oats in their feedbags, and they were munching away as they plodded dutifully along. Kelly knew they were making good time, and they'd probably pass Mike Cooper's sometime early this evening. She'd hoped to ask Papa about stopping by the store, but he'd been so cross during lunch, she'd lost her nerve.

Besides, what reason would she give for stopping? She sure couldn't tell her dad she wanted to make a few more drawings so Mike could try to sell them. Papa had made it clear the way he felt about Kelly wasting time on her artwork. If she told him her plans, Papa might make good on his threat and pitch her tablet into the stove.

"If he ever does that, I'll make another one or find some old pieces of cardboard to draw on," Kelly fumed.

A young boy about eight years old crossed Kelly's path. He carried a fishing pole in one hand and a metal bucket in the other. The child stopped on the path and looked at Kelly as though she was daft. Had he overhead her talking to herself?

Kelly stopped walking. "Goin' fishin'?" *What a dumb question. Of course he's goin' fishin'. Why else would he be carryin' a pole?*

The freckle-faced, red-haired lad offered Kelly a huge grin, revealing a missing front tooth. "Thought I'd try to catch myself a few catfish. They was bitin' real good yesterday afternoon."

"You live around here?" Kelly questioned.

"Yep. Up the canal a ways."

Kelly's forehead wrinkled. She didn't remember seeing the boy before, and she wondered why he wasn't in school. The youngster's overalls were torn and dirty, and when Kelly glanced down at his bare feet, she shuddered. It was too cold yet to be going without shoes. Maybe the child was so poor his folks couldn't afford to buy him any decent footwear.

"My pap's workin' up at Mauch Chunk, loadin' coal," the boy said before Kelly could voice any questions.

"But I thought you said you lived nearby."

53

He nodded. "For the last couple months we've been livin' in an old shanty halfway up the canal." He frowned. "Don't see Pap much these days."

"Do you live with your mother?" Kelly asked.

The boy offered her another toothless grin. "Me, Ma, and little Ted. He's my baby brother. Pap was outa work for a spell, but things will be better now that he's got a job loadin' dirty coal."

Kelly's heart went out to the young child, since she could relate to being poor. Of course, Papa had always worked, and they'd never done without the basic necessities. Still, she had no money of her own.

"Kelly McGregor, why have you stopped?"

Kelly whirled around at the sound of her dad's angry-sounding voice. He was leaning over the side of the boat, shaking his fist at her.

"Sorry, Papa," she hollered back. "Nice chattin' with you," Kelly said to the child. "Hope you catch plenty of fish today." She gave the boy a quick wave and started off.

As Kelly led her mules down the rutted path, she found herself envying the freckle-faced boy with the holes in his britches. At least he wasn't being forced to work all day.

Mike pulled a pocket watch from his pant's pocket. It was almost six o'clock. He needed to close up the store and head on over to the preacher's place for supper. All day long he'd hoped the McGregors would stop by, but they hadn't, and he'd seen no sign of their boat. Of course, they could have gone by without him seeing, as there were many times throughout the day when he'd been busy with customers. As tempting as it had been, Mike knew he couldn't stand at the window all day and watch for Amos McGregor's canal boat. He had a store to run, and that took precedence over daydreaming about Kelly or watching for her dad's boat to come around the bend.

Mike put the CLOSED sign in the store window and grabbed his jacket from a wall peg near the door. He was almost ready to leave when he remembered that tonight was Betsy's birthday and he should take her a gift.

He glanced around the store, looking for something appropriate. Mike noticed the stack of Bibles he had displayed on a shelf near the front of his store. He'd given plenty of them away, but he guessed Betsy, being a preacher's daughter, probably had at least one Bible in her possession.

As he continued to survey his goods, Mike's gaze came to rest on Kelly's drawings, tacked up on one wall. What better gift than something made by one of the locals? He chose the picture that showed two children fishing along the canal. He thought Betsy would like it. This would be Kelly's first sale, and he would give her the money she had coming as soon as he saw her again.

Since it was a pleasant spring evening with no sign of rain, Mike decided to walk to the Nelsons' rather than ride his horse or hitch up the buggy. He scanned the canal, looking for any sign of the McGregors' boat, but the only movement on the water was a pair of mallard ducks.

Mike filled his lungs with fresh air as he trudged off toward

Walnutport. Sometime later, he arrived at the Nelsons' front door.

Betsy greeted him, looking prim and proper in a crisp white blouse and long blue skirt. Her hair was pulled into its usual tight bun at the back of her head.

"Come in, Mr. Cooper—I mean, Mike," she said sweetly. "Supper is ready, so let me take your coat."

Mike stepped inside the small, cozy parsonage and slipped off his jacket. He was about to hand it to Betsy when he remembered the picture he'd rolled up and put inside his pocket. He retrieved it and handed the drawing to Betsy. "Happy birthday."

Betsy smiled and unrolled the picture. She studied it a few seconds, and her forehead creased as she squinted her eyes. "This isn't one of those drawings young Kelly McGregor drew, is it?"

Mike nodded. "I thought you might like it, seeing as how there are children in the picture."

Her frown deepened. "What makes you think I have a fondness for children?"

"Well, I. . .that is, doesn't everyone have a soft spot for little ones?" Mike thought about his desire to have a large family, and he remembered reading how Jesus had taken time to visit with children. It only seemed natural for a preacher's daughter to like kids.

Betsy scrunched up her nose, as though some foul odor had permeated the room. "Children are sometimes hard to handle, and I don't envy anyone who's a parent." She batted her eyelashes a few times. "I get along better with adults."

Mike wondered if there was something in Betsy's eye. Or maybe she had trouble seeing and needed a pair of spectacles.

"Do you like Kelly's charcoal drawing or not?" he asked.

Betsy glanced at the picture in her hand. "I'll find a place for it, since you were thoughtful enough to bring me a present."

Mike drew in a deep breath and followed Betsy into the next room, where a table was set for three. Preacher Nelson stood in front of the fireplace, and he smiled at Mike.

"Good to see you, son. Glad you could make it tonight."

Mike nodded and forced a smile in return. He had a feeling it was going to be a long evening, and he could hardly wait for it to come to an end.

Chapter 7

Kelly plodded along the towpath, tired from another long day, and feeling frustrated because they'd passed Mike's store without stopping. It was getting dark by the time they got to that section of the navigation system, and she hadn't seen any lights in the store windows. Maybe Mike was closed for the day.

It had been less than a week since Kelly had left three of her drawings with him. Chances were none of them had sold yet. By the time they did stop at Cooper's General Store, Kelly thought she would have a few more drawings to give Mike, and hopefully he'd have good news about the ones he was trying to sell. In the meantime, Kelly knew she needed to be patient.

"Patient and determined," she muttered into the night air. The moon was full, and Kelly could see some distance ahead. They were coming to another lock, and Papa was already blowing on his conch shell to announce their arrival to the lock tender.

Kelly looked forward to each lock they went through. It

gave her a chance to rest, tend to the mules, or draw.

She patted her apron pocket. *That's why I keep my tablet and a hunk of charcoal with me most of the time.*

Tonight, however, there were no boats ahead of them, and they went through the lock rather quickly. Kelly wasn't disappointed. It was too dark to draw anyway, and getting through the lock meant they would soon be on their way.

Kelly was hungry and tired. She could hardly wait to stop for the night. But she didn't smell the usual aroma of food coming from the boat. It made her wonder if Mama was tired and had decided to serve a cold meal. Maybe cheese and bread, with a piece of fruit or some carrot sticks. Anything would taste good.

When Kelly thought she'd die of hunger and couldn't take another step, Papa hollered for her to stop. With her dad's help, Kelly loaded the mules onto the boat, where they would be bedded down in the enclosed area reserved for them. If they'd been at a place where they could have stabled the mules, they wouldn't have to go through this procedure.

Kelly stretched her limbs with a weary sigh. "What's Mama got planned for supper, do ya know?"

Papa shook his head. "Your mama ain't feelin' well, and she's taken to her bed. You'll have to see about supper tonight."

Kelly felt immediate concern. "Mama's sick? What's wrong, and why didn't you tell me sooner?"

Papa shrugged. "Saw no need."

"But I could've come aboard and started supper. Maybe seen if there was somethin' I could do to make Mama more comfortable."

Papa grunted. "It's best you kept on walkin'. I don't wanna be late picking up my load of coal in Mauch Chunk tomorrow."

Kelly stared down at her clenched hands as anger churned in her stomach. All Papa cared about was hauling coal and making money he never shared. Didn't he give a hoot that Mama was sick in bed?

Feeling as though she carried the weight of the world on her shoulders, Kelly headed for their small kitchen. She would get some soup heating on the stove, then go below to see how Mama was doing.

A short time later, Kelly and her dad sat at the kitchen table, eating soup and bread—leftovers from their afternoon meal. Kelly had checked on her mother and found her sleeping. She didn't have the heart to wake her, so she tiptoed out of her parents' cubicle with the intention of offering Mama a bowl of soup later on.

"You'd better get to sleep right after ya clean up the dishes," Papa said. "I'm planning to head out at the first light of day tomorrow mornin'." He wiped his mouth on the edge of his shirtsleeve. "If your mama's still feelin' poorly, you'll need to get breakfast."

Kelly watched the flame flicker from the candle in the center of the table. More chores to do. Just what she didn't need. She'd better pray extra hard for Mama tonight.

Mike had never been so glad to see his humble home. The time he'd spent at the Nelsons' had left him feeling irritable and exhausted. Didn't Betsy ever stop talking or batting her eye-lashes? Reverend Nelson had acted a bit strange all evening, too. He kept dropping hints about his daughter needing a God-fearing husband, and he'd even asked Mike to sit on the sofa beside Betsy as they drank their coffee after dinner. Maybe the preacher was trying to link Mike up with his daughter, but it wasn't going to work. Mike had other ideas about who was the right woman for him.

Mike hung his jacket on a wall peg near the door, sank into an overstuffed chair by the stone fireplace, and looked around the room. He really did need someone to help fill his lonely evening hours. He'd been praying for a wife for some time now, but surely Betsy Nelson wasn't the one God had in mind for him. The woman got on his nerves, with her constant jabbering and opinionated remarks.

"It doesn't seem as if she likes children, either," Mike murmured. He didn't see any way he could be happily married to a woman who didn't share his desire for a family. Mike saw children as a gift from God, not a nuisance. He'd had customers come into his store who'd done nothing but yell at their kids, shouting orders or scolding them for every little thing.

Mike's thoughts went immediately to Kelly McGregor. Did she like children? Would Kelly make a good wife? Was she a believer in Christ? Mike knew so little about the young woman. The only thing he was sure of was that he was attracted to her.

I need to figure out some way for us to become better acquainted. With the McGregors' canal boat coming by every few days, there ought to be a chance to see Kelly more and get to know her.

Mike closed his eyes, and a few minutes later he fell asleep, dreaming about Kelly McGregor.

Kelly stretched her aching limbs and forced herself to sit up. Inky darkness enveloped her room, but Papa was hollering at her to get up. She needed to see if Mama was still ailing, and if so, fix some breakfast. Then she'd have to feed the mules, lead them off the boat, and get ready to head for Mauch Chunk. She hadn't slept well the night before, and she'd had several dreams—one that involved Mike Cooper.

Why do I think about him so often? Kelly fumed. *Probably because he has my drawings, and I'm anxious to see if he's sold any. Yep, that's all there is to it—nothin' more.*

After Kelly washed up and got dressed, she rolled up her finished drawings and placed them inside her apron pocket, just in case they made a stop at Cooper's store today. Then she tiptoed over to her folks' room to check on Mama.

Her mother was awake, but she looked terrible. Dark circles lay beneath her eyes, her skin was pasty white, and her forehead glistened with sweat.

"How are ya feelin' this mornin'?" Kelly whispered.

Mama lifted her head off the pillow and offered Kelly a weak smile. "I'll be back on my feet in no time a'tall. It's just a sore throat, and my body aches some, too."

Kelly adjusted the patchwork quilt covering her mother's bed. "I'll bring you a cup of hot tea and a bowl of cornmeal mush as soon as I get Papa fed. He might be less crabby if his belly is full."

Mama nodded, coughed, and relaxed against the pillow. "I'm sorry you're havin' to do more chores than usual. If Sarah were still here, your load would be a bit lighter."

Kelly shrugged. She didn't want to think about her runaway sister. "I'll manage. You just get well." She patted the quilt where Mama's feet were hidden. "I'll be back soon."

A short while later, Kelly was in the kitchen preparing breakfast.

"What about lunch and supper?" she asked her dad when she handed him a bowl of mush.

His forehead wrinkled. "What about it?"

"If I'm gonna be leadin' the mules all day, and Mama's still sick in bed—"

Papa grunted and pulled on the end of his mustache. "Guess that means I'll be stuck with the cookin'."

"But how will you do that, watch up ahead, and steer the boat, too?" she questioned.

"I'll manage somehow. Don't guess I've got much other choice." He snorted. "If that renegade sister of yours hadn't run off with Sam Turner, we wouldn't be shorthanded right now."

Kelly drew in a deep breath, feeling a bit put out with her sister, too.

Things seemed to go from bad to worse as the day progressed. Kelly kept an eye on the boat, and a couple times she spotted her dad racing back and forth between the woodstove sitting on the open deck and the stern of the boat. He would lift the pot lid and take a look at the beans he was cooking, run back to the stern and give the tiller a twist, and do it all over again.

Kelly wondered if he might collapse or run the boat aground from all that rushing around.

When it came time for lunch, Papa gulped down a hasty meal, leaped from the boat to the towpath, and took over leading the mules so Kelly could eat. She did all right getting into the boat, but when she jumped over the side again, she missed her mark and landed in the canal with a splash.

Now she was walking the towpath in a sopping wet skirt that stuck to her legs like a tick on a mule. She'd been forced to remove her boots because they were waterlogged, and she sure hoped no snakes came slithering across the path and nailed her bare feet.

To make matters worse, the drawings she'd put in her pocket that morning had gotten ruined when she fell in the water. Now she had nothing to give Mike if she saw him today.

The only bright spot in Kelly's day was when Papa told her they would be stopping by Cooper's General Store later on. He wanted to see if Mike had any cough syrup in stock. Papa thought it might make Mama sleep better if they could get her cough calmed down. Stopping at the store would be good for Mama as well as Kelly. She hoped her dress would be dry by the time they got there.

Chapter 8

For the past couple of days, Mike had tried unsuccessfully to sell some of Kelly's drawings. "Isn't there anyone in the area who can see her talent and needs something special to give as a gift?" he muttered as he studied the two remaining pictures displayed on the wall of his store. Was it possible that Kelly wasn't as talented as Mike thought? Maybe folks were put off by the simplicity of the paper she used. Maybe he was too caught up in his unexplained feelings for the young woman. He might have been thinking with his heart instead of his head when he'd agreed to try to sell some of her artwork. Now he was going to have to face Kelly when she stopped by the store again and tell her nothing had sold.

That's not entirely true, he reminded himself. *I took one of her pictures to give Betsy Nelson, and I plan to pay Kelly her share for it. Maybe I should buy a second picture, then frame it and hang it in my house.* Mike smiled, feeling a sense of satisfaction because of his idea. Kelly wouldn't have to know who'd bought the drawings. She'd probably be happy just getting the money.

With that decided, Mike removed the picture of Kelly's two mules and stuck it under the front counter. He would take it home when he was done for the day.

Mike pulled out an envelope and wrote Kelly's name on it. Then he withdrew some money from the cash box and tucked it inside. Hopefully he'd be able to sell her other drawing before Kelly came by the store again.

"I need to get busy and quit thinking about Kelly McGregor," Mike muttered as he grabbed a broom and started sweeping the floor. Thoughts of the young woman with dark brown eyes and long, coffee-colored hair were consuming too much of his time.

Mike had just put the broom away in the storage closet when the front door opened. He pivoted, and his heartbeat quickened. Kelly McGregor stood there, her straw hat askew, and her long gray skirt, wrinkled, dirty, and damp. She looked a mess, yet he thought she was beautiful.

Mike swallowed hard and moved toward her. "Kelly. It's good to see you again."

"Hello, Mike Cooper," Kelly said, feeling timid and unsure of herself.

He smiled, and the dimple in his chin seemed to be winking at her.

She took a tentative step forward. "Mama's sick and needs

some cough syrup. Have ya got any on hand?"

"I think there's still several bottles on the back shelf." Mike pointed to the other end of the store. "Would you like me to get one for you?"

She nodded. "If ya don't mind."

"Not at all." Mike headed in the direction he'd pointed, and Kelly turned her attention to the wall nearest the door. One of her drawings of children playing along the canal was there, but the other two were nowhere in sight. A feeling of excitement coursed through her veins. Had Mike sold them? Did she have some money coming now? Dare she ask?

When Mike returned a few minutes later, she was still studying her drawing. She glanced over at him. He held a bottle of cough syrup and stood so close she could smell the aroma of soap, which indicated that he at least was wearing clean clothes. Mike's hair was nicely combed, too. She, on the other hand, looked terrible. He probably thought she was a filthy pig. Should she explain about falling into the canal? Would he even care?

"You're quite talented," Mike said, bringing Kelly's thoughts to a halt. "Have you done any more pictures lately?"

"I did have three more ready, but Mama's been sick, so Papa and me have had to share all the chores." She glanced down at her soiled skirt and frowned. "As you can see, I fell in the canal earlier today, trying to jump from the boat back to the towpath. My drawings were in my pocket, and they got ruined."

Mike shook his head slowly. "Sorry to hear that. I did wonder why your skirt was so rumpled and wet." He moved toward the counter, and Kelly followed. "Sorry you're having to do double duty, but maybe this will make you feel better." He set the cough syrup down, pulled open a drawer beneath the counter, withdrew an envelope, and handed it to Kelly.

She took the envelope and studied it a few seconds. Her name was written on the front. "What's this?"

"It's your share of the money for two of the drawings you left with me."

She smiled up at him. "You really sold two of my pictures?"

Mike's ears turned slightly red, and he looked a little flustered. Was he embarrassed because he hadn't sold all three?

"I. . .uh. . .found someone who really appreciates your talent," he said, staring down at the wooden counter.

Kelly's smile widened. "I'm so glad. Once Mama gets better, I'll have a bit more time to draw, and maybe when we stop by here again I'll have a few more pictures to give you."

Mike's smile seemed to be forced, and his face had turned red like his ears. Something seemed to be troubling him, and Kelly aimed to find out what it was.

"Is everything all right? You look kinda upset."

Mike lifted his gaze. "Everything's fine. Feel free to bring me as many drawings as you like."

Kelly felt a sense of relief wash over her. If she could get Mama back on her feet, she'd have more time to draw. Mike wanted her to bring more pictures, she'd already sold two, and things were looking hopeful. She slipped the envelope into her apron pocket and turned toward the door.

"Aren't you forgetting something?" Mike called after her.

Kelly whirled around and felt the heat of a blush spread over her face when Mike held up the bottle of cough syrup. She giggled self-consciously and fished in her pocket for the coins to pay for her purchase.

Mike's fingers brushed hers as she dropped the money into his hand, and Kelly felt an unexpected shiver tickle her spine. What was there about Mike Cooper that made her feel so giddy and out of breath? Was it the crooked smile beneath his perfectly shaped mustache? Those hazel eyes that seemed capable of looking into her soul? The lock of sandy brown hair that fell across his forehead?

Kelly snatched up the bottle of cough syrup, mumbled a quick thanks, and fled.

Mike couldn't believe the way Kelly had run out of the store. Had he said or done something to upset her? He'd thought they were getting along pretty well, and Kelly had seemed pleased about her drawings being sold.

Maybe she suspects I'm the one who bought the pictures. But how could she know that? He'd been careful not to give her too much information, so she couldn't have guessed he was the one. He hadn't actually lied to her, but he didn't see the need to tell Kelly he was the one either. She might have taken it the wrong way.

Seeing Kelly again had only reinforced the strong feelings Mike was having for her. When their hands touched briefly during the money exchange, he had felt as though he'd been struck by a bolt of lightning. Had Kelly felt it, too? Could that have been the reason for her sudden departure? Or maybe she just needed to get back to work. The canal boaters always seemed to be in a hurry to get to and from their pickup and delivery points. That was probably all it was. Kelly's dad had no doubt told her to hurry, and she was only complying with his wishes.

How am I going to get to know Kelly better if she stops by the store only once in a while, then stays just long enough to buy something and hurries off again? Mike closed his eyes. *Lord, would You please work it out so Kelly and I can spend more time together?*

Mike was still standing behind the counter, mulling things over, when Amos McGregor entered the store.

"Mr. McGregor, your daughter was just here buying some cough syrup for your wife."

"Don'tcha think I know that?" the boatman snapped. His bright red hair stuck out at odd angles, like he hadn't combed it in a couple of days, and dark circles rimmed his eyes.

Mike shrugged. It was obvious the man wasn't in a good mood, and there was no point in saying anything that might rile him further.

"The wife's been sick for a couple of days," Amos mumbled. "That left me stuck doin' most of her chores." He stuffed his hands inside the pocket of his dark blue jacket and started for the back of the store.

"Can I help you find something?" Mike called after him.

"Need some of that newfangled soap that floats," came the muffled reply. "I told Kelly to get some, but as usual, she had her head in the clouds and forgot."

Mike skirted around the counter and went straight to the

shelf where he kept the cleaning supplies and personal toiletries. "Here's what you're looking for, sir," he said, lifting a bar of soap for the man's inspection.

"Yep. That's it, all right." Amos shook his head slowly. "I dropped our last bar overboard by mistake and didn't wanna take the time to stop and fish it outa the canal." He grabbed another bar of soap and marched back to the counter. "Better to have a spare," he muttered.

Mike nodded and slipped the cakes of soap into a paper sack. "Good idea." He handed the bag to Amos. "Need anything else?"

"Nope." Amos plunked some coins on the counter and started for the front door.

"Feel free to stop by anytime," Mike called after him. "And if you ever need a place to spend the night, I'll gladly let you stable your mules in my barn."

The boatman mumbled something under his breath and shut the door.

Mike shook his head. "I wonder why that man's such a grouch? No wonder Kelly acts like a scared rabbit much of the time. Guess I'd better pray for the both of them."

Chapter 9

On Saturday evening, much to Mike's surprise, Kelly and her mother stopped by the store.

"That cough syrup you sold Kelly a few days ago sure helped me sleep," Dorrie said as she stepped up beside Mike, who'd been stocking shelves near the front of the store.

Mike smiled. "I'm glad to hear that, Mrs. McGregor. Are you feeling better?"

She nodded. "I'm back to doin' most of my own chores, too."

Mike glanced at Kelly out of the corner of his eye. She was standing by the candy counter, eyeing something she was obviously interested in. He started to move toward the young woman, but Dorrie's next words stopped him.

"Amos is feelin' poorly now, so we need more medicine." Her forehead wrinkled, and she blinked a couple of times. "Sure hope you've got some, 'cause I used up the bottle of cough syrup Kelly bought."

Mike nodded toward the back of the store. "There's a couple bottles on the second shelf to the right. Want me to get one for you?"

Dorrie glanced over at Kelly, still peering inside the candy counter, and she shook her head. "Why don'tcha see what kind of sweet treat my daughter would like, while I fetch the medicine?"

Mike didn't have to be asked twice. He set the tin of canned peaches he'd been holding down on the shelf and then hurried over to Kelly.

"How are you?" he asked. "Sure hope you're not getting sick, too."

"Nope. I'm healthy as a mule."

"Glad to hear it, but I'm sorry about your dad. Is he able to keep on working?"

"He made it through the day, even with his fits of coughing and fever. I think he's plannin' to tie up here and spend the night. We'll stay all day Sunday, so he can rest." Kelly's gaze went to her mother, who was at the back of the store. "Mama doesn't have all her strength back yet, either, so a good day's rest should do 'em both some good."

And you, Kelly, Mike thought as he studied her face. The dark circles under her eyes gave evidence to how tired she was.

"The last time your dad was in the store, I told him I'd be glad to stable your mules in my barn anytime he wanted to dock here for the night."

"That's right nice of you." Kelly gazed at the candy counter with a look of longing on her face.

Mike wondered how long it had been since she had eaten

any candy. Without hesitation, he opened the hinged lid on the glass case. "Help yourself to whatever you like—my treat."

Kelly stiffened. "Oh, no. I couldn't let you do that. Thanks to you sellin' a couple of my charcoal drawings, I've got money of my own now." She shrugged. "Although, it's safely hidden in my room on the boat, and I'd have to go back and get it."

"Wouldn't you rather spend it on something more useful than candy?"

She pursed her lips. "Probably should be savin' my money, but I've sure got a hankerin' for some lemon drops."

Mike reached down and grabbed the glass jar filled with sugar-coated lemon drops. "Take as many as you like, and please consider it a present from me to you."

Kelly tipped her head to one side, as if contemplating his offer. Finally with a nervous giggle, she agreed.

He filled a small paper bag half full of candy and handed it to her, hoping she wouldn't change her mind.

She took the sack and stuffed it in her apron pocket. "Thank you."

"You're welcome."

Kelly shuffled her feet, and her boots scraped nosily against the wooden planks. Why did she seem so nervous? Was it because her mother was nearby and might be listening in on their conversation?

Hoping to put her at ease, Mike reached out and touched Kelly's arm. She recoiled like she'd been bitten by a snake, and he quickly withdrew his hand.

"Sorry, I didn't mean to startle you."

Kelly shrugged. What was wrong? They'd had such a

pleasant visit the last time she'd come by.

"Did you bring me any more drawings?" Mike asked, hoping the change of subject might ease the tension he felt filling up the space between them.

She shook her head. "I'm out of charcoal, and for the last couple of days, Papa's been burnin' coal instead of wood in our cook stove. I haven't come across any cold campfires along the canal lately neither."

So that was the problem. Kelly was feeling bad because she hadn't been able to draw and she'd promised Mike she would have more pictures the next time she came by.

Mike had a brand-new set of sketching pencils for sale, along with some tubes of oil paints. He would have gladly given them to her but was sure she would say no. It had taken some persuasion to get her to take a few lemon drops, and they weren't worth half as much as the art supplies. Since Kelly did have some money of her own, she could probably purchase a box of pencils, but she might be saving up for something more important.

Suddenly, Mike had an idea. "I've got some burned charcoal chips in my home fireplace at the back of the store," he announced. "How 'bout I run in there and get them for you?"

Kelly hesitated a moment but finally nodded. "That would be right nice."

Before she had a chance to change her mind, Mike hurried to the back of the store. He passed Kelly's mother on his way to the door leading to his attached house.

"I'll be right back, Mrs. McGregor. Take your time looking around for anything you might need."

Kelly watched Mike's retreating form as he disappeared behind the door at the back of his store. He seemed like such a caring young man. Probably would make someone a mighty fine husband. Maybe he and the preacher's daughter would link up. Betsy had seemed pretty friendly to him the last time Kelly saw the two of them together.

She frowned. Why did the idea of Mike and Betsy Nelson together make her feel so squeamish? She reached into the sack inside her pocket and withdrew a lemon drop, then popped the piece of candy into her mouth.

"We'll head on back to the boat as soon as the storekeeper returns and I pay for the cough syrup and a few other things I found," Mama said, driving Kelly's thoughts to the back of her mind.

Kelly slowly nodded her head.

"Mike Cooper seems like a nice young man," Mama remarked.

Kelly nodded again. "He offered to let us stable Herman and Hector in his barn for the night."

Mama's dark eyebrows lifted. "For free?"

"I think so. He never said a word about money."

"Hmm. . .guess as soon as we leave the store, you should get the mules fed and ready to bed down then."

"I'd be happy to," Kelly readily agreed. "I'm sure Hector and Herman will be right glad to have a bigger place to stay tonight than they have on board our boat."

"You're probably right." Mama smiled. "Say, I was thinkin'—since tomorrow's Sunday, and we won't be movin' on 'til early Monday morning, why don't the two of us head into town and go to church?"

Kelly opened her mouth to respond, but Mama rushed on. "It's been a good while since I've sat inside a real church and worshiped God with other Christian folks."

"Well, I. . .uh. . ." Kelly swallowed against the urge to say what was really on her mind. Being in church would make her feel uncomfortable—like others were looking down their noses at the poor boatman's daughter who wore men's boots and smelled like a dirty mule. Kelly had seen the way Betsy Nelson turned her nose up whenever the two of them met along the towpath. She wasn't good enough to sit inside a pretty church building; it was just that simple.

"I'm waitin' for your answer," Mama said, giving Kelly's shoulder a gentle tap.

"I was kinda hoping to get rested up tomorrow. Maybe do a bit of drawin'."

Mama's squinted eyes and furrowed brow revealed her obvious concern. "You ain't feelin' poorly, too, I hope."

Kelly shook her head. "Just tired is all."

"And well you should be," Mama agreed. "The last few days, you and your dad have been workin' real hard trying to do all my chores plus keeping up with your own jobs as well." She gave Kelly a hug. "I think you're right. It might be good for us all to spend the day restin'."

Kelly felt bad about not being willing to attend church with her mother. She could tell by Mama's wistful expression that she really did miss Sunday services inside a church building. Reading the Bible every night after supper was a good thing, but it wasn't the same as being in fellowship with other believers.

She and her mother went to wait for Mike by the wooden sales counter.

A few seconds later, Mike entered the store, carrying a large paper sack. He handed it to Kelly and grinned. "This should get you by for a while."

She peered inside the bag. Several large clumps of charcoal, as well as some smaller ones, completely filled it. Mike was right. These would last a good while, and tonight she planned to start putting them to use. "Thanks," she murmured.

He winked at her. "You're more than welcome."

Kelly cleared her throat, feeling kind of warm and jittery inside. Maybe she was coming down with whatever had been ailing her folks. A day of rest might do her more good than she realized.

Chapter 10

Sunday morning dawned with a blue, cloudless sky. It would be the perfect day for Kelly to enjoy the warm sun and draw. She hurried through her breakfast and morning chores, anxious for some time alone. Mama would be tending to Papa's needs for the next little while, and after that, she would probably take a rest herself.

Papa had taken to his bed last night and not even shown his face at the breakfast table. Kelly figured he must be pretty sick if he wasn't interested in food, for her dad usually had a ravenous appetite. She had taken him a tray with a cup of tea and bowl of oatmeal a little while ago, but Papa turned his nose up at both and said he wanted to be left alone—needed some sleep, that was all.

It seemed strange for Kelly to see her dad, who was usually up early and raring to go, curled up in a fetal position with a patchwork quilt pulled up to his ears. His breathing sounded labored, and he wheezed and coughed like the steam train that ran beside the canal, despite the medicine Mama had been spoon-feeding him since their visit to Mike's store last evening.

Thinking about Mike Cooper made Kelly remember their mules had been sleeping in his barn all night. She needed to feed and groom the animals, then take them outdoors for some fresh air and exercise. Wouldn't do for the mules to get lazy because they'd stopped for a bit. As soon as she was finished tending the critters, Kelly hoped to finally have some free time.

As she headed for the barn, which sat directly behind Mike's house, Kelly hummed her favorite song—"Hunks-a-go Pudding." Would Mama feel up to fixing a big meal today? Would it include a roast with some yummy hunks-a-go pudding? Kelly sure hoped so. It had been a good long while since she'd enjoyed the succulent taste of roast beef and hunks-a-go pudding, where the batter was put in the fat left over from the meat and then fried in a pan on top of the stove.

Forcing thoughts of food to the back of her mind, Kelly opened the barn door and peered inside. Except for the gentle braying of the mules, all was quiet. The sweet smell of hay wafted up to her nose, and she sniffed deeply. She stepped inside and was almost to the stall where Hector and Herman were stabled when she heard another sound. Someone was singing.

"Sweet hour of prayer, sweet hour of prayer, that calls me from a world of care."

Kelly plodded across the dirt floor, and the sound of the clear, masculine voice grew closer. She recognized it as belonging to Mike Cooper.

"And bids me at my Father's throne, make all my wants and wishes known."

Kelly halted, feeling like an intruder on Mike's quiet time alone with God. He must be deeply religious, for not only was he kindhearted, but he sang praises to God. Whenever Kelly sang, it was some silly canaler's song like "Hunks-a-go Pudding" or "You Rusty Canaler, You'll Never Get Rich." As a young child she would often sing "Jesus Loves Me," but she'd been a lot happier back then. Sarah had still been living with them, helping share the burden of walking the mules and visiting with Kelly for hours on end. Papa expected twice as much from Kelly now that Sarah was gone. But was that any excuse to quit worshipping the Lord?

Kelly knew the answer deep in her soul. She was angry with God for not changing Papa's heart. She was angry with Papa for being so stubborn and hot-tempered. And she was angry with Sarah for running off and leaving her to face Papa's temper and do all the work.

I'll show them. I'll show everyone that Kelly McGregor doesn't need anyone to get along in this world. I'm gonna make it on my own someday.

When Mike's song ended, Kelly moved forward again. She could see him sitting on a small wooden stool, milking a fat brown and white cow.

She cleared her throat real loud to make her presence known and stepped into the stall where Herman and Hector had bedded down for the night.

"Good morning," Mike called to her.

"Mornin'," she responded.

"Looks like it's gonna be a beautiful day."

"Yep. Right nice."

"What plans have you made for this Lord's Day?" he asked.

Kelly patted Herman's flank and leaned into the sturdy mule. "As soon as I get these two ready, I plan to take 'em outside for some exercise and fresh air."

Mike didn't say anything in reply, and Kelly could hear the steady *plunk, plink, plunk,* as the cow's milk dropped into the bucket. It was a soothing sound, and she found herself wishing she had a real, honest-to-goodness home with a barn, chicken coop, and maybe a bit of land. Nine months out of the year, her home was the inside of a canal boat, and during the winter, it was a cramped, dingy flat at a boardinghouse in Easton. Papa seemed to like their vagabond life, but Kelly hated it—more and more the older she got. Someday she hoped to leave it all behind. Oh, for the chance to fulfill her dreams.

Mike grabbed the bucket of milk and headed for the stall where Kelly's mules had been stabled. He was finally being given the chance to spend a few minutes alone with Kelly, and he aimed to take full advantage. If things went as he hoped, he would have the pleasure of her company for several hours today.

Mike leaned against the wooden beam outside the mules' stall and watched Kelly as she fed and groomed her beasts of burden. She wasn't wearing her usual straw hat this morning, and her lustrous brown hair hung down her back in long, loose waves. His fingers itched to reach out and touch those silky tresses.

"You're good with the mules," he murmured.

Kelly jumped, apparently startled and unaware that he'd been watching her. "Hector and Herman are easy to work with."

Mike drew in a deep breath. *May as well get this over with.* "I. . .uh. . .was wondering if you'd like to go on a picnic with me later today."

Kelly turned her head to look directly at him, and she blinked a couple of times. "A picnic? You and me?"

He nodded, then chuckled. "That's what I had in mind."

"Well, I was plannin' to spend some time drawin', and—"

"No reason you can't draw after we share our picnic lunch."

She hesitated a few seconds. "Mama may need my help with somethin', and my folks might not approve of me goin' on a picnic."

Mike smiled. At least she hadn't said no. He took that as a good sign. "While you finish up with the mules, how about I go talk to your parents?"

Kelly's forehead wrinkled. "I don't know if that's such a good idea."

"If they say it's all right, would you be willing to eat a picnic lunch with me?"

She nodded. Mike grinned. "Great! I'll take this milk into the house, get cleaned up a bit, and run down to the boat to speak with your folks."

"Papa's still in bed," Kelly said. "He ain't feelin' much better today than he was last night."

"Sorry to hear it. I'll ask your mother." Mike hurried out of the barn, and he hummed "Sweet Hour of Prayer" all the way. God was already answering his prayer for the day, and he felt like he was ten feet tall.

Kelly couldn't believe her mother had actually given permission for Mike Cooper to take her on a picnic. Maybe she felt bad because Kelly worked so hard and rarely got a day off. Or it might be that Mama needed some quiet time herself today, so she thought it would be good if Kelly were gone awhile.

The idea of a picnic did seem kind of nice. It would be a chance for Kelly to relax and enjoy Mike's company, as well as the good food he'd promised to prepare. On the other hand, spending time alone with the fine-looking storekeeper might not be such a good thing. What if he got the notion she was interested in him? Would Mike expect her to do more things with him when she was in the area? In some ways, she hoped they could. Life along the canal was lonely, especially when her only companions were a pair of mules.

Kelly stood in her tiny room and studied her reflection in the mirror that she kept in the trunk at the foot of her bed. Did she look presentable enough to accompany Mike Cooper on a picnic? Mike always smelled so clean, and he wore crisp trousers and shirts without holes or wrinkles. It was hard to believe he had no mother or wife caring for his needs. He must be very capable, she decided.

Mike had said he would meet Kelly in front of his store a

little before noon. This gave her plenty of time to get ready, and she'd even taken a bath in the galvanized tub and washed her hair, using that new floating soap Mama liked so well.

Kelly grabbed a lock of hair, swung it over her shoulder, and sniffed deeply. "Smells clean enough to me." She glanced down at her dark green skirt and long-sleeved white blouse with puffy sleeves. Both were plain and unfashionable, but Kelly didn't care a hoot about fashion, only comfort and looking presentable enough to be seen in public. Her clothes were clean; Mama had washed them yesterday. At least today she wasn't likely to offend Mike by smelling like one of her mules.

Kelly took out her drawing tablet and a piece of charcoal and stuffed them in her oversized skirt pocket. Then she grabbed her straw hat and one of Mama's old quilts. At least they would have something soft to sit on during their picnic lunch. She left the room and tiptoed quietly past her parents' bedroom. It wouldn't be good to wake Papa. He'd probably be furious if he knew she was taking the day off to go on a picnic—especially with a man. He might think she was going to up and run off the way Sarah had. Well, that would never happen!

As Kelly stepped off the boat, she caught a glimpse of Reverend Nelson and his daughter, Betsy. They were standing in front of Mike's store, and several boatmen and their families had gathered around.

It made no sense to Kelly. Shouldn't the preacher have been at his church, pounding the wooden pulpit and shouting at the congregation to repent and turn from their wicked ways? Instead, he was leading the group of people in song, and his daughter was playing along with her zither.

Kelly hoped to avoid the throng entirely, but Mike, who stood on the fringes, motioned her to join him. He was holding a wicker basket, and Kelly figured he was probably ready to head out on their picnic. If she hung back until the church service was over, they would lose some of their time together.

Mike crooked his finger at Kelly again, and she inched her way forward. *Guess I may as well see what he's plannin' to do.*

Chapter 11

*M*ike smiled at Kelly when she stepped up beside him.

"What's goin' on?" she whispered.

"Reverend Nelson finished his worship service early today, so he and Betsy decided to bring a bit of revival to the boatmen and their families who stayed in the area for the night."

"Do you attend their church in town?" Kelly asked.

Mike shrugged his shoulders. "Sometimes." The truth was, he used to go every Sunday, but here of late he'd been feeling mighty uncomfortable around Betsy Nelson. He'd stayed home the last couple weeks, praying and reading his Bible in solitude. He knew he shouldn't be using Betsy's overbearing, flirtatious ways as an excuse to stay away from church, but it was getting harder to deal with her. Especially since Kelly McGregor had come into his life.

He stared down at Kelly, small and delicate, yet strong and reliable. Where did she stand as far as spiritual things were concerned? He needed to find out soon, before he lost his heart to the beautiful young woman.

"Ready to head out on our picnic?" Kelly questioned.

Now was as good a time as any to see how interested she was in church.

"I thought maybe we'd stick around until Reverend Nelson is done preaching," Mike said. "It's been awhile since I've heard a good sermon." He studied Kelly's face to gauge her reaction. She looked a bit hesitant, but agreeably she nodded. He breathed a sigh of relief.

"Should we take a seat on the grass?" he asked, motioning to a spot a few feet away.

She followed him there and spread out the quilt she'd been holding so tightly.

Mike set the picnic basket down, and they both took a seat on the blanket. Leaning back on his elbows, Mike joined the group singing "Amazing Grace." His spirits soared as the music washed over him like gentle waves lapping against the shore. He loved to sing praises to God, and when the mood hit, he enjoyed blowing on the old mouth harp that had belonged to Grandpa Cooper.

He glanced over at Kelly. She wasn't singing, but her eyes were closed, and her face was lifted toward the sun. *She must be praying. That's a good indication that she knows the Lord personally.*

He smiled to himself. The day had started out even better than he'd expected.

Kelly opened her eyes and looked around. About two dozen

people were seated on the ground. Some were singing, some lifted their hands in praise, and others quietly listened. She couldn't believe she'd let Mike talk her into staying around for this outdoor church service. It was a beautiful spring day, and she wanted to be away from the crowd, where she could listen to the sounds of nature and draw to her heart's content. When she'd agreed to accompany Mike on a picnic, the plan hadn't included church.

Kelly knew her attitude was wrong. She'd asked Jesus to forgive her sins several years ago. She should take pleasure in worshipping God. Besides, out here among the other boatmen and their families, Kelly didn't stick out like a sore thumb. Nobody but the preacher and his daughter were dressed in fine clothes, so Kelly blended right in with her unfashionable long cotton skirt and plain white blouse.

The singing was over, and the reverend had begun to preach. Kelly's gaze wandered until she noticed a young boy who sat several feet away. He had bright red hair, and his face and arms were covered with freckles. The child's looks weren't what captured Kelly's attention, though. It was the small green toad he was holding in his grubby hands. He stroked the critter's head as though it were a pet.

He's probably poor and doesn't own many toys. If his papa's a boatman, they travel up and down the canal most of the year, so the little guy can't have any real pets.

Kelly knew that wasn't entirely true. Many canalers owned dogs that either walked along the towpath or rode in the boat. She figured the little red-haired boy's dad was probably too cranky or too stingy to let his son own a dog or a cat. *Kind of like my dad. He'd never allow me to have a pet.*

Kelly's thoughts were halted as Preacher Nelson shouted, "God wants you to turn from your sins and repent!"

She sat up a little straighter and tried to look attentive when she noticed Mike look over at her. Had he caught her daydreaming? Did he think she was a sinner who needed to repent?

After the pastor's final prayer, he announced, "My daughter, Betsy, will now close our service with a solo."

Betsy stood up and began to strum her zither as she belted out the first verse of "Sweet By and By." As the young woman came to the last note, her voice cracked, and her faced turned redder than a radish.

Kelly stifled a chuckle behind her hand. *Serves the snooty woman right for thinkin' she's better'n me.*

"He that is without sin among you, let him first cast a stone at her." Kelly gulped as she remembered that verse of scripture from the book of John. Mama had quoted it many times over the years.

The preacher's daughter might be uppity and kind of pushy at times, but Kelly knew she was no better in God's eyes. Fact of the matter, Kelly felt that she was probably worse, for she often harbored resentment in her heart toward Papa. She resolved to try to do better.

When the service was over, Mike stood and grabbed their picnic basket. Kelly gathered up her quilt and tucked it under one arm. She'd thought they would head right off for their picnic, but Mike moved toward Preacher Nelson. Not knowing what else to do, Kelly followed.

"That was a fine sermon you preached," Mike said, shaking Reverend Nelson's hand.

The older man beamed. "Thank you, Mike. I'm glad you enjoyed it."

Betsy, who stood next to her father, smiled at Mike and fluttered her eyelashes. "How about the singing? Did you enjoy that, too?"

Mike nodded. It was downright sickening the way Betsy kept eyeing him, as though she wanted to kiss the man, of all things.

Kelly nudged Mike in the ribs with her elbow. "Are we goin' on that picnic or not?"

"Yes. . .yes, of course," he stammered.

Why was Mike acting so nervous all of a sudden? Did being around Betsy Nelson do this to him? Kelly opened her mouth to say something, but Betsy cut her right off.

"You're going on a picnic, Mike?" Her eyelids fluttered again. "It's such a beautiful day, and I haven't been on a picnic since early last fall. Would you mind if I tag along?"

"Well, uh. . ." Mike turned to Kelly, as though he expected her to say something.

When she made no response, Betsy said, "You wouldn't mind if I joined you and Mike, would you, Kelly?"

Kelly's irritation flared up like fireflies buzzing on a muggy summer day. She didn't want to make an issue, so she merely shrugged her shoulders and made circles in the dirt with the toe of her boot.

"Great! It's all settled then." Betsy grinned like an eager child. "Have you got enough food for three, Mike?"

"Sure, I made plenty of fried chicken and biscuits."

Betsy turned to her father then. "I won't be gone long, Papa."

He smiled. "You go on with the young people and have yourself a good time. I want to visit with several folks, and if I'm fortunate enough to be invited to join one of the families for a meal, I probably won't be home until evening."

"Everything is perfect then. I'll see you at home later on." Betsy handed her father the zither and slipped her hand through the crook of Mike's arm. "So, where should we have this picnic?"

"Guess we'll look for a nice spot up the canal a bit." When Mike looked at Kelly, she noticed his face was a deep shade of red. Was he wondering why he'd invited her on a picnic? Did he wish he could spend time alone with Betsy Nelson? Should Kelly make up some excuse as to why she couldn't go? Maybe it would be best if she went off by herself for the day.

Mike pulled away from Betsy and grabbed hold of Kelly's hand. "Let's be off," he announced. "I'm hungry as a bear!"

Chapter 12

Kelly, Mike, and Betsy sat in silence on the quilt. The picnic basket was empty, and everyone admitted to being full. There had been plenty of food to go around.

Kelly leaned back on her elbows, soaking up the sun's warming rays and listening to the canal waters lapping against the bank. She felt relaxed and content and had almost forgotten her irritation over the preacher's daughter joining their picnic.

Seeing a couple of ducks on the water reminded Kelly that she'd brought along her drawing tablet and a piece of charcoal. She sat up and withdrew both from her skirt pocket, then quickly began to sketch. A flash of green on the mallard's head made her once again wish she could work with colored paints. Folks might be apt to buy a picture with color, as it looked more like the real thing.

"In another month or so the canal will be filled with

swimmers," Betsy said, her high-pitched voice cutting into the serenely quiet moment.

"You're right about that," Mike agreed. "It scares me the way some youngsters swim so close to the canal boats. It's a wonder one of them doesn't get killed."

"I hear there's plenty of accidents on the canal," Betsy put in.

"Kelly could probably tell us a lot of stories in that regard," Mike said.

Kelly's mind took her back to a couple years ago, when she'd witnessed one of the lock tender's children fall between a boat and the lock. The little boy had been killed instantly—crushed to death. It was a pitiful sight to see the child's mother weeping and wailing.

Kelly had seen a few small children fall overboard and drown. Most folks who had little ones kept them tied to a rope so that wouldn't happen, but some who'd been careless paid the price with the loss of a child.

"Yep," Kelly murmured, "there's been quite a few deaths on the Lehigh Navigation System."

Mike groaned. "I was afraid of the water when I was a boy, so I never learned to swim as well as I probably should have. So I don't often go in the canal except to wade or do a couple of dives off the locks now and then."

"If you can't swim too good, aren't you afraid to dive?" Kelly asked.

He shrugged his shoulders. "I can manage to kick my way to the surface of the water, then paddle like a dog back to the lock."

"Hmm. . .I see."

"What about you?" Betsy asked, looking directly at Kelly. "As dirty as you get trudging up and down the dusty towpath, I imagine you must jump into the canal quite frequently in order to get cleaned off."

Kelly sniffed deeply, feeling a sudden need to defend herself. "I learned to swim when I was a little girl, so I have no fear of drowning." *Just scared to death of water snakes*, her inner voice reminded. She saw no need to reveal her reservations about swimming in the canal. No use giving the preacher's daughter one more thing to look down her nose about.

Mike shifted on the quilt and leaned closer to Kelly. She could feel his warm breath against her neck and found it to be a distraction.

"That's a nice picture you're making," Mike whispered. "Is the charcoal I gave you working out okay?"

"It's fine," she answered as she kept on drawing.

"Maybe you can get a few pictures done today so I can take them back to the store and try to sell them."

She nodded. "Maybe so."

"How about you and me going for a walk, Mike?" Betsy asked, cutting into their conversation.

Mike moved away from Kelly, and she felt a keen sense of disappointment, which made no sense, since she wasn't the least bit interested in the storekeeper. She'd already decided Betsy Nelson would make a better match for Mike than someone like herself.

"Kelly, would you like to walk with me and Betsy?" Mike asked.

She shook her head. "I'd rather stay here with my tablet and charcoal. You two go ahead. I'll be fine."

Betsy stood up and held her hand out to Mike. "I'm ready if you are."

He made a grunting sound as he clambered to his feet. "We'll be back soon, Kelly."

Keeping her focus on the ducks swimming directly in front of her, Kelly mumbled, "Sure, okay."

Mike wasn't the least bit happy about leaving Kelly alone while he and Betsy went for a walk. This was supposed to be his and Kelly's picnic—a chance for them to get better acquainted. It should have been Kelly he was walking with, not the preacher's daughter.

Betsy clung to his arm like they were a courting couple, and she chattered a mile a minute. If only he could figure out some way to discourage her without being rude. Mike didn't want to hurt Betsy's feelings, but he didn't want to lead her on, either.

"Maybe we should head back," he said, when Betsy stopped talking long enough for him to get in a word.

She squeezed his arm a little tighter and kept on walking. "Why would you want to head back? It's a beautiful day, and the fresh air and exercise will do us both some good."

Mike opened his mouth to reply, but she cut him right off.

"I missed seeing you in church this morning."

He cleared his throat a few times, feeling like a little boy who was about to be reprimanded for being naughty. "Well, I—"

"Papa says we need young men like yourself as active members in the church," Betsy said, chopping him off again.

Mike shrugged as a feeling of guilt slid over him. He knew what the Bible said about men being the spiritual leaders. He also was aware that he needed to take a more active part in evangelizing the world. Maybe he would speak to Reverend Nelson about holding regular church services along the canal. Mike could donate some of his Bibles for people who didn't have one of their own. As far as attending the Nelsons' church, Mike wasn't sure that was such a good idea. It would mean spending more time with Betsy. It wasn't that he disliked the woman, but her chattering and pushiness got on his nerves.

"Mike, are you listening to me?"

He pushed his thoughts aside and focused on the woman who was tugging on his shirtsleeve. "What were you saying?"

"I was talking about mission work," Betsy replied in an exasperated tone. "I said we have a mission opportunity right here along the canal."

He nodded. "I agree. I was just thinking that if your father wanted to hold regular Sunday services out in front of my store, I'd be happy to furnish folks with Bibles."

Betsy's thin lips curled into a smile. "That sounds like a wonderful idea. I'll speak to Papa about it this evening."

Mike was amazed at Betsy's exuberance. She either shared his desire to tell others about Jesus or was merely looking forward to spending more time with him.

He grimaced. *I shouldn't be thinking the worst.* Mike knew he was going to have to work on his attitude, especially where the preacher's daughter was concerned. She did have some good points, but she wasn't the kind of woman Mike was looking for.

A vision of Kelly flashed into his mind. Dark eyes that bore right through him; long dark hair cascading down her back; a smile that could light up any room. But it was more than Kelly's good looks and winning smile that had captured Mike's attention. There was a tenderness and vulnerability about Kelly McGregor that drew Mike to her like a thirsty horse heads for water. Sometimes, she seemed like an innocent child needing to be rescued from something that was causing her pain. The next minute, Kelly appeared confident and self-assured. She was like a jigsaw puzzle, and he wanted to put all the complicated pieces of her together.

"Mike, you're not listening to me again."

He turned his head in Betsy's direction. "What were you saying?"

"I was wondering if you would like to come over for supper one night next week."

He groped for words that wouldn't be a lie. "I. . .uh. . .am expecting a shipment of goods soon, and I need to clean off some shelves and get the place organized before the load arrives."

Betsy's lower lip jutted out. "Surely you won't be working every evening."

Mike nodded. "I could be."

Her eyebrows drew together, nearly meeting at the middle. "I was hoping to tempt you with my chicken and dumplings. Papa says they're the best he's ever tasted."

"I'm sure they are." Mike gave Betsy's arm a gentle pat. "Maybe some other time."

"I hope so," she replied.

Should I be frank and tell her I'm not interested in pursuing a personal relationship? Mike stopped walking and swung around, taking Betsy with him, since she still held onto his arm. "We'd better head back now."

"Why so soon?"

"We left Kelly alone, and I don't feel right about that."

"I'm sure she's fine. She's not a little girl, you know."

Mike knew all right. Every time Kelly smiled at him or tipped her head to one side as she spoke his name, he was fully aware that she was a desirable young woman, not the child who used to drop by his store with her parents. He was anxious to get back to their picnic spot and see what Kelly had drawn.

"Mike, please slow down. I can barely keep up with you," Betsy panted when Mike started walking again.

"Sorry, but I invited Kelly to join me for a picnic today, and she probably thinks I've abandoned her."

Betsy moaned. "I didn't realize you two were courting. Why didn't you say so? If I'd known, I certainly would not have intruded on your time together."

Mike's ears were burning, and he knew they had turned bright red, the way they always did whenever he felt nervous or got flustered about something.

"Kelly and I are not officially courting," he mumbled. *Though I sure wish we were.*

Betsy opened her mouth as if to say something, but he spoke first.

"Even though we're not courting, I did invite her on a picnic. So, it's only right that I spend some time with her, don't you think?"

Betsy let out a deep sigh, but she nodded. "Far be it from me to keep you from your Christian duty."

"Thanks for understanding." Mike hurried up the towpath, with Betsy still clutching his arm. Soon Kelly came into view, and Mike halted his footsteps at the sight before him. Stretched out on the quilt, her dark hair fanned out like a pillow, Kelly had fallen asleep. The sketching tablet was in one hand, and a chunk of charcoal was in the other. She looked like an angel. Would she be his angel someday?

Chapter 13

*T*he following day, Mike was surprised when Kelly's dad entered his store shortly after he'd opened for business.

"Mr. McGregor, how are you feeling this morning?" Mike asked.

"I'll live," came the curt reply.

"I hope the days you spent docked here gave you ample time to rest up and get that cough under control."

Amos coughed and grunted in response. "As I said, I'll live, but it looks like we'll be stuck here another day or so, 'cause thanks to you, one of my mules came up lame this mornin'."

Mike frowned. "Really? They both seemed fine yesterday."

"Herman's not fine now. He went and got his leg cut up on a bale of wire you carelessly left layin' around." Kelly's dad leveled Mike with a challenging look.

Feeling a headache coming on, Mike massaged his forehead with his fingertips. "Weren't your mules in their stalls last night?"

"Yeah, in your barn."

"Then I don't understand how one of them could have gotten cut with the wire, which was nowhere near the stalls."

"Guess the door wasn't latched tight and they got out. At least Herman did, for he's the one with the cut leg."

Mike opened his mouth to respond, but Amos rushed on. "You got any liniment for me to put on the poor critter?"

"I'm sure I do." Mike hurried to the area of the store where he kept all the medicinal supplies, and Amos stayed right on his heels. The man seemed grumpier than usual today. Was it because he was so upset about the mule's injury and blamed Mike for the mishap?

Mike had no more than taken the medicine off the shelf, when Amos snatched it out of his hands. The older man stomped up to the counter and demanded, "How much do I owe ya for this?"

"I normally charge a quarter for that liniment, but since you feel the accident was my fault, there'll be no charge," Mike answered as he moved to the other side of the counter. He knew the McGregors weren't financially well off, and now that they couldn't travel because of a lame mule, they would be set back even further.

Amos slapped a quarter down. "I won't be beholdin' to no man, so I'll pay ya what the stuff is worth." He grimaced. "I'm losin' money with each passing day. First I got slowed down when Dorrie was sick and I was tryin' to cook, clean, and steer the boat. Then I came down with the bug and was laid up for a couple of days. Now I've got me a lame mule, and it should never have happened!"

"I'm sorry for your inconvenience, Mr. McGregor," Mike said apologetically.

"Yeah, well, at the rate things are goin', it'll be the end of the week before I can get back up to Mauch Chunk for another load of coal."

"Could you go on ahead with just one mule? I'd be happy to stable Herman until you come back this way."

Amos scowled at Mike. "Hector might be strong enough to pull the boat when it's empty, but not with a load of coal. Don'tcha know anything, boy?"

Mike clenched his teeth. Even though he didn't know everything about canal boating, he wasn't stupid. Should he defend himself to Kelly's dad or ignore the discourteous remark? Mike opted for the second choice. "I hope your mule's leg heals quickly, Mr. McGregor, and I'm sorry about the wire. If you need anything else, please don't hesitate to ask."

Amos coughed, blew his nose on the hanky he'd withdrawn from the pocket of his overalls, and sauntered out the door, slamming it behind him.

Mike sank to the wooden stool behind the counter and shook his head. At least one good thing would come from the McGregors being waylaid another day or two. It would give him a chance to see Kelly again. Yesterday's picnic had been a big disappointment to Mike. First, Betsy had invited herself to join them, and then, she'd hung onto him most of the day. Kelly had fallen asleep while she was waiting for him and Betsy to return from their walk. He'd wakened her when they got back to the picnic site, but Kelly seemed distant after that and said she needed to head for the boat. Mike offered to walk with her, but she handed him her finished picture of two ducks on the water and said she could find her own way. She'd even insisted that Mike see the preacher's daughter safely home.

Mike reached up to scratch the back of his head. He had to let Kelly know he wasn't interested in Betsy. He cared about Kelly, and he wanted her to realize that. He just had to figure out how to go about revealing his true feelings without scaring her off.

Kelly couldn't believe they were stranded in front of Mike's store yet another day, possibly more. And as she followed Papa's curt instructions to get off the boat and put some medicine on Herman's leg, she shook her head over Papa's refusal to let the mules be stabled in Mike's barn any longer. It wasn't Mike's fault Herman had broken free from his stall and cut his leg on a roll of wire that had been sitting near the barn door. Now Herman and Hector were both tied to a maple tree growing several feet off the towpath, not far from where their boat was docked. Tonight, they would be bedded down in the compartment set aside for them in the bow of the boat.

Kelly squatted beside Herman's right front leg and slathered on some of the medicine. "I don't see why I have to do this," she muttered. "I'd planned to get some drawin' done today, but Papa will probably find more chores for me to do when I return to the boat."

A sense of guilt for her selfish thoughts washed over Kelly. She knew her dad still wasn't feeling well, and he had a right to get some rest while they were laid over. Trouble was, she wanted to draw. At the rate she was going, she would never have anything to give Mike to try to sell in his store. She had given him the picture of the ducks she'd drawn during yesterday's picnic, but that was all.

Thinking about the picnic caused an ache in Kelly's soul. She didn't understand why Mike had invited her, then asked Betsy Nelson to join them.

Well, not asked, exactly, she reminded herself. If Kelly's memory served her right, it was Betsy who had done the asking. Mike only agreed she could accompany them on the picnic. Might could be that he had no real interest in Betsy at all.

" 'Course I don't care if he does," she murmured.

Herman brayed, and Hector followed suit, as if in answer to her complaints.

When Kelly stood up, Herman nuzzled her arm with his nose. She chuckled and patted his neck. "You should be good as new in a day or so, Herman the Determined. Then we can be on our way again."

On impulse, Kelly reached into her apron pocket and withdrew the drawing pad and piece of charcoal she often carried with her. She flopped onto the ground and began to sketch the two mules as they grazed on the green grass.

Some time later, she stood up. She had two pictures of Herman and Hector to take over to Mike's.

When she entered the store, Kelly was pleased to see that Mike had no customers, and he seemed genuinely glad to see her.

"I was sorry to hear about Herman's leg," he said, moving

toward Kelly. "Your dad thinks it's my fault because there was a roll of wire by the barn door."

She pursed her lips. "Papa always looks for someone to blame. Don't fret about it, 'cause it sure wasn't your doin'. If anyone's to blame, it's Papa. He's the one who fed and watered the mules last night, so he probably didn't see that the door to their stall was shut tight." She frowned. "Of course, he'd never admit it."

Mike grinned at Kelly, and her stomach did a little flip-flop. She licked her lips and took a step forward. "I. . .uh. . .brought you a couple more drawings."

She held the pictures out to Mike, and he took them. "Thanks, these are nice. I'll get them put on display right away."

"Sure wish they had a little color to 'em. Herman and Hector are brown, not black, but my picture don't show it."

"Maybe you could buy a set of watercolors or oil paints," Mike suggested.

She shook her head. "Don't have enough money for that yet." Kelly knew she needed to save all her money if she was ever going to earn enough to be on her own or open an art gallery.

"Have you considered making your own watercolors?"

Her forehead wrinkled. "How could I do that?"

"I noticed some coffee stains on my tablecloth this morning," Mike said. "Funny thing was, they were all a different shade of brown."

"Hmm. . .guess it all depends on the strength of the coffee how dark the stain might be."

He nodded. "Exactly. So, I was thinking maybe you could try using old coffee to paint with. I've got some brushes I could let you have."

Kelly considered his offer carefully. It did sound feasible, but she wouldn't feel right about taking the brushes without paying something for them. If Papa had taught her anything, it was not to accept charity.

"How much would the brushes cost?" she asked Mike.

"I just said I'd be happy to give them to you."

She shook her head. "I either pay, or I don't take the brushes."

He shrugged. "I'll let you have three for a nickel. How's that sound?"

She nodded. "It's a deal."

A few minutes later, Kelly was walking out the door with three small paintbrushes, a jar of cold coffee, and an apple for each mule. Mike had insisted the coffee was a day old and he would have to throw it out if she didn't accept it. Kelly decided stale coffee didn't have much value, so she agreed to take it off his hands. The apples she paid for.

"Come back tomorrow and let me know how your new watercolors work out," Mike said.

She smiled and called over her shoulder, "I may have more pictures for you in the mornin'."

Chapter 14

*T*hat night after Kelly went to her room, she worked with the coffee watercolors. It was the first time she'd ever used a paintbrush, and it took awhile to get the hang of it. But once she did, Kelly found it to be thoroughly enjoyable. She decided to try a little experiment.

In her bare feet, she crept upstairs to the small kitchen area. She knew her folks were both asleep. She could hear Mama's heavy breathing and Papa's deep snoring.

Kelly lifted the lid from the wooden bin where Mama kept a stash of root vegetables. She pulled out a few carrots, two onions, and a large beet. Next, she heated water in the cast-iron kettle on the cookstove. When it reached the boiling point, she placed her vegetables in three separate bowls and poured scalding water over all. One by one Kelly carried the bowls back to her room. She would let them sit overnight, and by morning, she hoped to have colored water in three different shades.

The following day, Herman's leg was no better, and Papa was fit to be tied.

"I'm losin' money just sittin' here," he hollered as he examined the cut on Herman's leg.

Kelly stood by his side, wishing she had some idea what to say.

"Do you know how many boats I've seen goin' up and down the canal?" he bellowed. "Everyone but me is makin' money this week!"

Kelly thought of the little bit of cash she'd made when Mike paid her for those first few drawings. If Papa were really destitute, she would offer to turn the money over to him. That wasn't the case, though. Her dad was tightfisted with his money, and truth be told, he probably had more stashed away than Kelly would ever see in her lifetime. Besides, she didn't want Papa to know she had any money. If he found out, he would most likely demand that she give it all to him—and any future money she made as well.

So Kelly quietly listened to her father's tirade. He would soon calm down. He always did.

"Should I check with Mike Cooper and see if he has any other medicine that might work better on Herman's cut?" she asked when Papa finally quit blustering.

His face turned bright red, and his forehead wrinkled. "I ain't givin' that man one more dime to take care of an injury that he caused in the first place. We'll sit tight another day and see how Herman's doin' come morning." Papa turned and stomped off toward the boat.

Kelly reached up to stroke Herman behind his ear. "He's a

stubborn one, that papa of mine," she mumbled. Yes, they were losing time and money by waiting for the mule's leg to heal, but didn't Papa realize if he spent a little more on medicine, Herman's leg would probably heal faster? Then they could be on their way to Mauch Chunk and be making money that much sooner. Papa was just being mulish.

Kelly dipped her hand into the deep apron pocket where she kept her drawing tablet. At least one good thing had happened this morning. She'd gotten up early and painted a couple of pictures, using her homemade watercolors. The first one was another pose of the mules, only now they were coffee colored, not black. The second picture was of a sunset, with pink, orange, and yellow hues, all because of her vegetable watercolors. She was proud of her accomplishment and could hardly wait to show the pictures to Mike.

"I think I'll head over to his store right now," Kelly said, giving Hector a pat, so he wouldn't feel left out. The mule brayed and nudged her affectionately. Herman and Hector really were her best friends.

A short time later, Kelly entered Mike's store. He was busy waiting on a customer—Mrs. Harris, one of the lock tenders' wives. Kelly waited patiently over by the candy counter. It was tempting to spend some of her money on more lemon drops, but she reminded herself that she still had a few pieces of candy tucked safely away inside the trunk at the foot of her bed. She would wait until those were gone before she considered buying any more.

"Can I help you with something?" Lost in her thoughts, Kelly hadn't realized Mike had finished with his customer and now stood at her side. She drew in a deep breath as the fresh scent of soap reminded her of Mike's presence. He always smelled so clean and unsullied. His nearness sent unwanted tingles along her spine, and she forced herself to keep from trembling.

"I wanted to see what you thought of these." Kelly held out her drawing tablet to Mike.

He studied the first painting of Herman and Hector, done with coffee water. "Hmm. . .not bad. Not bad at all." Then he turned to the next page, and his mouth fell open. "Kelly, how did you make such beautiful colors?"

She giggled, feeling suddenly self-conscious. "I poured boiling water over some carrots, onions, and a beet; then I let it stand all night. This mornin', I had some colored water to paint with."

Mike grinned from ear to ear. "That's really impressive. I'm proud of you, Kelly."

Proud of me? Had she heard Mike right? In all her seventeen years, Kelly didn't remember anyone ever saying they were proud of anything she'd done. She felt the heat of a blush creep up her neck and flood her entire face. "It was nothin' so special."

"Oh, but it was," Mike insisted. "My idea of using coffee water was okay, and your picture of the mules is good, but you took it even further by coming up with a way to make more colors." He lifted the drawing tablet. "You've captured a sunset beautifully."

She smiled, basking in his praise. If only Mama and Papa would say things to encourage her the way Mike did. Mama said very little, and Papa either yelled or criticized.

"I think I'll come up with a better way to display your artwork," Mike announced.

"Oh? What's that?"

"I'm going to make a wooden frame for each of your pictures, and then I'll hang them right there." He pointed to the wall directly behind the counter where he waited on customers. "Nobody will leave my store without first seeing your talented creations."

Talented creations? First Mike had said he was proud of her, and now he'd called her talented. It was almost too much for Kelly to accept. Did he really mean those things, or was he only trying to be nice because he felt sorry for her? She hoped it wasn't the latter, for she didn't want anyone's pity.

"Kelly, did you hear what I said?"

She jerked her head toward Mike. "What did ya say?"

"I asked if you thought framing the pictures would be a good idea."

She nodded. "I suppose so. It's worth a try if you want to go to all that trouble."

"I like working with my hands, so it won't be any trouble at all." Mike looked down at the tablet he still held. "Mind if I take the two colored pictures out now?"

"It's fine by me," she replied, feeling a sense of excitement. "If we stay around here another day or so, maybe I can get a few more drawings done."

He smiled and moved toward the counter. Kelly followed. "That would be great. I hope you do stay around a bit longer—for more reasons than one."

Mike felt such exuberance over Kelly's new pictures done on

newsprint, not to mention the news of her staying for another day or so. He'd been asking God to give him the chance to get to know Kelly better, and it looked as if he might get that opportunity. But he did feel bad that her father was losing money because of the mule's leg. If there was some way he could offer financial assistance, he would, but Mike knew it wouldn't be appreciated. Amos McGregor was a proud man. He'd made that abundantly clear on several occasions.

"Guess I should get goin'," Kelly announced. "Papa left me to tend Herman's leg, and that was some time ago. He'll probably come a-lookin' for me if I don't get back to the boat pretty soon."

Mike carefully removed Kelly's finished pictures and handed her the tablet. "Keep up the good work, and when you get more paintings done, bring them into the store." He chuckled. "If you give me enough, I'll line every wall with your artwork. Then folks won't have any choice but to notice. And if they notice, they're bound to buy."

Kelly snickered, and her face turned crimson. "I like you, Mike Cooper." With that, she turned around and bounded out the door.

Mike flopped down on his wooden stool. "She likes me. Kelly actually said she likes me."

Chapter 15

*I*t took three days before Herman's leg was well enough so he could walk without limping. Even then, Papa had said at breakfast that they'd be taking it slow and easy. "No use pushin' things," he told Kelly and her mother. "Wouldn't want Herman to reinjure his leg."

As Kelly connected the towline to the mules' harnesses, a sense of sadness washed over her soul. These last few days had been so nice, being in one place all the time, visiting with Mike Cooper whenever she had the chance, and painting pictures. She'd used up all her homemade watercolors and would need to make more soon. Kelly figured as she journeyed up the towpath she might come across some plants, tree bark, or leaves she could steep in hot water to make other colors. It would be an adventure to see how many hues she could come up with.

"You all set?" Papa called from the boat.

Kelly waved in response, her signal that she was ready to go.

She'd only taken a few steps when she heard someone holler, "Kelly, hold up a minute, would you?"

She whirled around. Mike Cooper was heading her way, holding something in his hands.

Kelly stopped the mules, but Papa shouted at her to get them going again. She knew she'd better keep on walking or suffer the consequences. "I've gotta go," she announced when Mike caught up to her. "Papa's anxious to head out."

"I'll walk with you a ways," he said.

"What about your store?"

"I haven't opened for the day yet."

Kelly clicked her tongue, and the mules moved forward. Then she turned to face Mike as she moved along. The item he held in his hand was a wooden picture frame, and inside was her sunset watercolor.

"What do you think?" Mike asked as she looked at the piece of artwork.

"You did a fine job makin' that frame."

He laughed. "The frame's nothing compared to the beauty of your picture, but it does show off your work really well, don't you think?"

Kelly nodded but kept on walking. If she stopped, the mules would, too.

"When do you think you'll be coming by my store again?" Mike asked.

She shrugged her shoulders. "Can't say for sure. Since Papa lost so much time because of his cough and Herman's leg gettin' cut, he probably won't make any stops that aren't absolutely necessary."

"Guess we could always pray he knocks a few more bars of soap overboard."

Kelly snickered. "With the way things have been goin' these days, Papa would probably expect me to jump in the canal and fetch 'em back out."

Mike reached out and touched Kelly's arm. She felt a jolt and wondered if he had, too.

"I'm sorry you have to work so hard, Kelly," he murmured.

She nodded and kept moving forward. "I'm used to it, but someday, when I make enough money of my own, I won't be Papa's slave no more."

"I'm sure he doesn't see you as his slave."

She snorted. "I don't get paid for walkin' the mules. Not one single penny had I ever made 'til you sold my two drawings." She glanced at Mike out of the corner of her eye and noticed his shocked expression.

"That will change," he said with a note of conviction. "By the time you stop at my store again, I'm sure several more of your pictures will be gone."

They were coming to a bend in the canal, and Kelly and the mules would be tromping across the changing bridge soon. Kelly knew it was time to tell Mike good-bye, although she hated to see him go. She was beginning to see Mike Cooper as a friend.

"Guess I'd better head back and open up the store," Mike said, "but I wanted to ask you something before you crossed to the other side."

"Oh? What's that?"

"I was wondering if you've ever accepted Christ as your

personal Savior. You know—asked Him to forgive your sins and come live in your heart?"

"I did that when I was twelve years old," she said as a lump formed in her throat. Why was Mike asking about her relationship to God, and why was she getting all choked up over a simple good-bye? She'd be seeing Mike again; she just didn't know when.

Mike took hold of Kelly's hand and gave it a gentle squeeze. She glanced back at the boat, hoping Papa couldn't see what was going on.

"I'm awful glad to hear you're a believer. See you soon, Kelly," he whispered.

"I hope so," Kelly said; then she hurried on.

Mike stood watching Kelly until she and the mules disappeared around the bend. She looked so forlorn when they parted. Was she going to miss him as much as he would miss her? He hoped so. These last few days had been wonderful, with her popping into the store a couple of times and the two of them meeting outside on several occasions. Mike felt as though he were beginning to know Kelly better, and he liked what he'd discovered. Not only was the young woman a talented artist, but she was clever. She had figured out how to make her own watercolors, and Mike had a hunch she would probably have come up with even more colors by the time he saw her again.

"Sure hope I've sold some of her artwork by then," he muttered as he turned toward his store. "I can't keep buying them myself, and I wouldn't want Kelly to find out about the two I did pay for."

An image of Kelly lying on the patchwork quilt they'd used at the Sunday picnic flashed across Mike's mind. If Betsy hadn't been there, he might have taken a chance and kissed his sleeping beauty, for he was quickly losing his heart to Kelly McGregor.

Kelly had to hold up the mules at the changing bridge, as two other boats passed and their mules went over. While she waited, she decided to take advantage of the time, so she reached into her apron pocket and pulled out her drawing pad and a stick of charcoal. Kelly had just begun to sketch the boat ahead of her when Reverend Nelson and his daughter came walking up the towpath.

"Good morning," the preacher said. "It's a fine day, wouldn't you say?"

Kelly nodded in reply.

"Daddy and I are walking a stretch of the towpath today," Betsy remarked. "We're calling at people's homes who live near the canal, as well as visiting with those we meet along the way." She stuck out her hand and waved a piece of paper in front of Kelly's face. "We're handing these out. Would you like one?"

"What is it?" Kelly asked.

"It's a verse of scripture," Reverend Nelson answered before his daughter could respond.

Kelly took the Bible verse with a mumbled thanks, then stuffed it into her apron pocket. She would look at it later.

"What's that you're drawing?" the pastor asked.

"One of the canal boats."

Reverend Nelson glanced at her tablet and smiled. "It's a good likeness."

Kelly shrugged her shoulders. "I've only just begun."

"Betsy has one of your drawings. It's quite well done, considering what you have to work with."

Kelly's mouth dropped open. Betsy had one of her drawings? But how? A light suddenly dawned. The preacher's daughter must have gone into Mike's store and purchased one of Kelly's pictures. She smiled at Betsy and asked, "Which one did you buy?"

Betsy's pale eyebrows drew together as she frowned. "The picture is of a couple children fishing on the canal, but I didn't buy it."

"You didn't?"

Betsy shook her head. "Mike Cooper gave it to me as a birthday present. A few weeks ago he came over to our house for supper and to help me celebrate. He presented it to me then."

Kelly felt as though someone had punched her in the stomach. If Mike had given one of the drawings away, then he must have bought it himself. Her fingers coiled tightly around the piece of charcoal she still held in her hand. Who had bought the other picture Mike had paid her for? Was it him? He hadn't actually said so, but he'd given her the impression that he'd sold the pictures to some customers who'd come into the store.

The ground beneath her feet began to rumble as a steam train lumbered past. Billows of smoke from the burning coal poured into the sky, leaving a dark, sooty trail.

"Guess we'd better be moving on," the preacher said with a wave of his hand.

Kelly nodded. Her heart was hammering in her chest like the *clickety-clack* of the train's wheels against the track.

Just wait until I drop by Mike's store again, she fumed. *I'm gonna give that man a piece of my mind, and that's for certain sure!*

For the rest of the day Kelly fretted about the pictures Mike had supposedly sold. At supper that night, she was in a sour mood and didn't feel much like eating, even though Mama had made Irish stew, a favorite with both Kelly and her dad.

"What was that storekeeper doing, walkin' along the towpath with you this mornin'?" Papa asked, sending Kelly a disgruntled look.

She shrugged and switched her focus to the bowl of stew in front of her. "He was showin' me something he made and plans to sell in his store."

"What did he make?" Mama questioned.

Kelly had hoped neither of her parents would question her further. She didn't want them to know she'd given Mike some of her drawings and paintings to sell in his store. And she sure wasn't about to tell them the storekeeper had been the only person to buy any of her work.

"It was a picture frame," she said, her mind searching for anything she could say to change the subject. She took a bite of stew and smacked her lips. "This is delicious, Mama. Good as always."

Her mother smiled from ear to ear. She was a good cook; there was no denying it. Mama could take a few vegetables and a slab of dried meat and turn it into a nutritious, tasty meal.

"I don't want that storekeeper hangin' around you, Kelly. Is that understood?"

At the sound of her dad's threatening voice, Kelly dropped the spoon, and it landed in her bowl, splashing stew broth all over the oilcloth table covering.

"You don't have to shout, Amos," Mama said in her usual soft-spoken tone.

"I'll shout whenever I feel like it," he shot back, giving Kelly's mother a mind-your-own-business look.

Mama quickly lowered her gaze, but Kelly, feeling braver than usual, spoke her mind. "Mike and I are just friends. I don't see what harm there is in us havin' a conversation once in a while."

"Humph!" Papa sputtered. "From what I could see, the two of you was havin' more than a little talk."

So he had seen Mike take her hand. Kelly trembled, but she couldn't let her father know how flustered she felt. She was glad Mama hadn't said anything about her and Mike going on a picnic together, for that would surely get Papa riled.

Mama touched Kelly's arm. "I think your dad is concerned that you'll run off with some man, the way Sarah did."

"You needn't worry about that," Kelly was quick to say. "I don't plan on ever gettin' married." *Besides, Mike Cooper's not interested in me. It's Betsy Nelson he's set his cap for.*

"I'm glad to hear that." Papa tapped his knife along the edge of the table. "Just so you know, if I catch that storekeeper with his hands on you again, I'll knock his block off. Is that clear enough?"

Kelly nodded, as her eyes filled with tears. She might be mad as all get-out at Mike, but she couldn't stand to think of him getting beat up by her dad. She would have to make sure Mike never touched her when Papa was around. Not that she wanted him to, of course.

She reached into her pocket for a hanky and found the slip of paper Betsy Nelson had given her instead. Holding it in her lap, so Papa couldn't see it, Kelly silently read the verse of Scripture: *"Jesus said, 'If ye forgive men their trespasses, your heavenly Father will also forgive you'" Matthew 6:14.*

Kelly swallowed hard. She knew she needed to forgive Papa for the way he acted toward her. It sure wouldn't be easy, though.

Chapter 16

On Thursday morning, a sack of mail was delivered to Mike's store, brought in by one of the canal boats. This was a weekly occurrence, as Mike's place of business also served as the area's post office.

While sorting through the pile of letters and packages, Mike discovered one addressed to him. He recognized his brother Alvin's handwriting and quickly tore open the envelope.

Mike hadn't heard from either Alvin or John in several months, so he was anxious to see what the letter had to say:

Dear Mike,

John and me are both fine, and our fishing business is doing right well. I wanted to let you know that I've found myself a girlfriend, and we plan to be married in

December, when we'll be done fishing for the season.
Hope things are good for you there at the store.

Your brother,
Alvin

Mike was happy for his brother, but he couldn't help feeling a pang of envy. He wanted so much to have a wife and children, and he wasn't any closer to it now than he had been several weeks before, when he'd prayed earnestly for God to send him a wife. He was still hoping Kelly McGregor might be that woman, but so far, she'd given him no indication that she was interested in anything beyond friendship. At least he knew she had a personal relationship with Christ, even though she had been in a hurry when he'd asked her so they couldn't really discuss it.

Mike turned and glanced at the wall directly behind the counter. He'd framed all of Kelly's pictures and hung them there. One had sold yesterday, and the man who'd bought it seemed interested in the others. No doubt Kelly had talent, but she was also young and probably insecure when it came to men. Maybe she didn't know how to show her feelings. Maybe she was afraid. Mike had noticed how Amos McGregor often yelled at Kelly and his wife. Kelly might think all men were like her dad.

"I'll go slow with Kelly and win her heart over time," Mike murmured as he continued to study her artwork. "And while I'm waiting, I'll try even harder to get some of these pictures sold."

Papa had kept true to his word and taken it slow and easy on the trip to Mauch Chunk. On a normal run, they would have been there by Wednesday night. Instead, they'd spent Wednesday night outside the small town of Parryville.

They arrived in Mauch Chunk on Thursday afternoon, with Herman doing well and his leg in good shape. Then they loaded the boat with coal from the loading chutes, which descended 250 feet to the river. They spent the night in Mauch Chunk, surrounded by hills that were covered with birch, maple, oak, and wild locust trees.

The next morning, they were heading back toward Easton to deliver their load. They'd be passing Mike's store either that evening or the next morning, depending on how hard Papa pushed. Since Herman was doing well, Kelly suspected they would move faster than they had on Wednesday and Thursday.

"Probably won't be stopping at Mike's store this time," Kelly mumbled. "Sure wish we were, though. I need to talk to him about the picture he gave Betsy Nelson."

As the wind whipped against her long skirt, Kelly glanced up at the darkening sky. They were in for a storm, sure as anything. She hoped it would hold off until they stopped for the night. She hated walking the towpath during a rainstorm.

Hector's ears twitched, as though he sensed the impending danger a torrential downpour could cause—fallen trees, a muddy towpath, rising canal waters. And there was always the threat of being hit by lightning, especially with so many trees lining the path. A few years back, a young boy leading his dad's mules had been struck by a bolt of lightning and was killed instantly.

Kelly shivered. Just thinking about what was to come made her feel jumpy as a frog. The mules would be harder to handle once the rain started because they had no depth perception and hated walking through water, even small puddles. If they came to a stretch of puddles, they would tromp clear around them. There was no fear of the mules jumping into the canal to get cooled off on a hot day the way a horse would have done. Kelly's mules liked water for drinking, but that was all.

Forcing her mind off the impending storm, Kelly thought about how glad she was that Papa had chosen mules, not horses, to pull his boats. It was a proven fact that mules, with their brute strength and surefooted agility, were much less skittish and far more reliable than any horse could be. If horses weren't stopped in time, they would keep on pulling until they fell over dead. Mules, if they were overly tired or had fallen sick, would stop in the middle of the path and refuse to budge. A mule ate one-third less food than a horse did as well, making the beast of burden far more economical.

By noon, rain began falling. First it arrived in tiny droplets, splattering the end of Kelly's nose. Then the lightning and thunder came, bringing a chilling downpour.

Kelly cupped her hands around her mouth and leaned into the wind. "Are we gonna stop soon?" she hollered to Papa, who stood at the stern of the boat, already dripping wet. He was just getting over a bad cold and shouldn't be out in this weather.

"Keep movin'!" Papa shouted back to her. "We won't stop unless it gets worse."

Worse? Kelly didn't see how it could get much worse. Thunder rumbled across the sky, and black clouds hung so low she felt as if she could touch them. "I–I'm cold and wet," she yelled, wondering if he could hear her. The wind was howling fiercely, and she could barely hear herself. Then Kelly's straw hat flew off her head, causing long strands of hair to blow across her face. She ran up ahead, retrieved the hat, and pushed it down on her head, hoping it would stay in place.

Papa leaned over the edge of the boat and tossed a jacket over the side. Kelly lunged forward and barely caught it in time. If it had fallen into the canal, it would have been lost forever, as the murky brown water was swirling and gurgling something awful.

Kelly slipped her arms into the oversized wool jacket and buttoned it up to her neck. It helped some to keep out the wind, but she knew it was only a matter of time until the rain leaked through and soaked her clean to the skin.

On and on Kelly and the mules trudged, through the driving rain, pushing against the wind, tromping in and out of mud puddles, murk, and mire. Several times, the mules balked and refused to move forward. Kelly coaxed, pushed, pleaded, and pulled until she finally got them moving again.

By the time Papa signaled her to stop, Kelly felt like a limp dishrag. She glanced around and realized they were directly in front of Mike's store. Lifting her gaze to the thunderous sky, Kelly prayed, "Thank You, God, for keepin' us safe and for givin' Papa the good sense to stop."

"We're stayin' here for the night," Papa shouted. "Help me get the mules on board the boat."

"Can't they bed down in Mike Cooper's barn tonight?" Kelly asked. "I could care for 'em better there."

"Guess it wouldn't hurt for one night," Papa surprised her by saying.

Mike was about to close up his store, figuring no one in their right mind would be out in this terrible weather, when the door flew open, and Kelly practically fell into the room. She looked like a drowned rat. Her hair, wet and tangled, hung in her face. Her clothes were soaked with rainwater, and her boots were covered in mud. Her straw hat, pushed far over her forehead, resembled a hunk of soggy cardboard.

Mike grabbed hold of Kelly as a gust of wind pushed her forward. The door slammed shut with so much force that the broom, lying against one wall, toppled over, while several pieces of paper blew off the counter and sailed to the floor.

"Kelly, what are you doing here?" he questioned.

"We've stopped for the day because of the storm." She leaned into him, and he had the sudden desire to kiss her.

Why was it that every time they were together anymore, Mike wanted to find out what her lips would feel like against his own?

He drew in a deep breath and gently stroked her back. "Are you okay? You look miserable."

She pulled away. "I'm fine, but we were wonderin' if we could stable the mules in your barn tonight."

He nodded. "Of course. I'll put on my jacket and help you get them settled in."

"I can manage," she said in a brisk tone of voice. She'd been so friendly a few minutes ago. What had happened to make her change?

Mike studied Kelly's face. It was pinched, and tears streamed down her face. At least he thought they were tears. They might have been raindrops.

"Kelly, what's wrong?" Mike touched her arm, and she recoiled as if some pesky insect had bitten her.

As she moved toward the door, her gaze swung to the pictures on the wall.

"How do you like the way I've got your artwork displayed?" he questioned.

She squinted her eyes at him. "How could you, Mike?"

"How could I what?"

"Buy my drawing and give it to Betsy Nelson for her birthday?"

"Her dad invited me to their house for supper to help her celebrate. I wanted to take something, and I thought Betsy

129

would like one of your wonderful charcoal drawings."

She continued to stare at him, and Mike felt his face heat up. Why was she looking at him as though he'd done something wrong? He'd paid her for the picture; same as if someone else had bought it.

"And the other drawing?"

"Huh?"

"You gave me money for two drawings and said you'd sold them both."

The heat Mike felt on his face had now spread to his ears. "I...that is...I bought both of the pictures," he admitted. "One for Betsy's birthday and the other to hang in my living room."

She shook her head slowly. "I figured as much."

"How did you find out about the picture I gave the preacher's daughter?"

"Reverend Nelson told me when I ran into him and Betsy on the towpath the other day." Kelly bit down on her lower lip, like she might be about to cry. "Why'd ya lead me to believe you'd sold my pictures, Mike?"

"I did sell them," he defended. "I don't see what difference it makes who bought them."

"It makes a lot of difference," Kelly shouted before she turned toward the front door. "I may be poor but I don't need charity from you or anyone else!"

He couldn't let her leave like this. Not without making her understand he wasn't trying to hurt her. Mike grabbed Kelly's arm and turned her around. "Please forgive me. I never meant to upset you, and I really did want those drawings." He pointed to the wall where her other paintings hung. "I sold one of your watercolors this morning to a man who lives in Walnutport."

She squinted her dark eyes at him. "Really?"

"Yes. He was impressed with your work and said he may be back to buy more."

Kelly's eyes were swimming with tears. "I—I can't believe it."

"It's true. Mr. Porter knows talent when he sees it, and so do I." Mike reached for her hand and gave it a gentle squeeze. "Am I forgiven for misleading you?"

She hesitated a moment, then her lips curved up. "Yes."

"Good. Now will you let me help you stable the mules?"

She nodded.

Mike grabbed his jacket off the wall peg by the door. "You lead one mule, and I'll take the other."

A moment later, they stepped into the driving rain, but Mike paid it no mind. All he could think about was spending the next hour or so in the company of Kelly McGregor.

Chapter 17

*D*uring the next half hour, Kelly and Mike got the mules fed and bedded down for the night. Kelly was grateful for his help and the loan of the barn. It meant Herman and Hector had a warm, dry place to rest, without the bouncing and swaying from the rough waters caused by the storm.

Truth be told, Kelly dreaded going to her own room. It would be hard to sleep with the boat bobbing all over the place. She'd probably have to tie herself in bed in order to keep from being tossed onto the floor.

"I was wondering if you and your folks would like to stay at my place tonight," Mike said, as he rubbed Herman down with an old towel.

"Your place?"

"My house. I've got plenty of room."

Kelly wondered if Mike had been able to read her mind. Or was he smart enough to figure out how difficult it would be to spend the night on a boat riding the waves of a storm?

"I'd have to ask Papa and Mama," she said. "They might agree, but I'm not sure."

"Would you prefer it if I asked them instead?"

"That probably would be best. Papa's usually more open to things if it comes from someone other than me."

Mike hung the towel on a nail and moved toward Kelly, who'd been drying Hector off with a piece of heavy cloth. "I take it you and your pa don't get along."

Kelly lowered her gaze to the wooden floor. "I used to think he liked me well enough, but ever since Sarah left, he's been actin' meaner than ever."

Mike's heart clenched. He hated to see the way Kelly's shoulders drooped or hear the resignation in her voice. "Are you afraid of him, Kelly?"

She nodded slowly. "Sometimes."

"Has he ever hit you?"

"Not since I was little. Then it was only a swat on the backside." Kelly's eyes filled with tears, and it was all Mike could do to keep from kissing her. "Papa mostly yells, but sometimes he makes me do things I know are wrong."

"Like what?"

She sucked in her lower lip. "The other day, a bunch of chickens was runnin' around near the towpath. He insisted I grab hold of one and give it to Mama to cook for our supper that night."

Mike drew in a deep breath and let it out in a rush. "But that's stealing. Doesn't your dad know taking things that don't belong to you is breaking one of God's commandments?"

"Papa don't care about God. He thinks Mama is plain silly for readin' her Bible every night."

"What do you think would have happened if you'd refused to do what your dad asked?"

"I don't know, but I didn't think I should find out."

Mike could hardly believe Kelly's dad had asked her to do something so wrong, but it was equally hard to understand why she wouldn't stand up to him. If he didn't threaten her physically, what kind of hold did the man have on her?

"Does your dad refuse to pay you if you don't do what he asks?" Mike questioned.

Kelly planted her hands on her hips. "I told you the other day, Papa has never paid me a single penny for leadin' the mules."

Mike reached up to scratch the side of his head. He'd forgotten about their conversation about Kelly's lack of money. That was why she wanted to sell some of her artwork. And it was one more reason Mike had to help make it happen.

"It's all Sarah's fault for runnin' off with one of the lock tender's sons. She made Papa angry and left me with all the work." Kelly balled her fingers into tight fists, and Mike wondered if she might want to punch someone. He took a few steps back, just in case.

Before he had a chance to respond to her tirade, Kelly announced, "I'm afraid men are all the same, and I ain't never gettin' married, that's for certain sure!"

Mike felt like he'd been kicked in the gut. Never marry? Had he heard her right? If Kelly was dead set against marriage, what hope did he have of winning her hand? About all he could do was try to be her friend, but he sure wished he could figure out some way to prove to her that all men weren't like her dad.

Kelly felt the heat of embarrassment flood her face. What had possessed her to spout off like that in front of Mike? He'd been helping her with the mules and sure didn't deserve such wrath. She knew she should apologize, but the words stuck in her throat.

She grabbed a hunk of hay and fed it to Hector. Maybe if she kept her hands busy, she wouldn't have to think about anything else.

"Why don't you finish up with the mules while I go talk to your folks and see if they'd like to spend the night at my place?" Mike suggested.

Kelly nodded. "Sounds good to me."

She heard the barn door close behind Mike, and she dropped to her knees. "Oh, Lord, I'm sorry for bein' such a grouch. Guess I'm just tired and out of sorts tonight 'cause of the storm and all."

Tears streamed down Kelly's cheeks. Mike thought she was a sinner for taking that chicken. He didn't understand how things were with Papa, either. To make matters worse, Mike had been kind to her, and she'd yelled at him in return. What must he think of her now?

"I'm sorry for stealin' the chicken, Lord. Give me the courage to tell Papa no from now on."

Kelly dried her eyes with the backs of her hands and was

about to leave the barn when Mike showed up with Mama.

"Where's Papa?" Kelly questioned.

Her mother sighed deeply. "He's bound and determined to stay on the boat tonight. Never mind that it's rockin' back and forth like a bucking mule." She wrinkled her nose. "And now the roof's leaking as well."

"So are you and me gonna stay at Mike's house?" Kelly asked.

"Yes, and it was a very kind offer, wouldn'tcha say?"

Kelly nodded in response and smiled at Mike. "Sorry for snappin' like a turtle."

He winked at her. "Apology accepted."

For the next two days, the storm continued, and Papa refused to leave the boat. He said he might lose it if he did, but Kelly knew the truth. Her dad didn't want to appear needy in front of Mike. He'd rather sit on his vessel and be tossed about like a chunk of wood thrown into a raging river than accept anyone's charity.

Sitting at Mike's kitchen table with her drawing tablet, Kelly thought about Proverbs 12:27, a verse of scripture she'd learned as a child: *The substance of a diligent man is precious.* Papa was diligent, that was for sure. Too bad he wasn't kinder or more concerned about his family.

The last two nights, she and Mama had shared a bed inside a real home, and Kelly found herself wishing even more that she could leave the life of a mule driver behind.

"Aren't you gonna eat some breakfast?" Mama asked, pushing a bowl of oatmeal in front of Kelly.

"I will, after I finish this drawing."

Mama leaned forward with her elbows on the table. "What are you makin'?"

"It's a picture of our boat bein' tossed by the rising waters. I took a walk down to the canal this morning so I could see how things were lookin'." Kelly frowned. "The rain hasn't let up one little bit, and I figure God must be awful angry with someone."

Mama looked at Kelly as if she'd taken leave of her senses. "What would make ya say somethin' like that?"

"Doesn't God cause the rain and winds to come whenever He's mad?"

Reaching across the table, Mama took hold of Kelly's hand. "Storms are part of the world we live in, but I don't believe God sends 'em to make us pay for our sins."

"Really?"

Mama nodded. "The Bible tells us in Psalm 34:19, 'Many are the afflictions of the righteous: but the Lord delivereth him out of them all.' Everyone goes through trials, and some of those come in the form of storms, sickness, or other such things. That don't mean we're bein' punished, but we can have the assurance that even though we'll have afflictions, God will deliver us in His time."

Kelly tried to concentrate on her drawing, but Mama's words kept rolling around in her head. *When's my time comin' to be delivered, Lord? When are You gonna give me enough money so I can leave this terrible way of life?*

She grabbed the hunk of charcoal and continued to draw, not wanting to think about her situation. It was bad enough that the storm wasn't letting up and Papa refused to get off the boat. She didn't wish to spend the rest of the day worried about God's direction for her life. If more of her drawings didn't sell soon, she'd have to figure out some other way to make money on her own. When they wintered in Easton, Kelly might get a job in one of the factories. Then she'd have plenty of money, and Papa could find someone else to lead the mules.

A few minutes later, the door flew open, and Papa lumbered into the room. Mama jumped up and moved quickly toward him.

"Oh, Amos, it's so good to see you. Can I fix ya a bowl of oatmeal or maybe some flapjacks?"

He stormed right past Mama as though she hadn't said a word about food. "Stupid weather! It ain't bad enough we lost so much time with sickness and mule problems; now we're stuck here 'til the storm passes by. I'm gettin' sick of sittin' around doin' nothin', and I can't believe my family abandoned me to come get all cozy-like over here at the storekeeper's place!"

Kelly tried to ignore her dad's outburst, but it was hard, especially with him breathing down her neck, as he was now. She could feel his hot breath against her cheek, as he leaned his head close to the table. "What's that you're doin'?" he snarled.

"I'm drawin' a picture of our boat in the storm."

"Humph! Ain't it bad enough I have to endure the torment of bein' tossed around like a cork? Do ya have to rub salt in the wounds by makin' a dumb picture to remind me of my plight?"

Kelly opened her mouth to reply, but Papa jerked the piece of paper right off the table. "This is trash and deserves to be treated as such!" With that, he marched across the room, flung open the door on the woodstove, and tossed Kelly's picture into the fire.

She shot out of her seat, but it was too late. Angry flames of red had already engulfed her precious drawing.

"How could you, Papa?" she cried. "How could you be so cruel?" Kelly rushed from the house, not caring that she wasn't wearing a jacket.

Chapter 18

Mike glanced out the store window and was surprised to see Kelly run past. She wasn't wearing a jacket, and the rain was still pouring down. She would be drenched within seconds.

He yanked the door open and hurried out after her. She raced into the barn, and Mike was right behind her.

"Kelly, what are you doing out here without a coat?" he hollered as he followed her into the mules' stall.

She kept her head down, and he could see her shoulders shaking.

Mike rushed over to her. "What's wrong? Why are you crying?"

She lifted her gaze to his, her dark eyes filled with tears. He ached to hold her in his arms—to kiss away those tears. He might have, too, if he hadn't been afraid of her response.

"I was working on a drawing of our boat this mornin', and Papa got mad and threw it into the fire," she sobbed.

Mike took hold of Kelly's arms. "Why would he do such a thing?"

"He stormed into your kitchen, yelled about the weather, and said I was rubbin' salt into his wounds by makin' a picture of the boat in the storm. Then he said my picture was trash and deserved to be treated as such. That's when he turned it to ashes." Tears streamed down Kelly's face, and Mike instinctively reached up to wipe them away with the back of his hand.

"I'm so sorry, Kelly. I promise someday things will be better for you."

"How can you say that? Are you able to see into the future and know what's ahead?" she wailed.

Mike shook his head slowly. Kelly was right; he couldn't be sure what the future held for either of them. He wanted things to be better and wished she would allow him to love her and help her. If Kelly were to marry him, Mike would gladly spend the rest of his life taking care of her. If only he felt free to tell her that.

"God loves you, Kelly, and He wants only the best for you."

She glared up at him. "If God loves me so much, then why do I have to work long hours with no pay? And why's Papa so mean?"

"God gives each of us a free will, and your dad is the way he is by his own choosing. We can pray for him and set a good example, but nobody can make him change until he's ready."

Kelly sniffed deeply. "I don't care if he ever changes. All I care about is earnin' enough money to make it on my own. I need that chance, so if you want to pray about somethin', then ask God to help *me*."

Mike's hand rested comfortably on her shoulder. With only a slight pull, she would be close enough for him to kiss. The urge was nearly overwhelming, and he moved away, fighting for control. Kelly had made clear how she felt about marriage. Even if she were attracted to him—and he suspected she was—they had no hope of a future together. He wanted marriage and children so much. All she seemed to care about was drawing pictures and making money so she could support herself. Didn't Kelly realize he was more than willing to care for her needs? As long as he was able to draw breath, Mike would never let his wife or children do without.

"I'll be praying, Kelly," he mumbled. "Praying for both you and your dad."

The following Monday, the rain finally stopped, and the canal waters had receded enough so the McGregors could move on. Kelly felt a deep sense of sadness as she said good-bye to Mike. He truly was her friend, and as much as she hated to admit it, she was attracted to him. She would miss their daily chats as she cared for the mules. She would miss his kind words and caring attitude. As the days of summer continued, she hoped they would stop by his store on a regular basis—not only to see if any of her paintings had sold, but also so she could spend more time with Mike.

With Mike's encouragement over the last few days, she'd done several more charcoal drawings, always out of Papa's sight.

"Get up there," Kelly said as she coaxed the mules to get going. They moved forward, and she turned to wave at Mike one last time. She didn't know why she should feel so sad. She'd see him again, probably on their return trip from Easton.

They'd only traveled a short ways when Papa signaled her to stop. They were between towns, and no other boats were around. She had a sinking feeling her dad was up to something. Something he'd done a few times before when he'd lost time due to bad weather or some kind of mishap along the way.

Sure enough, within minutes of their stopping, Papa had begun to shovel coal out of the compartment where it was stored and was dumping it into the canal. He did this to lighten their load, which in turn would help the boat move faster. Of course, it also meant Kelly would be expected to keep the mules moving at a quicker pace.

She shook her head in disgust. "I don't see why Papa has to be so dishonest."

Hector brayed loudly, as though he agreed.

"It's not fair for him to expect the three of us to walk faster," she continued to fume. "It's hard enough to walk at a regular pace, what with the mud and all, but now we'll practically have to run."

Kelly's thoughts took her back to what Mike had told her the other morning in his barn. He'd said they needed to pray for Kelly's dad and set him a good example. That was a tall order—especially since Papa seemed determined to be ornery and didn't think twice about cheating someone. She knew from experience that, shortly before they arrived in Easton to deliver their load, Papa would wet the coal down, making it weigh more. Since he was paid by weight and not by the amount, no one would be any the wiser.

She sighed deeply and turned her head away from the canal. There was no use watching what she couldn't prevent happening. Someday, maybe she wouldn't have to watch it at all.

For the next several weeks, Kelly trudged up and down the towpath between Easton and Mauch Chunk, but they made no stops that weren't absolutely necessary. Papa said they'd lost enough time, and he didn't think they needed to dally. When Mama complained about needing fresh vegetables, Papa solved the problem by turning the tiller over to her. Then he jumped off the boat and helped himself to some carrots and beets growing near the towpath. The garden belonged to someone who lived nearby, but Papa didn't care. He said if the people who'd planted the vegetables so close to the canal didn't want folks helping themselves, they ought to have fenced in their crops.

Kelly had been praying for Papa, like Mike suggested, but it seemed the more she prayed, the worse he became. The effort appeared to be futile, and she had about decided to give up praying or even hoping Papa might ever change.

That morning at breakfast, Mama had asked Papa if they could stop at Mike's store later in the afternoon. She needed more washing soap, some thread, flour for baking, and a few other things she couldn't get by without. After a few choice words, Papa had finally agreed, but now, as they neared the spot in front of Cooper's General Store, Kelly wondered if he might change his mind. His face was a mask of anger, but he signaled her to stop.

She breathed a sigh of relief and halted the mules. At last she could see Mike again and ask if any of her pictures had sold. She didn't have more to give him. She'd been too busy during the days to draw, and at night, she was too tuckered out. At the rate things were going, Kelly doubted she'd ever get the chance to earn enough money to buy any store-bought paint, much less to open an art gallery.

"A dream. That's all it is," she mumbled moments before Mama joined her to head for the store.

Mike stood behind the front counter, praying and hoping Kelly would stop by his store soon. He'd just sold another one of her paintings, and he could hardly wait to tell her the good news. It had been two whole weeks since he'd spoken with her, although he had seen the McGregors' boat go by on several occasions. Each time, he'd had customers in the store, or else he would have dashed outside and tried to speak with Kelly—although it probably would have meant running along the towpath as they conversed, for that's pretty much what it looked like Kelly had been doing. Her dad was most likely trying to make up for all the time he'd lost during the storm, but Mike hated to see Kelly being pushed so hard. It wasn't right for a young woman to work from sunup to sunset without getting paid.

Mike was pleasantly surprised when the front door opened

and in walked Dorrie and Kelly McGregor. They both looked tired, but Kelly's face showed more than fatigue. Her dark eyes had lost their sparkle, and her shoulders were slumped. She looked defeated.

Mike smiled at the two women. "It's good to see you. Is there something I can help you with?"

Dorrie waved a hand. "Don't trouble yourself. I can get whatever I'm needin'." She marched off in the direction of the sewing notions.

Kelly hung back, and she lifted her gaze to the wall where her artwork was displayed.

"I sold another picture this morning," Mike announced.

"That's good," she said with little feeling. "Sorry I don't have any more to give you right now. There's been no time for drawin' or paintin' here of late."

"It's all right," he assured her. "I'm sure you'll find some free time soon."

She scowled at him. "Why do you always say things like that?"

"Like what?"

"You try to make me think things are gonna get better when they're not."

"How do you know they're not?"

"I just do, that's all."

Mike blew out his breath. It was obvious nothing he said would penetrate her negative attitude this afternoon. He offered up a quick prayer. *Lord, give me the right words.*

"Would it help if I had a talk with your dad?"

Kelly looked horrified. "Don't you dare! Papa would be

furious if he knew I'd been complaining." She squared her shoulders. "I'll be fine, so there's no reason to concern yourself."

"But I am concerned. I'm in—" Mike stopped himself before he blurted out that he was in love with her. He knew it would be the worst thing he could say to Kelly right now. Besides the fact that she was in a sour mood and would probably not appreciate his declaration of love, her mother was in the store and might be listening to his every word.

Mike moved over to the candy counter. "How about a bag of lemon drops? I'm sure you're out of them by now."

Kelly's frown faded, and she joined him at the counter. "Since I sold a painting and have some money comin', I'll take two bags of candy—one lemon drops, and the other horehounds."

"I didn't know you fancied horehounds."

"I don't, but Papa likes 'em. Maybe it'll help put him in a better mood."

So she was trying to set a good example for her dad. At least one of Mike's prayers was being answered. If Kelly's dad found the Lord, then Kelly might be more receptive to the idea of marriage.

Mike reached into the container of horehound drops with a wooden scoop. "You think you might be stopping over come Sunday?"

She shrugged her shoulders. "If we make it to Mauch Chunk in good time, Papa might be willin' to stop on our way back. Why do you ask?"

"I'd like to take you on another picnic." He grinned at her. "Only this time it'll be just you and me."

She tipped her head to one side. "No Betsy Nelson?"

"Nope."

She smiled for the first time since she'd come into the store. "We'll have to wait and see."

Chapter 19

When Mike asked Kelly about going on another picnic, she never expected her family's canal boat would be stopped in front of his store the next Sunday. They'd arrived the evening before, and Papa had decided to spend the night so he could work on the boat the following morning. He'd accidentally run into one of the other canal boats and put a hole in the bow of his boat. It wasn't large, and it was high enough that no water had leaked in, but it still needed to be repaired before it got any worse. Papa would be busy with that all day, which meant Kelly could head off with Mike and probably go unnoticed.

Not wishing to run into Betsy again, Kelly waited until the crowd had dispersed from Reverend Nelson's outdoor preaching service before she walked to Mike's store. They'd talked briefly the night before and had agreed to meet sometime after noon in front of his place.

It was a hot summer day in late August, and Kelly wished

she and Mike could go swimming in the canal to get cooled off. She dismissed the idea as quickly as it popped into her mind when she remembered Mike had said he didn't swim well, and she, though able to swim, was afraid of water snakes. They would have to find some other way to find solace from the oppressive heat and humidity.

Mike was waiting for her in front of the store, a picnic basket in one hand and a blanket in the other. "Did you bring along your drawing tablet?" he asked.

She nodded and patted the pocket of her long gingham skirt.

"I thought we'd have our picnic at the pond behind Zach Miller's house. There's lots of wildflowers growing there, and maybe we can find some to brew into watercolors," he said, offering Kelly a smile that made her skin tingle despite the heat of the day.

"That would be good. Mama's runnin' low on carrots and beets, so I haven't been able to make any colors for a spell, other than the shades I've gotten from leftover coffee and tree bark."

Mike whistled as they walked up the towpath, heading in the direction of the lock tender's house.

"You seem to be in an awful good mood this afternoon," Kelly noted.

He turned his head and grinned at her. "I'm always in fine spirits on the Lord's day. I looked for you at the preaching service but didn't see you anywhere."

"Mama needed my help with some bakin'." Kelly felt a prick of her conscience. She had helped her mother bake oatmeal bread, but truth be told, that wasn't the real reason she hadn't attended the church service. She didn't want to hear God's Word and be reminded that her prayers weren't being answered where Papa was concerned. Besides, Mama hadn't attended church, either, and if she didn't feel the need to go, why should Kelly?

"Sure wish you could have heard the great message the reverend delivered this morning. It was a real inspiration."

"I'm sure it was."

"Summer will be over soon," Mike said, changing the subject. "Won't be long until the leaves begin to turn and drop from the trees."

Kelly nodded, feeling suddenly sad. When fall came, they'd only have a few months left to make coal deliveries. Winter often hit quickly, and Papa always moored the boat for the winter and moved them to Flannigan's Boardinghouse in Easton, where they would live until the spring thaw. That meant Kelly wouldn't be seeing Mike for several months. She would miss his smiling face and their long talks.

A lot could happen in three months. Mike and Betsy might start courting and could even be married by the time they returned to the canal. And Kelly was acutely aware that lots of coal was now being hauled via steam train, which meant fewer boats were working the canals in eastern Pennsylvania. How long would it be before Papa gave up canaling altogether and took a year-round job in the city?

"A lemon drop for your thoughts," Mike said.

"What?"

"I brought along a bag of your favorite candy, and I'd gladly give you one if you're willin' to share your thoughts with me."

She snickered. "I doubt anything I'd be thinkin' would be worth even one lemon drop."

Mike stopped walking and turned to face her. "Don't say that, Kelly. You're a talented, intelligent woman, and I value anything you might have to say."

She pursed her lips. "I'm not sure 'bout my talents, but one thing I do know—I'm not smart. I've only gone through the eighth grade, and that took me longer than most, 'cause I just attended school during the winter."

"A lack of education doesn't mean you're stupid," Mike said with a note of conviction. "My dad used to say he graduated from the school of life and that all the things he learned helped him become a better man. We grow from our experiences, so if we learn from our mistakes, then we're smart."

Kelly contemplated Mike's words a few seconds. "Hmm. . . I've never thought about it that way before."

"I hope to have a whole passel of kids someday, and when I do, I want to teach them responsibility so they can work hard and be smart where it really counts."

Kelly wasn't sure she liked the sound of that, but she chose not to comment.

Mike started walking again, and Kelly did as well. Soon they were at the pond behind the Millers' house. Nobody else was around, so Kelly figured they weren't likely to be interrupted, and she might even get some serious drawing done.

Sitting on the blanket next to Kelly, his belly full of fried chicken and buttermilk biscuits, Mike felt content. He could spend the rest of his life with this woman—watching her draw, listening to the hum of her sweet voice, and kissing away all her worries and cares. Should he tell her what he was feeling? Would it scare her off? He drew in a deep breath and plunged ahead. "Kelly, I was wondering—"

"Yes?" she murmured as she continued to draw the outline of a clump of wildflowers.

"Would it be all right if I wrote to you while you're living in the city this winter?"

She turned her head to look at him. Her dark eyes looked ever so serious, but she was smiling. "I'd like that."

"And will you write me in return?" he asked hopefully.

She nodded. "If I'm not kept too busy with my factory job."

"Do you know where you'll be working?"

"Not yet, but I'll be eighteen on January 5, and I'm gettin' stronger every year. I can probably get a job at most any of the factories. Even the ones where the work is heavy or dangerous."

Mike's heart clenched. "Please don't take a job that might put you in danger. I couldn't stand it if something were to happen to you, Kelly."

She gave him a questioning look.

"I love you, and I—" Mike never finished his sentence. Instead, he took Kelly in his arms and kissed her upturned mouth. Her lips tasted sweet as honey, and it felt so right to hold her.

When Kelly slipped her hands around his neck and returned his kiss, Mike thought he was going to drown in the love he felt for her.

Kelly was the first to pull away. Her face was bright pink, and her eyes were cloudy with obvious emotion. Had she enjoyed the kiss as much as he?

She placed her trembling hands against her rosy cheeks. "I. . .I think it's time to go."

"But we haven't picked any wildflowers for you to use as watercolors," Mike argued.

She stood and dropped her art supplies into the pocket of her skirt. "I shouldn't have let you kiss me. It wasn't right."

Mike jumped to his feet. "It felt right to me."

She hung her head. "It wasn't, and it can never happen again."

Mike's previous elation plummeted clear to his toes. "I'm sorry you didn't enjoy the kiss."

"I did," she surprised him by saying. "But we can never be more than friends, and I don't think friends should go around kissin' each other."

So that's how it was. Kelly only saw him as a friend. Mike felt like a fool. He'd read more into her physical response than there was. He'd decided awhile back to take it slow and easy with Kelly—be sure of her feelings before he made a move. He'd really messed things up, and it was too late to take back the kiss or his declaration of love.

"Forgive me for taking liberties that weren't mine," he said, forcing her to look him in the eye, even though it pained him to see there were tears running down her cheeks.

When she didn't say anything, Mike bent to retrieve the picnic basket and blanket. "I think you're right. It's time to go."

All the way back to the boat, Kelly chided herself for being foolish enough to allow Mike to kiss her. Now she'd hurt his feelings. It was obvious by the slump of his shoulders and the silence that covered the distance between them. On the way to the pond, he'd been talkative and whistled. Now the only sounds were the call of a dove and the canal waters lapping against the bank.

I was wrong to let him kiss me, but was I wrong to tell him we could only be friends? Should I have let him believe I might feel more for him than friendship? Do I feel more?

Kelly's disconcerting thoughts came to a halt when they rounded the bend where the canal boats could be seen. In the middle of the grassy area between Mike's store and the boats that had stopped for the day, two men were fistfighting. One was Patrick O'Malley. The other was Kelly's dad. Several other men stood on the sidelines, shouting, clapping, and cheering them on. What was the scuffle about, and why wasn't someone trying to stop it?

As though Mike could read her thoughts, he set the picnic basket and blanket on the ground, then stepped forward. "Please, no fighting on the Sabbath. Can't you two men solve your differences without the use of your knuckles?"

Pow! Papa's fist connected on the left side of Patrick's chin. "You stay outa this, boy!" he shouted at Mike.

Smack! Patrick gave Papa a head butt that sent him sprawling on the grass.

"Stop it! Stop it!" Kelly shouted. Tears were stung the backs of her eyes, and she felt herself tremble. Why must Papa make such a spectacle of himself? What did Mike and the others who were watching think of her dad?

The men were hitting each other lickety-split now, apparently oblivious to anything that was being said. Closer and closer to the canal they went, and when Papa slammed his fist into Patrick's chest, the man lost his footing and fell over backward. He grabbed Papa's shirtsleeve, and both men landed in the water with a splash.

Mortified, Kelly covered her face with her hands. How could a day that started out with such promise end on such a sour note?

After the fight was over and the two men settled down, Kelly learned the reason behind the scuffle. It had all started over something as simple as whose boat would be leaving first come Monday morning.

After the way her dad had caused such a scene, Kelly didn't think she could show her face to Mike or anyone else without suspecting they were talking behind her back. It was embarrassing the way her dad could fly off the handle and punch a man for no reason at all. Men didn't make a lick of sense!

Chapter 20

*A*s summer moved into fall, Kelly saw less of Mike. Papa kept them moving, wanting to make as many loads as possible before the bad weather. He refused to stop for anything that wasn't necessary.

It was just as well she wasn't spending time with Mike, Kelly decided as she sat upon Hector's back, bone tired and unable to take another step. After Mike's unexpected kiss the day they'd had a picnic by the Millers' pond, Kelly hadn't wanted to do or say anything that might cause Mike to believe they had anything more than a casual friendship. What if Mike was thinking about marriage? What if he only felt sorry for her because she worked so hard? Kelly wasn't about to marry someone just to get away from Papa.

"I wish I didn't like Mike so much," Kelly murmured against the mule's ear.

It had been a long day, and Mike was about ready to close up his store when Betsy Nelson showed up. She seemed to have such good timing. Mike had just finished going through a stack of mail brought in by the last boat, and he was feeling lower than the canal waters after a break. He'd gotten another letter from his brother Alvin. This one said his other brother John had also found himself a girlfriend. There was even mention of a double wedding come December.

"Sorry to be coming by so late in the day," Betsy panted, "but Papa's real sick, and I need some medicine to help quiet his cough." Her cheeks were red, and it was obvious by her heavy breathing that she'd probably run all the way to Mike's store. Mike knew Preacher Nelson didn't own a horse, preferring to make all his calls on foot.

"Come inside, and I'll see what kind of cough syrup I've got left in stock." Mike stepped aside so Betsy could enter, and she followed him to the back of the store.

"I haven't seen you for a while," Betsy said as Mike handed her a bottle of his best-selling cough syrup.

"I've been kinda busy."

Her eyelids fluttered. "I've missed you."

Mike swallowed hard. Betsy was flirting again, and it made him real nervous. He didn't want to hurt her feelings, but the simple fact was he didn't love Betsy. Even though Kelly had spurned his kiss, he was hoping someday she would come to love him as much as he did her.

As lonely as Mike was, and as much as he desired a wife, he knew he couldn't marry the preacher's daughter. She was too self-centered and a bit short-tempered, which probably meant she wouldn't be a patient mother. Kelly, on the other hand, would make a good wife and mother. It wasn't just her lovely face or long brown hair that had captured Mike's heart. Kelly had a gentle spirit. He'd witnessed it several times when she tended the mules. If only she seemed more willing.

Maybe I should quit praying for a wife and get a dog instead.

"Mike? Did you hear what I said?"

Betsy's high-pitched voice drove Mike's musings to the back of his mind. "What was that?"

"I said, 'I've missed you.'"

Mike felt his ears begin to warm. "Thank you, Betsy. It's nice to know I've been missed."

She looked at him with pleading eyes. No doubt she was hoping he would respond by saying he missed her, too. Mike couldn't lie. It wouldn't be right to lead Betsy on.

He moved quickly to the front of the store and placed the bottle of medicine on the counter. "Is there anything else you'll be needin'?"

Betsy's lower lip protruded as she shook her head.

He slipped the bottle into a brown paper sack, took her money, and handed Betsy her purchase. "I hope your dad is feeling better soon. Give him my regards, will you?"

She gave him a curt nod, lifted her head high, and pranced out the door. Mike let out a sigh of relief. At least she hadn't invited him to supper again.

The last day of November arrived, and Kelly couldn't believe it was time to leave the Lehigh Navigation System until spring. When Mama said she needed a few things, Papa had agreed to stop by Cooper's General Store. Kelly felt a mixture of relief and anxiety. Even though she wanted the chance to say good-bye, she dreaded seeing Mike again. Ever since the day he'd kissed her, things had been strained between them. She was afraid Mike wanted more from her than she was able to give. He'd said once that he wanted a whole passel of children so he could teach them responsibility. Did he think making children work would make them smart?

"I wonder if he wants kids so he can force 'em to labor with no pay," Kelly fumed to the mules. All the men she knew who put their kids to work paid them little or nothing. It wasn't fair! No wonder Sarah ran away and got married.

" 'Course if Sarah hadn't run off, I wouldn't have been left with all the work. Maybe the two of us could have come up with a plan to make money of our own."

They stopped in front of Mike's store, and Kelly secured the mules to a tree while she waited for her parents to get off the boat. A short time later, Mama disembarked.

"Where's Papa?" Kelly asked her mother.

Mama shrugged her shoulders. "He said he thought he'd take a nap while we do our shoppin'. He gave me a list of things he needs and said for us not to take all day."

Kelly followed her mother inside the store. She was glad to

see Mike was busy with a customer. At least she wouldn't have to speak with him right away. It would give her time to think of something sensible to say. Should she ask if he still planned to write her while she was living in Easton? Should she promise to write him in return?

She thought about the paintings she had in her drawing tablet, which she hoped to give Mike before she left. Trouble was, she didn't want Mama to see. Could she find some way of speaking to Mike alone?

As if by divine intervention, the man Mike had been waiting on left the store, and about the same time, Mama decided to go back to the boat. She said something about needing to get Papa's opinion on the material she planned to use for a shirt she'd be making him soon.

Kelly knew she didn't have much time, so when the door closed behind her mother, she moved over to the counter where Mike stood.

"Hello, Kelly," he said, offering her a pleasant smile. "It's good to see you."

She moistened her lips with the tip of her tongue. "We're on our way to Easton for the winter and decided to stop by your store for a few items."

When Mike made no comment, Kelly rushed on before she lost her nerve. "I've got a few more paintings to give you. That is, if you're interested in tryin' to sell them." She reached into her pocket and withdrew the tablet, then placed it on the counter.

Mike thumbed through the pages. "These are great, Kelly. I especially like the one of the two children playing in a pile of fallen leaves."

Kelly smiled. That was her favorite picture, too. She'd drawn it in charcoal, then used a mixture of coffee shades, as well as some carrot, onion, and beet water for the colored leaves.

"I've sold a couple more pictures since you were last here," Mike said, reaching into his cash box and producing a few bills, which he handed to Kelly.

"What about your share of the profits?" she asked. "Did ya keep out some of the money?"

Mike gave her a sheepish grin. "I thought with you going to the big city and all, you'd probably need a little extra cash. I'll take my share out of the next batch of pictures I sell."

Kelly was tempted to argue, but the thought of having more money made her think twice about refusing. She nodded instead and slipped the bills into her pocket.

"When do you think you'll be back?" Mike asked.

"Sometime in March, whenever the ice and snow are gone."

"Is there an address where I can write to you?"

"We'll be staying at Mable Flannigan's Boardinghouse. It's on the corner of Front Street in the eight hundred block."

"And you can write me here at Cooper's General Store, Walnutport, Pennsylvania."

"I'll try to write if there's time." That was all Kelly could promise. She had no idea where she might be working or how many hours she'd be putting in each day.

"Mind if I give you a hug good-bye?" Mike asked. "Just as friends?"

Kelly wasn't sure what to say. She didn't want to encourage Mike, yet she didn't want to be rude, either. She guessed one little hug wouldn't hurt. He did say it was just as friends. She nodded and held out her arms.

Mike skirted around the counter and pulled her into an embrace.

Kelly's heart pounded against her chest, and she feared it might burst wide open. What if Mama came back and saw the two of them? What if Mike decided to kiss her again?

Her fears were relieved when Mike pulled away. "Take care, Kelly McGregor. I'll see you next spring."

Chapter 21

Winter came quickly to the Lehigh Valley, and a thick layer of snow soon covered the ground. Mike missed Kelly terribly, and several times a week he walked the towpath, as he was now, thinking about her and praying for her safety. He knew she cared for him, but only as a friend. If he just hadn't allowed himself to fall in love with her. If only she loved him in return.

Kelly had been gone a little over a month, and still not one letter had he received. He'd written to her several times, but no response. Was she too busy to write? Had she found a man and fallen in love? All sorts of possible explanations flitted through Mike's mind as he trudged along, his boots crunching through the fresh-fallen snow.

God would need to heal his heart if Kelly never returned, because Mike was in love with her, and there didn't seem to be a thing he could do about it.

I shouldn't have let myself fall for her, Lord, he prayed. *What*

I thought was Your will might have only been my own selfish desires.
Maybe You want me to remain single.

Shivering against the cold, Mike headed back to his house.
There was no point in going over this again and again. If Kelly
came back to the canal in the spring with a different attitude
toward him, Mike would be glad. If she didn't, then he would
have to accept it as God's will.

When Mike stepped inside the house a short time later, a
blast of warm air hit him in the face. It was a welcome relief
from the cold. As he hung his coat on a wall peg, he noticed
the calendar hanging nearby. Today was January 5, Kelly's
eighteenth birthday. He remembered her mentioning it before
she left for the city. He'd sent her a package several days ago
and hoped she would receive it on time. Even more than that,
Mike hoped she liked the birthday present he'd chosen.

Kelly couldn't believe how bad her feet hurt. She was used
to walking the towpath every day, but trudging through the
hilly city of Easton was an entirely different matter. Papa had
insisted Kelly get a job to help with expenses, and she'd been
out looking almost every day since they had arrived at the
boardinghouse in Easton. No one seemed to be hiring right
before Christmas, and after the holidays, she was told either
that there was no work or that she wasn't qualified for any of
the available positions. Kelly kept looking, and in the evenings
and on weekends, she helped Mama sew and clean their small,
three-room flat.

Kelly hated to spend her days looking for work and longed to be with their mules that had been left at Morgan's Stables just outside of town. It wasn't cheap to keep them there, but Papa said they had no choice. Needing money for the mules' care was one of the reasons he'd taken a job at Glendon Iron Furnace, which overlooked the canal and Lehigh Valley Railroad. The work was hard and heavy, but pay was better than at many other manual jobs.

Every chance she got, Kelly went to see her animal friends. Today was her eighteenth birthday, and she'd decided to celebrate with a trip to the stables right after breakfast. It might be the only thing special about her birthday, since neither Mama nor Papa had made any mention of it. They'd been sitting around the breakfast table for ten minutes, and no one had said a word about what day it was. Papa had his nose in the *Sunday Call,* Easton's newspaper, and Mama seemed preoccupied with the scrambled eggs on her plate.

Kelly sighed deeply and drank some tea. It didn't matter. She'd never had much of a fuss made on her birthday anyway. Why should this year be any different?

Maybe I'll take some of the money I earned sellin' paintings and buy something today. Kelly grimaced. She knew she should save all her cash for that art gallery she hoped to open some day. Even as the idea popped into her mind, Kelly felt it was futile. She'd only sold a few paintings so far, and even if she sold more, it would take years before she'd have enough to open any kind of gallery. She would need to pay rent for a building, and then there was the cost of all the supplies. It wouldn't be enough to simply sell her paintings and drawings; she'd want to offer her customers the chance to purchase paper, paints, charcoal pencils, and maybe some fancy frames. All that would cost a lot of money. Money Kelly would probably never see in her lifetime.

I may as well give up my dream. If I can find a job in the city, it would probably be best if I stay here and work. Papa can hire a mule driver to take my place. It would serve him right if I never went back to the canal.

A loud knock drove Kelly's thoughts to the back of her mind. She looked at Papa, then Mama. Neither one seemed interested in answering the door.

Kelly sighed and pushed her chair away from the table. Why was she always expected to do everything? She shuffled across the room, feeling as though she had the weight of the world on her shoulders.

She opened the door and was greeted by their landlord, Mable Flannigan. A heavyset, middle-aged woman with bright red hair and sparking blue eyes, Mable had told them that her husband was killed in the War Between the States, and she'd been on her own ever since. The woman had no children to care for and had opened her home to boarders shortly after the war ended nearly twenty-seven years ago. Kelly always wondered why Mrs. Flannigan had never remarried. Could be that she was still pining for her dead husband, or maybe the woman thought she could get along better without a man.

"This came for you in the mornin's mail," Mrs. Flannigan said, holding out a package wrapped in brown paper.

Kelly's forehead wrinkled. "For me?" She couldn't imagine who would be sending her anything.

The older woman nodded. "It has your name and the address of my boardinghouse right here on the front."

Kelly took the package and studied the handwriting. Her name was there all right, in big, bold letters. Her heart began to pound, and her hands shook when she saw the return address. It was from Mike Cooper.

Remembering her manners, Kelly opened the door wider. "Would ya like to come in and have a cup of coffee or some tea?"

Mrs. Flannigan shook her head. "Thanks, but I'd better not. I've got me some washin' to do today, and it sure won't get done if I lollygag over a cup of hot coffee."

The woman turned to go, and Kelly called, "Thanks for deliverin' the package."

A few seconds later, Kelly sat on the sofa, tearing the brown paper away from the box. With trembling hands, she lifted the lid. She let out a little gasp when she saw what the box contained. Her eyes feasted on a tin of store-bought watercolor paints, a real artist's tablet, and three brushes in various sizes. There was also a note:

Dear Kelly,

I wanted you to have this paint set for your eighteenth birthday. I only wish I could be with you to help celebrate. I hope you're doing all right, and I'm real anxious for you to return to the canal.

Fondly, your friend,
Mike Cooper

P.S. Please write soon.

Kelly sat for several seconds, trying to understand how Mike could have known today was her birthday and relishing the joy of owning a real set of watercolors, not to mention a store-bought tablet that she hadn't put together herself. She would be able to paint anything she wanted now, using nearly every shade imaginable.

An image of Mike's friendly face flashed into Kelly's mind. She might have mentioned something to him about her birthday being on January 5. The fact that he'd remembered and cared enough to send her a present was almost overwhelming. No one had ever given her a gift like the one she held in her hands.

"Kelly, who was at the door?" Papa hollered from the next room.

She swallowed hard and stood up. Her dad might be mad when he saw the present Mike had sent her, but she wouldn't lie or hide it from him. While Papa was at work, and after Kelly got home from searching for a job every day, Mama had been reading the Bible out loud, and Kelly had fallen under deep conviction. She'd strayed from God and knew she needed to make things right. It was wrong to lie or hide the truth from her parents. It had been a sin to harbor resentment toward Papa, and with the Lord's help, she was doing much better in that regard.

Grasping the box with her birthday present inside, Kelly walked back to the kitchen. "Mrs. Flannigan was at the door with a package for me." Kelly placed the box on the table.

"Who would be sendin' you anything?" Papa asked, his eyebrows drawing together.

"It's from Mike Cooper."

"The storekeeper along the canal?" Mama questioned as she peered into the box.

Kelly nodded. "It's for my birthday." She sank into her chair, wondering when the explosion would come.

Mama pulled the tin of watercolors out of the box and held it up. Papa frowned but didn't say a word. Kelly held her breath.

"What a thoughtful gift," Mama said. "Now you'll be able to paint with real colors instead of makin' colored water out of my vegetables."

Kelly felt her face heat up. So her mother had known all the time that she was taking carrots, beets, and onions out of the bin. Funny thing, Mama had never said a word about it until now.

"Humph!" Papa snorted. "I hope that man don't think his gift is gonna buy him my daughter's hand in marriage."

"Mike and I are just friends, Papa," Kelly was quick to say. She turned to face him. "Can I keep it? I promise not to paint when I'm supposed to be workin'."

"You've gotta find a job first," Papa grumbled. "We've been in the city for a whole month already, and not one red cent have you brought in."

"I'll look again on Monday," Kelly promised.

"Why don'tcha try over at the Simon Silk Mill on Bushkill Creek?" Mama suggested. "I hear tell they're lookin' to hire a few people there."

Kelly nodded. "I'll go first thing on Monday."

Papa took a long drink from his cup of coffee, wiped his mouth with the back of his hand, and stood up. "I need to get to work."

"But it's Saturday," Mama reminded.

He leveled her with a disgruntled look. "Don'tcha think I know that, woman? They're operatin' the plant six days a week now, and I volunteered to come in today." His gaze swung over to Kelly. "You can keep the birthday present, but I'd better not find you paintin' when ya should be out lookin' for work."

"Thank you, Papa, and I promise I won't paint until all my chores are done for the day, neither." Kelly felt like she could kiss her dad. She didn't, though. Papa had never been very affectionate, and truth be told, until this moment, Kelly had never felt like kissing him.

Papa grunted, grabbed his jacket off the wall peg, and sauntered out the door.

Mama patted Kelly's hand. "Tonight I'm fixin' your favorite supper in honor of your birthday."

"Hunks-a-go pudding and roast beef?" Kelly asked hopefully.

Mama nodded and grinned. "Might make a chocolate cake for dessert, too."

Kelly smiled in return, feeling better than she had in weeks. Today turned out to be a better birthday than she'd ever imagined. Now if she could only find a job.

Chapter 22

As Kelly stood in front of the brick building that housed the Simon Silk Mill, she whispered a prayer, petitioning God to give her a job. She didn't know any other kind of work besides leading the mules, but Mama had taught her to sew, and she figured that's what she would be doing if she were hired here. All the other times they'd wintered in Easton, Papa had never demanded Kelly find a job. That was probably because Mama insisted Kelly go to school. She was older now and done with book learning, so it was time to make some money. If only she didn't have to give it all to Papa. If she could keep the money she earned, Kelly would probably have enough to open her art gallery in no time at all. Of course, she didn't think she would have the nerve to tell Papa she wasn't going back to the canal in the spring.

Pushing the door open, Kelly stepped inside the factory and located the main office. She entered the room and told the receptionist she needed a job. Disappointment flooded Kelly's soul when she was told all the positions at the mill had been taken.

Kelly left the office feeling a sense of frustration. What if she never found a job? Papa would be furious and might make her throw out her art supplies. She couldn't let that happen. There had to be something she could do.

Kelly was almost to the front door when she bumped into someone. Her mouth dropped open, and she took a step back. "Sarah?"

The young woman with dark brown hair piled high on her head looked at Kelly as if she'd seen a ghost. "Kelly, is that you?"

"It's me, Sarah. I'm so surprised to see you."

"And I, you," her sister replied.

"Do you work here?"

Sarah nodded. "Have been for the last couple of months. Before that, I was home takin' care of little Sam."

"Little Sam?"

"Sam Jr."

"You have a son?" Kelly could hardly believe her sister had a baby they knew nothing about. For that matter, they hadn't heard anything from Sarah since that one letter telling the family she and Sam had gotten married and were living in New Jersey.

"The baby was born six months ago," Sarah explained. "Sam was workin' at Warren Soapstone, but one day he lost his temper with the boss and got fired. So I had to find work, and he's been home takin' care of the baby ever since."

Kelly stood, studying her sister and trying to let all she'd said sink in. Sarah was dressed in a beige-colored cotton blouse and plain brown skirt covered with a black apron. Her shoulders were slumped, and she looked awful tired.

The fact that Sam Turner would allow his wife to work while he stayed home was one more proof for Kelly that men only used women. Sam was no better than Papa. Sarah had run off with Sam to get away from working, and now she was being forced to support not only herself, but her husband and baby as well. It made Kelly sick to the pit of her stomach.

"Are you and the folks stayin' at the boardinghouse like before?" Sarah's question drove Kelly's thoughts to the back of her mind.

"Yes, we've been there since early December." Kelly gave her sister a hug. "I'm sure Mama and Papa would like to see you and the baby. . .Sam Sr., too."

When Sarah pulled away, tears stood in her dark eyes. "Oh, please don't say anything to the folks about seein' me today."

"Why not?"

"Papa always hated Sam, and when we tried to tell him we were in love and wanted to get married, he blew up and said if we did, he'd punch Sam in the nose."

Kelly flinched at the memory. She'd been there and could understand why her sister might be afraid to confront their dad now.

"I won't say a word," Kelly promised, "but I would sure like to see my nephew. You think there's any way that could be arranged?"

Sarah gave a tired smile. "I'd like you to meet little Sam. Mama, too, for that matter. Maybe the two of you can come by our apartment sometime soon. Let me talk it over with my husband first, though."

"How will we get in touch with you?"

Sarah looked thoughtful. "Is Papa workin' every day?"

Kelly nodded. "Over at Glendon Iron Furnace, even Saturdays now."

"Then how about if the baby and I come by the boardinghouse next Saturday?"

"That would be great. Should I tell Mama ahead, or do you want to surprise her?"

"Let's make it our little surprise." Sarah squeezed Kelly's arm. "I need to get back up to the second floor where I work on one of the weavin' looms."

Kelly gave her sister another hug. "Sure is good to see you, Sarah."

"Same here." Sarah started for the stairs, and Kelly headed for the front door, feeling more cheerful than she had all morning. Even if she didn't have a job, at least she'd been reunited with her sister. That was something to be grateful for.

For the third time that morning, Mike sorted through the stack of mail he'd dumped on the counter after it arrived by canal boat. There was nothing from Kelly. Wasn't she ever going to respond? Had she received his birthday present? Did she like the watercolor set, sketching pad, and paintbrushes, or was she mad at him for giving them to her? If only she'd written a note to let him know the package had arrived.

"I've got to get busy and quit thinking about Kelly." Mike slipped each letter into the cubbyholes he'd made for his postal customers. The packages were kept in a box underneath. As local people dropped by the store, he would hand out their mail and be glad he'd taken the time to organize it so well. Any mail that came for the boatmen who were working in the city and wanted their parcels to be held until they returned to the canal was stored safely in a wooden box under the front counter. Most canalers lived in homes nearby, and those, like Amos McGregor, would be getting their mail forwarded to their temporary address during the winter months.

Thinking about Amos caused Mike's mind to wander back to Kelly. Whenever he closed his eyes at night, he could see her smiling face, hear her joyous laughter, and feel her sweet lips against his own. Had it been wrong to kiss her? He hadn't thought so at the time, but after she'd pulled away and cooled off toward him, Mike figured he'd done a terrible thing.

"I kept telling myself I would go slow with Kelly, but I moved too fast." Mike moaned. "Why must I always rush ahead of God?" He reached for one of the Bibles he had stacked near the end of the counter and opened it to the book of Hebrews. He found chapter 10 and read verses 35 and 36: *"Cast not away. . .your confidence, which hath great recompense of reward. For ye have need of patience, that, after ye have done the will of God, ye might receive the promise."*

Mike closed his eyes and quoted Genesis 2:18: " 'And the Lord God said, It is not good that the man should be alone; I will make him an help meet for him.'" He dropped to his knees behind the counter. "Oh, Lord, if I have patience and continue to do Your will, might I receive the promise of an help meet?"

Except for the eerie howling of the wind against the eaves of the store, there was no sound. Patience. Mike knew he needed to be more patient. With God's help he would try, but it wouldn't be easy.

Chapter 23

On Saturday afternoon, Sarah, with baby Sam tucked under one arm, came by the boardinghouse. Kelly was shocked at her sister's haggard appearance. Sarah had looked tired the other day, but it was nothing like this. Puffiness surrounded her sister's red-rimmed eyes, indicating she had been crying. Something was wrong. Kelly could feel it in her bones.

Mama, who hadn't been told about Sarah's surprise visit, rushed to her oldest daughter's side when Kelly stepped away and closed the door. "Sarah!" Mama exclaimed. "I can't believe it's you. Where have you been livin'? How did you know we'd be here?" She reached out to touch the baby's chubby hand. "And who is this cute little fellow?"

Sarah emitted a small laugh, even though her expression was strained. "Too many questions at once, Mama. Can I come in and be seated before I answer each one?"

Mama's hands went to her flushed cheeks. "Yes, yes. Please,

let me have your coats, then go into the livin' room and get comfortable."

Sarah turned to Kelly, who so far hadn't uttered a word. "Would ya mind holdin' Sam while I take off my coat?"

Kelly held out her arms to the child, but little Sam buried his head against his mother's chest and whimpered.

"He's a bit shy around strangers," Sarah said. "I'm sure he'll warm up to you soon." She handed the baby over to Kelly despite the child's protests.

Feeling awkward and unsure of herself, Kelly stepped into the living room and took a seat on the sofa. Baby Sam squirmed restlessly, but he didn't cry.

A few minutes later, Sarah and their mother entered the room. Mama sat beside Kelly on the sofa, and Sarah took a seat in the rocking chair across from them.

"Mama, meet your grandson, Sam Jr.," Sarah announced.

Mama's lips curved into a smile, and she reached out to take the infant from Kelly. He went willingly, obviously drawn to his grandma.

"I can't believe you have a baby, Sarah. How old is he, and why didn't ya write and tell us about him?"

Sarah hung her head, and Kelly noticed tears dripping onto her sister's skirt, leaving dark spots in the gray-colored fabric. "I—I knew you and Papa were angry with me for runnin' off with Sam, so I figured you wouldn't want to know anything about what I was doin'."

Kelly closed her eyes and offered up a prayer on her sister's behalf as she waited for her mother's reply.

Mama's eyes filled with tears, and she hugged the baby to

her chest. "I could never turn my back on one of my own, Sarah. I love both my girls." She glanced over at Kelly, who was also close to tears.

"I love you, too, Mama," Kelly murmured.

"So do I," Sarah agreed. "Now as to your questions, Sam is six months old, and we've all been livin' in a flat across the bridge in Phillipsburg. Up until a few weeks ago, Sam worked at Warren Soapstone, but he got fired for shootin' off his mouth to the boss." Sarah paused and drew in a deep breath. "I've been workin' at the Simon Silk Mill ever since, and Sam *was* takin' care of the baby."

Was? What did Sarah mean by that? Before Kelly could voice the question, her sister rushed on.

"Sam's been drinkin' here of late, and actin' real funny. Last night when I got home from work, he had his bags packed and said he was leavin' me and the baby." Sarah's eyes clouded with fresh tears, and she choked on a sob. "I've got no place to leave Sam Jr. while I'm at work now, and I can't afford to hire a babysitter and pay the rent on my flat, too."

"I could watch the baby for you," Kelly spoke up. "I haven't been able to find work anywhere yet, so I have nothin' else to do with my time." *Except paint and dream impossible dreams,* she added mentally.

Sarah shot Mama an imploring look. "Would ya allow Kelly to come live with me?"

"I'm not sure that would set well with your papa." Mama pursed her lips. "Why don't you and the baby move in here with us?"

Sarah glanced around the room. "This is the same place

you've always rented from Mable Flannigan, right?"

Their mother nodded.

"Mama, it's so small. There's not nearly enough room for two extra people." She nodded at Kelly. "If you could come stay with me and Sam Jr., I couldn't pay you, but I could offer free room and board. You'd also have a small room, which you'd need to share with the baby."

As sorry as Kelly was to hear the news that Sarah's husband had left, the idea of moving in with her sister sounded rather pleasant. It would give her more time to paint without Papa breathing down her neck or hollering because she still hadn't found a job. She touched her mother's arm gently. "Please, Mama. I'd like to help Sarah out in her time of need."

Mama shrugged. "If Papa says it's all right, then I'll agree to it as well."

The next few months were like none Kelly had ever known. Much to her surprise, Papa had given permission for her to move in with Sarah. Kelly spent five days a week taking care of little Sam while Sarah was at work. This gave her some time to use her new watercolor set, since she could paint or draw whenever the baby slept.

Besides babysitting, Kelly cleaned the apartment, did most of the cooking, and even sewed new clothes for her fast-growing nephew. She and little Sam had become good friends, and Kelly discovered she was more capable with children than she'd ever imagined.

As Kelly sat in the rocking chair, trying to get the baby to sleep, she let her mind wander back to the general store outside of Walnutport. A vision of Mike Cooper flashed across her mind. He was good with children. Kelly had witnessed him giving out free candy to several of the kids who played along the canal and to many who visited his store, as well. Mike wanted a whole houseful of children; he'd told her so.

"I never did write and thank Mike for the birthday gift," Kelly whispered against little Sam's downy blond head. The baby looked a lot like his papa, but Kelly hoped he didn't grow up to be anything like the man. How could Sam Turner have left his wife and child? Just thinking about it made Kelly's blood boil. Was Mike Cooper any different than Papa or Sam? Could he be trusted not to hurt her the way Papa often did or the way Sam had done to Sarah?

Mike had promised to write, and he'd done so several times. He'd also sent her a wonderful present. He might not be the same as other men she knew. Kelly guessed she'd have to make up her mind about Mike when they returned to the canal sometime in March.

She bent her head and kissed the tip of little Sam's nose. "You and your mama might be goin' with us this spring. I don't rightly see how the two of you can stay on here by yourselves." She giggled at the baby's response to her kiss. He'd scrunched up his nose and wiggled his lips, almost as if he was trying to kiss her back.

"Of course, I could always stay on here, I suppose. Papa can't make me return to the canal if I don't want to." Even as the words slipped off her tongue, Kelly knew what she would do when Papa said it was time to return to their boat. She would go along willingly because she missed her mule friends, missed the smell of fresh air, and yes, even missed Mike Cooper.

Mike stared at his empty coffee cup. He should clear away the breakfast dishes and get his horse hitched to the buckboard. He was expecting a load of supplies to be delivered to Walnutport today by train, and it would be good if he were there when it came in. Mike knew that Gus Stevens, who ran the livery stable next to the train station, would be happy to take the supplies to his place and hold them for him, but Mike didn't like to take advantage of the older man's good nature.

With that thought in mind, Mike scooped the dishes off the table and set them in the sink. He'd pour warm water over them and let them soak until he returned from town.

A short time later, Mike climbed into his wagon, clucked to the horse, and headed toward Walnutport. During the first part of the trip, he sang favorite hymns and played his mouth harp. It made the time go quicker and caused Mike to feel a bit closer to his Maker. It also made him feel less lonely.

As the days had turned into weeks, and the weeks into months, Mike's yearning for a wife had not diminished. He'd been feeling so lonely here of late, he'd actually considered accepting one of Betsy Nelson's frequent supper invitations. The woman was persistent, he'd give her that much. Persistent and pushy. Nothing like Kelly McGregor.

"I've got to quit thinking about Kelly," Mike berated himself.

"She obviously feels nothing for me. If she did, she would have written by now." Mike wasn't sure he'd ever see Kelly again. For all he knew, she'd decided to stay in the city of Easton. She'd probably found a job and a boyfriend. She could even be married.

By the time Mike arrived at his destination, he was sweating worse than his horse. He'd let the gelding run and had enjoyed the exhilarating ride. It helped clear his thinking. Nothing else had mattered but the wind blowing against his face. Tomorrow would be a new day. Another time to reflect on God's will for Mike's life.

Chapter 24

On Monday morning, the third week of March, the McGregors boarded their boat. The canal was full of water again, and Papa was most anxious to get started hauling coal. Sarah and baby Sam had come along, since Sarah didn't want to stay in Easton by herself and couldn't talk Kelly into staying on. Besides, Mama could use Sarah's help on the boat and would be available to watch the baby whenever Kelly's sister took over walking the mules.

Kelly felt bad that Sarah was returning to the canal she'd hated so much, but it would be nice to have her sister's help, as well as her companionship.

Kelly looked forward to stopping by Cooper's General Store Tuesday afternoon. While they'd picked up some supplies at Dull's Grocery Store in Easton, Papa had forgotten a couple of things and was planning on getting them at Mike's store. Kelly planned to give Mike several more pictures to try to sell, as she'd been able to paint many during her stay in the city. She was also anxious to see whether he'd sold any of her other pieces. She hoped she could continue their business relationship without Mike expecting anything more.

Kelly pulled the collar of her jacket tightly against her chin as she tromped along the towpath, singing her favorite song and not even minding the chilly March winds.

"Hunks-a-go pudding and pieces of pie; my mother gave me when I was knee-high. . . . And if you don't believe it, just drop in and see—the hunks-a-go pudding my mother gave me."

Mike felt better than he had in weeks. He'd had several customers and given away a couple of Bibles to some rough-and-tumble canalers who were desperately in need of God. Mike had witnessed these two men fighting on more than one occasion, and the fact that they'd willingly taken a Bible gave him hope that others might also be receptive to the Gospel.

As Mike washed the store windows with a rag and some diluted ammonia, he thought about Kelly's dad. Now there was a man badly in need of the Lord. Mike had witnessed Amos McGregor's temper several times. If Amos found forgiveness for his sins and turned his life around, maybe Kelly would be more receptive to Mike's attentions. He was sure the main reason Kelly was so standoffish was because she was afraid of men.

He glanced at the wall behind his front counter. Only two of Kelly's pictures had sold since she'd left for Easton, and those had both been bought before Christmas. No one had shown any interest in her work since then, even though Mike often pointed the pictures out to his customers, hoping they would take the hint and buy one.

Mike studied the window he'd been washing, checking for any spots or streaks. To his surprise, Amos McGregor's boat was docked out front, and the man was heading toward the store. Trudging alongside of Amos was his wife, Dorrie, Kelly, and another woman carrying a young child.

Mike climbed off his ladder and hurried to the front of the store. Kelly had returned to the canal! He opened the door and greeted his customers with a smile and a sense of excitement. "It's sure nice to see you folks again."

Amos grunted in reply, but Kelly returned his smile. "It's good to be back," she said.

"And who might this little guy be?" Mike asked, reaching out to clasp the chubby fingers of the little boy who was held by the other young woman.

"That's baby Sam," Kelly said. "In case you don't remember, this is my sister, Sarah. She and Sam Jr. are gonna be livin' with us for a while."

"Yes, I remember Sarah." Mike nodded and smiled at Kelly's sister. He didn't ask for details. From the pathetic look on Sarah's face, he figured her marriage to Sam Turner was probably over.

"Do you have any soft material I might use for diapers?" Sarah asked. "Sam seems to go through them pretty fast, and I don't have time to be washin' every day."

Mike pointed to the shelf where he kept bolts of material.

"I'm sure you'll find something to your liking over there."

Sarah moved away, and her mother followed. Amos was across the room looking at some new shovels Mike had recently gotten in, so apparently Kelly felt free to stare up at her paintings.

Mike positioned himself so he was standing beside Kelly. "How have you been? I've missed you," he whispered.

Her gaze darted from her dad, to the paintings, and back to Mike. "I'm fine, and I've brought you more pictures." She frowned. "But from the looks of it, you still have quite a few of my old ones."

He nodded. "Sorry to say I only sold two while you were gone." He leaned his head close to her ear. "Did you get the birthday present I sent? I'd hoped you would write and let me know."

"Yes, I got the package and put it to good use." Kelly averted his gaze. "Sorry for not writing to say thank you. I kept meaning to write, but I got busy takin' care of little Sam while Sarah went to work each day."

"That's okay. I understand." Mike touched her arm briefly, but then he pulled his hand away. "Do you have the new pictures with you now?"

She nodded, reached into her pocket, retrieved the drawing tablet he'd sent her, and handed it to him. "I was able to make things look more real usin' things you sent me."

Mike thumbed quickly through the tablet. Pictures of row housing, tall buildings, and statues in the city of Easton covered the first pages. There were also some paintings of the bridge that spanned the river between Easton, Pennsylvania, and Phillipsburg, New Jersey, as well as a few pictures of people.

They were all done well, and Mike was glad he'd sent Kelly the paint set, even if she hadn't chosen to write and tell him she'd received it. He was even happier that she'd accepted the gift and put it to good use.

"These are wonderful," he said. "Would you mind leaving them with me to try and sell?"

Kelly's eyebrows furrowed. "But you still have most of my other pictures. Why would ya be wantin' more?"

"Because they're good—really good," he asserted. "I've always admired your artwork, and I believe you've actually gotten better."

Her expression turned hopeful. "You really think so?"

"I do."

She pointed to the tablet. "And you think you can sell these?"

"I'd like to try."

She nodded her consent. "Do as you like then."

"Will you be spending the night in the area?" Mike asked.

Kelly opened her mouth, but her dad spoke up before she could say anything. "We'll be headin' on up the canal. Won't be back this way 'til probably late Saturday."

Mike turned his head to the left. He hadn't realized Kelly's dad was standing beside him, holding a shovel in one hand.

"You think you might stay over on Saturday night?"

"Could be," Amos said.

Mike smiled to himself. If the McGregors were here on Sunday, then he might get the chance to spend some time alone with Kelly. Even though the weather was still a bit chilly, it was possible that they'd be able to go on another picnic.

Kelly left Mike's store with mixed feelings. It was wonderful to see him again, but her spirits had been dampened when he'd told her he'd only sold two pictures during her absence. Mike had given her the money for those paintings as she was on her way out the door. He'd also whispered that he wanted to take her on another picnic and hoped it would be this Sunday, if they were near his store.

"Mind if I walk with you a ways?" Sarah asked, breaking into Kelly's musings. "Sam's ready for a nap, and Mama doesn't need me for anything. I thought the fresh air and exercise might do me some good."

Kelly was always glad for her sister's company. "You wanna be in charge of the mules or just offer me companionship?"

"You can tend the mules," Sarah was quick to say. "I think they like you better than they do me."

"They're just used to me, that's all." Kelly adjusted the brim of her straw hat, which seemed to have a mind of its own. "Truth be told, I think old Herman kinda likes it when I sing silly canal songs."

"You sing to the mules?"

Kelly nodded. "Guess it's really for me, but if they enjoy it, then that makes it all the better."

Sarah chuckled. It was good to see her smile. She'd been so sad since her husband had run off, and Kelly couldn't blame her. She would be melancholy, too, if the man she'd married had chosen not to stay around and help out. Sam Turner ought to be tarred and feathered for walking out on his wife and baby. He probably never loved Sarah in the first place. Most likely he only married her just to show her folks that he could take their daughter away.

"Tell me about Mike Cooper," Sarah said.

Kelly jerked her head. "What about him?"

"Have you and him been courtin'?"

"What would make you ask that?"

Sarah gave Kelly a nudge in the ribs with her bony elbow. "He couldn't take his eyes off you the whole time we were in the store." She eyed Kelly curiously. "I'd say it's as plain as the nose on your face that you're smitten with him as well."

What could Kelly say in response? She couldn't deny her feelings for Mike. She enjoyed his company, and he was the best-looking man she'd ever laid eyes on. That didn't mean they were courting, though. And it sure didn't mean she was smitten with him.

"Mike and me have gone on a few picnics, but we're not a courtin' couple," Kelly said, shrugging her shoulders.

"But you'd like to be, right?" her sister prodded.

"We're just friends; nothin' more."

Sarah wiggled her dark eyebrows, then winked. "Whatever you say, little sister. Whatever you say."

Chapter 25

*E*arly Saturday afternoon, Mike went outside to help one of the local boatmen load the supplies he had purchased onto his boat. They had no more than placed the last one on deck when Mike saw the McGregors' boat heading their way.

His heart did a little flip-flop. Would they be stopping for the night? Mike stepped onto the towpath, anxious for Kelly to arrive. While he waited, he slicked back his hair, finger-combed his mustache, and made sure his flannel shirt was tucked inside his trousers.

A few minutes later, Kelly and her mules were alongside him. The animals brayed and snorted, as if they expected him to give them a handout, as he'd done a few times before.

"Sorry, fellows, but I didn't know you were coming, so there aren't any apples or carrots in my pockets today." Mike gave each mule a pat on its flank, then he turned and smiled at Kelly. "I'm glad you're here. Are you planning to stay overnight?"

She shook her head. "Now that Sarah's here to help, Papa has us movin' twice as fast as before. He says there's no time to waste. Especially when we never know if there's gonna be trouble ahead that might slow us down."

Mike felt his anticipation slip to the toes of his boots. He'd been waiting so long to be with Kelly again, and now they weren't stopping? How was he ever going to tell her what was on his mind if they couldn't spend any time together?

"I'm sorry to hear you're not staying over," he muttered. "I was really hoping we'd be able to go on a picnic tomorrow afternoon."

"Isn't it a mite chilly for a picnic?"

Mike shrugged his shoulders. "I figured we could build a fire and snuggle beneath a blanket if it got too cold."

When Kelly smiled at him, he wanted to take her into his arms and proclaim his intentions. He knew now wasn't the time or the place, so he drew on his inner strength and took a step back. "When do you think you might be stopping long enough so we can spend a few minutes together?"

She turned her palms upward. "Don't know. That's entirely up to Papa."

Mike groaned. "Guess I'll just have to wait and ask God to give me more patience."

"Get a move on, would ya, girl?"

Kelly and Mike both turned. Amos McGregor was leaning over the side of the boat, and he wasn't smiling.

"I need to get the mules movin' again," Kelly said to Mike.

He stepped aside but touched her arm as she passed by. "See you soon, Kelly."

"I hope so," she murmured.

The next few weeks sped by, as Kelly and Sarah took turns leading the mules, and Papa kept the boat moving as fast as the animals would pull. They stopped only once for supplies, and that was at a store in Mauch Chunk. Kelly was beginning to think she'd never get the chance to see Mike Cooper again or find out if any of her paintings had sold. On days like today, when the sky was cloudy and threatened rain, Kelly's spirits plummeted, and she didn't feel much like praying. All the while they'd been living in Easton, she'd felt closer to God, reading her Bible every day and offering prayers on behalf of her family and her future. It didn't seem as if any of her prayers were going to be answered, and she wondered if she should continue to ask God for things He probably wouldn't provide.

She'd prayed for her sister, and look how that had turned out. She had prayed for Papa's salvation, yet he was still as moody and cantankerous as ever. She'd asked God to allow her to make enough money to support herself and open an art gallery, but that wasn't working out, either. So far, she'd only made a few dollars, which was a long ways from what she would need. It was an impossible dream, and with each passing day, Kelly became more convinced it was never going to happen.

She looked up at the darkening sky and prayed, "Lord, if walkin' the mules is the only job You have in mind for me, then help me learn to be content."

It was the end of April before Kelly saw Mike again. They'd arrived in front of his store at dusk on Saturday evening, so Papa decided to stay for the night. Since the next day was Sunday and the boatmen were not allowed to pull their loads up the canal, they would be around for the whole day.

Kelly settled into her bed, filled with a sense of joy she hadn't felt in weeks. Tomorrow she planned to attend the church service on the grassy area in front of Mike's store. Afterward she hoped to see Mike and talk to him about her artwork. She'd managed to do a few more paintings—mostly of little Sam—so she would give those to Mike as well.

Sam was growing so much, and soon he'd be toddling all over the place. Then they would have to be sure he was tied securely to something, or else he might end up falling overboard. Canal life could be dangerous, and precautions had to be taken in order to protect everyone on board. Even the mules needed safeguarding from bad weather, insects, freak accidents, and fatigue.

Kelly closed her eyes and drew in a deep breath as she snuggled into her feather pillow. She fell asleep dreaming about Mike Cooper.

Sunday morning brought sunshine and blue skies. It was perfect spring weather, and Kelly had invited her sister and mother to join her for the church service that had just begun. Mama said she'd better stay on the boat with Papa, but Sarah left the baby behind with her parents and joined Kelly.

The two young women spread a blanket on the grass and took a seat just as Betsy Nelson began playing her zither, while her father led those who had gathered in singing "Holy Spirit, Light Divine."

Kelly lifted her voice with the others. The first verse spoke to her heart:

Holy Spirit, Light divine,
Shine upon this heart of mine.
Chase the shades of night away;
Turn my darkness into day.

The song gave Kelly exactly what she needed. A reminder that only God could turn her darkness into day. As difficult as it was, she needed to keep praying and trusting Him to answer her prayers.

Kelly felt her sister's nudge in the ribs. "Psst. . .look who's watchin' you."

Kelly glanced around and noticed Mike sitting on a wooden box several feet away. He grinned and nodded at her, and she smiled in return.

"I told you he likes you."

Kelly put her fingers to her lips. "Shh. . .someone might hear."

Sarah snickered, but she stopped talking and began to sing. Kelly did the same.

A short time later, the preacher gave his message from the book of Romans.

"'And we know that all things work together for good to them that love God, to them who are the called according to his purpose,'" Reverend Nelson read in his booming voice.

"All things. . . . For them that love God and are called according to His purpose." Kelly was sure that meant her. The preacher was saying all things in her life would work together for good because she loved God. Surely He wanted to give her good things. The question was, would those good things be what she'd been praying for?

Kelly hadn't realized the service was over until Sarah touched her arm. "You gonna sit there all day, or did ya plan to go speak to that storekeeper who hasn't taken his eyes off you since we sat down?"

Kelly wrinkled her nose. "You're makin' that up."

"Am not." Sarah stood up. "I'd better get back to the boat and check on little Sam. Got any messages you want me to give the folks?"

Kelly got to her feet as well. "What makes you think I'm not returnin' to the boat with you?"

"Call it a hunch." Sarah bent down and grabbed the blanket. She gave it a good shake, then folded it and tucked it under Kelly's arm. "Should I tell Mama you won't be joinin' us for the noon meal?"

Kelly felt her face heat up. Was Sarah able to read her mind these days?

"Well, I. . .uh. . .thought I might speak to Mike about my paintings. See if any more have sold."

197

"And if he invites you to join him for lunch?"

Kelly chewed on her lower lip. "You think I should say yes?"

Sarah swatted Kelly's arm playfully. "Of course, silly."

"What about the folks? Shouldn't I check with them first?"

"Leave that up to me."

"Okay, then. If I don't return to the boat in the next half hour, you can figure I'm havin' a picnic lunch with Mike. He did mention wantin' to do that the last time we talked."

Sarah gave Kelly a quick hug, hoisted her long skirt, and trudged off in the direction of the boat. Kelly turned toward the spot where Mike had been sitting, but disappointment flooded her soul when she realized he was gone. With a deep sigh, she whirled around and headed the same way Sarah had gone. There was no point in sticking around now.

Kelly had only taken a few steps when she felt someone touch her shoulder. She whirled around, and her throat closed with emotion. Mike was standing so close she could feel his warm breath on her neck. She stared up at him, her heart thumping hard like the mules' hooves plodding along the hard-packed trail.

"Kelly." Mike's voice was low and sweet.

She slid her tongue across her lower lip, feeling jittery as a june bug. "I came to hear the preaching."

"Reverend Nelson delivered a good message today, didn't he?"

Kelly nodded in response. It was hard to speak. Hard to think with him standing there watching her every move.

"Can you join me for a picnic?" Mike asked. "It will only take me a few minutes to throw something in the picnic basket, and it's the perfect day for it, don't you think?"

"Yes, yes, it is," she replied, glad she'd found her voice again.

"Then you'll join me?"

"I'd be happy to. Is there anything I can bring?"

"Just a hearty appetite and that blanket you're holding."

Kelly glanced down at the woolen covering Sarah had tucked under her arm. Her sister must have been pretty certain Mike would be taking her on a picnic. "Where should I meet you?"

"How about at the pond by the lock tender's house? That way you won't have to worry about anyone seeing us walk there together."

Kelly knew Mike was probably referring to her dad, and he was right. It would be much better if Papa didn't know she was going on a picnic with the storekeeper.

"Okay, I'll head there now, and maybe even get a bit of sketching done while I'm waitin' for you."

Mike winked at her. "See you soon then."

"Yes, soon."

Chapter 26

The warmth of the sun beating down on her head and shoulders felt like healing balm as Kelly reclined on her blanket a few feet from the pond. She always enjoyed springtime, with its gentle breezes, pleasantly warm temperatures, and flowers blooming abundantly along the towpath. Summer would be here soon, and that meant hot, humid days, which made it more difficult to walk the mules. So she would enjoy each day of spring and try to be content when the sweltering days of summer came upon them.

"Are you taking a nap?"

Kelly bolted upright at the sound of Mike's voice. "I...uh... was just resting and enjoyin' the warmth of the sun."

He took a seat beside her and placed the picnic basket in the center of the blanket. "It's a beautiful Lord's day, isn't it?"

She nodded and smiled.

"I hope you're hungry, because I packed us a big lunch."

Kelly eyed the basket curiously. "What did ya fix?"

Mike opened the lid and withdrew a loaf of bread, along with a hunk of cheese and some roast beef slices. "For sandwiches," he announced.

Kelly licked her lips as her mouth began to water. She hadn't realized how hungry she was until she saw the food.

"I also brought some canned peaches, a bottle of goat's milk, and a chocolate cake for dessert."

"Where did you get all this?" Surely the man hadn't baked the cake and bread, canned the peaches, and milked a goat. When would he have had the time? Papa always said cooking and baking were women's work, although he had been forced to do some of it when Mama had taken sick last year.

Mike fingered his mustache as a smile spread across his face. "I must confess, I bought the bread and cake from Mrs. Harris, the wife of one of our lock tenders living along the canals. I often buy her baked goods and sell them in my store. The peaches came from Mrs. Wilson, who lives in Walnutport."

"And the goat's milk?"

He wiggled his eyebrows. "I recently traded one of my customers a couple of kerosene lamps for the goat."

"Couldn't they have paid for the lamps, or were you actually wantin' a goat?"

He chuckled. "Truth of the matter, they didn't have any cash, and even though I offered them credit, they preferred to do a bit of bartering." He poured some of the goat's milk into a cup and handed it to Kelly. "I enjoy animals, so Henrietta is a nice addition to the little barnyard family I adopted this winter."

"Your barnyard family? How many other animals do you have?"

"Besides Blaze, my horse, and Henrietta the goat, I also own a cat, a dozen chickens, and I'm thinking about getting a pig or two."

Kelly shook her head. "Sounds like a lot of work to me."

"Maybe so, but a man can get lonely living all by himself, and taking care of the critters gives me something to do when I'm not minding the store."

Kelly was about to take a sip of her goat's milk, when Mike took hold of her hand. "Shall we pray?"

"Of course."

After Mike's simple prayer, he sliced the bread and handed Kelly a plate with a hunk of cheese, some meat, and two thick pieces of bread. She made quick work out of eating it, savoring every bite.

When they finished their sandwiches, Mike opened the jar of peaches and placed two chunks on each of their plates.

"Don't you ever get lonely walking the towpath by yourself?"

"I'm not really alone," Kelly replied. "Herman and Hector are good company, and of course now that Sarah's back, she sometimes walks with me."

His eyebrows drew together. "Mind if I ask where Sarah's husband is?"

Kelly felt her stomach tighten. She didn't want to think of the way Sam had run off and left his family, much less talk about it.

"I guess it's none of my business," Mike said, before she could make a reply. "Forget I even asked."

Kelly reached out and touched the sleeve of his shirt. "It's all right. Others will no doubt be askin', so I may as well start by telling you the facts." She swallowed hard, searching for the right words. "Shortly after we arrived in Easton, I ran into my sister at the Simon Silk Mill, where I'd gone looking for a job."

Mike nodded.

"Sarah told me Sam had lost his job at Warren Soapstone. Said it was because he'd gotten mad at his boss and talked back." Kelly paused a moment and was surprised when Mike reached for her hand. She didn't pull it away. His hand was warm and comforting.

"Sarah said Sam had been staying home with the baby while she worked," Kelly continued. "I invited her to drop by the boardinghouse where we were staying, so Mama and me could meet Sam Jr."

"And did she stop by?" Mike asked.

"Yes, the next Saturday. But as soon as I laid eyes on her, I knew somethin' was wrong."

"What happened?"

"She said Sam up and left her, which meant she had no one to watch the baby." Kelly's eyes filled with tears, just thinking about how terribly her sister had been treated. "I agreed to move in with Sarah and watch the little guy while she was at work."

"So that's how you were able to get so many paintings done." Mike squeezed Kelly's hand. "That was a fine thing you did, agreeing to help care for your sister's child." He frowned. "I'm sorry to hear Sam Turner couldn't face up to his responsibilities. Guess maybe he wasn't ready to be a husband or father."

Kelly snorted. "I'd say most men aren't ready."

"That's not true," Mike said, shaking his head. "I'm more than ready. Have been for a couple of years." He eyed Kelly in a curious sort of way. What was he thinking? Why was he smiling at her like that?

She didn't know what to say, so she withdrew her hand and popped a hunk of peach into her mouth.

"Ever since my folks passed away, I've felt an emptiness in my heart," Mike went on to say. "And after Alvin and John left home to start up their fishin' business in New Jersey, I've had a hankering for a wife and a houseful of kids." He stared down at his plate. "I've been praying for some time that God would give me a Christian wife, and later some children who'd take over the store some day." His gaze lifted to her face, and she swallowed hard. "I feel confident that God has answered my prayer and sent the perfect woman for my needs."

Kelly's heart began to pound. Surely Mike couldn't mean her. He must be referring to someone else. . .maybe Betsy Nelson, the preacher's daughter. It was obvious that the woman had eyes for Mike. Maybe the two of them had begun courting while Kelly was away for the winter months.

"I think the preacher's daughter would make any man a fine wife," Kelly mumbled.

"The preacher's daughter?" Mike's furrowed brows showed his obvious confusion.

"Betsy Nelson. I believe she likes you."

Mike set his plate on the blanket, then took hold of Kelly's and did the same with it. He leaned forward, placed his hands on her shoulders, and kissed her lips so tenderly she thought she might swoon. When the kiss ended, he whispered, "It's you I plan to marry, and it has been all along."

Kelly's mouth dropped open, but before she could find her voice, he spoke again. "Ever since that day you and your folks came into my store so you could buy a pair of boots, I've been interested in you. I thought you might feel the same."

"I...I...," she sputtered.

"We can be married by Preacher Nelson whenever you feel ready," Mike continued, as though the matter was entirely settled. "I'm hoping we can start a family right away, and—"

Kelly jumped up so quickly she knocked over the jar still half-full of peaches. "I won't be anyone's wife!" she shouted. "Especially not someone who only wants a woman so he can have children he can put to work and never pay!"

Mike scrambled to his feet, but before he had a chance to say one word, she turned on her heel and bounded away, not caring that she'd left her blanket behind.

Mike stood staring at Kelly's retreating form and feeling like his breath had been snatched away. What had gone wrong? What had he said to upset her so?

Taking in a deep breath of air, Mike tried to sort out his tangled emotions. Kelly had to be the one for him. After all, she'd appeared at his store last year only moments after his prayer for a wife. He'd thought they'd been drawing closer each time they spent alone. She'd allowed him to kiss her. Had Kelly really believed he was interested in Betsy Nelson? And what had she meant by shouting that she didn't want to be anyone's wife—especially not someone who wanted a woman so he could have children he could put to work and never pay?

"I would never do such a thing," Mike muttered. "I can't imagine why she would think so, either."

An image of Amos McGregor popped into Mike's mind. The man was a tyrant, and he remembered Kelly saying on several occasions that her dad had refused to pay her any money for leading the mules. That was the reason her sister, Sarah, had run off with Sam Turner a couple years ago.

Mike slapped the side of his head and moaned. "How could I have been so stupid and insensitive? I should have realized Kelly might misunderstand my intentions."

He closed his eyes and lifted his face toward the sky. "Father in heaven, please guide me. I love Kelly, and I thought by her actions she might have come to love me. Help me convince her, Lord."

Chapter 27

Kelly knew her face must be red and tear-stained. Her parents would want to know where she'd gone after the church service, but she couldn't face anyone now or answer any questions. She just wanted to be alone in her room, to cry and sort out her feelings.

Kelly climbed onto the boat and hurried to her bedroom, relieved that nobody was in sight. They were probably all taking naps. She flung the door of her room open and flopped onto the bed, hoping she, too, might be able to nap. But sleep eluded her as she thought about the things that had transpired on her picnic with Mike.

Did the man really expect her to marry him and bear his children, just so they could work in his store? Mike hadn't really said it would be without pay, but then she'd run off so fast there hadn't been a chance for him to say anything more. Maybe she should have asked him to explain his intentions.

Maybe she should have admitted that she'd come to care for him in a special way.

A fresh set of tears coursed down Kelly's cheeks, and she sniffed deeply while she swiped at them with the back of her hand. *I can never tell Mike how he makes me feel. If I did, he would think I wanted to get married and raise his children. I won't marry a man just to get away from Papa's mean temper or the hard work I'm expected to do. I want the opportunity to support myself. I need the chance to prove I can make money of my own.*

She squeezed her eyes shut. "Dear God, please show me what to do. Help me learn to be content with my life, and help me forget how much I enjoyed Mike's kiss."

For the next several weeks, Kelly avoided Mike's store. Even when they stopped for supplies, she stayed outside with the mules. She couldn't face Mike. He probably thought she was an idiot for running out on their picnic, and it was too difficult for her to explain the way she'd been thinking. She was pretty sure she loved him, but she couldn't give in to her feelings. No way did she want to end up like Mama, who had to endure Papa's harsh tongue and controlling ways. Nor did Kelly wish to be like her sister, raising a baby alone and continuing to work for their father with no pay.

Today was hotter than usual, especially since it was only the end of May. Kelly looked longingly at the canal as she plodded along the towpath, wishing she could stop and take a dip in the cooling waters. Even though she was leery of water moccasins,

Kelly would have set her fears aside and gone swimming if they'd stopped for any length of time.

A short time later, Kelly's wish was granted. A long line of boats waited at the lock just a short way past Mike's store. No telling how long they might be held up. Kelly decided she would take off her boots and go wading. No point in getting her whole body wet when all she needed was a bit of chilly water on her legs to get cooled off.

She made sure both mules had been given a drink of water, then secured them to a nearby tree. She thought about asking Sarah to join her in the water, but the baby was down for a nap, and Sarah and Mama had taken advantage of the stop and begun washing clothes.

Kelly plunked herself on the ground, slipped off her boots and socks, and stood up. It was time to get cooled off.

Mike closed the door behind a group of tourists from New York who were traveling by boat up the canal. They'd dropped by his store in search of food supplies, but to his surprise, they'd been favorably impressed with Kelly's artwork. So much so that Mike had sold all of Kelly's paintings, and two of the travelers had asked if he would be getting any more, saying they would stop by the store on their return trip.

Mike promised to try to get more, but after the customers left, he wondered how it would be possible. He hadn't seen Kelly since their picnic, when he'd been dumb enough to announce that he wanted to make her his wife. Her folks had stopped by a couple of times, but Kelly never came inside.

He'd been tempted to seek her out, but after a time of prayer, Mike decided to leave their relationship in God's hands. He had tried to take control of the matter before, and it only left him with an ache in his heart. From now on, he'd let God decide if Kelly McGregor was meant for him. If she showed an interest, he would know she was the one. If not, then he needed to move on with his life. Maybe he wasn't meant to have a wife.

Feeling a headache coming on, Mike closed his store a bit early and went outside for some air. Even though he had never learned to swim well and couldn't do much more than dive in the water and paddle back to the lock, today seemed like the perfect day for getting wet. Wearing only a pair of trousers he'd rolled up to the knees, Mike jumped into the canal near the stop gate.

With her skirt held up, Kelly plodded back and forth along the bank by the lock tender's house. Several swimmers had been there earlier, but most had gone for the day. It would be awhile until Papa was ready to go, as there had been a break in the lock and all the boats were still held up. Kelly decided to take advantage of this free time to get some sketching done. She'd left her drawing tablet on the grass next to her boots and was about to reclaim it when she noticed Mike Cooper in the water. He dove from one dock, then crossed the gates and grabbed hold of the dock on the other side. She was surprised to see him, as she remembered Mike saying once that he wasn't a good swimmer and didn't go into the canal very often.

Kelly stood still, watching in fascination as Mike took another dive. She waited for him to resurface on the other side, but he didn't come up where he should have.

A sense of alarm shot through her body when she noticed small bubbles on top of the water. They seemed to be coming from a large roll of moss about ten feet above the gates. With no thought for her own safety, Kelly jerked off her skirt, and wearing only her white pantalets and cotton blouse, she dove into the water and swam toward the spot where she'd seen the bubbles. Her scream echoed over the water. "Hold on, Mike! I'm comin'!"

A few seconds later, Kelly dove under the water and spotted Mike, thrashing about while he tried to free his hands and feet from the twisted moss. Visions of them both being drowned flashed through her mind as Kelly tried to untangle the mess. Mike wouldn't hold still. He was obviously in a state of panic. At one point, he grabbed Kelly around the neck, nearly choking her to death.

Her lungs began to burn, and she knew she needed air quickly. Desperation surged within. Her insides felt as if they would burst. She sent up a prayer and did the only thing that came to mind.

Pop! Kelly smacked Mike right in the nose. Blood shot out in every direction, but Mike loosened his grip on her neck. Using all her strength and inner resolve, Kelly managed to get his hands and feet free from the moss, and she kicked her way to the surface, pulling Mike along.

When Mike's face cleared the water, she breathed a sigh of relief. Gasping for breath, Kelly propelled them through the murky water until at last they were both on the shore. Mike lay there, white as a sheet, and Kelly worried that he might be dead. She rolled him over and began to push down on his back. A short time later, he started coughing and sputtering.

A great sense of relief flooded Kelly's soul. She grabbed hold of the skirt she'd left on the grass, ripped off a piece, and held it against Mike's bleeding nose. How close she'd come to losing the man she loved. The realization sent shivers up Kelly's spine, and she trembled and let out a little sob.

Mike opened his eyes and stared up at her, a look of confusion on his face. "What happened? Where am I?"

"You were trapped in a wad of moss," she rasped. "I'm awful sorry, but I had to punch you in the nose to get you to stop fightin'."

He blinked several times. "You hit me?"

She nodded. "Sorry, but I didn't know what else to do."

Mike reached up and touched her hand where she held the piece of material against his nose. "Is it broken?"

She pulled the cloth back and studied the damage. "I don't think so. The bleedin' seems to be almost stopped."

"You saved my life."

"I guess I did, but it was God who gave me the strength to do it."

He clutched her hand. "Why would you do that if you don't care about me?"

She frowned. "Who says I don't care?"

"Do you?" Mike's eyes were seeking, his voice imploring

her to tell the truth.

Kelly's heart was beating so hard she thought it might burst wide open. She'd been fighting her feelings for Mike all these months, yet seeing him almost drown made her realize she wouldn't know what to do if he wasn't part of her life. Was love enough? If she were to marry Mike, would he expect her and their children to work for free at his store?

"Kelly, my love," Mike murmured. "You're the answer to my prayers."

"You were prayin' someone would find you in the moss and save your life?"

He laughed, coughed, and tried to sit up.

"You'd better lie still a few more minutes," she instructed. "That was quite an ordeal you came through."

"I'm okay," he insisted as he pulled himself to a sitting position in front of her.

"Are you sure?"

"I'm sure about one thing."

"What's that?"

He pulled her into his arms. "I'm sure I love you, and I believe God brought us together. Will you marry me, Kelly McGregor?"

Before Kelly could answer, Mike leaned over and kissed her upturned mouth. When the kiss was over, he said, "I promise never to treat you harshly, and I won't ask you or any children we may be blessed with to work for free. If you help me run the store, you'll earn half the money, same as me. If our kids help out, they'll get paid something, too."

She opened her mouth, but he cut her off. "There's more."

"More?" she echoed.

He nodded. "This morning, a group of tourists came by the store, and they bought the rest of your paintings."

"All of them?"

"Yes, and they said they'd be stopping by the store on their return trip to New York, so if you have any more pictures, they'll probably buy those as well."

Kelly could hardly believe it. All her pictures sold? It was too much to digest at once. And Mike asking her to be his wife and help run the store, agreeing to give her half of what they made? She pinched herself on the arm.

"What are you doing?" Mike asked with a little scowl.

"Makin' sure I'm not dreaming."

He kissed her again. "Does this feel like a dream?"

She nodded and giggled. "It sure does."

"Kelly, I've been thinking that I could add on to the store. Make a sort of gallery for you to paint and display your pictures. Maybe you could sell some art supplies to customers, as well."

Her mouth fell open. She'd been dreaming about an art gallery for such a long time, and it didn't seem possible that her dream could be realized if she married Mike. "I'd love to have my own art gallery," she murmured, "but I won't marry you for that reason."

"You won't? Does that mean you don't love me?"

Mike's dejected expression was almost her undoing, and Kelly placed both her hands on his bare shoulders. "I do love you, and I will marry you, but not because of the promise of a gallery."

"What then?"

"I'll agree to become your wife for one reason and only one." Kelly leaned over and gently kissed the tip of Mike's nose. "I love you, Mike Cooper—with all my heart and soul. This is finally my chance for real happiness, and I'm not about to let it go."

Mike looked up and closed his eyes. "Thank You, Lord, for such a special woman."

Epilogue

*I*t was a pleasant morning on the last Saturday of September. So much had happened in the last four months that Kelly could hardly believe it. From her spot in front of an easel, she glanced across the room where her husband of three months stood waiting on a customer.

Mike must have guessed Kelly was watching him, for he looked over at her and winked.

She smiled and lifted her hand in response. Being married to Mike was better than she ever could have imagined. Not only was he a kind, Christian man, but he'd been true to his word and had added on to the store so Kelly could have her art gallery. Whenever she wasn't helping him in the store, she painted pictures, always adding a verse of scripture above her signature. This was Kelly's way of telling others about God, who had been so good to her and the family.

Sam Turner had returned to the canal a few weeks ago,

apologizing to Sarah and begging her to give him the chance to prove his love for her. Rather than going back to the city, the couple and the baby were living with Sam's parents. Sam assisted his dad with the lock chores, and Sarah helped her mother-in-law make bread and other baked goods, which they sold to many of the boaters who came through. They'd also begun to take in some washing, since many of the boatmen were either single or didn't bring their wives along to care for that need.

Kelly had finally seen the seashore along the coast of New Jersey, where Mike's brothers lived. They'd gone there for their honeymoon, and she'd been able to meet Alvin, John, and their wives.

The most surprising thing that had happened in the last few months was the change that had come over Kelly's dad. He'd accepted one of Reverend Nelson's cards with a Bible verse written on it, and Papa's heart was beginning to change. Not only was he no longer so ill-tempered, but Papa had given money to Kelly and Sarah, saying they'd both worked hard and deserved it. Since neither of them was available to work for him any longer, he'd willingly hired two young men—one to drive the mules, the other to help steer the boat. Kelly figured if she kept praying, in time Papa would turn his life completely over to the Lord.

When the front door opened and Betsy Nelson walked in, Kelly smiled and waved. What had happened in the life of the preacher's daughter was the biggest surprise of all.

"That's a beautiful sunset you're working on," Betsy said, stepping up beside Kelly.

"Thanks. Would ya like to have it?"

Betsy shook her head. "I'm afraid where I'm going there will be no use for pretty pictures."

Kelly nodded, knowing Betsy was talking about South America, where she'd recently decided to go as a missionary. "No, I suppose not."

"I'm leaving tomorrow morning for Easton, and then I'll ride the train to New York. From there, I'll board a boat for South America," Betsy said.

"Everyone will miss your zither playin' on Sunday mornings," Kelly commented.

Betsy gave her a quick hug. "Thanks, but I'll be back someday, and when I return, I expect you and Mike will have a whole houseful of little ones."

Kelly smiled and placed one hand against her stomach. In about seven months the first of the Cooper children would make an appearance, and she couldn't wait to become a mother. God had given her a wonderful Christian man to share the rest of her life with, and she knew he would be an amazing father.

As soon as Betsy and the other customer left, Mike moved across the room and took Kelly into his arms. "I sure love you, Mrs. Cooper."

"And I love you," she murmured against his chest.

Mike bent his head to capture her lips, and Kelly thanked the Lord for giving her the chance to find such happiness. She could hardly wait to see what the future held for Cooper's General Store on the Lehigh Canal.

RECIPE FOR HUNKS-A-GO PUDDING

Make a batter with the following ingredients:
1 cup flour
1 tsp. salt
1 cup milk
2 eggs

Pour the batter into hot grease left over from cooked roast beef. Cover with a lid and cook on top of the stove until done.

Discussion Questions for Kelly's Chance

1. During the canal era, many young men and women were forced to work for their parents with no pay, so they often married young in order to get away. What would you say to someone who wanted to get married just so they could leave home?

2. Kelly didn't like leading the mules that pulled her father's canal boat. She prayed that God would fulfill her dream of getting away from the canal and opening her own art gallery. Since that was her only goal, she shied away from love and romance. Have you ever had such determination to reach a goal that you didn't see other possibilities?

3. One of the reasons Kelly was against marriage was because her father was so harsh with her and her mother. What are some ways we can move past the things that happened to us during our childhood?

4. Most of the time Kelly preferred to be alone. Being around the people in town made her feel nervous and self-conscious. What are some ways a shy person might overcome their self-consciousness? How can we help someone who's shy and has no self-esteem?

5. As a new Christian, Kelly knew her negative attitude about certain things was wrong. The resentment Kelly harbored toward her father kept her from worshipping God as she

should. Has there ever been a time in your life when you let resentments interfere with your walk with Lord? What steps can we take to work through our resentments?

6. Kelly was envious of Betsy Nelson, the preacher's daughter, who had fine clothes and good manners. Have you ever struggled with jealousy? What does God's Word tell us about being envious of others? How can we deal with jealousy?

7. Kelly's father had no appreciation for her artistic talent and often ridiculed her for the drawings she did. How can a child rise above ridicule from their parents? What are some ways we can encourage others to make use of their talents, despite negative comments that have been made by their parents?

8. Mike wanted nothing more than to find a good woman and get married. When he met Kelly, he felt that she was the one. But Kelly seemed to be holding back, and he felt sure he'd pushed her away when she moved to the city. Have you ever been in a relationship where you felt you had pushed too hard? Perhaps it was the other person who'd done the pushing. What's the best way to deal with someone who doesn't seem ready for a close relationship? Is there ever a time when it's right to push ourselves on someone in order to make them our friend?

9. When Betsy Nelson let it be known that she was interested in Mike, he tried to be nice without leading her on. However,

on more than one occasion, Betsy took Mike's politeness to mean that he had an interest in her. Would there have been a better way for Mike to have handled things with Betsy?

Betsy's
RETURN

BRIDES *of* LEHIGH CANAL

BOOK TWO

DEDICATION/ACKNOWLEDGMENTS

To my husband, who's also my pastor,
and to pastors everywhere who give so much of themselves
in order to minister to the needs of their congregations.

Chapter 1

Summer 1896

*O*h, Papa, I'm so sorry." Betsy Nelson dabbed at her tears and sank to the bed in the small room she occupied in New York City. She had just received a telegram saying that her father had suffered a heart attack and would have to resign his position as pastor of the community church in Walnutport, Pennsylvania.

"It isn't fair," Betsy moaned, as she let her mind take her back to the days when Papa, newly widowed, had begun his ministry at the small church not far from the Lehigh Canal. Betsy had been a young girl then, barely out of pigtails. Grieving over her mother's untimely death, she had been an angry, disagreeable child, often saying spiteful things so others would feel as badly as she did. Even as an adult she had made cutting remarks and looked down her nose at those she thought were beneath her.

She remembered when she had tried to get Mike Cooper's attention. Besides being young, handsome, and single, Mike ran a general store along the Lehigh Canal. There'd been one problem—Mike was interested in Kelly McGregor, an unkempt young woman who led the mules that pulled her father's canal boat.

Betsy grimaced at the memory of the harsh words that had come from her mouth the day she'd invited herself to join Mike and Kelly on a picnic. They'd been talking about swimming, and Mike had admitted that he'd never learned to swim well. Betsy had turned to Kelly and asked, "What about you? As dirty as you get trudging up and down the dusty towpath, I imagine you must jump into the canal quite frequently in order to get cleaned off."

Five years later Betsy could still picture Kelly's wounded expression and see the look of horror on Mike's face.

"They must have thought I was terrible. I'm surprised the board of deacons didn't fire Papa because of me," she murmured. Yet despite Betsy's curt, self-righteous ways, the church leaders had remained patient with her, just as her dear father had.

Betsy closed her eyes, and a vision of Papa standing behind the pulpit came to mind. In his younger days he'd been a handsome man with curly, dark hair and gray blue eyes that reflected the concern and compassion he felt for others. He'd preached strong sermons from the Bible and played the fiddle with enthusiasm, and despite his disagreeable daughter, everyone in the congregation respected and admired the Reverend Hiram Nelson.

Betsy squeezed her fingers around the telegram, crumpling it into a tight ball and letting it fall to the floor. "It's not right that Papa should have to give up something he's done for so many years. If only his heart had remained strong. If only God would give us a miracle."

She stood and moved over to the window, staring at the street below. An ice wagon rolled past, probably heading to one of the nearby stores to make a delivery. Several horses plodded down the street, pulling various-sized buggies transporting businessmen to their office jobs. A newspaper boy stood on one corner, heralding the news of the day. A peddler selling his wares ambled down the road, pushing his cart full of pots and pans. New York City was always busy, even in these early morning hours.

Betsy leaned against the window casing and thought about how much her life had changed over the last four years. She'd left Walnutport in 1892, and soon after her arrival in New York City, where she was to meet with the mission board, she had been beaten and robbed. A gentle, caring woman named Abigail Smith, an officer in the Salvation Army, had taken Betsy into her home and nursed her back to health. By the time Betsy's wounds had healed, she knew the Salvation Army was a worthy cause and she wanted a part in it. Since that time she'd found a closer relationship with Christ and had joined others from the Salvation Army in numerous street meetings, often playing her zither, singing, and proclaiming the Word of God to anyone who would listen. She'd also spent many hours at the Cheap Food and Shelter Depot, which helped the poor and downtrodden obtain a new lease on life.

Betsy's ties with the Salvation Army had also presented her with an opportunity to volunteer at a local orphanage. She, who had previously been uncomfortable around children, now found pleasure in working with under-privileged orphans so in need of love and attention. For the first time in Betsy's thirty-one years she found herself wishing she had children of her own. She supposed some women were destined to be old maids, and she was convinced that she would be one of them.

Betsy's mind snapped back to the present situation with her father's ill health and his resignation from the church. A new preacher would soon be assigned to take Papa's place, and that didn't feel right to Betsy. Neither did Papa being sick.

A spark of anger ignited a flare of determination in her heart as she moved away from the window and knelt in front of the trunk at the foot of her bed. "I must set my work in New York City aside and return home. Papa needs me to care for him now."

Dear William Covington:
The board of deacons from the Walnutport
Community Church in Pennsylvania would like to
interview you, for our previous pastor, the Rev. Hiram
Nelson, recently suffered a heart attack and has been
forced to retire. If you're willing to meet with us, please
notify me as soon as possible.

Sincerely,
Ben Hanson
Head Deacon

William folded the letter he'd received yesterday and placed it on the rolltop desk sitting in the far corner of his father's study. It had only taken him a few hours to deliberate before he'd sent a telegram to Deacon Hanson, letting him know that he would arrive at the train depot in Easton, Pennsylvania, on Friday and would rent a carriage to make the trip to Walnutport. That would give him the opportunity to meet with the board of deacons on Saturday, as well as tour the church and parsonage. On Sunday he would meet the members of his prospective congregation and give them a sample of his preaching.

William strolled back across the room and took a seat on the elegant sofa his mother had purchased on her recent trip to England. He leaned back, stretching his arms overhead, and yawned. He was glad for this opportunity to be alone with his thoughts. His parents had gone to the opera tonight, and even though William's mother had tried to convince him to go along, he had politely declined, saying he needed time to pack for the trip and prepare his sermon.

William's gaze came to rest on the massive portrait of his father, hanging on the far wall. William Covington Jr. had been born into a wealthy family and had inherited all his father's business ventures after William Sr. died several years ago. William III had no desire to follow in his father's or grandfather's footsteps as a successful entrepreneur. The fact that William's father owned a thriving newspaper in Buffalo, New York, as well as several hotels, the new music hall, and numerous specialty stores, meant nothing to William. He had accepted Christ as his Savior when he was twelve years old, and ever since then, his strongest desire had been to become a minister. Three and a half months ago he'd graduated from the seminary in Boston, full of hope for the future and anxious to marry Beatrice Lockhart, his high school sweetheart.

William groaned as a vision of Beatrice came to mind— ebony hair and eyes the color of dark chocolate. Soon after they'd begun courting, Beatrice had agreed to marry him. The wedding had been set for the week after William graduated from seminary, and his future bride had seemed excited about the idea of being the wife of a "prominent minister," as she liked to refer to William whenever they were with her friends. But when William had informed Beatrice that his first church might be small and unable to pay him much money, she'd insisted that he give up the idea of becoming a preacher and go to work for his father. Certain that God had called him to the ministry, William had refused her request. Beatrice pouted at first, the way she'd always done whenever she didn't get her way. Then she'd finally given in and said she would abide by whatever William decided.

"She lied to me!" William shuddered at the memory of standing at the altar, waiting for a bride who never showed up. A note had been delivered by Beatrice's father. Beatrice had changed her mind; she didn't want to be a minister's wife after all. *"Too many demands,"* she'd written. *"It might take years before you're hired at a church that would be able to support us adequately."*

William folded his arms and leaned forward, a deep groan escaping his lips. He could never trust another woman or get over the humiliation of being jilted by Beatrice. He'd thought she loved him for better or worse, richer or poorer, but he'd been sorely mistaken.

He stood, prepared to return to the desk and work on the sermon he would deliver to the people in Walnutport, but raucous yapping distracted him. His mother's Siamese cat raced into the room, with his father's English setter nipping at her tail. The dog had obviously sneaked into the house, probably because William had left the door ajar when he'd gone out for some fresh air after his parents left. Thanks to his carelessness, muddy paw prints now covered Mother's Persian rug.

"Lucius, come here!"

The dog ignored William and kept chasing the hissing, spitting cat.

William quickly joined the chase, hoping to capture his father's prized hunting dog and remove him from the house. But each time Lucius was within William's grasp, the animal eluded him. In the meantime, Princess, the pampered feline, hopped onto a small table, and Lucius leaped into the air and swiped at Princess with his large, muddy paw. The cat jumped to the floor, eluding the setter, but Mother's Parisian vase crashed to the floor.

"I'll never hear the end of this," William groaned. When his mother saw the mess, she would tell him that it would never have happened if he had gone to the opera as they had asked.

William looked up. "Oh Lord, I pray the church in Walnutport accepts me as its pastor, because I need to get away—away from Father's unreasonable demands, from Mother's persnickety ways, and from the memory of the woman who left me standing at the altar."

Chapter 2

*A*s Betsy stepped through the front doorway of the parsonage, a feeling of nostalgia swept over her like a cool wind on a hot summer's day. She had spent the better part of fifteen years in this home, and she and her father had created enough memories to fill up a lifetime.

"Papa, I'm home!" she called.

"I–I'm in the sitting room" came his feeble reply.

Betsy placed her suitcase beside the umbrella stand and rushed into the next room. The sight made her halt in midstride. Her father reclined on the sofa, his face pale and drawn, his hair, once full and shiny, now dull and thinning. He offered a weak smile and pulled himself to a sitting

233

position. "Betsy, it's so good to see you."

She hurried across the room and dropped to her knees in front of the sofa. "Oh, Papa, it's good to see you, too. If I'd known how things were with your health, I would have come much sooner."

He reached out and wiped the moisture from her cheeks with his thumb. "Don't waste your tears on me, daughter. I'm in God's hands, and He will see me through to the end."

The end? Did Papa believe he was dying? Could Papa's heart be so weak that he might not live much longer?

Betsy reached for her father's hand and was saddened by the lack of strength in his grip. Papa used to be so energetic; now he was a mere shell of a man.

"I wish you hadn't felt the need to come home," he said. "Your work with the Salvation Army is important, and people check on me regularly."

Betsy gently massaged his bony fingers. "I'm needed here right now. It's my place to care for you."

Tears welled in Papa's eyes. "You're a good daughter, and I'm much obliged."

Late-afternoon shadows bounced off the walls as Betsy glanced around the room, noting the thick coating of dust on the end tables and fireplace mantle. "Is there anything I can get for you, or would you rather I do some cleaning?"

He shook his head, easing himself back to the sofa pillows. "You're probably tired from your train trip, and the cleaning can wait. Why don't you sit awhile so we can visit?"

Betsy rose from her knees. "All right, but first let me fix you a cup of tea."

"That would be nice."

"What kind would you like, herbal or black?"

"A couple of ladies from church came by yesterday and brought some things for the pantry. So whatever you come up with is fine."

"I'll be back soon." Betsy leaned over and kissed his forehead then hurried to the kitchen. A knock sounded at the back door. When she opened it, she was greeted by two of the church deacons, Ben Hanson and Henry Simms.

"Afternoon, Betsy," Ben said with a nod. "We heard you were coming and thought we'd better get over here and explain things to you."

Betsy opened the door wider, bidding them enter. "Your telegram said my father had a heart attack and that his health has failed so much that he must resign as pastor."

"That's right," Henry said, combing his stubby fingers through his thinning hair. "A minister's on his way here from Buffalo, New York, to interview for the position."

Betsy clenched her teeth. It grieved her to hear them speak of hiring someone to take Papa's place. Yet it wasn't their fault Papa's health had failed. Even though it had been the board of deacons' decision to ask for her father's resignation, the board had had no choice. If Papa could no longer fulfill his duties, it was time for him to step aside.

Ben cleared his throat and shuffled his feet. "The

thing is, once we've hired a new preacher and he moves to Walnutport, he's going to need a place to live."

Henry nodded in agreement. "Since the parsonage was built by the founding church members and is owned by the church, I'm afraid we'll have to ask you and your father to move."

Betsy stood still as she let the deacons' words register. Her father would not be preaching in Walnutport anymore. A minister was coming for an interview. She and Papa would have to look for another place to live.

"You won't have to move until we've hired a new preacher and he's able to relocate." Ben gave the end of his handlebar mustache a quick flick. "It could take several months to find the right man for the job."

"That's right," Henry put in. "I—I'm sure it won't be easy to fill your pa's shoes."

Betsy bit her lip so hard she tasted blood. "Is that all you gentlemen wanted?"

"Yes, yes. I believe we've said all that needs to be said. Give the good preacher our regards!" Ben called over his shoulder as he and Henry hurried out the door.

"I'll do that." Betsy closed the door behind them and headed for the pantry. She found several glass jars filled with vegetables and fruit, a jar of coffee, and a bag of flour on the floor, but no tea.

She released a sigh. "Looks like I'll need to make a trip to Cooper's store and see about getting some tea and a few other things we'll need," she mumbled. "I'd better tell Papa where I'm going."

When she entered the sitting room, she found her father asleep, so she scrawled him a note and left it on the low table in front of the sofa. She didn't think it would take long to get the things she needed, and she'd probably be back long before Papa woke up.

As William guided the horse pulling his rented carriage down the dusty road toward Walnutport, he thought about his mother's predictable reaction when he'd told her that he was interviewing to be pastor in a small town near the Lehigh Canal in Pennsylvania.

"Why can't you wait until a church opens here in Buffalo?" she had questioned. "Why would you want to minister to a bunch of country folks?"

"Don't you think I'll be a good enough preacher to shepherd the flock?" William had asked.

"That's not what I meant at all," she had said in a defensive tone.

"What your mother is trying to say is that a small church in the middle of nowhere won't be able to pay you much because there won't be enough people," his father had interjected, giving his goatee a couple of quick pulls.

William gripped the reins tighter. "I shouldn't have

expected them to understand. All Mother cares about is her socialite friends, and all Father worries about is his money."

He drew in a quick breath and blew it out with a huff. "It would have been nice if one of them had been supportive about me going to Walnutport for this interview."

William rounded a bend and spotted a store near the canal, so he decided to stop and get himself something cold to drink. It wouldn't do for the prospective pastor to show up in Walnutport hot, sweaty, and feeling as out of sorts as a dog with a tick on his backside. Maybe a bottle of sarsaparilla was what he needed.

"It's so nice to see you again," Kelly Cooper said, as she wrote up Betsy's purchases. "It's a shame you had to come home under such gloomy conditions though."

Betsy lifted her shoulders and let them drop with a sigh. There was no point giving in to her emotions, for it wouldn't change a thing.

"If there's anything we can do to help, be sure to let us know," Kelly's husband, Mike, offered as he joined his wife behind the counter.

"I appreciate that." Betsy hoped her smile didn't appear forced. She appreciated their concern, but it was hard to think about Papa leaving the ministry, much less to see the pity on Mike's face when he offered support. "What Papa and I need most is your prayers."

"You've sure got those," Kelly said.

Mike nodded his agreement.

"If you hear of anywhere we can move once we're ousted from the parsonage, be sure to let us know."

"I'll keep my eyes and ears opened—you can be sure of that," Mike said.

"Thanks." Betsy was pleased she had developed a pleasant relationship with the Coopers over the years in spite of the way she'd behaved before Mike and Kelly had gotten married. *I'll never throw myself at another man the way I did at Mike,* she determined. *It would be better to remain an old maid for the rest of my life than to embarrass myself like that.*

She glanced around the room. "Where are your two little ones, Kelly?"

"They're over at my sister Sarah's, playing with her kids."

The bell above the front door jingled, and Betsy turned her head. A young man with neatly combed, chestnut-colored hair and the bluest eyes she had ever seen stepped into the store. He wore a dark brown suit and a pair of leather shoes that looked as out of place in Cooper's General Store as a fish trying to make its home on dry land.

"Can I help you, sir?" Mike asked, stepping quickly around the counter.

The man nodded. "I'd like a bottle of sarsaparilla, if you have some."

"Sure do. If you'll wait here, I'll get one from the ice chest."

"I'll do that." The man seemed a bit uncomfortable as he shifted his weight from one foot to the other.

Betsy offered him the briefest of smiles then quickly averted her gaze to the food Kelly was packaging for her.

"I don't recollect seein' you around before," Kelly said, nodding at the man. "Are you visiting someone in the area or just passing through?"

"My name is William Covington, and I've come from Buffalo, New York. I'll be meeting with the board of deacons at the Walnutport Community Church tomorrow about the possibility of becoming their new minister."

Betsy's mouth dropped open, and Kelly glanced her way with a shrug. Betsy had known the board would be interviewing a minister from Buffalo; she just didn't think he would be so young—or so handsome.

Chapter 3

"Can you tell me how much farther it is to Walnutport?" William asked, directing his question to the young woman who stood behind the counter, with long, dark hair hanging down her back.

"It's a short drive from here." She nodded toward the other woman, whose ash-blond hair was worn in a tight bun at the back of her head. "This is Betsy Nelson, the preacher's daughter. She could probably show you the way to town."

"You're. . .Rev. Nelson's daughter?"

She nodded. "My father's the man you'll be replacing if the board of deacons hires you."

William swallowed. "I–I'm sorry about your father's

health problems, and if you would feel awkward about showing me the way to Walnutport, I'll certainly understand."

Miss Nelson lifted her package into her arms. "It would be no bother. I'm going there anyway, and it's not your fault my father has been asked to resign."

William winced, feeling as though he'd been slapped. It might not be his fault Rev. Nelson had been asked to step down from the pulpit, but he was the one who might be taking the poor man's place.

"Here's your sarsaparilla," the young man who ran the store said, handing the bottle to William.

"How much do I owe you?"

The man flashed William a friendly grin. "It's free. Consider it my welcome to our community."

William was tempted to say that he hadn't been hired as the new minister yet and might not be moving to Walnutport, but he took the sarsaparilla gratefully and expressed his thanks.

"I'm ready to head out if you are," Miss Nelson said, nodding toward the front door.

"Yes, I suppose we should." William extended his hand toward the storekeeper. "It was nice to meet you. I'll be preaching at the community church on Sunday, so maybe I'll see you there."

The storekeeper nodded as he shook William's hand. "My name's Mike Cooper, and my wife, Kelly, and I, as well as our two children, attend regularly. We'll look forward to seeing you on Sunday morning."

William smiled. "Good day then." He held the door for Miss Nelson and followed her to a dilapidated buckboard. If the town's minister couldn't afford to drive anything better than this, the church probably didn't pay its pastor much at all.

But I won't be coming here for the money, he reminded himself. *This is my chance to make a fresh start and serve God's people.*

Miss Nelson leaned into the wagon and placed her package on the floor behind the seat. Lifting her long, brown skirt, she started to step up. William was quick to offer his hand, but she shook her head and mumbled, "I've been climbing into this old wagon since I was a girl in pigtails."

William shrugged and headed for his carriage. By the time he'd gathered the reins, Miss Nelson was already heading down the road at a pretty good clip.

"She's either in a hurry, or she has made up her mind that she doesn't like me," he mumbled.

I shouldn't have been so rude to Rev. Covington, Betsy reprimanded herself as she headed down the dusty road toward Walnutport. *I'll need to apologize as soon as we get to town.* She glanced over her shoulder and pulled slightly back on the reins to slow the horse. The reverend's buggy was way behind, and if she didn't allow him to catch up, he might think she didn't want to show him the way to town.

As Betsy continued to travel, she thought about her father. Had he awakened in her absence and found the note she'd left him? Should she tell Papa about the new minister who'd come to interview for his position? Maybe it would be better not to say anything. The interview might not go well, and then the Rev. William Covington would be on his way back to Buffalo, leaving the board of deacons to begin the process of finding another prospective minister.

"Whoa! Whoa! Hold up there, boy!"

Betsy turned in her seat to see what was going on in the minister's rig and was surprised to discover that he'd stopped the horse and was climbing out of his carriage. She halted her horse, stepped down from the buckboard, and walked back to where he stood, holding up his horse's right front foot.

"Is there a problem?"

He nodded. "My horse has thrown a shoe and seems to have picked up a stone. I'm afraid if I keep going along this road he might turn up lame."

Betsy's forehead wrinkled as she mulled over her options. She could leave the reverend here with his rig while she headed for town to see about getting the blacksmith to come shoe the horse, or she could suggest that Rev. Covington tie the horse to a tree, push his carriage off the road, and ride with her. When she got to town, she would drop him off at the blacksmith's shop and let the smithy take things from there. The second option seemed like the polite thing to do, so she suggested it.

"Yes, yes. I suppose it would be wise." He pushed a wayward strand of thick hair off his damp forehead. "If you're sure you don't mind."

"I wouldn't have suggested it if I'd minded." Betsy could have bit her tongue. She was being rude again. "I'm sorry for snapping," she apologized. "And I'm sorry if I sounded curt with you back at the store." She released a sigh. "I'm concerned about my father, and I'm afraid my fears have caused my tongue to be sharper than usual."

"Apology accepted. I understand this must be a difficult time for you and your father," Rev. Covington said, as he unhitched his horse and led him to the closest tree.

"Yes it is," Betsy agreed. "When I got the telegram saying my father had suffered a heart attack and had been forced to retire from the ministry, I knew I should leave my job in New York City and return to Walnutport in order to care for him."

"You were working in New York?"

She nodded. "For the Salvation Army. I've been with them the past four years."

"I see." He tied the horse and moved back to his buggy, which he pushed off the road with little effort.

No questions or comments about the Salvation Army? Was a quick "I see" all the man was capable of offering?

Maybe he sees the work I did as inferior. Betsy couldn't believe how inconsequential she felt in this man's presence. She, who used to look down her nose at those she thought were beneath her, felt as out of place standing beside Rev. Covington as one of the canal mules trying to take up residence inside a church.

"Shall we be on our way?" he asked, pulling her thoughts back to the present.

She offered a quick nod then led the way to her buckboard.

This time Betsy allowed the reverend to help her climb aboard. She even offered to let him take the reins, but he declined, saying he could enjoy the scenery more if he wasn't driving.

Betsy took up the reins and got the horse moving again. They rode in silence for a time, until he turned to her and said, "The lay of the land is quite different here than in Buffalo. The navigation system is a whole different world, isn't it?" He pointed to a flat-roofed boat making its way up the canal with a load of coal.

"Yes it is, but there used to be a lot more action on the canal than there is now."

"Many things that were once hauled by the canal boats are now being transported by train," he said with a nod.

Her eyebrows lifted as she stared at him.

"When I was asked to interview here, I made an effort to learn about the area," he explained.

"I see." Betsy drew in a deep breath and decided to broach the subject she dreaded the most. "What kind of congregation are you looking for, Rev. Covington?"

"A needy one. A caring one." He paused and reached up to rub his chin. "A congregation that works together, plays together, and most importantly, prays together."

Betsy couldn't argue with that. She'd heard her father stress the importance of prayer to his flock many times.

"Now I have a question for you," he said.

"What's that?"

"How did you get involved with the Salvation Army, and what took you to New York City in the first place?"

Betsy spent the next little while telling William about her call to the mission field, how she'd been beaten and robbed when she first got to New York, and the details of Abigail nursing her back to health, then introducing her to the work and mission of the Salvation Army. "There are so many needy people in New York City, and if we can help even one find his way to Christ, it's worth every hour we spend serving others at the soup kitchens and conducting street meetings," she added.

"Any form of ministry that leads people to God is a worthy endeavor," he said with a note of conviction.

"I agree."

"I imagine your father missed you when you left for New York."

"I suppose he did. I was very involved at our church until

I went away." Betsy nodded toward the canal. "My father and I even held some services down here so the boatmen could hear God's Word. Papa would preach, and I played my zither and led the people in singing."

His eyebrows lifted high on his forehead. "Why don't the boatmen attend church in town?"

"Some do, but others aren't comfortable inside a church building."

"I see." He stared straight ahead. "That would make it hard for the church to grow. This could be a difficult ministry."

Betsy shrugged, wondering if he might have second thoughts about coming here to interview. "If the board of deacons asks you to take the church, how would your family feel about moving here?" she asked.

He turned and looked at her. "I have no family except my mother, father, and older brother who is married. If I take this church, none of my family will be coming with me, only Frances Bevens, an older widow who used to be my nanny and might be coming as my housekeeper."

"Oh, I see. I thought you might have a wife and children."

He grimaced, and the light in his eyes faded. "No, I'm as single as any man can be."

Chapter 4

As William headed down Main Street after leaving the small hotel where he'd spent the previous night, he thought about his meeting with Betsy Nelson the day before. She was obviously a devoted daughter, having left New York and given up a work she seemed passionate about in order to care for her father. William was sure it must have been difficult for her to meet him yesterday, since he could possibly be the one to take her father's place as shepherd of the community church.

His thoughts went to Betsy's father, the Rev. Hiram Nelson. The process of the church finding someone to replace him had to be even harder on the ailing man than it was on his daughter. Not only did Rev. Nelson have a serious health problem, but he'd been asked to give up his ministerial duties.

I haven't even begun my ministry as a pastor, William thought, *yet I would feel horrible if someone said I couldn't do it. Maybe I should stop by the reverend's house to speak with him and offer a word of encouragement.*

He reached into his jacket and withdrew the pocket watch that had once been his grandfather's. His meeting with the board of deacons was scheduled for ten o'clock at the church, and it was quarter to ten now. *I'd better wait to call on Rev. Nelson until after my interview,* he decided. *By then I'll know if I'll be taking his place.*

Betsy took one last look at her sleeping father and closed the door to his room. Dr. McGrath had been there earlier to examine Papa and give him some medicine to help him sleep.

Downstairs in the kitchen, Betsy stoked the woodstove and set a kettle of water on to heat. Maybe a cup of chamomile tea and some time in God's Word would help calm her nerves. She certainly needed something to take her mind off the interview that was going on in the church next door.

If Rev. Covington is asked to take Papa's position, I wonder how long it will be before he moves to Walnutport and we'll be expected to find a new home, she fretted.

Bristle Face, the shaggy terrier that had been her father's trusted friend for the last four years, flipped his tail against Betsy's long skirt and whined.

"What's the matter, boy?" she asked, reaching down to pet the animal's silky head. "Are you hungry, or do you need to go outside?"

The dog whimpered and padded across the room.

"All right then, out you go." Betsy hurried across the room, opened the door, and let out a squeal when she discovered Rev. Covington standing on the porch, dressed in a dark blue suit.

"Sorry if I startled you," he said. "I was getting ready to knock when you opened the door."

Before Betsy had a chance to respond, the little terrier stood on his hind legs and pawed at the man's pant leg.

"Bad dog! Get down," Betsy scolded as she gave Bristle Face a nudge with the toe of her shoe.

"It's okay. My father has an English setter, so I'm used to dogs." William chuckled. "Cats, too, for that matter."

Betsy bent down and scooped Bristle Face into her arms; then she stepped off the porch and placed him on the ground. "Now do your business, and be quick about it."

The dog turned, hopped back onto the porch, and pawed at William's pant leg again.

"Bristle Face, no!" she shouted. "I told you to stay down!"

William leaned over and picked up the terrier. "Bristle Face, huh? Interesting name."

Betsy gave a quick nod.

"I think the little guy has taken a liking to me."

"He can be a pest, but my father likes him." She smiled. "The dog showed up at the parsonage shortly after I moved to New York, and he's been Papa's friend ever since."

"Speaking of your father," William said, "I was wondering if I might have a few words with him."

"He's taking a nap right now."

"Would you mind if I wait until he wakes up? I'd like to speak with him about a few things."

"Is. . .is it about the church? Have the deacons decided to hire you?"

He nodded. "We've just finished the interview, and it was a unanimous decision."

Betsy felt the pounding of her heart against her rib cage, and she drew in a calming breath. "Have you accepted the call?"

"Yes. Yes I have."

Her heart continued to thud, and then it felt like it had sunk all the way to her toes. A new shepherd would soon lead Walnutport Community Church, and she and Papa would have to move.

William, still holding Bristle Face, took a step toward Betsy. "Are you all right? You look pale. Maybe you should sit down."

Betsy didn't want to sit. She didn't want to continue this discussion with the new minister. All she wanted to do was run into the house and have a good cry. But what good would that do? It wouldn't alter the fact that her father's life was about to change and hers right along with it. For Papa's sake she needed to remain strong.

Stepping onto the porch, Betsy nodded at the wooden bench positioned near the railing. "Won't you have a seat? I'll run inside and get some refreshments."

"Please, don't go to any bother."

"It's no bother. I'll be right back." She rushed into the house before Rev. Covington could say anything more.

When she returned a few minutes later with some tea and a plate of ginger cookies, she found Rev. Covington sitting on the bench with Bristle Face in his lap.

Betsy placed the tray on the small table near the bench and handed him a cup of tea.

He smiled and took a sip. "Umm...this is good."

She leaned against the porch railing and folded her arms. "Help yourself to some cookies."

"Aren't you having any?"

"I'm not really hungry."

He tapped the empty space beside him. "Then please have a seat. It makes me feel uncomfortable to watch you stand while I enjoy the fruits of your labor."

Betsy shrugged and seated herself on one end of the bench, being careful to put a respectable distance between them. "How soon will you be moving into the parsonage?"

"Probably not for another month. I'll need to return

home to pack whatever things I'll need for the trip."

"When will you be heading to Buffalo?"

"On Monday morning. I'll be preaching tomorrow morning as planned. That way I'll have the chance to meet my new congregation before I head back."

Betsy flinched. Everything was happening so fast, and she dreaded having to give her father the news of the board's decision.

"When I asked one of the deacons about music in the church, he said his wife had been playing the organ while you were in New York, but now that you're back, she would prefer having you take over that responsibility again," William said.

"I. . .I suppose I could play on the Sundays Papa feels well enough to be in church or is up to staying home by himself." She sighed. "I'll make sure we're moved out of the parsonage by the time you get back from Buffalo."

Bristle Face woke up just then and jumped onto the porch. Rev. Covington shifted on the bench and turned to face Betsy. "If it were only me to worry about, I'd be happy to stay at one of the boardinghouses in town, but as I mentioned before, I'll be bringing my housekeeper along." His face turned a light shade of red. "It was Mother's idea. The moment I told her I was coming for an interview, she started planning things. She insists that, since I'm not married, I'll need to have someone to cook and keep house for me."

"Well, you needn't worry," Betsy was quick to say. "Papa and I will be moved out of the parsonage well before you and your housekeeper arrive."

A flutter of nervousness tickled William's stomach as he stepped onto the platform at the community church the following morning. In one month, this would be his church and the men and women staring back at him would be his people. It would be an exciting venture, yet a frightening one, since this was his very first church. He wanted to make a good impression.

He took a seat in one of the chairs near the back of the platform as Ben Hanson, the head deacon, stepped up to the pulpit. "Good morning," the man said in a booming voice, nodding at the congregation. "Yesterday the board of deacons met with Rev. Covington, and I'm happy to say that our vote was unanimous to call him as our new pastor." Ben motioned William to step forward. "I'm pleased to say that Rev. Covington has accepted that call."

William joined the deacon behind the pulpit, hoping his smile didn't appear forced and that his suit wasn't showing the signs of the perspiration he felt under his arms. "I'm glad to be here this morning," he said, nodding at the congregation. His gaze went to the first row of pews, where Betsy Nelson sat, dressed in a pale yellow frock that matched the color of her hair. He noted that Betsy's father wasn't with her, and William figured the man either wasn't feeling well enough to attend church this morning or couldn't tolerate the idea of seeing someone else standing behind his pulpit.

Yesterday, when Rev. Nelson had awoken from his nap, William had been able to speak with him, and he'd been impressed by the man's friendliness. Yet he'd sensed a sadness that went deeper than Rev. Nelson's health problems, and William wondered what it could be.

"There wasn't time to plan a welcome dinner in honor of our new pastor today, but we'll have a short time of fellowship with coffee and cookies after the service so everyone has a chance to greet Rev. Covington," Ben said, giving William's shoulder a squeeze. "Tomorrow morning the good reverend will return to his home in Buffalo, but he'll back within the month to begin his ministry here in our little church."

The congregation clapped—everyone except Betsy Nelson, who sat stiff and tall with her hands folded in her lap. *She's probably not happy about me taking her father's place, and hearing the deacon's exuberant introduction must have been difficult for her.*

"Now, if you'll take your songbooks and turn to page 15, our song leader, Bill Hamilton, will lead us in praising the Lord." Ben stepped aside, and a young, dark-haired man wearing a well-worn suit stepped onto the platform. William returned to his seat behind the pulpit, Betsy took her place at the organ, and everyone rose to their feet.

When the first song, "The Solid Rock," began, William was surprised at the congregation's zeal for singing. Apparently this was a foot-stomping, hand-clapping group of people he'd agreed to pastor, and that would take some getting used to. The church William had grown up in back in Buffalo was full of people who barely smiled on Sunday mornings, and they certainly never would have shouted, "Hallelujah! Praise the Lord!"

He glanced over at Betsy, who was matching the rhythm of the music as her head bobbed up and down, and her feet pumped the pedals of the well-used organ that sat near the front of the room.

Yes indeed, William said to himself as he tapped his foot against the wooden platform, *this will surely take some getting used to.*

Chapter 5

"I think you and your father will be comfortable here," Freda Hanson said as she opened the door to the small cottage she'd offered to show Betsy. "Since my niece has recently married and moved to Boston, the house is empty, and Ben and I would be happy to have good people like you and your father living here."

Betsy followed the tall, slender woman inside. Ben and Freda, a middle-aged, childless couple, were among the few people living in Walnutport who had been educated past high school. Soon after he'd become a successful businessman in Boston, Ben had decided to return to his hometown of Walnutport and open a few businesses. The bank was one of them, as well as a hotel, a restaurant, and a few small cottages.

"How much would the rent be?" Betsy asked as her gaze traveled around the small, partially furnished living room. "I don't have a job yet, and Papa won't be getting any more money from the church, so—"

Freda put her arm around Betsy's shoulder and gave it a gentle squeeze. "Now don't fret, dear. Ben and I have talked this over, and we want you and your father to live here rent free for as long as necessary. All we ask in return is that you keep the place clean and in good condition." She smiled. "It's the least we can do for the kindhearted man who pastored our church for so many years."

Betsy swallowed around the lump in her throat. "Your offer is so generous, but I was planning to get a job and—"

"Your father needs you to be close to him now," Freda interrupted. "Perhaps you can do sewing or laundry for some of the boatmen. That would be something you could do from home."

Betsy nodded as she fought to keep her emotions under control. "That might be best since I couldn't afford to hire someone to look out for Papa if I took a job away from home."

Freda gave Betsy's shoulder another squeeze. "Anytime you need to go shopping, run errands, or just take a break, be sure to let me know. I'll ask one of the ladies from church to stay with your father while you're gone."

"That's kind of you. I. . .I can't tell you how much I appreciate all you and Mr. Hanson have already done."

"Ben and I realize how hard this must be for you and your father. We want to do all we can to make this transition as smooth as possible." Freda motioned to the door leading to the next room. "Why don't I show you the rest of the house? Then if you think it's acceptable, we'll see about getting some of the men from church to move your things over right away. Our new preacher and his housekeeper will be in Walnutport by the end of the week, so we'll need to see that the parsonage is vacated before then."

Betsy didn't need any reminder that the new preacher was coming. It had been on her mind every day since Rev. Covington had left Walnutport after his call to their church. She blinked against stinging tears and bit her bottom lip, determined not to break down in front of Freda. *Papa and I will make it through this. With God's help, we can do it.*

"This is the home the church has provided for the minister?" Mrs. Bevens's voice raised a notch as William followed her into the kitchen.

"It seems to be adequate for my needs." William and his housekeeper had arrived in Walnutport a short time ago, and he was showing her around the parsonage. "Having the home right next to the church makes it quite handy."

"You will no doubt want to entertain some of the town's more prominent business people in the hopes of getting them to support your church financially." She made a swooping gesture with one hand and cast a mournful look at the faded blue curtains hanging on the window above the sink. "This place isn't large enough or nice enough for entertaining a mere commoner, much less someone of higher standing."

"Most of the people living in Walnutport are not well-to-do, and this house is all the church has to offer, so we shall make the best of it." William leaned against the table and folded his arms. "If you're not happy with the arrangements, then perhaps you should catch the next train back to Buffalo and tell my mother you've changed your mind about being my housekeeper."

Mrs. Bevens patted the sides of her graying brown hair, pulled back into a perfectly shaped bun, and squinted her hazel eyes. "I'll simply have to make do. I'm sure that, once we're able to fill the house with some decent furniture and hang some proper curtains at the windows, the place will be a bit more livable."

William's gaze went to the ceiling. He could only imagine what kind of plans Mrs. Bevens had for this simple, warm home. Maybe if she kept busy with her remodeling projects, she wouldn't have time to smother him, the way she had done during his childhood.

A knock at the back door drove William's thoughts aside, and before Mrs. Bevens had a chance to respond, he strode across the room and opened the door. He discovered a middle-aged, dark-haired woman standing on the porch, holding a wicker basket.

"Afternoon, Pastor," she said with a friendly grin. "I'm Alice Clark, and my husband, Garth, and I are members of your church. We met on the Sunday after your interview, but you might not remember us, since that was a whole month ago."

William returned her smile. "I do remember, Mrs. Clark. If I'm not mistaken, you were the lady who made those wonderful oatmeal cookies."

Her head bobbed up and down as she held the basket out to him. "Those were mine, all right. I've brought you a tasty potato casserole today, along with a loaf of freshly baked bread."

"Thank you, Mrs. Clark. That was thoughtful of you." William opened the door wider. "Won't you come in and meet my housekeeper?"

"Only for a minute. I promised to do some shopping with my daughter Mabel this afternoon. Mabel teaches school here in Walnutport, and she's not married." Alice's pale blue eyes fairly twinkled. "We'll have you over for supper soon, so the two of you can get better acquainted."

William grimaced internally and stepped aside. If his role as minister was going to include lots of supper invitations, he might have to keep an eye on his weight. And if his ministerial duties included dodging matchmaking mothers and their available daughters, then at some point he might need to let his congregation know that he was a confirmed bachelor and planned to stay one.

As William stepped into the church on his first Sunday as pastor, deacons Ben Hanson and Henry Simms met him in the foyer. "Good morning, Rev. Covington," Ben said with a hearty handshake. "My wife wanted me to inform you that the ladies have planned a potluck dinner today, and it will be served on the lawn out behind the church after the service."

William smiled. "That's fine with me. My housekeeper isn't feeling well this morning, which is why she didn't accompany me to church, so I'm sure she won't feel up to cooking or attending the potluck."

Henry draped his arm across William's shoulder. "What you need is a wife, not a housekeeper, Rev. Covington."

A sour knot formed in William's stomach. *Don't tell me the men in this church want to match me up with their daughters, too. Maybe I should make the announcement about being a confirmed bachelor at the close of my sermon today.*

"Are you sure you're feeling up to going to the worship service this morning?" Betsy asked as she strolled down the sidewalk with one hand in the crook of her father's arm. In the other hand she carried a basket full of muffins she had made for the potluck dinner. Papa seemed a little stronger this morning, but being back in church and seeing his successor standing behind the pulpit might be hard on him. She'd wanted him to stay home, but he'd adamantly refused, saying he was anxious to hear the new preacher deliver his sermon.

Papa gave Betsy's hand a reassuring squeeze. "I feel better today than I have in weeks."

"Maybe that's because you've been sleeping more lately."

"And maybe it's because my daughter is taking such good care of me."

She smiled. "I enjoy taking care of you. I'm just not looking forward to seeing someone else take your place."

"I'd like to see you get involved in some church activities," he said, making no reference to his replacement. "A bit of socializing would be good for you, Betsy."

"I didn't return to Walnutport so I could socialize. I'm here to see to your needs."

"Be that as it may, you still need to make time for some fun."

They were approaching the church, so Betsy decided to drop the subject.

A short time later they entered the sanctuary where several others had already gathered. Rev. Covington was seated in one of the chairs near the back of the platform.

Betsy escorted her father to a seat and hurried to take her place at the organ. When the song leader announced the first hymn, "Rescue the Perishing," Betsy's heart sank clear to her toes. This was a song she had often sung while she played her zither during street meetings in New York. It was a reminder of the call God had placed on her heart four years ago. Though she might not have gone to a foreign country as a missionary, she'd certainly met the challenge of spreading God's Word during her years with the Salvation Army, and she missed it.

What can I do to serve You here in Walnutport? Betsy beseeched the Lord as she opened her songbook to the proper page. *Is there anyone besides Papa to whom I can minister?*

Chapter 6

"Yoo-hoo, Pastor Covington! Could you please come here a minute?"

William set his cup of coffee on the table and turned to see who had called him. Clara Andrews was waving frantically and looking wide-eyed and desperate. Maybe if he acted as if he hadn't heard, she would get busy talking to someone else and forget she had called him.

Ever since the potluck had begun, several women, and even a few men, had bombarded William with supper invitations and introduced their eligible daughters. It seemed to be a hazard of his chosen profession—at least the supper invitations. If he were married, dealing with desperate mothers and tethering young women wouldn't be a problem.

Maybe I should have made that announcement that I'm not a candidate for marriage. That would have saved these hopeful parents the trouble of introducing their daughters and planning some special meal in my honor. William grimaced. If he had made such an announcement, he might have some explaining to do. More than likely, people would have wanted to know why he was opposed to marriage, and he wasn't ready to share the shame of being left at the altar. Still, he wasn't willing to pretend he hadn't heard Mrs. Andrews call his name either.

As William stood, he glanced at Rev. Nelson, who sat beside his daughter at the next table. Hiram was probably the only parent present who hadn't tried to pawn his daughter off on the new preacher.

"Pastor Covington, are you coming?" Clara called again. This time she held a white hankie above her head and waved it as though it were a flag of surrender.

With a sigh of resignation, William ambled across the yard to see what the determined woman wanted.

When he arrived at the place where she and several other women stood, Clara pointed to a cluster of wooden boxes sitting beside one of the tables. "As a welcome gift, our church folks have put together some food items for you to take home so your pantry will be well stocked."

"Thank you," he said with a nod. "That was generous of

you." At least it wasn't another supper invitation in hopes of him getting together with someone's daughter.

"What's all this?" Mrs. Bevens asked as William entered the kitchen, carrying one of the boxes he'd been given during the potluck.

"Donations of food." He set the box on the sideboard near the sink. "Several more like it are on the porch."

Mrs. Bevens peeked into the box and wrinkled her nose. "Ten jars of blackstrap molasses! What am I supposed to do with those?"

"Use them for baking."

"Humph! I prefer to use honey when I bake."

William started for the door but turned when she spoke again.

"I see some home-canned vegetables in here, too. How do you know they were properly prepared and won't make us sick?"

He clenched his teeth. "I'm sure we won't die from food poisoning, Mrs. Bevens. But just to be sure, I'll say an extra prayer over each of our meals."

"I think to be on the safe side, I'll throw away the jars that don't look right to me."

"I wouldn't want to hurt anyone's feelings by throwing away what they've worked so hard to prepare."

Mrs. Bevens compressed her thin lips and squinted at the box, but before she could comment, William said, "By the way, what are you doing out of bed? You said you weren't feeling well this morning, and since you couldn't go to church, I figured you would spend the day resting."

Mrs. Bevens straightened to her full height, and her cheeks turned pink. "I *was* feeling under the weather, but I got up in order to fix your lunch."

"That was kind of you, but I have already eaten. We had a potluck meal after church." William patted his much-too-full stomach and grinned. "It didn't take me long to discover that there are some fine cooks in my congregation."

"Too many potlucks like that, and you'll end up looking like your father's friend Eustace Landers." Mrs. Bevens released an undignified grunt. "His stomach's so big that he has to sit a foot away from the table in order to eat. It's a wonder the poor man can even walk."

William went out the door, shaking his head. He returned to the kitchen moments later with another box of food, which he placed on the table.

Mrs. Bevens was immediately at his side, peering into the box as if it had been packed full of snakes. "You should see how many containers of salt are in here. Too much salt's not good for anyone."

"Too little salt makes everything taste flat," William mumbled under his breath.

She glared at him. "Are you insinuating that my cooking is flat?"

"Your cooking is fine, Mrs. Bevens." William rushed out of the room before she could say anything more.

"Are you sure you won't take a nap?" Betsy asked her father soon after they arrived home from church. "You look awfully tired."

He shook his head. "I'll just sit in my chair and read a few passages of scripture. If I get sleepy, I'll lie down on the sofa."

"All right. I'll go make some tea."

Betsy had just reached the door leading to the other room when he called out to her. "Do you know where Bristle Face is? I haven't seen him since we got home from church!"

"I tied him to a tree in the backyard before we left this morning. Since he's not used to our new home yet, I didn't want to take a chance that he might run off."

"Would you mind bringing my furry friend inside? I'd like to hold him awhile."

"Sure, Papa. I'll get him right now." Betsy scurried out of the room and went out the back door. When she reached the end of the porch, she halted. The rope she'd tied around Bristle Face's neck was still connected to the tree, but the dog wasn't on the other end of it.

She scanned the yard but didn't see Bristle Face anywhere. She cupped her hands around her mouth and hollered, "Bristle Face! Where are you, boy?"

No whine. No bark. No sign of the dog.

She ran around the side of the house, checking behind the shrubs, calling the dog's name, looking under the porch, and searching every nook and cranny. No Bristle Face. She was getting worried. What if the animal had run off and couldn't find his way back? She knew her father would be heartsick if he lost his loyal companion.

Betsy moaned and went back inside.

"Did you find him?" Papa asked as soon as she had entered the sitting room.

She shook her head. "Bristle Face broke free from his rope and took off. I searched the entire yard, but there was no sign of him."

Papa frowned. "It's not like my dog to take off. I wonder if. . ."

"What is it, Papa? What are you thinking?"

"Do you suppose Bristle Face went back to the parsonage? That's been his home ever since he was a pup. He might have gotten confused once he broke the rope, so he could have headed for the place he knows best."

"You might be right about that. Would you like me to go over there and see?"

He nodded. "If Bristle Face isn't there, would you ask the new preacher to keep an eye out for him—in case he shows up on his doorstep?"

"Of course." Betsy leaned over and kissed her father's forehead. "I'll be back soon."

As Betsy walked over to the parsonage, she searched for Bristle Face along the way. She saw no sign of the scruffy little black terrier, and none of the people she spoke with had seen the dog either.

Soon she reached the parsonage, and when she stepped onto the porch, the boards creaked under her feet. She lifted her hand and was about to knock when the door swung open. Rev. Covington stepped out, still wearing the dark gray suit he'd worn to church that morning. "I didn't realize anyone was here," he said.

"Actually I was about to knock when you opened the door."

She held his gaze for a moment, then, feeling a bit uncomfortable, looked away. The young minister's neatly trimmed hair and finely chiseled features seemed to fit his refined personality, and being in his presence made her feel like a commoner. "I hope I haven't interrupted anything," she mumbled, forcing herself to look at him again.

"No no. I was just on my way over to the church to get my Bible." His ears turned pink. "I got busy carrying the boxes of food and forgot it."

"I see."

"What can I do for you?" he asked. "Is it about your father? Is he doing all right this afternoon?"

She nodded. "He says he's fine, although I think the long day took a bit out of him."

"That's understandable."

Betsy shifted her weight and leaned against the porch railing. "The reason I came by is to ask if you've seen Papa's dog. I tied him to a tree in our backyard this morning, but he broke free while we were at church, and I thought he might have come here."

"He wasn't here when I got home, but I suppose he could be now. Shall we go around back and take a look?"

"Sure."

They stepped off the porch, and Rev. Covington's footsteps quickened through the tall grass as they made their way around the side of the house. They had just reached the backyard when Betsy's steps slowed, and she halted. "Look, there he is!" She pointed to the overgrown flower bed near the porch, where the dog lay curled in a tight ball.

The pastor patted the side of his knee. "Here, Bristle Face. Come here, little fella."

The dog lifted his head, stretched his front feet in front of him, and plodded across the yard. Rev. Covington bent down and scooped the animal into his arms. "You don't live here anymore," he said, ruffling the wiry hair on the terrier's head. "You've got to stay at your new home with your master now."

Betsy reached over and rubbed one of Bristle Face's silky ears. "I don't know if he showed up here because he still thinks it's his home or if it's because he's taken a liking to you, Rev. Covington."

"I'd appreciate it if you would call me Pastor William." He smiled, and the dimples in his cheeks seemed to deepen.

"All right, Pastor William," she murmured.

"It's nice to know someone likes me today," he said as he continued to pet the dog. "I think my housekeeper is ready to disown me."

Betsy tipped her head. "Why's that?"

He shrugged, and his ears turned even pinker. Betsy had a hunch it didn't take much to make the young minister blush.

"I shouldn't have asked," she said. "It's none of my business."

William handed her the dog. "Let's just say Mrs. Bevens and I had a difference of opinion."

Betsy didn't press the issue. She figured whatever had caused the rift between William and his housekeeper was between them. "I guess I'd better take this little guy home."

Pastor William placed his hand on Betsy's wrist. The innocent contact sent unexpected shivers up her arm.

"Did your father say anything about my sermon today?" he asked, apparently unaware of her reaction.

She blinked a couple of times. "Uh. . .no, he didn't. Why do you ask?"

"I wanted to be sure I didn't say anything he disapproved of."

Betsy drew in a couple of shallow breaths. "I. . .I'm sure Papa found no fault in your message."

A look of relief flashed onto his face, and he nodded. "That's good to hear."

She moistened her lips with the tip of her tongue. "I thought you did well with the delivery of your sermon, and the congregation can always use a reminder of the importance of unity."

"Thanks," he said with a smile that reached all the way to his dark blue eyes. "I appreciate hearing that."

Bristle Face stirred restlessly in Betsy's arms. "I. . .uh. . . really should go. Have a good afternoon, and I hope you locate your Bible as easily as I found Papa's dog."

He snickered, and they walked away in opposite directions. *I can see why so many women in church are anxious to match the new pastor with their daughters,* Betsy thought. *Despite the fact that I wish he weren't taking Papa's place, he is quite charming.*

Chapter 7

*T*he following morning, after Betsy had finished cleaning the kitchen and had washed a batch of clothes one of the boatmen had brought her, she decided to check on Bristle Face. She had tied him to a tree in the backyard again, being careful to make sure the knot was more secure than it had been the day before.

As Betsy stepped out the back door, the morning sun struck her shoulders with such intense heat that she grimaced. "I'll be glad when summer is over and fall brings in cooler weather." She squinted against the harsh light and scanned the yard until her gaze came to rest on the maple tree where she'd tied Bristle Face. The dog wasn't there. "Oh no," she moaned. "Not again."

Betsy trudged back to the house, mumbling all the way. She found her father in the sitting room, reclining on the sofa with his Bible in his hands. "Bristle Face has broken free from his rope again," she said. "I've a pretty good hunch where he's gone."

Papa turned his head toward her. "Maybe we should see if some of the men from church would be willing to put a fence around our yard. That's probably the only way we're going to keep that renegade dog from running back to the parsonage all the time."

"I'll speak to the new pastor about it when I go over to get Bristle Face. Hopefully he'll be willing to round up a crew of men to do the work." Betsy nodded at her father. "I'm sure you would do the same thing for someone if you were still the pastor."

"I'd do more than that. I would be the first one in line to do the work."

A pang of regret stabbed Betsy's heart as she was reminded once more of the reality of her father's declining health. The doctor had told her that any day Papa could have another heart attack and the next one could be his last. "Will you be all right on your own? I really should go over to the parsonage and retrieve Bristle Face before he makes a nuisance of himself."

He smiled. "I'll be fine, so there's no need to hurry back if you decide to stay and visit awhile."

"I shouldn't be too long." Betsy leaned over and kissed the top of his head before she left the room.

A short time later she found herself on the front porch of the parsonage, knocking on the door.

When the door opened, she was greeted by a tall, older woman with hazel eyes and graying brown hair worn in a tight bun at the back of her head. "May I help you?"

"Is Pastor William in? I need to speak with him."

"He's not here right now." The woman nodded curtly. "I'm his housekeeper, Mrs. Bevens. Is there something I can help you with?"

The intensity in the woman's eyes made Betsy feel like a bug about to be squashed. She shifted her weight from one foot to the other. "I'm Betsy Nelson, and I'm here about my father's dog, Bristle Face. He broke free from his rope again, and I thought he might have come here."

Mrs. Bevens squinted as she stared at Betsy. "Are you sure you're not using the dog as an excuse to see William?"

"What? I assure you that—"

"Two other young women have already called on the pastor this morning," Mrs. Bevens said, cutting Betsy off in midsentence. She lifted her chin and held her shoulders rigid. "Of course, they made up some excuse about needing to know if the pastor planned to begin a choir, and if so, they wanted him to know they were willing to be in it."

"I only came to see if my father's dog is here," Betsy said with a shake of her head. "He came over to the parsonage yesterday afternoon, and since he's broken free again, I thought he might have—"

"I don't know anything about a dog." Mrs. Bevens pursed her lips. "Rev. Covington is at the church going over some music, so I'm sure he won't want to be disturbed. Good day to you, Miss Nelson." With that, the woman pivoted on her heel and shut the door.

Betsy stood with her mouth hanging open. She'd never met such a rude, irritating woman. Even during her most self-centered days, she hadn't acted that unpleasantly. At least she hoped she hadn't.

She turned and started down the porch steps. *Maybe I'll head over to the church and speak to Pastor William. At least I can let him know that Bristle Face has escaped again and might turn up on his doorstep.*

For the last half hour, William had been sitting on a back pew in the sanctuary, looking through the hymnbook, and he still hadn't found the song he was searching for. His message next week would be on the subject of hope, and he'd planned to sing a solo before he spoke to the congregation.

When William heard a door open and close, he set the hymnal aside and walked to the foyer. Betsy Nelson stood there, her flaxen hair hanging down her back in soft, gentle waves, rather than being pulled back in its usual bun, and he drew in a quick breath, surprised by her beauty. "Good—good morning, Betsy." His voice sounded strained, and he cleared his throat a couple of times, giving himself a good mental shake. "How may I help you?"

Her cheeks blushed crimson, and she averted her gaze. "Bristle Face is missing again. I stopped by the parsonage to see if he'd gone there, but your housekeeper said she hadn't seen him."

William tapped his chin with the tip of his finger. "Mrs. Bevens doesn't much care for dogs. If Bristle Face did show up there, she probably chased him away."

Betsy's stunned expression made him wish he could take back his words, so he quickly added, "I'm sure she would have told you if she'd seen him though."

"I hope he hasn't run away or become lost," she said. "It would break Papa's heart if something happened to his little terrier."

Betsy looked so forlorn that, for one crazy moment, William had the impulse to give her a hug. *Take control of your thoughts,* he reprimanded himself. *She might misinterpret the gesture, and besides, it wouldn't be appropriate.* "Is there any place the dog might have gone?" he asked. "Somewhere he's run off to before?"

"The only place he ever went when we lived next door was over here to the church," she said with a shrug.

William's eyebrows lifted in surprise. "Really? The dog came to church?"

"He didn't actually come to church; he just liked to follow my father over here when he came to prepare his sermons. Papa sometimes let Bristle Face into his study." Betsy chuckled. "Of course, no one but the two of us knew about that."

William grinned and touched his lips. "You can count on me to keep it a secret."

"So I take it you haven't seen any sign of the dog today?"

He shook his head. "I've been here for the last half hour, trying to find a song to share with the congregation before my message next Sunday."

"Are you looking for anything in particular?"

"I'll be speaking on the subject of hope."

"How about 'I Know Whom I Have Believed'? I'm quite sure it's on page 35 in our songbooks."

"That's impressive. You must be quite familiar with the hymnal."

"I've sung it several times at various Salvation Army street meetings."

He motioned toward the sanctuary. "Would you be willing to sing it for me now?"

Betsy nodded, although her face had turned quite pink.

He opened the door to the sanctuary and allowed her to go in first, then he followed her up front.

Betsy took a seat on the organ bench, and William sat on the front pew. He watched as she set the hymnal on the music rack and turned to the proper page. Her legs began pumping, her fingers pressed down on the keys, and the room swelled with mellow music. He closed his eyes and rested against the pew as her voice sang out:

> *"I know not why God's wondrous grace*
> *To me He hath made known,*
> *Nor why, unworthy, Christ in love*
> *Redeemed me for His own.*

> *"But I know whom I have believed,*
> *And am persuaded that He is able*
> *To keep that which I've committed*
> *Unto Him against that day."*

When she began the second verse, he joined in:

> *"I know not how this saving faith*
> *To me He did impart,*
> *Nor how believing in His Word*
> *Wrought peace within my heart."*

He stood and moved over to the organ.

> *"But I know whom I have believed,*
> *And am persuaded that He is able*
> *To keep that which I've committed*
> *Unto Him against that day."*

They finished the next three verses as a duet, and when the song was over, William sank to the bench beside her. "You have the voice of an angel, do you know that? It should be you singing the solo next Sunday, not me."

"Maybe we could sing the song together," she said in a voice barely above a whisper.

"I would like that."

Chapter 8

On Sunday morning, as Betsy secured the rope that would tie Bristle Face to the maple tree in their backyard, she thought back to Monday and what had happened after she and William had finished practicing their song. Betsy had said she needed to get home to check on her father, and as she left the church, she'd found Papa's dog crouched in the bushes near the front porch of their cottage. She was relieved to see that Bristle Face wasn't hurt, but from the way he whined and crawled to her on his belly, she could tell something had traumatized him. It had made her wonder if the poor animal had gone over to the parsonage and been chased off by Pastor William's disagreeable housekeeper.

"You'd better stay put today," Betsy warned Bristle Face. "If you don't, I'll ask someone to build you a cage." She shook her head as she walked away, realizing she'd been so busy with laundry and mending jobs all week she'd forgotten to ask the pastor about finding someone to put a fence around their backyard. *I'll do that sometime this week,* she promised herself.

Returning to the house, Betsy found her father sitting on the sofa with his Bible lying open in his lap. It seemed as if he was always reading God's Word. "Are you sure you don't want to take the buckboard to church today?" she asked. "There's still time for me to hitch up the horse."

He shook his head. "I'd rather walk. The fresh air and sunshine are good for me; the doctor said so."

"All right then, but we still have plenty of time before church starts, so let's not be in a hurry getting there." Betsy touched his pale cheek. "Those dark circles under your eyes lead me to believe you didn't sleep well last night."

"I'll be fine." Papa closed his Bible and stood. "Shall we go?"

She nodded and slipped her hand into the crook of his arm.

As Betsy and her father headed to church, she became more concerned, because he had to stop every few feet in order to catch his breath.

"Maybe we should go back and get the buckboard," she suggested. "Or better yet, why don't you stay home from church today and rest?"

He shook his head. "And miss hearing you sing?"

Betsy smiled despite her growing concerns. Ever since Mama had died, Papa had doted on her. *Guess maybe he spoiled me a bit, too,* she mused, gripping her father's arm a little tighter as they proceeded down the street.

They were nearly at the church when Betsy halted. A trickle of perspiration rolled down her forehead and onto her nose. "Papa, do you think anyone in the congregation will get the wrong idea when Pastor William and I sing our duet?"

He stared at her like she'd taken leave of her senses. "Of course not, Betsy. Think of all the times you've sung with other people in our church, including me."

"But I wasn't sharing a song with a handsome, single minister."

Papa raised his bushy eyebrows. "Are you saying I'm not handsome?"

"Certainly not. You're the most handsome man I know." She smiled up at him. "But seriously, some people might wonder why the minister chose to sing with me. There might be those who will think there's something going on between Pastor William and me."

Papa grinned. "Is there something going on?"

"Absolutely not. We barely know each other, and I have no intention of—"

"You deserve to be happy, daughter. And when I'm gone,

you'll need to begin a life of your own."

She patted his arm. "I have a life, right here with you."

"I appreciate your devotion, but it's past time for you to find a husband and start a family of your own."

Betsy shook her head. "If the Lord was going to give me a husband, I'm sure He would have done so by now. I'm thirty-one years old, Papa, and no man has ever shown the slightest interest in me."

"What about Mike Cooper? He seemed interested for a time."

"Puh! It was me who was interested in Mike, not the other way around. He only had eyes for Kelly, and I was a fool to throw myself at him the way I did." Betsy lifted her chin as they walked up the steps leading to the church. "I'm older and wiser now, and I shall never do such a humiliating thing again."

William was glad Mrs. Bevens had come to church today, but he wasn't pleased with the dour expression on her face as she stood off to one side of the foyer, watching him greet people as they entered the building. *She's probably scrutinizing everything I say and do. I think if she didn't have something in which to find fault, she would be miserable.*

Turning away from Mrs. Bevens and her accusing stare, William stepped forward and greeted Betsy and her father.

"Good morning. How are you feeling today, Rev. Nelson?"

"I'm a bit winded from the walk over here, but I'm sure I'll be fine once I'm seated."

William glanced at Betsy to gauge her reaction.

"I tried to talk him into staying home today, but he insisted on coming." She frowned. "I couldn't get him to agree to take the buckboard, either."

"My daughter worries too much," Hiram said before William could offer a reply. He squeezed Betsy's shoulder. "I'm anxious to hear the song you and Betsy will be singing today. She has a beautiful voice, and from what I hear, so do you."

William smiled, and he glanced at Mrs. Bevens again. She gave him an angry glare, as if to remind him of what she had told him that morning during breakfast. "I'm concerned about how your duet with Miss Nelson will look to the congregation," she had said. When he asked what she meant, she had pursed her lips, then replied, "Some people might get the impression that you're romantically interested in Betsy, and if you choose to sing with her, it might set off some ugly rumors."

He had assured Mrs. Bevens that he had no romantic interest in any woman and that he'd only asked Betsy to help with the song because she sang it so well and would keep him on key. He'd also said that he didn't believe the people in Walnutport were like those who lived in the larger cities, where vicious gossipers seemed to be everywhere. He'd ended the conversation by saying that if he got wind of any gossip in his church, he would be quick to nip it in the bud.

When William glanced at Mrs. Bevens again, he was relieved to see that she was now engaged in a conversation with Sarah Turner, one of the lock tenders' wives.

"We should get into the sanctuary," Betsy said, taking hold of her father's arm. "Pastor William has other people to greet, and I need to get the organ warmed up."

As Betsy and her father moved away, the room seemed stuffy all of a sudden, and William slid one finger under the back of his shirt collar, noticing that it felt kind of tight. *Oh Lord,* he prayed, *please tell me I didn't do the wrong thing by asking Betsy to sing with me this morning.*

Betsy hadn't been sure if she could get through the music part of the service without making obvious mistakes, but she'd managed to play all the hymns as well as the offertory without missing a note. The pastor had offered a lengthy prayer after the congregational singing, and he'd just announced that he and Betsy would now sing a duet.

Dear Lord, she prayed, *please still my racing heart and help my voice not to crack in the middle of our song.*

As William stepped up to the organ, Betsy glanced at the congregation and noticed her father slouched on the front pew. He seemed to be struggling to keep awake, and she wished once more that he had stayed home in bed. Her gaze went to the other side of the room, where Mrs. Bevens sat rigid without a hint of a smile on her face.

Betsy grimaced internally. *For some reason that woman doesn't like me. Either that or she had a bowl of sour cherries for breakfast this morning.*

"I'm ready when you are," William whispered, bending close to Betsy's ear.

She nodded, and a shiver tickled her spine.

Betsy sang the first verse alone, and William joined her on the chorus. Their voices blended in perfect unison, and Betsy soon forgot her nervousness as she allowed the music and the words of the beautiful hymn to lift her spirits. As they reached the last note, she felt as if God was looking down from heaven and smiling His approval.

The room exploded with applause and numerous *amen*s, and everyone but William's housekeeper and a few of the young, single women smiled back at them.

When the service ended and Betsy and her father headed for the door, she was stopped by several people who said how much they enjoyed the duet. Some even commented on how well the pastor's and Betsy's voices blended, and Kelly Cooper had been bold enough to whisper that she thought Betsy and the preacher looked real handsome together.

"Please don't tell that to the pastor or anyone else," Betsy whispered back. "I wouldn't want any false rumors getting started."

"Oh, don't worry," Kelly said as she ushered her two children out the door behind their father. "I would never embarrass you that way."

Betsy turned to her father, who looked even paler than he had earlier. "Should I see if someone can give us a ride home?"

He nodded. "That's probably a good idea. I'm feeling a bit weak and shaky."

"Why don't I walk you back to the sanctuary so you can have a seat? Then I'll see who might be available to take us home."

Papa took hold of Betsy's arm and offered her a feeble-looking smile. "You're such a thoughtful daughter, and you've got the voice of an angel. I know everyone enjoyed the song you and the pastor sang today."

"Thank you, Papa." Betsy saw that her father was situated on a back pew, and then she headed back to the foyer. She was about to ask Sarah Turner and her husband, Sam, if they could catch a ride in their wagon, when she overheard Clara Andrews invite the preacher over to her house for Sunday dinner. "It will give you and my daughter, Hortence, a chance to get better acquainted," the woman said, clasping the pastor's arm.

"I—I don't know." Pastor William looked kind of flustered. Had he made other plans for the afternoon? "I'll have to check with my housekeeper and see what plans she's made for our dinner today."

"Mrs. Bevens is welcome to join us. In fact, that will work out real well. She and I can visit while you and Hortence spend some time together."

And I was worried that someone might think I'd set my cap for the pastor, Betsy thought with a shake of her head. *I would say Pastor William is the one who needs to worry.*

Chapter 9

"I'm heading out to make a few calls on some people in my congregation," William told Mrs. Bevens as he grabbed his Bible and started for the back door.

She looked up from the letters she'd been writing at the kitchen table and frowned. "Can't that wait? I was hoping you would help me measure the windows in the sitting room today. The curtains are terribly faded, and they should have been replaced before we moved in. I want to have some new ones put up as soon as possible."

"I don't think new curtains are a priority right now," he said with a wave of his hand.

"Oh, but they are," Mrs. Bevens argued. "If you're going

to entertain properly, you'll need the parsonage to look as nice as possible." She wrinkled her nose, as though some foul odor had permeated the room. "This house is a disgrace."

William grimaced. It was a shame that the persnickety woman put so much emphasis on material things and didn't seem to care about people or their needs. *And she calls herself a Christian*, he thought with dismay. *But then, it's not my place to judge. Only God has the right to do that.*

"I need to go, Mrs. Bevens. We'll talk about the curtains some other time." Without waiting for her reply, he rushed out the door.

Betsy pushed a strand of hair away from her face and bent to pick up a pair of trousers. She'd spent four hours last night at the treadle sewing machine, mending several shirts, which had left the muscles in her shoulders sore and tense. This morning after breakfast she'd come out to the backyard, where she'd spent several more hours stooped over the washtub, scrubbing trousers, shirts, and socks that had been dropped off by some of the boatmen on their way up the canal to Mauch Chunk. It was amazing how quickly the news had gotten out that Betsy was taking in clothes to wash and mend. While she wasn't earning a lot of money, it was enough for their basic needs, and since Papa had saved a little from his years of preaching, they could fall back on that if the need arose. Betsy felt sure that God would provide for their needs, and as much as she missed her work with the Salvation Army, at least she was doing something meaningful.

In order to make the time pass more quickly and to take her mind off the pain that had settled in her lower back, Betsy decided to sing a few hymns. She'd just finished "Almost Persuaded" and had just begun to sing "Only Trust Him," when a deep voice coming from the other side of the yard sang out, " 'Come, every soul by sin oppressed; there's mercy with the Lord, and He will surely give you rest by trusting in His Word.' "

Betsy turned and saw Pastor William walking across the grass, holding his Bible in one hand. "It's a beautiful song. Let's sing the refrain together," he said, as he approached her.

Betsy strummed the washboard, keeping time to the music as her voice blended with Pastor William's. " 'Only trust Him, only trust Him, only trust Him now; He will save you, He will save you, He will save you now.' "

When the song was over, she straightened and faced him, feeling the heat of a blush sweep over her face. "What brings you by on this hot, sticky morning?" she asked the smiling preacher.

He lifted his Bible. "I've been out calling on people. I hope to get into a routine of doing that at least once a week. I'll be setting certain hours aside for studying my sermon, too, of course."

Betsy resumed her scrubbing. "Have you given any thought to holding services along the canal for the boatmen and their families who don't come to the church?"

"I have considered the idea, but I'm wondering if it wouldn't be better if I went down to the canal, introduced myself, and invited those people to attend our regular Sunday services here in town. I understand that none of the canal boats run on Sunday, so I don't see why the boatmen can't come to the church."

Betsy grabbed another pair of trousers and sloshed them up and down in the soapy water. "I know many of the men who work the canals, and most wouldn't feel comfortable sitting inside a church building."

The pastor's eyes narrowed. "Why is that?"

"Most of the canalers don't have a lot of money. They wear simple, plain clothes, speak crudely, are uneducated, and would feel as out of place sitting on a polished pew as a duck trying to make its nest in a tree." She reached around to rub the kink in her back and winced.

"Are you in pain?" he asked, kneeling beside her with a look of concern.

"I'll be all right. It's just a little crick."

He glanced at the pile of wet clothes in the wicker basket beside the laundry tub. "Surely these can't all be your father's."

She shook her head. "I'm taking in washing and mending for some of the boatmen who don't have wives traveling with them. It was the only way I could think of to earn money."

He cringed, as though it were his back that hurt and not hers. "In the home where I grew up, we had servants to do our washing, mending, and other chores around the house. The most menial tasks I ever saw my mother do was to tend her rose garden and crochet lace doilies." He shook his head. "You shouldn't have to work so hard, Betsy. Not when you have your father to care for."

"I'm managing," she mumbled.

"Maybe my housekeeper could come by once a week to help you."

Betsy straightened to her full height, ignoring the pain that shot through her back. "Absolutely not! I can't afford to pay anyone, and I'm getting by fine on my own." She knew her tone was harsh, and she bit her bottom lip, wishing she could retract the words. "I–I'm sorry for snapping."

"It is I who should apologize. I'm sorry if I've offended you by my suggestion." Pastor William took a step closer to Betsy, and the scent of his spicy cologne stirred something deep within her.

"I tend to be a little too sensitive," she admitted, leaning away. "I think it comes from years of self-reproach."

He squinted his blue eyes. "Would you care to explain?"

Betsy stared at the ground. How could she admit that she used to be a flirt and had actually tried to manipulate men in order to get her way? She would be too embarrassed to confess that she'd once thrown herself at Mike Cooper, only to be rebuffed by him.

"I'm thinking the real reason you're a bit sensitive has more to do with your concern for your father than anything else. You seem like a loving, caring daughter, and your willingness to do such hard work is proof of that." He motioned to the washtub.

She shrugged. "Maybe, but I must confess that I wasn't always so loving or caring. In my younger days I was a selfish, spoiled girl, and my tongue was sharper than any fisherman's knife."

"People change, and you obviously have, for I don't see a trace of selfishness in you now."

Betsy rinsed the trousers in the bucket of water sitting beside the washtub, wrung them out, and placed them in the wicker basket. "Papa's in the house, resting on the sofa. I assume you came by to see him."

He nodded and raked his fingers through the back of his hair. "I also came to ask you a favor."

"Oh?"

He shifted from one foot to the other. "I was talking with Kelly Cooper when I stopped by the store this morning, and she mentioned that you used to do volunteer work at an orphanage in New York City."

"That's right. Several women from the Salvation Army helped out there."

He cleared his throat and rubbed his hand across his chin. "I figure if you've worked with orphans that you must have a special way with children."

"I never used to like children much. They made me feel uncomfortable," Betsy admitted. "But my work at the orphanage changed that, and now I realize how special children are."

"Yes, they're all precious in God's sight." Pastor William cleared his throat. "The thing is I paid a call on Andy and Mae Gates this morning. Mae is in a family way and hasn't been feeling well, so she's going to give up teaching her Sunday school class." He kicked a small stone with the toe of his shoe. "I was wondering if you might be willing to take over that class."

Betsy thought about the puppets she'd made to entertain the children at the orphanage and wondered if something like that might work for a Sunday school class of young girls. "I would be willing to teach," she finally said, "but my only concern is that I might not be able to be in church every week."

"You mean because of your father's health?"

She nodded.

"On the Sundays you feel you must stay at home, perhaps one of the other ladies from church could fill in as your substitute teacher." He smiled. "Or maybe someone could sit with your father while you're at church."

"I'd feel better staying with him when he's having a bad day," she said, nearly choking on the words. Betsy hadn't admitted it to anyone, but she was worried that Papa might not have much longer to live. She wanted to spend as much time with him as possible and was concerned that he might become extremely ill or could even die while she was away.

"I understand." Pastor William glanced at the house. "I'd best see how your father is doing now. Think about the Sunday school class and let me know, all right?"

"Yes, I will. Thank you for stopping by."

"You're welcome." He started for the house, whistling a hymn, and Betsy resumed her work, praying that the Lord would help her make a wise decision. She also prayed that God would allow her to spend many more days with her father.

Chapter 10

I'm glad you were able to come over for supper tonight," Clara Andrews said as William entered her modest but pleasant home. "But I'm sorry that your housekeeper isn't with you."

William nodded, wishing he didn't have to offer an explanation. "Mrs. Bevens sends her greetings, but she's been fighting a headache all day and didn't think she would be good company this evening." While it was true that Mrs. Bevens had told William she had a headache, he was pretty sure the real reason she hadn't come with him tonight was because she didn't want to socialize with anyone from his congregation. She thought she was better than them and had tried to convince William that most of the people he'd come to pastor in Walnutport were uneducated and lacked all the social graces she felt were so important.

"My daughter, Hortence, is in the sitting room," Clara said, gesturing to the room on her right. "Please, make yourself comfortable, and the two of you can visit while I get supper on the table."

William scanned the hallway, then he glanced into the sitting room. Seeing no sign of Clara's husband, Frank, he asked, "Where's Mr. Andrews?"

"Frank's out in the barn, feeding the animals. He should be done soon, I expect."

"Maybe I should go out and keep him company or see if I can help in any way."

"No no, that's not necessary. My husband prefers to do his chores alone." Clara grabbed hold of William's arm and practically shoved him toward the sitting room.

William felt like a bug trapped in a spider's web as he entered the room and took a seat in the chair closest to the door. Hortence, who sat on the sofa across from him, looked up from the needlepoint lying in her lap and smiled.

William nodded and forced a smile in return.

"You two have a nice visit." Clara ducked quickly out of the room before William had a chance to respond.

He shifted uncomfortably on the straight-backed chair as Hortence stared at him, the ends of her thin lips turning up, and her lashes blinking rapidly against her faded blue eyes. While the young woman wasn't what William would refer to as homely, she was certainly no beauty, either. Hortence's pale skin made him wonder if she ever spent any time outdoors, and her mousy brown hair, parted straight down the middle and pulled back into a tight bun, looked dry and brittle.

Say something, he admonished himself. *Anything to break the silence.* He cleared his throat a couple of times. "What's that you're working on, Hortence?"

Her smile widened as she lifted the piece of material and held it at arm's length. "It's going to be a pillow top—for my hope chest."

"I see." He loosened the knot on his tie a bit and squinted at the colorful needlepoint. "Is that a cluster of red roses?"

She nodded. "I hope to carry a bouquet of roses like this when I get married. Of course, I have to find a husband first," she added with an unladylike snicker.

William cringed. He hoped she wasn't hinting that he might be a candidate as her future husband. "I'm. . .uh. . . sure when the right man comes along, you'll make a lovely bride," he mumbled.

Hortence's eyes brightened, and she sat a little straighter, lifting her chin. "You really think so, Pastor William?"

"Of course. I've never seen a bride who wasn't lovely." An uninvited vision of Beatrice popped into his mind. William had never seen his fiancée in her wedding gown, but he was sure she would have been a beautiful bride. Even though it had happened several months ago, the thought of her leaving him at the altar still hurt like a festering sliver. Hardly a day went by that he didn't relive that discomforting moment, and he wondered once more if he would ever get over the humiliation of being rejected by the woman to whom he had pledged his undying love.

William clenched and unclenched his fingers around the arm of the chair. If he needed to remind himself a hundred times a day, he would never allow that to happen again.

"Mother says that because of my planning and organizational skills I would make a good preacher's wife," Hortence said, pulling his thoughts aside.

Unsure of how best to reply to the woman's bold comment, William stood and moved quickly to the unlit fireplace. He peered at the clock on the mantel. "I wonder what's keeping your father," he said when the clock bonged six times. "I thought he would have joined us by now."

Hortence sighed, and William turned to face her again. "Daddy always goes out to feed the animals just before supper, and he usually takes his time doing it. I would never say this to Mother, but I think he dawdles on purpose, just to get under her skin."

William glanced toward the adjoining room, which he assumed was the kitchen. He wondered if the Andrews couple might be having some kind of marital discord and, if so, whether they would feel comfortable talking to him about it.

He shifted his weight and glanced at the clock again. When he'd accepted the call to Walnutport, he hadn't given much thought to all the details that went with a minister's job. During his time at seminary, he'd concentrated on Bible studies, theology, church history, and learning how to deliver a sermon properly. He knew that counseling and being available to the people in his flock during illness and bereavement were an important part of his ministry, but until he'd taken a church, he hadn't realized how unprepared he was for it all.

He glanced over at Hortence again, who kept staring at him in such a peculiar way, and wondered if he might have a spot of dirt on his suit coat. He opened his mouth, prepared to ask, when she blurted out, "I'm wondering why such a handsome man as yourself isn't married yet, Pastor."

Heat flooded William's face, and he drew in a quick breath, hoping to diffuse the blush he knew must be covering his cheeks. "I'm...uh...that is...."

"Don't you think it would make your ministry stronger if you had a helpmate?"

A trickle of sweat rolled down his face and dribbled under his shirt collar. "The biblical account of the apostle Paul leaves us with the impression that he wasn't married, yet he had a very successful ministry," he said in defense.

"That may be true, but—"

"Don't you usually help your mother with supper, Hortence?"

Hortence's mouth dropped open like a broken hinge. "Of course, but Mother said I should entertain you and that she would manage without my help this evening."

"I see." William sank into the chair, resigned to the fact that this was going to be a long evening. He hoped not all his supper invitations would turn out like this, and he prayed that God would help him remember to be friendly and sociable with everyone in the congregation, even the outspoken members like Hortence Andrews.

Betsy picked up the small, oval-shaped looking glass from her dressing table and peered at her reflection. Not wishing to appear too stiff and formal, she'd decided to wear her hair down today, secured at the back of her neck with a green ribbon that matched the high-necked, full-skirted cotton dress she had chosen.

"I hope I was right to agree to teach a Sunday school class," she murmured as she set the mirror down and moved across the room to fetch her shawl and the satchel full of teaching supplies.

For most of the week, Betsy had wrestled with the idea of whether it would be good for her to teach the girls' class.

Not until Papa said he thought she should do it and had assured her that he would be fine at home on the days he felt too tired to go to church had Betsy finally decided to give it a try. She knew she could either call on a substitute to teach the class or ask one of the ladies from church to come to their house and sit with Papa should it become necessary.

On Friday afternoon Betsy had gone to the parsonage and given the pastor her answer. He'd seemed pleased and said that if Betsy felt ready, she could begin teaching this Sunday.

"I'm ready," she murmured, gathering her hand puppets and slipping them into the satchel. She moved back to the dresser and, with one last look in the mirror, hurried out of the room.

She hoped Papa might feel up to going to Sunday school with her this morning, but when she stepped into the living room and found him asleep in his favorite chair, she felt a keen sense of disappointment. How different things were now than when she was a young girl. Back then, Papa had risen early every Sunday morning and had never missed teaching the men's Sunday school class or preaching to the congregation he cared so much about.

I'd best let him sleep, she decided. *Maybe he will feel up to coming to church if he rests awhile.*

Betsy tiptoed out of the room and opened the front door, feeling a mixture of excitement and apprehension about teaching a group of girls she barely knew. Would the children be eager to learn the Bible story she planned to tell them? Would they welcome her as their new teacher?

"I guess there's only one way to find out," Betsy said with a lift of her chin; then she stepped out the door.

Chapter 11

*I*f you won't let me take you to see the doctor, then I'm going to ask him to come over here and examine you," Betsy told her father Monday morning as they sat at the breakfast table.

"I'll be fine. I'm just a little more tired than usual, that's all."

"A little more tired?" Betsy pointed to the bowl of oatmeal sitting before him, untouched. "You stayed home from church yesterday because you felt tired; you ate very little supper last night; and you've been sitting at the table for half an hour without touching your tea, oatmeal, or your favorite cinnamon muffins."

"I'm not hungry." Papa's face looked paler than normal, and dark circles had formed beneath his eyes. He leaned forward, placing his elbows on the table and resting his forehead against the palms of his hands.

"Are you in pain?"

"Just some pressure in my chest, and I'm having a hard time getting my breath."

Betsy jumped up from the table. "That doesn't sound good to me, Papa. You need to see the doctor today!"

Betsy paced in front of her father's bedroom door as she waited in the hallway for Dr. McGrath to finish examining him. She was glad the doctor had been available to make a house call, because Papa had been feeling so poorly that Betsy didn't think he was up to riding to the doctor's office in their buckboard.

Oh Lord, she silently prayed, *please help Dr. McGrath think of something that might help Papa's heart grow stronger. I've only been home a few weeks, and I can't stand the thought of losing him.* She stopped in front of his bedroom door, tempted to poke her head inside and see what was taking so long.

Loud barking from outside drew Betsy's attention, and she moved over to the window at the end of the hall to look into the backyard. She spotted Bristle Face running back and forth, pulling on his rope, and yapping at two young boys who were walking by the house.

"I still need to see if someone will build us a fence. If something's not done, that dog will keep breaking free and running back to the parsonage." She shook her head. "That sure wouldn't set well with William's housekeeper."

The door to Papa's bedroom opened just then, and Betsy whirled around. "Dr. McGrath, how's my father doing?"

The doctor joined her at the window. "I'm afraid his heart has become weaker."

"Is. . .is he going to die?" Betsy hated to ask the question, but it had been on her mind ever since she'd returned to Walnutport.

"Short of a miracle, I'm afraid his heart won't hold out much longer." The doctor pursed his lips. "What Hiram needs is a new heart, but since that's not possible, the best we can do is make him comfortable and see that he gets plenty of rest."

Betsy drew in a shuddering breath. She thought she had prepared herself for this, but hearing the truth hurt worse than she could have imagined. "It doesn't seem right to give up hope," she said in a quavering voice.

"Perhaps we should go into the sitting room," Dr. McGrath said. "I'd like to discuss something with you."

Betsy nodded and led the way down the hall. When they entered the sitting room, the doctor placed his leather bag on the table by Papa's chair and took a seat. Betsy seated herself on the sofa across from him. "What is it you wish to talk to me about?" she asked.

"I recently read an article that was published in the *New York Medical Journal*," Dr. McGrath replied. "It's about an extract made from hawthorn berries, and it's used to treat various heart conditions."

Betsy leaned forward as a feeling of hope welled in her soul. "Has there been some success with this extract?"

"Some. Of course, it's still in the experimental stages, and all the tests are not conclusive."

"Even so, it offers a ray of hope, doesn't it?"

He nodded. "The article said the berry juice is not a cure-all for every heart condition, but in weak hearts with capillary congestion, it's been proven to have great benefit."

"Will you try some of this extract on my father?"

"As soon as I get back to my office, I'll see about getting some hawthorn berries. Then I'll ask my nurse to pulverize them and make a tea."

"Thank you, Doctor. I hope this is the miracle I've been praying for."

As William came up the walk in front of the Nelsons' place, he could hear Bristle Face barking in the backyard. He was tempted to go around and greet the dog but figured he'd better make his call on Betsy's father first. Hiram hadn't been in church yesterday, and when Betsy said she'd left her father asleep in his chair, William had become concerned and decided to visit.

Just as he walked up the porch steps, the front door opened and Dr. McGrath stepped out. "Good afternoon, Reverend. I'm sorry I missed church yesterday, but I had a baby to deliver."

"One of the women at church told me that Mae Gates had gone into labor. Did the delivery go well?"

"Mae had a healthy baby boy. Her husband, Andy, said he thought his son might make a good preacher someday because he's got such a good set of lungs." The doctor chuckled. "Andy said he could hear the lad squalling all through the house."

William smiled, then motioned toward the house. "How's Hiram doing? I assume you were making a call on him."

"Yes, and I'm sorry to say that he's not doing well. His heart seems weaker today than it has on any of my previous visits."

"I'm sorry to hear that."

"I plan to try a new remedy, but a good dose of prayer wouldn't hurt either."

William nodded. "That's what I've come for. That and to offer some encouraging words to Hiram and his daughter."

"They'll appreciate that, I'm sure." Dr. McGrath lifted his hand in a wave and stepped off the porch.

William rapped on the front door, and moments later Betsy opened it. "I came to see your father. Is he up to some company?"

She opened the door wider, bidding him to enter. "He's very tired, but I'm sure he'll be pleased to see you."

William followed her inside. "Dr. McGrath mentioned something about a new medication he hopes to try on your father."

She nodded. "It's a tea made with hawthorn berries. The doctor read about it in a medical journal." Betsy's smile appeared hopeful. "Papa still needs a lot of prayer though."

"I've been praying for him and will continue to do so." William touched Betsy's shoulder. "I'll try to come by more often, and if you ever need anything, please don't hesitate to ask."

She paused outside her father's bedroom door and leaned against the wall. "Actually, there is something I've been meaning to ask you."

"What's that?"

"I was wondering if you might speak to some of the men from church about the possibility of putting a fence around our yard so I won't have to keep tying Bristle Face to a tree." Betsy grimaced. "That animal seems determined to break free and run over to the parsonage, and I'm sure it's become quite a nuisance for you."

William thought about the last time the dog had shown up at his door. Mrs. Bevens had threatened to chase him away with a broom. "I'm sure some of the men would be willing to build a fence," he said to Betsy. "I'll be happy to help out, too."

"Thank you." Betsy released a sigh. "I have one more favor to ask."

"What's that?"

"It's about my Sunday school class."

"I heard that it went quite well on Sunday. The McDougal girls told me they liked your puppets."

Betsy nodded. "I enjoyed teaching them, but with Papa taking a turn for the worse, I'm not sure I'll be able to continue teaching. I was hoping you might find someone else to take the class and maybe play the organ, too."

"I'm sure some of the women from church would be glad to sit with your father while you're teaching."

Betsy nibbled on her lower lip as she stared at the floor.

"Your help is much appreciated, and everyone at church benefits from your musical talents." He took a step forward. "I don't think it would be good for you to stay cooped up in the house all the time, and I'm sure your father would agree with me on that."

She lifted her gaze to meet his, and he noticed tears in her eyes. "I...I guess maybe I should take one week at a time and see how it goes."

William nodded. "Is there anything else you wish to discuss before I see your father?"

"That was all."

He turned toward her father's room and grasped the doorknob.

"Wait. There is one more thing."

He pivoted back around. "What is it, Betsy?"

"Please don't say anything to Papa about the hawthorn berry tea Dr. McGrath wants to try. I don't want to get his hopes up."

William shook his head. "Of course not. I'll merely offer some words of encouragement and pray with him."

"Thank you, Pastor William."

Chapter 12

*B*etsy bent over the washtub she'd set up on the back porch and grabbed a pair of overalls. It was time to do laundry again. Today she had her and Papa's clothes to do, as well as some from the boatmen. She'd been getting more business lately, which was a good thing because she needed the money. The washing and mending, however, kept her busier than ever, leaving less time to spend with her father.

For the last few weeks some of the women from church had taken turns relieving Betsy so she could teach Sunday school, play the organ during church, and go shopping whenever it was needed. During those weeks Dr. McGrath had been giving Betsy's father a dose of hawthorn berry

317

tea every day, and they were waiting to see if it helped his heart any.

A fence had been put up around their backyard as well. Since Ben Hanson owned the house Betsy and her father lived in, he'd agreed to pay for the needed supplies. Several of the men from church, including Pastor William and Mike Cooper, had been involved in building the fence. Bristle Face was now safe and secure, and he couldn't make a pest of himself by going over to the parsonage and bothering Mrs. Bevens or the pastor anymore.

At the moment, the dog was sleeping on the porch, but when he let out a noisy yap, Betsy spotted Harriet Miller coming up the walk, carrying a wicker basket.

"I brought lunch over for you and your father," Harriet said once she'd reached the gate. "Would you like me to hand it over the fence, or should I come into the yard?"

Betsy dropped a just-washed pair of trousers into the rinse bucket and straightened. "If you'd like to go around front, I'll meet you there. If you come into the backyard, you'll have to deal with Bristle Face, which probably won't be pleasant."

Harriet's eyebrows lifted, and a blotch of pink erupted on her cheeks. "Oh dear, does the animal bite?"

"To my knowledge, Bristle Face has never bitten anyone, but he does like to jump up, and I'm sure you wouldn't appreciate his dirty paw prints all over your clean skirt."

Harriet nodded. "I'll head around front."

Betsy's RETURN

A few minutes later Betsy joined Harriet on the front porch. "It was kind of you to bring us a meal," she said, taking the basket from the elderly woman. "Would you care to come inside and say hello to my father while you're here?"

"Is he feeling up to company today?"

"I think so. He was relaxing on the sofa when I went outside to do the laundry, but I'm sure he would enjoy a visit from you."

Harriet smiled. "I'll go in to see him in a few minutes, but first, I'd like to have a little chat with you, if you have the time."

Betsy motioned to the two wicker chairs sitting near the door. When they were both seated, she placed the wicker basket on the porch by her chair. "Was there anything in particular you wished to speak with me about?"

"As a matter of fact, there is." Harriet smoothed the wrinkles in her long, gray skirt. "I've been meeting with some of the other women from church on Monday mornings, so we can pray, study our Bibles, and discuss the needs of our congregation."

"There seems to be many needs among us these days," Betsy said with a nod.

"You're so right, and one of the needs we've been praying about is a husband for you."

Betsy's mouth dropped open. "What?"

Harriet reached over and took hold of Betsy's hand.

"Look how red and wrinkled your skin has become since you started taking in washing. And I saw the way you grimaced in pain when you stood up from that washtub earlier." She clicked her tongue. "If you had a husband to provide for your needs, you wouldn't have to slave over a hot tub of water in order to earn money."

Betsy gripped the arms of her chair until her fingers dug into the wicker. "Are all the women in your group praying that I find a husband?"

Harriet nodded. "Most of us have attended the community church for a good many years, and we've known you since you were a little girl."

"That's true, but—"

"What about our handsome young preacher?"

"What about him?"

"I think you and Pastor William would make the perfect match."

"Oh, I don't believe—"

Harriet patted Betsy's hand in a motherly fashion. "Several of us think you would make a good minister's wife. After all, you've grown up in the ministry and know what's expected of a pastor and his family. Your musical abilities are certainly a plus, too."

Betsy swallowed hard. "Have I said or done anything to make you believe I've set my cap for the preacher?"

Harriet blinked. "Why, no, dear. I just think that the two of you are well suited, and—"

Betsy shook her head. "I'm not looking for a husband, Harriet."

"Haven't you noticed how kind and caring the pastor seems to be? He's such a handsome man, don't you think?"

Betsy didn't know how to respond. She had noticed how handsome the pastor was, and if she were still the old flirtatious Betsy, she might be tempted to let her interest in the man be known. But she had changed and would not throw herself at any man, no matter how much he might interest her. If God ever decided that she should have a husband, then He would have to cause that man to make the first move.

William couldn't get over all the invitations he'd recently received to share lunches and suppers with various people from his congregation. Yet here he was, stepping into another house for a noon meal. It was the third invitation in two days. Mrs. Bevens had been invited, too, but as usual she'd declined.

"Fred and I are so glad you could join us for lunch today," Doris Brown said as she led William into her roomy kitchen. "Why, when I told Fred you were coming over to eat, he said, 'I'll just knock over a chicken or two, and you can get out some flour doin's, and then we'll feed that new pastor of ours some tasty chicken fixin's.'" She offered William a wide grin and pointed to the table. "Fred's upstairs changing out of his dirty work clothes, but he'll be down soon, so why don't you pull up a chair and make yourself comfortable?"

William smiled and took the chair closest to him.

"Too bad your housekeeper couldn't have come over," Doris said. "She's not such a friendly type, is she?"

"What makes you think that?"

"Some of us women have been having ourselves a little Bible study on Monday mornings, and when I saw Mrs. Bevens at church a couple of Sundays ago, I asked if she'd like to join us."

"I see." William didn't bother to ask what reply his housekeeper had given, because he already knew Mrs. Bevens had declined the invitation. The snooty woman had mentioned that she didn't care much for people like Doris Brown, a plain, simple woman, lacking in education and social graces.

"I haven't been able to figure out if your housekeeper is stuck on herself or is just shy around folks she don't know so well." Doris reached around William to pour water into his glass. "The lady doesn't say much, and some of the women from church think she seems kind of hoity-toity, which makes no sense, seeing as to how she's workin' as your housekeeper and all."

William grimaced. Hoity-toity. That was exactly the impression Mrs. Bevens left with people.

Doris pulled out a chair on the other side of the table and

sat down, apparently in no hurry to get lunch on the table. "Can you tell me why Mrs. Bevens keeps her distance?"

William drew in a deep breath and released it quickly. "I've known Mrs. Bevens since I was a boy—when she was my nanny. It's my understanding that her father was once a successful businessman, but soon after his wife died, he started drinking and lost all his assets."

"Assets?"

"All his business holdings—his money."

"I see."

"So Mrs. Bevens, being an only child, was sent away to live with her old maid aunt because her father could no longer care for her." William paused. He hoped he wasn't speaking out of turn or that the information would appear to be gossip. But Doris had asked a direct question, and he felt she deserved an honest answer.

"Do you think Mrs. Bevens might've become bitter 'cause her daddy was a louse?" Doris leaned forward with her elbows on the table and blinked her eyelashes several times.

William shrugged. "Maybe so, but it's not my place to judge. I've probably spoken out of turn by telling you what I have about Mrs. Bevens."

"I'm glad you shared what you did 'cause it helps me understand the woman a little better." Doris pushed away from the table and lumbered over to the stove. She opened the oven door and peeked inside. "Chicken looks brown enough now, so we can eat as soon as my man shows up."

"If it tastes half as good as it smells, I'm sure I'll be in for a treat."

"Oh, it will—I can guarantee that," Doris's husband, Fred, said as he sauntered into the room with a towel slung over his shoulder. He stepped up beside his wife and planted a noisy kiss on her cheek. "My Doris is the best cook in the whole state of Pennsylvania."

"I think we have a church full of good cooks." William patted his stomach. "I've eaten several meals prepared by the ladies already, and I enjoyed every one."

Fred plodded over to the table and pulled out a chair. "Know what I think you need, Preacher?"

William opened his mouth to respond, but Doris cut him off. "He needs a wife, that's what he needs."

Fred's bald head bobbed up and down. "That's just what I was gonna say. It ain't good for a preacher man to be single."

Doris placed a platter full of chicken on the table and patted William on the back. "I know exactly who the perfect wife for you would be."

William fiddled with the knife beside his plate as his face heated up. Was everyone in the church determined to see him married?

"It's Frank Andrews's daughter, Hortence, huh?" Fred jiggled his bushy eyebrows and gave William a silly grin. "I've seen the way that little gal looks at you on Sunday mornings."

William's ears burned, and a trickle of sweat rolled down his forehead.

"Oh no, Fred," Doris said as she set a bowl of mashed potatoes in front of William. "I think Betsy Nelson would be more suitable as a pastor's wife, don't you?"

William cringed. *I think it's time for me to nip this talk of marriage in the bud.* This Sunday, before he began his sermon, he would let everyone in the congregation know that he was perfectly happy being single and that he planned to stay that way.

Chapter 13

On Sunday morning as William stepped into the pulpit, he reminded himself what his first announcement should be. His only concern was in choosing the right words. He didn't want to hurt anyone's feelings, yet he couldn't allow the folks who had been trying to play matchmaker to continue inviting him to dinner with the hope of getting him married off to their daughters.

He placed his Bible on the pulpit, collected his thoughts as best he could, and smiled at the congregation. "Good morning. This is the day that the Lord hath made."

Several *amen*s went up around the room, and many people nodded their heads in agreement.

"I. . .uh. . .have an announcement to make." William loosened his tie a notch and swallowed around the constriction in his throat. Everyone wore expectant looks, even Betsy, who sat at the organ with her hymnbook in her hands. Would he embarrass someone if he said this in front of the entire congregation? He didn't want to cause hard feelings or draw attention to anyone in particular. Maybe it would be better if he spoke one-on-one to the individuals who were determined to play matchmaker, rather than announcing to the whole group that he was a confirmed bachelor.

William gripped the edge of the pulpit for support. Why did the room feel so hot all of a sudden? The windows were open, so a breeze must be coming in. These people were expecting him to make an announcement, so if he wasn't going to say what was on his mind, then he needed to come up with something else to say.

He cleared his throat a couple of times. "My. . .uh. . . announcement this morning is that. . .uh. . . ."

"What's the matter, Preacher? Are you gonna chew us out because we've done somethin' wrong?" Abe Rawlings, one of the few canalers who came to church whenever his boat passed through the area, shouted from the back of the room.

William shook his head, feeling more frustrated than ever. He needed to think of something to announce, and it had better be quick. "No one has done anything wrong.

I just wanted to announce that—" An idea suddenly popped into his head, and he practically shouted out the rest of his sentence. "Next Sunday, after the worship service is over, I want to conduct another service down by the canal, and a...a picnic will follow."

Several heads bobbed up and down, and smiles spread across most of the people's faces.

"Shortly after I came here, it was brought to my attention that the boatmen might enjoy some singing and preaching down at the canal, where their boats are tied up for their day of rest." He glanced over at Betsy, knowing this had been her idea, and added, "I hope all of you will come and be part of this special service."

"You can count on me, Pastor."

"I'll be there."

"Yeah, me, too."

"A picnic sounds like fun."

Everyone seemed to be talking at once, and William rapped his knuckles on the edge of the pulpit to get their attention. "Perhaps some of you ladies can get together and discuss what you might want to bring for the picnic. I think it would be nice if each family brought enough food to share with some of the canalers, don't you?"

Several heads nodded in agreement, and a couple of women started whispering to those who sat near them.

William tapped on the pulpit again. "Rather than taking time to discuss the details of the picnic right now, I think it would be better if we waited until after church is over."

"The preacher man's right!" Abe hollered. "We came here to sing God's praises and hear His Word, not talk about food!"

Everyone quieted, and William looked over at Betsy again. "Perhaps you could meet with me for a few minutes after church today, along with any others who might want to sing a special song or play a musical instrument during our canal service."

Betsy nodded and smiled.

When church was over and the final prayer had been said, Betsy stood near the organ, waiting for the pastor to finish greeting the people so he could meet with her and any others who might want to contribute to the music next Sunday during the canal service. She was pleased that Pastor William had decided to hold church there. It had meant a lot to the boatmen whenever Papa walked the canal to hand out Bible verses or conducted a Sunday service in the grassy area near the towpath. Many men, including Kelly and Sarah's father, Amos McGregor, had found a personal relationship with the Lord because of those informal meetings. Now whenever Amos and his wife were near Walnutport on a Saturday evening, they would tie up for the night and come to church on Sunday morning. Betsy knew how pleased Kelly and Sarah were when their folks were able to be in church, and the look of pride on Dorrie McGregor's face as she sat on a pew, holding one of her grandchildren in her lap, was a joy to behold.

"Excuse me," Ruby Miller said as she stepped up beside Betsy, "but I was wondering if I might speak to you a minute."

Betsy nodded. "Of course. Were you wanting to sing a special song at our canal service next Sunday?"

Ruby's face turned pink, and she fanned her face with her hands. "Oh my, no. I'd scare folks away if I tried to sing a solo."

Betsy smiled at the middle-aged woman and gently squeezed her arm. "You wouldn't have to sing a solo. You could do a duet with me or someone else from the congregation."

Ruby shook her head. "My husband says I squawk like a chicken whenever I sing, so I wouldn't think of embarrassing anyone by asking them to do a duet with me."

"So what did you wish to speak with me about?"

Ruby leaned closer to Betsy and whispered, "I was hoping you and your father might come to supper at our place one night next week."

"It's nice of you to ask, but I don't think Papa's up to going anywhere right now." Betsy gestured to the empty pews. "You've probably noticed he hasn't been in church for the last couple of weeks."

Ruby nodded. "I'm sorry he's not doing any better. We're all praying for him, you know."

"We appreciate that."

"Would your father be okay with you coming to dinner without him? I could ask someone to sit with him while you're gone, if that would help." Ruby touched Betsy's shoulder. "You really do need a break once in a while."

"I'll think about it and let you know." Betsy offered Ruby what she hoped was a pleasant smile.

"I'll stop by your house on Tuesday for an answer, and if you decide to accept my invitation, we'll have you over for supper on Friday evening."

Ruby walked away, and a few minutes later Pastor William showed up. "Was Ruby talking to you about the music for our canal service next week?"

Betsy shook her head. "She had something else on her mind."

"I see. Well, I hope you'll be able to take part in the services. I would like it if you brought your zither along to accompany the songs."

"As long as my father isn't any worse and I can find someone to spend the afternoon with him, I'll be there," Betsy said with a nod.

"It would be wonderful if he felt up to going along that day."

"Yes, it would."

"Does the doctor think the new treatment is helping at all?"

Betsy shrugged. "He's not sure. There are days when Papa

seems a bit stronger and doesn't have as much chest pain, but other days he can barely walk across the room without having to stop every few seconds to catch his breath."

"The last time I spoke with your father, he informed me that he's ready to die if the Lord chooses to take him home rather than heal his heart."

A shiver started at the base of Betsy's neck and ran all the way down her spine. She could hardly think about Papa dying, much less speak the words.

"I apologize if I've spoken out of turn. I can see that you're shaken." Pastor William nodded toward the organ bench. "Would you like to sit awhile?"

"I'm fine." Betsy grabbed the hymnbook from the end of the organ where she had placed it after the service. "Should we pick some songs for next Sunday now?"

"Yes. Yes, of course."

Chapter 14

I'm sorry you couldn't come over to our place for supper last week," Ruby said to Betsy as they both pulled their buckboards into a clearing near the section of the canal closest to the lock tender's house.

Betsy glanced over at her father, who sat in the seat beside her. "Papa wasn't feeling well that night, and—"

"I tried to get her to go, but my daughter can be so stubborn sometimes." Papa nodded at Betsy. "I love you and appreciate your dedication, but you worry about me too much."

Betsy couldn't argue with that. She did worry about her father and wanted him to get well so they could spend more time together.

"I'm glad you're feeling up to attending our church service and picnic at the canal today," Ruby said. "Sure wish my husband would have been able to come."

"Is Clem sick?" Betsy asked. "I didn't see him at our service in town."

"He's not sick, but yesterday morning that determined man put a kink in his back when he tried to move a huge rock in our backyard." Ruby pursed her lips. "He was still hurtin' this morning and didn't want to get out of bed. Said I should go to church without him."

"Clem should have asked some of the men from church to help him move that rock," Betsy's father put in. "That's how we got our fence put up. Isn't that right, Betsy?"

She nodded and reached over to touch his hand. "Are you sure you're up to this outing today?"

He squeezed her fingers. "I'm fine, and I wouldn't have missed seeing my canal friends here—not to mention sampling some of the tasty food the ladies from church have brought along to share."

"I baked some apple pies," Ruby said. "That's always been a favorite of yours."

He grinned and patted his stomach. "Yes, Ruby, I do love your sweet apple pies."

Betsy smiled. The fact that Papa seemed so pleased gave her hope that he might be feeling better. If God provided a miracle and healed Papa's heart, he might be able to start preaching again. Of course, now there was a new pastor standing in his pulpit, so either William would have to leave or Papa would need to look for some other church to pastor. The thought of them moving away from Walnutport didn't set well with Betsy, and thinking about the new pastor leaving wasn't much better. Betsy wouldn't have admitted it to anyone, but in the short time Pastor William had been in town, she'd become quite fond of him. He seemed kind, caring, and smart, and he was extremely good-looking. She was sure he would make a fine husband.

Betsy's shoulders tensed as a pain shot up her neck, and her musings came to a halt. What on earth had she been thinking? Friendship was all she could offer right now, and she was sure the pastor saw her only as a friend as well.

"Shall we climb down from the buckboard and join the others?" Papa asked.

Betsy nodded. "Let me put a blanket on the grass so you'll have a comfortable place to sit, and then I'll come back to the buckboard to get you."

"I'm not an invalid, Betsy. And I don't plan to sit on a blanket all day."

Betsy knew her father's words weren't meant to be harsh, but she felt the sting of them nonetheless. "I just don't want you overdoing it. This is the first day in a long while that you've been outside the house."

He patted her arm. "I'll be fine."

A short time later as Betsy, her father, and Ruby headed for the canal, she spotted Mike and Kelly along with their two children: Anna, who was four, and Marcus, who had just turned two.

"Pastor Nelson, it's so good to see you," Mike said, taking Betsy's father by the arm.

"I wouldn't have missed coming here today for anything," Papa replied. The two men wandered off, Ruby joined Freda Hanson, who stood nearby, and Betsy followed Kelly and her children across the grass.

"I think I'm going to set out my blanket and picnic basket before the service begins," Kelly said. "That way we'll be sure to have a good place to sit when it's time to eat."

Betsy nodded. "Guess I'll do the same."

The children sat on the grass and watched as Kelly and Betsy spread out their blankets. They'd just gotten everything situated when Kelly's mother and sister—Dorrie and Sarah—showed up. Sarah's three children—Sam Jr., age six; Willis, who was four; and two-year-old Helen—tagged along behind them.

Kelly's children scurried over to their grandmother, and she gave them each a hug. "I'm so glad the new pastor has decided to hold services down here by the canal." She smiled at Betsy. "Since your father retired from preaching, those of us who spend most of the week on our boats have missed this time of singing, Bible teaching, and fellowship."

"That's right," Sarah said with a nod. "Even though my family usually makes it to church in town most Sundays, we've always enjoyed the services held here along the water."

"Mike and I have enjoyed that, too," Kelly agreed.

"Betsy, did you bring your zither?" Dorrie asked.

Betsy nodded and pointed to the leather case she'd set on one end of the blanket. "I'm just waiting for our pastor to arrive."

Sarah glanced at the group of people who had already congregated. "I would think he would have been here by now. I hope he didn't change his mind about holding the service down here."

"I'm sure Pastor William is coming," Betsy said. "He helped me pick out the songs we're going to sing today, and he seemed excited about the opportunity to preach to the boatmen."

Kelly poked Betsy gently on the arm and motioned to the left. "Here he comes now, and he's got his housekeeper with him."

William was amazed at how many people had gathered along the grassy banks near the canal. He recognized several from church, but lots of faces were new to him.

"I don't see why you insisted that I be here for this," Mrs. Bevens said through tight lips as she tromped through the tall grass beside him. "I attended services at your church this morning; that ought to be good enough."

"I thought you might use this time as an opportunity to

get to know the people in the community a little better," he said, patting her arm. "It's a warm, sunny afternoon with not much humidity, and it's the perfect day for a picnic."

"Perfect for the ants and buzzing insects maybe." Mrs. Bevens lifted the edge of her long, gray skirt and frowned. "If I get grass stains on my dress, it will be your fault."

William clenched his teeth and kept on walking. He was nervous enough about conducting his first outdoor service, and he didn't need Mrs. Bevens's negative attitude to put a damper on things. He spotted Betsy standing beside Kelly and her sister and was relieved to see that she'd brought her zither along.

"Should we begin with some singing?" he asked, moving away from Mrs. Bevens and stepping up to Betsy.

She nodded. "That's the way Papa always began his services." She motioned to a log lying a few feet from the towpath. Her father was sitting there with Mike Cooper on one side of him and Sam Turner on the other side.

"I'm glad your father could make it. I didn't see him in church this morning, so I assumed he wasn't feeling well."

"He says he's feeling better today, but he knew it would be too long of a day if he went to church in town and came here, too." Betsy smiled. "So he chose to attend this service and the picnic that will follow."

"Our dad's here today, too," Sarah put in.

"That's right. Preacher Nelson led Papa to the Lord some time ago," Kelly added. "He's not as comfortable comin' into town to the fancy church building, but ever since he accepted Christ as his Savior, Papa has enjoyed the services held along the canal."

"That's good to hear. If things go well today, I'll try to hold services down here on a regular basis."

Kelly and Sarah smiled, and Betsy fairly beamed. "I'm ready to get started with the singing whenever you are, Pastor," she said.

William moved over to the crowd of people and lifted his hands. "Good afternoon. For those of you who haven't met me yet, I'm Pastor William Covington, and I'm pleased to see so many of you here today."

There were several *amen*s, a few people snickered, and a couple of the canalers shouted, "Nice to meet ya, Preacher!"

William's cheeks warmed, and he knew it wasn't from the summer sun. The people at the church he'd attended in Buffalo were so formal and stuffy compared to these plain, simple folks who weren't afraid to show enthusiasm or say whatever was on their mind. Nothing William had learned in seminary had prepared him for preaching to a group of unpretentious, uneducated canalers, but he was ready and willing to do the Lord's work, no matter what it took.

William opened the service with a word of prayer then announced the first song they would sing: "Shall We Gather at the River?" He nodded at Betsy, and she began to strum her zither. Everyone's voices blended together as they sang out, "Shall we gather at the river, where bright angel feet have trod, with its crystal tide forever flowing by the throne of God?'"

William was pleased to see a look of joy on the people's faces, as they lifted their heads toward the sky and sang with gusto. He led them in two more songs, "What a Friend We Have in Jesus" and "Wonderful Words of Life," and was about to launch into his sermon when a voice from the crowd shouted, "I would like it if we sang, 'I Feel Like Traveling On'!"

William turned to see Hiram Nelson walking toward him, his face fairly glowing and his eyes shimmering with tears. "Of course we can sing that song. Would you like to lead us, Rev. Nelson?"

Hiram nodded, and in a surprisingly steady voice he began, "'My heavenly home is bright and fair. I feel like traveling on. Nor pain nor death can enter there. I feel like traveling on.'" He motioned to the crowd, and they joined him on the chorus: "'Yes, I feel like traveling on. I feel like traveling on. My heavenly home is bright and fair. I feel like traveling on.'"

When the song ended, Rev. Nelson lifted his hands and looked upward. "I'm ready to go home whenever You're ready to take me, Lord!"

Chapter 15

Betsy didn't know how she'd managed to sit through Pastor William's message when the singing ended, because after Papa's song and him telling God that he was ready to go home to be with Him, she felt numb. Just this morning Papa had told her that he was feeling better. Yet his choice of song and the prayer that followed made it clear that he was ready to die.

Papa sat on the blanket beside her now, smiling and licking his lips as he ate a chicken wing he'd pulled from the covered dish Betsy had taken from their picnic basket a few minutes ago. Didn't he realize how much he'd upset her with that song and prayer?

"This is sure tasty," he said with a smile. "You're going to make some man a mighty fine wife some day."

Betsy shook her head. "I'm an old maid, Papa, and I'm quite likely to stay one."

"You never know what the future holds." He glanced over at her half-eaten plate of food and frowned. "You've barely touched a thing. I can't eat all this by myself, you know."

She shrugged, wishing she felt free to tell her father all the things that were on her mind. "I'm not so hungry right now."

His eyebrows furrowed. "How come? Are you feeling sick?"

"No, I'm not sick."

"That's good to hear." Papa took another bite of chicken and wiped his mouth on the napkin she'd just handed him. "That young pastor sure preached a good sermon on forgiveness this afternoon, didn't he?"

Betsy shifted uncomfortably on the blanket. "I'm. . . uh. . .glad Pastor William decided to hold services down here." She didn't want to admit that she hadn't heard more than a few words of the pastor's message. "Several of the boatmen have told me how much they've missed the meetings you used to hold along the canal."

Her father nodded and reached for the cup of water Betsy had placed on the lid of the picnic basket. "I'm pleased to see such a good turnout, and I'm hoping Pastor William will continue to hold services here on a regular basis."

"I'm sure he will, as long as the weather cooperates."

Betsy sighed and set her plate aside.

He cast her a furtive glance. "Are you sure you're all right?"

She nodded and offered him what she hoped was a reassuring smile.

"I can tell by the wrinkles in your forehead that something is bothering you, so you may as well tell me what it is."

Betsy drew in a deep breath and released it quickly, glancing around to be sure no one sitting nearby was listening. "I'm worried about you, Papa."

"Now, Betsy, you know what the Bible says about worry. 'Therefore I say unto you, Take no thought for your life, what ye shall eat, or what ye shall drink; nor yet for your body, what ye shall put on. Is not the life more than meat, and the body than raiment?' Matthew 6:25."

Betsy grimaced. "I'm not worried about what I shall eat or wear, Papa. After hearing that song you sang earlier and listening to your prayer, I became worried that you might have given up on life and were preparing to die."

"We're all going to die sometime." Papa reached over and patted her hand. "You must remember that no matter what happens in the days ahead, my life is in God's hands."

Betsy opened her mouth to comment, but he rushed on. "No one but God knows what the future holds, but we do know that our heavenly Father holds the future, so let us remember to be loyal to Him and leave our destiny in His hands."

Betsy swallowed hard, trying to dislodge the lump that had formed in her throat. "I know, Papa, and I'll try not to worry."

"That's my girl," he said with a wink. "Now why don't you let your old papa take a nap while you visit with some of your friends?"

Betsy didn't feel like visiting with anyone right now, but because she knew her father needed to rest, she gathered up their plates and leftover food, placed them inside the picnic basket, and stood. Smoothing the wrinkles in her long, green skirt, she smiled down at him. "I'll come back in half an hour to check on you."

He reclined on the blanket, placing both hands behind his head. "No need to worry about me. I'll be fine."

"I'm going over to talk with Rev. Nelson for a bit," William said to Mrs. Bevens as she began putting away their leftover picnic food. "While I'm gone, why don't you try to get to know some of the ladies here a little better?"

Mrs. Bevens's mouth drooped at the corners. "I'd rather be alone. Maybe I will take a walk along the canal."

He released a frustrated groan. "Suit yourself, but you'll never feel at home in Walnutport unless you learn to mingle."

She pursed her lips and kept piling things into the wicker basket.

William rose from the blanket. "Have a nice walk, Mrs. Bevens."

A short time later he found Hiram Nelson lying under the shade of a leafy maple tree. The man's eyes were closed, and his steady, even breathing indicated that he must be sleeping. William was about to walk away, when the reverend said, "Don't run off. I'd like to talk to you."

William jumped. "I thought you were sleeping."

"Nope. Just resting my eyes." Hiram sat up and motioned William over to the blanket. "Have a seat, and we can visit awhile."

"Are you sure I'm not interrupting your nap?"

"I can sleep any old time." He chuckled. "To tell you the truth, I only said I wanted to take a nap so my daughter would feel free to leave my side and spend some time with her friends."

William glanced across the grassy area near the towpath and spotted Betsy sitting on a blanket beside Kelly and her sister, Sarah. "A couple of women from church have mentioned to me that Betsy doesn't socialize much."

"That's because she spends all her time washing and mending clothes for the canalers and, of course, tending to my needs."

"Betsy takes good care of you. It's obvious that she loves you very much."

"And I love her." Hiram pointed to the towpath where Mrs. Bevens walked alone. "Your housekeeper takes care of your basic needs, too, but she'll never take the place of a wife."

William's mouth dropped open. Surely Rev. Nelson wasn't in on the plot to see him married off, too.

"I wouldn't be so bold as to try and pick a wife for you," Hiram continued, "but I do think if you found the right helpmate it would benefit your ministry."

"But—but you have no wife, and from what I've heard, you got along just fine," William sputtered.

Hiram pulled his fingers through his thinning brown hair. "I was widowed when Betsy was a young girl, and many people thought I should find another wife."

"But you stayed single and did okay in your ministry. Am I right about that?"

Hiram nodded. "Yes, but that was because I never found a woman I could love as much as Betsy's mother. Abigail was a special lady, and she made me feel complete in so many. . ." His voice trailed off, as he stared into space.

William sat there a few seconds, allowing Hiram the privilege of reminiscing. After a few minutes he touched the man's arm. "I suppose I should let you get back to your nap. Unless there was more you wanted to say."

"Actually, there is one thing I'd like to mention."

"What's that?"

The older man cleared his throat. "This is. . .uh. . .a bit difficult for me to say, but I get the feeling that you might be putting a safe distance between you and your flock."

He moistened his lips with the tip of his tongue. "At first I thought it was because you thought you were better than them, since you're more educated and all."

A shock wave spiraled through William, but before he could offer a retort, Hiram added, "Now that I've gotten to know you better, I no longer believe that is true. I think the real reason you're keeping your distance is because you've been hurt by someone—perhaps a woman."

William clasped his hands together so hard that two of his knuckles popped. "I don't see what this has to do with anything."

Hiram laid a hand on William's shoulder. "If you want your ministry in Walnutport to succeed, then you're going to have to do more than preach a good sermon. You'll need to become part of the congregation—bring yourself down to their level: laugh with them, cry with them, become one of them. You must ask God to help you set your fears aside and become vulnerable enough to love and be loved by these people—and maybe by some special woman."

William blinked rapidly. "I don't know what to say."

"Just say you'll think about what I've said and also pray about it."

"Yes. Yes, of course I will." William rose. "You look tired, and I probably should mingle a bit and get to know some of the boatmen."

Hiram smiled, and William noticed the moisture clinging to the man's eyelashes. "Good for you, Pastor. Good for you."

347

As William started to walk away, two young boys raced past, shouting and tossing a ball back and forth as they zigzagged around the blankets where people sat visiting. "It's a wonder those two don't bump into someone," he muttered.

The boys kept running past the grassy area and onto the towpath. One threw the ball, and the other ran ahead to catch it, laughing and hollering as he went. William caught sight of his housekeeper again, standing along the edge of the canal, apparently deep in thought. He was about to call out a warning that a ball might be coming her way when the sphere of white whizzed through the air and smacked Mrs. Bevens on the back. She let out a muffled grunt and tumbled into the canal.

William rushed toward the water, but Harvey Collins, one of the canalers, jumped in first. William stood on the bank of the canal, watching as Mrs. Bevens flailed about, hollering, "I'm drowning!" while poor old Harvey struggled to drag her to shore.

Mrs. Bevens came out of the water, looking like a soggy scarecrow, and the unpleasant words she spewed told William she saw the incident as anything but funny. The finicky woman's hair had come loose from its perfect bun and stuck out in odd directions. Her stylish dress that had once been neatly pressed and stiffly starched at the collar clung to her body like it had been soaked with glue.

"Who did this to me?" Mrs. Bevens bellowed, as she spit water out of her mouth and stumbled onto shore. "I knew

I should not have come here today!"

"That dunk in the canal sure took the wind out of your snooty sails, didn't it?" Harvey chuckled as he squeezed water out of his own sopping clothes.

"Maybe what she needed was a good lesson in humility!" one of the other canalers called.

William couldn't argue with that. Mrs. Bevens did need to be taught a lesson, but he couldn't help feeling sorry for her as she spluttered away. Even Mrs. Bevens didn't deserve this kind of embarrassment.

Betsy rushed forward with a quilt and wrapped it around Mrs. Bevens's trembling shoulders. Not a word of thanks came from the woman's quivering lips—not to Betsy for the quilt or to Harvey for saving her life. Mrs. Bevens needed a lot of prayer, and William knew that was one thing he could do without her scolding him for it. He stepped forward and offered his arm. "I think it's time we went home, don't you?"

She gave a curt nod then tromped off toward William's buggy.

He nodded at Betsy and then at Harvey. "Thank you both for your kindness."

Chapter 16

I'll be on the back porch, washing some clothes, if you need me for anything," Betsy told her father as she positioned a small pillow behind his head, where he reclined on the sofa. He had come to the sitting room to read his Bible soon after breakfast, saying he wanted to spend time praying and meditating over God's Word.

I need to do that more often, too, Betsy thought, bending over to kiss his forehead.

"Don't work too hard, daughter. And always remember that I love you and wish you nothing but God's best."

"I love you, too, Papa." Betsy hurried out to the porch, anxious to get the washing out of the way so she could spend time with her father. She had convinced herself that if she cared for him properly, he would get well and things would be as they had been before his heart had started acting up. After seeing how well he'd done yesterday at the canal service, Betsy was beginning to believe that God might answer her prayers for a miracle.

Returning to the kitchen, Betsy hauled a kettle of hot water out to the porch, poured it into the washtub, added some lye soap, and dropped in one of the canalers' shirts. She reached into the hot, soapy water and dipped the shirt up and down several times, making sure it was sufficiently wet.

An image of Mrs. Bevens popped into her mind, and she bit back a chuckle. If she lived to be ninety, she didn't think she would ever forget seeing William's prim and proper housekeeper falling into the canal. Mrs. Bevens hadn't offered Harvey Collins any thanks at all for saving her life. For that matter, she hadn't thanked Betsy for the quilt she'd put around her shoulders.

A prick of conscience made Betsy shake her head. "It's not my place to judge Mrs. Bevens. Forgive me, Lord, for thinking such thoughts."

Betsy scrubbed the shirt against the washboard and gritted her teeth as she reflected on the way she used to be— self-centered and snobbish, always wanting her own way. She could have ended up just like Mrs. Bevens if she hadn't turned her life over to God and allowed Him to soften her heart.

She closed her eyes and offered up a heartfelt prayer. *Dear Lord, help me remember to set a good example to others and remind me whenever necessary that, but for Your grace, I could still be a snooty, selfish woman.*

Some time later, when all the clothes had been washed and hung on the line to dry, Betsy entered the kitchen. She filled a kettle with water and placed it on the stove with the intent of making her father his daily cup of hawthorn berry tea. While the water heated, she took a hunk of salt pork from the cooler, cut it into small pieces, and fried it in a pan to get the grease out, then she set it aside. She would add some potatoes, onion, tomatoes, and corn to the pot and then get some pork float cooking for their noon meal as soon as she had served Papa his tea.

Betsy placed a teacup on a wooden tray, filled it with water and the proper amount of the herb, and then headed for the sitting room. She stepped through the doorway, halted, and gasped. Papa lay facedown on the floor.

As William strolled down the sidewalk, prepared to make a few pastoral calls, he hummed his favorite hymn, "Where He Leads, I'll Follow," and thought about Sunday's service and the picnic that had followed. Most events during the day had encouraged his soul. He'd gotten to know several of the boatmen, become better acquainted with those who attended his church, had a pleasant conversation with Betsy's father, and filled his stomach with enough food to last him all week. The only sour note had been Mrs. Bevens's unplanned dip in the Lehigh Canal.

William couldn't help but feel sorry for the poor woman as he remembered how pathetic she'd looked when she came out of the water with porcupine hair and waterlogged clothes. The hoity-toity woman who'd gotten knocked into the canal had stepped onto dry land looking like an ordinary commoner. Unfortunately the incident hadn't done anything to soften Mrs. Bevens's heart.

I wish I could think of some way to get my dear housekeeper to move back to Buffalo, he thought ruefully. *Unless the Lord changes that frustrated woman's heart, she will never fit in here.*

Reminding himself that he needed to focus on something positive, William continued his trek down the street with a firm resolve. *I think I'll make my first call at the Nelsons' home and see how Hiram is doing.*

He had just turned onto Elm Street, when he almost collided with Betsy running at full speed. Her face looked pale, and her eyes were wide and full of fear.

"Betsy, what's wrong?" William clasped her shoulders.

"It—it's Papa. I was bringing him a cup of tea, and I f—found him lying on the floor. I couldn't get him to respond, and I'm afraid he might be—" Betsy choked on the words, and William instinctively drew her into his arms. "I've—I've got to get Dr. McGrath to come now. He needs to see Papa right away," she sobbed.

Realizing how shaken she was, he said, "I'll go with you to Dr. McGrath's."

Betsy pulled free from his embrace and darted down the street. William followed at a fast pace, reaching for Betsy's hand when he caught up to her. By the time they arrived at the doctor's office, Betsy could barely speak. "It's Papa. It's Papa. I think he's dead!" she gasped.

The doctor grabbed his black bag, said a few words to his nurse, and ushered them quickly out the door. "Let's take my carriage; it's around back." He nodded toward the back of the small building that served as his office.

When they stepped inside the Nelsons' home a short time later, William halted inside the door. Hiram lay on the sitting room floor, unmoving. Betsy rushed to her father's side. Dr. McGrath knelt next to her, opened his bag, and removed a stethoscope. "Help me turn him over, would you, Rev. Covington?"

William rushed across the room and dropped to his knees. Once they'd gotten Hiram turned onto his back, he could see that the man's face was deathly pale. There was no movement in his chest. William waited as the doctor placed the stethoscope over Hiram's heart so he could listen for a heartbeat.

Several minutes went by, which seemed like an eternity, then Dr. McGrath removed the stethoscope and placed his thumb over Hiram's wrist. He shook his head slowly as he looked over at Betsy. "There's no pulse, and I detected no heartbeat either. I'm sorry, but your father is dead."

Betsy sat there staring at her father. "Papa," she murmured.

William reached for her hand. "Your father's at peace now. He's gone home to be with Jesus."

Betsy blinked. Tears welled in her eyes, spilling onto her flushed cheeks. "Just yesterday Papa said he was feeling better." She squeezed her eyes shut. "But his song and prayer during the canal service were an indication that he knew he was going to die."

William winced, feeling her pain as though it were his own. Apparently Betsy's father had used the last of his strength to attend that service, and the song he'd sung and the prayer he'd prayed had been his final testimony.

"Lord, help Betsy in the days ahead," William prayed aloud. "Give her the strength and courage to go on." He gulped. The Rev. Hiram Nelson's funeral would be the first such service he'd ever conducted.

Chapter 17

*A*s Betsy stood near her father's coffin, she squeezed her eyes shut, willing herself not to break down during his graveside service. She'd held up fairly well during the service at the church, so she must maintain control of her emotions here. Despite her resolve, she wasn't sure how long she could hold out, for the pain in her heart was worse than any physical agony she'd ever endured. There seemed to be no answers to the questions filling her mind, and that only fueled her frustration. Why hadn't God healed Papa's heart? Why couldn't He have given them a few more years together?

"Dearly beloved, we have gathered today to pay our

final tribute and respects to the Rev. Hiram Nelson." Pastor William's deep voice broke into Betsy's thoughts, and her eyes snapped open.

I must not break down. I must remain strong.

"Forasmuch as the spirit of our departed loved one has returned to God, who gave it, we therefore tenderly commit his body to the grave." William paused long enough to open his Bible. "In John 14:1–3, we are told: 'Let not your heart be troubled: ye believe in God, believe also in me. In my Father's house are many mansions: if it were not so, I would have told you. I go to prepare a place for you. And if I go and prepare a place for you, I will come again, and receive you unto myself; that where I am, there ye may be also.'"

Papa's in heaven. That thought should have offered Betsy comfort, but she only felt grief.

"In John 11:25–26, Jesus said, 'I am the resurrection, and the life: he that believeth in me, though he were dead, yet shall he live: and whosoever liveth and believeth in me shall never die.'" William closed the Bible, and his gaze swept over the crowd of mourners. "May each of us find comfort in the knowledge that, while Hiram's body is dead, his soul lives on. Because this dedicated man believed in Jesus and accepted Him as his personal Savior, he now abides with the heavenly Father, where there are many mansions."

In spite of Betsy's resolve not to cry, tears flooded her eyes and streamed down her face, dripping onto the front of her black mourning dress. She felt all stirred up—as if her churning insides were as hot as coals. It was a comfort to know Papa no longer suffered and was now with Jesus, but oh, how she would miss him.

As Pastor William led the group in reciting the Lord's Prayer, Betsy pressed her lips together in an effort to keep from sobbing out loud. Instead of concentrating on the prayer, she thought about the funeral dinner Freda Hanson would be hosting at her house after the committal and wondered how she could get through the rest of the day.

William didn't know how he'd made it through Hiram's funeral, but God had graciously given him the words he needed for the message he'd shared at the church and then at the cemetery. He hoped the words of condolence he'd offered to Hiram's grieving daughter had been helpful, but he felt there was more he should have said.

As the group of mourners entered the Hansons' house, William prayed that God would show him, as well as others in the church, how to comfort Betsy in the days ahead.

"You did a fine job conducting the funeral today," Mike said, handing William a cup of coffee and steering him toward one of the tables that had been set up in the living room.

Once he was seated, William took a tentative sip. Realizing the coffee was cool enough to drink, he gulped some down. "Thank you. As you may have guessed, this was the first funeral I've ever done, and I was a little nervous."

Mike thumped William lightly on the back. "It didn't show. You seemed to be in perfect control." He glanced across the room to where Betsy stood talking to Kelly. "Betsy seems to be holding up well, don't you think?"

William nodded but made no comment. Despite the fact that Betsy appeared to be doing all right, her eyes looked hollow and tired, like she hadn't slept much since her father's death.

"I wonder if now that her father's gone, Betsy will return to New York and her work with the Salvation Army."

William's hand jerked, and some of the coffee spilled onto the table. If Betsy left, who would play the organ on Sunday mornings? And what about the girls' Sunday school class she'd been teaching? "Has she said anything to you or your wife about leaving?"

"Well, no, but I just assumed—"

"Walnutport is her home, is it not?"

Mike nodded.

"I would think she would want to stay close to the place where her father is buried and where she has friends to offer comfort."

"Maybe she will." Mike smiled. "I guess the only way to know what plans she might make is to come right out and ask her. What do you think, Pastor?"

William set his cup down and reached up to loosen his

tie. "Are you suggesting that I ask what her plans are?"

"I don't see why not." Mike's head bobbed up and down. "You are her pastor, after all."

"Well, yes, that's true, but—"

"I didn't see your housekeeper at the funeral this morning," Clara Andrews interrupted as she plunked down beside William. "That was some tumble she took into the canal last Sunday. I hope she didn't come down with a cold because of it."

"Mrs. Bevens is fine. She's a little embarrassed by what happened, and I don't think she's ready to socialize with anyone yet," William replied.

"Humph!" Clara folded her arms across her ample chest and frowned. "A funeral service is hardly a social function. I would think she would have had the decency to offer her condolences to Rev. Nelson's grieving daughter."

William couldn't argue with that. He had told Mrs. Bevens the same thing this morning when she'd refused to accompany him to the funeral service. "I came to Walnutport to look out for your needs, not to socialize with the people in your congregation," Mrs. Bevens had said.

William figured that with Mrs. Bevens's dour attitude, it was better that she wasn't here today. He was sure she wouldn't have offered Betsy much comfort, and she might have said something rude or condescending.

He glanced across the room again and noticed that Kelly had moved away and Betsy now stood alone. "If you'll excuse me, Clara, I think I should see how Miss Nelson is doing."

Betsy was about to head into the kitchen to see if she could find something that would keep her hands busy, when Pastor William stepped up to her. "I was wondering if there's anything you might need—anything I can do for you."

She bit her bottom lip to stop the flow of tears. Why did it make her feel worse when someone offered help or sympathy? "I'll be fine," she replied, not really believing it. The truth was, Betsy didn't know if she could make it through the next minute, let alone the next hour, day, or week. The future looked bleak and frightening without Papa. She felt like a canal boat that had broken free from its towrope and had no purpose, no sense of direction, no haven of rest.

William touched her arm. "You don't have to go through this alone. The people at the Walnutport Community Church had a great love and respect for your father, and it's obvious that they care about you as well."

"I. . .I appreciate everyone's concern, but I'll be fine."

"You're in the valley right now, Betsy." His tone was comforting. "When we're walking through the valley, we must learn to reach out to God and His people."

She gazed into his dark blue eyes, so full of compassion,

and swallowed around the lump in her throat. "Thank you for that reminder, Pastor William. I've said the same thing to others I've ministered to through the Salvation Army, but it's much harder to accept help than it is to give it."

"I know." He took her hand, and his warm fingers wrapped around hers in a gentle squeeze. "Never be afraid to ask any of us for help. And if ever you need to talk, I'm willing to listen."

Chapter 18

A steady *tap, tap, tap* roused Betsy from her slumber. She yawned, stretched, and pulled herself to a sitting position. She'd curled up on the sofa shortly after breakfast and must have fallen asleep. It had been a week since Papa's death, and still she wasn't sleeping well, so an occasional catnap was probably good for her.

The tapping continued, and Betsy stumbled to the front door, unmindful of her wrinkled dress or tangled hair. When she opened the door, she discovered Kelly standing on the porch, holding a wicker basket.

"I hope I'm not interrupting anything, but I brought a hot meal for your lunch," Kelly said with a friendly smile.

Despite her best efforts, Betsy released a noisy yawn. "Thanks. I haven't felt like cooking much lately, and I've appreciated all the meals the ladies from church have brought in this week." Remembering her manners, she opened the door wider. "Won't you come in, Kelly?"

"You look as if you've been sleeping, and I don't want to disturb you. I can just leave the meal and be on my way."

Betsy pushed a wayward strand of hair out of her face and tried to smile. "That's okay. I was just dozing on the sofa, but I need to get some things done yet today." She stepped aside and motioned Kelly to follow her down the hall.

"Is there anything I can do to help?" Kelly asked when they entered the kitchen. She placed the basket on the table and took a seat.

"Don't you have things to do at the store?"

"Mike said he could manage while I came to see you."

"What about your children? Who's watching them?"

"They're visiting my sister and her family today, so I'd be pleased to stay awhile if you need help with anything."

Betsy paced the length of the kitchen floor, feeling frustrated and kind of jittery. "I guess you could help me pack."

Kelly's eyebrows lifted in obvious surprise. "Pack? Are you going somewhere?"

Betsy stopped pacing and leaned against the counter. "I suppose I'll return to New York. Now that's Papa's gone, there's really no reason for me to stay here."

"Yes there is." Kelly stood and moved over to stand beside Betsy. "Our church needs you—I need you."

Tears welled in Betsy's eyes, blurring her vision. She used to see Kelly as her rival, but since she'd returned to Walnutport, they'd become friends. "That's nice to hear," she murmured. "But the church got along fine without me during the four years I lived in New York, and so did you."

Kelly gave Betsy a hug. "We didn't know what we were missing."

It felt good to be appreciated, and Betsy was about to comment when a knock sounded at the front door again. "Guess I'd better see who that is."

Kelly nodded. "I'll put the stew I brought on the stove so it stays warm."

"Thanks." Betsy hurried out of the room and down the hall. When she opened the door, she found Pastor William standing on the porch with his Bible tucked under his arm.

"Hello, Betsy," he said. "I missed seeing you in church Sunday morning, so I decided to check up on you today."

"I didn't feel up to coming to church, so I was glad Sarah Turner was willing to teach my Sunday school class."

A look of understanding flashed across his face. "It had only been a few days after your father's funeral, so I'm sure you weren't up to going anywhere yet."

Betsy nodded. The truth was, she still felt uncomfortable seeing people or trying to make idle conversation. She missed Papa terribly, and all she wanted to do was crawl into bed, pull the covers over her head, and sleep until the pain subsided.

"How are you doing today, Betsy?"

Instinctively she reached up to smooth the tangles in her hair, which she hadn't bothered to put up in a bun this morning. "I'm doing all right. Kelly Cooper's out in the kitchen, heating some stew she brought for lunch."

William shifted from one foot to the other. "Well, since you've already got company, I guess I should probably be on my way."

"Don't leave on my account," Kelly said as she stepped into the hallway. "There's more than enough stew for the three of us. So if you have the time, Betsy and I would be pleased to have you join us for lunch."

William sniffed the air and grinned. "It does smell good. Sure, I'd be happy to join you."

As William sat at the kitchen table with a bowl of stew and a plate of biscuits sitting before him, he glanced across the table at Betsy. Her face looked drawn, and her eyes were dark and hollow, as if she hadn't slept in several days. He figured she probably hadn't had a good night's rest since her father died. He grimaced. This was one area of the ministry where he fell seriously short. He'd always had trouble knowing what to say to someone who was grieving.

He glanced over at Kelly, who sat beside Betsy. "This is good stew. It's real flavorful."

She grinned back at him. "Thanks. It's one my mama used to make a lot when I was a girl leading Papa's mules up the towpath."

"That must have been hard work for a child."

"It was."

"Do you ever miss it?"

She shook her head. "I'm happy to spend my days raising our children and helping Mike at the store. When I have the time, I like to draw and paint pictures, too."

"Kelly's quite the artist," Betsy spoke up. "Mike even added a small art gallery onto their store so Kelly could paint and sell her artwork there." She smiled, although it never quite reached her eyes. "Several years ago I was the recipient of one of Kelly's beautiful charcoal drawings."

"It was just a silly old picture of two children fishing along the canal," Kelly said. "I'd given a couple of my pictures to Mike to sell in his store, and he ended up giving one of them to Betsy for her birthday."

William looked back at Betsy and noticed her flushed cheeks. It made him wonder if she and Mike had been boyfriend and girlfriend at one time.

"Papa invited Mike to dinner to celebrate my birthday one year." Betsy toyed with the handle of the spoon lying next to her half-eaten bowl of stew. "I think the poor man felt obligated to bring me a present."

"Betsy used to have her eye on Mike," Kelly said. "Then I came along and stole him away."

Betsy's blush deepened, and she stared at the table. "I was a terrible flirt back then, and I'd give anything if I could undo the past."

"It's okay," Kelly said, reaching over to pat Betsy's arm. "I might never have fallen for Mike if you hadn't made me feel so jealous."

"There was nothing to be jealous about. Mike only had eyes for you, and you're a much better wife for him than I could have been."

All this talk about love and marriage conjured up memories of the woman William had once loved and had almost married. Maybe Beatrice had done him a favor by breaking things off. Maybe she wouldn't have made a good preacher's wife.

"Did you know that Betsy's thinking of returning to New York?"

Shock spiraled through him as he turned to face Betsy. "You want to leave Walnutport?"

She shrugged. "I only came back to care for my father. Now that he's gone, there doesn't seem to be any reason for me to stay."

"That's not true. You're needed at church—as the organist and as a Sunday school teacher."

Betsy took a sip of water. "I'm sure you'll find someone to fill those positions after I'm gone."

"Does that mean you're definitely planning to leave?" He wondered how he could talk her out of going and why it mattered so much.

Betsy opened her mouth as if to reply, but Kelly cut her off. "I think she should pray about it, don't you, Pastor?"

He gave a quick nod. "I'll be praying, too."

Chapter 19

*A*s Betsy sat on the top porch step with Bristle Face in her lap, she reflected on her situation. Almost two weeks had passed since her father's death, and still she hadn't made a decision. If she went back to New York, she could continue with her work for the Salvation Army, which she knew would give a sense of purpose to her life. If she stayed in Walnutport, she could continue to play the organ for church and teach Sunday school, and both activities would help to further the Gospel.

"If I leave here, who's going to take care of you, little guy?" Betsy murmured as the terrier nuzzled her hand with his cold, wet nose. "You miss Papa, too, don't you, boy?"

The dog responded with a grunt, and she rubbed his silky ears. "I could see if Pastor William might be willing to take you, but there's the problem of his cranky housekeeper." Mrs. Bevens had never given any indication that she liked Bristle Face. She'd seemed quite upset when the dog kept running over to the parsonage before the fence was built, and she'd been adamant about Betsy keeping Bristle Face at home.

Betsy knew that if she stayed in Walnutport, she might lose her heart to a man who saw her as nothing more than a member of his congregation. And if she wasn't careful, she might end up throwing herself at him, or at least it could appear as if she was doing that.

She squeezed her eyes shut as the truth hit her full in the face. She didn't know when it had happened, but she had fallen in love with the new pastor. *Oh Lord, what would You have me to do? Should I move back to New York or stay here in Walnutport?*

"Yoo-hoo, Betsy! Can you hold on to your dog so I can come into the yard and speak with you about something important?"

Betsy's eyes snapped open, and she squinted against the glare of the afternoon sun. Freda Hanson stood on the walkway in front of the house, frantically waving her hand.

"Come on in. I'll put Bristle Face in the backyard." Betsy hoisted the terrier into her arms and hurried around back. When she returned, she found Freda sitting in one of the wicker chairs on the porch, so she took a seat in the other chair. "What did you wish to speak with me about?"

Freda leaned close to Betsy. "There's a rumor going around that you're thinking of leaving Walnutport. Is it true?"

Betsy nodded. "I've considered going back to New York and resuming my work with the Salvation Army."

"From the accounts I've read in the newspapers, the Salvation Army is a fine organization that does plenty of good deeds." Freda pursed her thin lips. "But you can serve the Lord here in this community, don't you think?"

Freda was the third person since Papa's death to suggest that Betsy was needed here. Could this be God's way of letting her know that He wanted her to stay? Wasn't it what she wanted, too?

"If you decide to stay, Ben and I will allow you to keep living in this house for as long as you like." Freda turned in her chair and motioned toward the front door.

"I know you only gave us the house to use because Papa was ill and had served as your pastor for so many years." A lump formed in Betsy's throat. "If I do stay on, I'll insist on paying you something for the rent."

"Does that mean you've decided to stay?"

"I suppose so. At least for now."

"That's wonderful, and there's no hurry about you paying any rent either. We can talk about that some other time." Freda reached over and clasped Betsy's hand. "Now, I must tell you about the box social our church ladies are planning for next Saturday. We're hoping you will take part in it."

Betsy shook her head. "I'm really not up to socializing yet."

"Oh, but this is for such a good cause. All the money that comes in during the bidding will go to our mission fund."

The words *mission fund* struck a chord with Betsy. How could she ignore something as important as that? At one time she had planned to serve in the mission field herself, and she knew missionaries who were sent to foreign countries needed all the funds they could get. "You can count on me to make a box lunch for the social, but I may not be there to see it bid on."

Freda frowned. "Not be there? Betsy, every woman who donates a box lunch should be in attendance that day. Please say you will come."

Betsy sat there a moment, mulling things over. Finally she released a sigh and nodded. "All right, I'll be at the box social."

The church basement was abuzz with activity, as everyone took a seat to await the bidding at the box social. Boxes and baskets in various sizes and shapes adorned the long wooden table at one end of the room, while the men who'd come to bid and the women who'd donated box lunches sat around the room in segregated groups. William had been asked to oversee this event, and though he'd hoped to act as the auctioneer, Freda Hanson insisted that her husband fill that role. She'd told William he needed a chance to bid on a lunch, and she'd sweetened the deal by letting him know that one of the lunch boxes included a piece of peach pie, which William had told Freda was his favorite kind.

As William took a seat beside Patrick O'Grady, the town's young, able-bodied blacksmith, he glanced across the room and noticed Betsy Nelson sitting beside Hortence Andrews. He was surprised to see Betsy, knowing she was still in mourning and hadn't attended church since her father's death. He'd heard through Freda that, for the time being, Betsy planned to remain in Walnutport, and that pleased him more than he cared to admit. He told himself he was just doing his pastoral duties by being attentive to her needs, but deep down he knew better.

When someone tapped William on the shoulder, he drew his gaze away from Betsy and turned. "Look for a white hatbox with a yellow ribbon, Pastor," Freda whispered in his ear. Before he could comment, she skirted across the room to join the married women.

Once again William focused on the colorful boxes sitting on the table. He spotted a white hatbox, but the ribbon tied around it was green, not yellow. His gaze went from one box to the next: a wicker basket with flowers tied to the handle; a short, square box covered with a red-and-white checkered cloth; a small silver bucket with two purple ribbons attached to the handle; a white hatbox with a bright yellow ribbon— that must be the one Freda spoke of—the one with the peach pie inside. *That's the one I'll bid on,* he decided.

Ben took his place behind the table and held up one hand to get everyone's attention. "The bidding's about to begin. We'll start with this one first." He held up a yellow basket.

William watched with interest as the bidding began. Various boxes went from fifty cents all the way up to three dollars. Since it was for a worthy cause, he was prepared to bid as much as five dollars for the box with the yellow ribbon.

When Ben got to the box William wanted, the auctioneer started the bidding at one dollar. Lars Olsen took the price up to two dollars. William quickly bid three, and from there the cost went to four. "We've got a four-dollar bid on this lovely hatbox!" Ben hollered. "Who'll give me five?"

William's hand shot up. He could almost taste the savory sweetness of that peach pie, and he licked his lips in anticipation.

"The bid's at five dollars. Now who'll give me six?"

The room became silent.

"Five, going once. Five, going twice." Ben slapped his hand on the table. "This lunch box has been sold to the preacher for five dollars!"

William stepped forward and picked up the hatbox,

bending down to sniff the lid. A delicious peach aroma tickled his nose, and he smiled with satisfaction. He hoped there were two pieces in there, because it would be hard to divvy up that peach pie with the woman who'd prepared the box lunch and with whom he knew he must share the meal.

Ben motioned to the women's side of the room. "Will the person who made the lunch inside the box our pastor just purchased please step forward?"

All heads turned, and William's mouth went dry when Betsy Nelson stood and walked slowly toward him.

Lars elbowed William in the ribs. "Sure hope she's got somethin' in that box worth five dollars."

Chapter 20

Betsy squirmed as she watched William spread a quilt on the grass behind the church, knowing they would be sharing a meal together. When she'd agreed to make a lunch for the box social, it hadn't occurred to her that the man who'd buy her lunch would turn out to be Pastor William.

"There, it's all ready. Won't you have a seat?" He nodded toward the quilt.

She smiled. At least she hoped it was a smile. Her knees knocked so badly and her face had heated up so much that she wasn't sure what her expression looked like.

Once they were seated on the quilt, Pastor William offered a blessing, and Betsy opened the hatbox lid. "I hope you like cold chicken," she said, chancing a peek at him.

"Has it been cooked?" he asked with a mischievous twinkle in his eye.

"Of course." She giggled and noticed that, for the first time all day, she felt relaxed. "The dill pickles and coleslaw are the only raw items in this meal."

"If I didn't know better, I'd think you had prepared this special lunch just for me."

"What do you mean?"

"Fried chicken, dill pickles, peach pie—all my favorites."

Betsy squinted, while pointing to the hatbox. "How did you know there's peach pie in there?"

A shadow crossed his face, and he quickly looked away. "Uh—a little birdie informed me."

"Freda Hanson is the only one I told that I'd made peach pie."

The pastor nodded. "Right before the bidding started, Freda whispered in my ear that the white hatbox with a yellow bow had peach pie in it." He glanced across the yard where Ben and Freda sat on a blanket, sharing the lunch Freda had prepared for them.

Betsy gritted her teeth.

Pastor William chuckled. "Oh well, at least I get to have my pie and eat it, too."

She smiled. It was nice to know the pastor had a sense of humor, and Betsy was overcome with the realization that this was the first time since Papa's death that she'd been able to find joy in something.

She reached inside the hatbox and removed the main course, a jug of cold tea, and two thick slices of peach pie for dessert. Then she took out plates, silverware, and a cup for each of them.

"If this tastes half as good as it looks, I'm in for a real treat," Pastor William said, reaching for a drumstick.

"Papa always said I was a good cook, almost as good as Mama used to be."

He bit into the chicken and smacked his lips. "I can't imagine anyone's chicken tasting better than this."

Betsy's neck heated up, and the warmth spread quickly to her cheeks. She wasn't used to getting such compliments—especially from such an attractive man. She felt something for Pastor William, no matter how hard she tried to deny it.

"I heard from the Hansons that you've decided to stay in Walnutport," he said, taking their conversation in another direction.

Betsy nodded. "For now, anyway."

"I'm glad to hear that."

She poured some tea and took a quick drink, hoping it might help calm her nerves. Was it possible that Pastor William wanted her to stay because he had feelings for her? No, that couldn't be. He was just being kind. He probably wanted her to stay so he wouldn't have to look for someone else to play the organ and teach the girls' Sunday school class.

Betsy dismissed her thoughts and decided to enjoy the meal as she listened to Pastor William talk about various needs in the church and how he was finally getting to know the people in his congregation.

They'd just begun clearing away their dishes when Kelly and Mike showed up. Mike suggested the pastor join him in checking on a broken window in the church that needed to be replaced.

Pastor William thanked Betsy for the delicious lunch and excused himself, then Kelly dropped to the quilt beside Betsy. "How did your lunch go?"

"Fine. How was yours?"

"It was good."

Betsy glanced around to be sure no one was listening. "I think Freda Hanson planned it so Pastor William would bid on my hatbox and end up having to eat lunch with me."

Kelly's eyebrows lifted. "Really? You think she's trying to get the two of you together?"

Betsy nodded. "From a couple of things Freda has said to me recently, I get the feeling that she thinks I would make a good pastor's wife."

"She's right. You would."

"I don't think so. I'm too outspoken, and besides, the pastor's not romantically interested in me."

"Then how come he seemed to be having such a good time over here this afternoon?"

"He was being kind and polite, like any good preacher

would be with someone from his congregation."

"Puh!" Kelly waved her hand, as though she were batting at a pesky fly. "If you can't see the way that man looks at you, then you'd better make an appointment with Dr. McGrath and ask him to check your eyes."

Betsy picked at a piece of lint on her dark blue skirt and remained silent. If Kelly wanted to think the preacher had eyes for her, that was Kelly's problem. Betsy was sure he'd only been acting polite today, and the kindness he'd shown toward her was no different than what he would have shown to any of his church members.

Kelly nudged Betsy's arm. "Changing the subject, I was wondering if you'd be free to have supper at our house next Friday."

At first Betsy was tempted to turn down the invitation, but then she thought about how much fun it would be to spend time with Kelly's two little ones. "I'd be happy to join you for supper next week," she said with a nod. "Is there anything I can bring?"

"Just a hearty appetite. Oh, and why don't you wear your hair down that night? It looks so pretty when it's hanging down your back."

Betsy didn't see what difference it made how she wore her hair when she went to the Coopers' house, but she agreeably nodded.

"Great." Kelly patted Betsy's hand. "It will be a fun evening, I'm sure."

Chapter 21

"I t was nice of you to invite me to join you and your family for supper tonight," Betsy said as she stepped into Kelly's cozy kitchen. It was a large room with blue- and white-checkered curtains hanging at the windows and a matching cloth draped over the wooden table. "I know how busy you are with the store and all, so I hope it wasn't too much trouble to fix this meal."

Kelly shook her head and moved over to the counter, where an abundance of fresh vegetables lay beside a huge wooden bowl. "Since our home is attached to the back of the store, it's easy for me to pop over here and get something going on the stove." She nodded toward the table. "Have a seat, and we can visit while I finish getting supper ready."

Betsy glanced around the room. "What needs to be done? I'd be happy to help in any way I can."

Kelly grabbed a head of lettuce and started tearing off the leaves then dropping them into the bowl. "The ham and potatoes are staying warm in the oven, and I just need to finish making the salad, so there's not much else to do right now."

Betsy was about to pull out a chair and sit down when a thought popped into her head. "What about the children? Do they need someone to keep them entertained until supper is ready?"

Kelly looked over her shoulder and grinned. "The little ones are in the living room with their papa, so I'm sure they're bein' well cared for." She nodded toward the cupboard across the room. "I guess you could set the table though."

Betsy pushed the chair in and hurried across the room, glad for the opportunity to do something useful.

When Kelly opened the oven door, the tantalizing aroma of baked ham floated into the room. It was at that moment that Betsy realized she hadn't eaten anything since breakfast, and even that had been a meager meal. Since Papa had died, she hadn't felt much like cooking. Besides, her appetite had diminished. But standing in this warm, welcoming kitchen with such a delicious smell teasing her nose, she realized hunger pangs gnawed at her insides.

Betsy reached into the cupboard and removed five plates.

She'd just begun to place them on the table when Kelly said, "Oh, I forgot to mention that you'll need to put out six place settings."

"Six? But there's only five of us—you, Mike, Anna, Marcus, and me."

"Pastor William will be joining us, too."

Betsy whirled around. "He—he will?"

"Uh-huh." Kelly closed the oven door and moved back to the counter; then she grabbed a tomato, sliced it, and added it to the bowl of lettuce.

"But I thought I was the only one you had invited. I didn't realize the pastor was coming, too." Betsy struggled with her swirling emotions as she leaned against the table. She had enjoyed spending time with Pastor William when they'd shared the box lunch last week, but it concerned her that some people from church had been trying to get her and the pastor together.

"You're okay with Pastor William coming, I hope. I mean, you like him, don't you?"

"What?" Betsy drew in a quick breath and fanned her face with her hand. The room had become so warm all of a sudden.

"Do you like Pastor William or not?"

"Of course I like him, but—"

"Mama, Marcus is botherin' me!" Anna shouted as she dashed into the kitchen from the other room. "Make him give my dolly back!"

"Where's your papa?" Kelly asked, reaching down to hug her fair-haired little girl. "Did you tell Papa that Marcus took your doll?"

Anna's lower lip jutted out. "I tried, but Papa's sleepin' on the sofa."

Kelly glanced at Betsy with an apologetic look. "Would you excuse me a minute so I can tend to this?"

Betsy nodded. "Of course."

Kelly wiped her hands on a towel, and she and Anna scurried out of the room.

Betsy moved back to the cupboard in order to get another plate. She followed that with glasses and silverware for everyone and had just finished setting the table when a knock sounded on the back door. "That's probably Pastor William. Oh I hope I look okay." She took a quick peek at herself in the oval looking glass hanging near the sink and hurried to the door.

When the door opened and William saw Betsy standing inside the Coopers' kitchen with her hair hanging around her shoulders in long, golden waves, his mouth went dry. He couldn't think of a thing to say, and all he could do was stand there, gaping at her.

"H–hello, Pastor William," she said, her voice quavering slightly.

"Betsy. I–I didn't expect to see you here," he stammered.

"Kelly invited me for supper, and only moments ago I found out she'd invited you, too."

He nodded slowly. Had he been set up? Was Kelly in on the little game that some of the other women from church had been playing while trying to match him up with a prospective wife?

"Come in," she said, stepping aside.

As a tantalizing aroma tickled his nose and made his stomach rumble, he shrugged his concerns aside and sniffed the air appreciatively. "Something smells good."

Betsy nodded and began to fill the glasses with water from a pitcher.

William glanced around the room, noting that he and Betsy were the only two people in the kitchen. Was Kelly planning for them to spend the evening alone? "Uh...where's the Cooper family hiding?"

"Kelly's in the living room, tending to a squabble between her two children."

"What about Mike?"

"Anna said her papa had fallen asleep on the sofa, so I guess Kelly will be waking him for supper, too."

"I see." William cleared his throat a couple of times. He didn't like the way he felt whenever he and Betsy were alone—all jittery and filled with a desire to be with her all the time. His heart, which he had vowed never to let love again, pounded away like the blacksmith's anvil every time Betsy was near. It made him wonder if he might be falling in love with her. He'd had those same feelings toward Beatrice. All that had left him with was a broken heart— and a determination never to fall in love again. Betsy seemed sincere and sweet, but he didn't know if she could be trusted. He'd trusted Beatrice, and what had that gotten him? He needed to hold on to what was left of his good sense, because Betsy was threatening to tear his defenses down.

"If you'd like to have a seat, I'm sure the Coopers will be joining us soon," Betsy said motioning to the chair nearest William.

He smiled despite the churning in his stomach and sat down.

"Have you chosen the songs for this Sunday yet?" Betsy asked, taking the chair opposite him.

He nodded. "They're all familiar hymns, so that's why I didn't bring you any music to practice this week." The truth was, he had purposely chosen those hymns so he wouldn't have to be alone with Betsy while they practiced the music. Each time they were together, he found himself wanting something he knew he couldn't have and didn't want. Or so he told himself.

"You're right. I probably don't need to practice the easier hymns." She smiled, and the dimple in her right cheek seemed to be winking at him.

William glanced at the door separating the Coopers' kitchen from their living room. *I wonder what's taking them so long?*

As if she could read his mind, Betsy pushed away from the table and stood. "Maybe I should let Kelly know you're here."

He nodded in reply.

Betsy had made it only halfway across the kitchen when the door flew open and the Cooper children zipped into the room. Anna held a rag doll in one hand and wore a smile that stretched from ear to ear. "I got my dolly back," she said, holding it up to Betsy. "And Marcus got a swat on his backside."

William stifled a chuckle as the two-year-old boy marched over to the table with a lift of his chin. Kids were sure cute. Too bad he would never have any of his own.

"Where's your mama?" Betsy asked, reaching out to touch one of Anna's golden curls.

"In there, tryin' to get Papa off the couch." The child pointed to the door then skipped across the room and climbed onto a chair. "I'm hungry."

Mike entered the room then, rubbing his eyes and yawning, and Kelly strolled in behind him. She smiled when she saw William. "I'm glad you could make it for supper, Pastor. Has Betsy been keeping you company?"

William's face heated. *I think I'm being set up. I'll bet Kelly stayed out in the living room just so Betsy and I could spend a few minutes alone.* He loosened the knot on his tie. *Well, it won't work. I will not give in to my feelings for Betsy Nelson, no matter how much I enjoy being with her.*

Chapter 22

As Betsy stared out her kitchen window at the driving rain, her thoughts took her back to the supper she and Pastor William had shared at the Coopers' house two weeks ago. Despite her apprehension, the meal had turned out quite well. After they'd enjoyed some of Kelly's delicious apple pie for dessert, the children were put to bed, while the two couples spent the rest of the evening sitting around the kitchen table, drinking hot chocolate, playing dominoes, and visiting. Betsy had felt so comfortable with Pastor William that it had almost seemed as if she'd known him all her life.

"I wonder if he felt the same way about me," she

murmured. "He seemed much more at ease than he has in the past."

Bristle Face, who lay curled in a tight ball in front of the woodstove, lifted his head and whimpered, as if in response.

Ever since Papa's death, Betsy had found companionship and comfort in the dog. There were times when she wondered if Bristle Face actually felt her pain. Or maybe it was just that the dog missed Papa, too.

The window rattled from a rumble of thunder that shook the morning sky, and Betsy shuddered. She disliked storms, and this was one of the worst they'd had in quite some time. It had rained continuously for almost a week, and it didn't look as though it would let up anytime soon.

"Sure hope the canal walls hold together," she said with a shake of her head. If the canal was shut down, even for a short time, it would affect the boatmen, as well as everyone who lived or worked near the canal. It had happened several times during the years Betsy and her father had lived in Walnutport, but the community had always banded together and overcome even the worst of storms.

Another clap of thunder sounded, and Betsy moved away from the window. She had several shirts to mend for some of the canalers and figured she'd better get busy, since she had promised to have them done by tomorrow. She opened her mending basket, took a seat in the rocking chair by the woodstove, and set to work on one of the most tattered shirts.

Bristle Face lifted his head again and grunted.

"It's okay, boy. Go back to sleep. I'm just going to sit here awhile and sew."

The dog lowered his head and nestled his paws, but a sudden knock on the back door brought him quickly to his feet. He darted to the door, barking frantically, until Betsy shushed him.

She was surprised to discover Pastor William on the porch, wearing a heavy black jacket and a pair of dark trousers. It was the first time she'd seen him out of his suit, and his sopping wet clothes dripped water all over the porch.

"I just got the news that the canal has broken in several places," he panted. "Water's rushing everywhere, the towpath is completely covered, and already several homes have been flooded."

Betsy grimaced. "I'm sorry to hear that."

He nodded. "I know you don't have a lot of room here, but I was wondering if you might be able to put a few people up, should it become necessary."

"Of course," Betsy answered without hesitation. "I'm sure others in town will help, too. In the past when we've had a storm such as this, Papa opened the church for meals and lodging to accommodate those who had no other place to go."

"I've already discussed that idea with the board of deacons, and cots are being set up in the church basement as we speak."

"Would you like to come inside for a cup of hot tea?"

Betsy asked. "I've got a fire going in the woodstove, and it will give you a chance to get dried off a bit before you head out into this nasty weather again."

Pastor William glanced over his shoulder. "I appreciate the offer, but I should probably get back to the church and help the men set up those cots."

Betsy nodded and was about to tell him good-bye when Bristle Face darted out the door and pawed at Pastor William's knees with an excited whine. "Get down, Bristle Face," she scolded. "You know better than to jump on anyone like that."

Pastor William bent down and patted the dog's head. "I think he misses his regular visits to the parsonage."

Betsy shook her head. "I believe it's you he misses. I've never seen Bristle Face take to anyone the way he has you."

He smiled and swiped at the raindrops that had dripped from his hair onto his chin. "Maybe I will take you up on that cup of tea. It'll give me and Bristle Face a chance to visit a few minutes."

"Right." Betsy opened the door farther and bid him entrance as a sense of disappointment flooded her soul. Why couldn't it be *her* Pastor William wanted to visit? Was she so unappealing that he would prefer a dog to her company? Well, she wouldn't flirt in order to get his attention—that much she knew.

"It's nice and warm in here," Pastor William said, stepping into the kitchen behind her. "I've never cared much for damp weather, and this drenching rain is enough to chill me clear to the bone."

"I know what you mean." Betsy motioned to the row of wall pegs near the door. "Why don't you hang up your jacket and take a seat at the table? I'll put a kettle of water on the stove and have a cup of tea ready in no time."

William did as she suggested, and as soon as he'd taken a seat, Bristle Face hopped into his lap. Before Betsy could holler at the dog, William smiled. "It's okay. I like the little fellow."

"That's fine, but he will have to get down once I put the tea and cookies on the table," she said with a shake of her head.

William's eyebrows lifted, and he wiggled them up and down. "Cookies? What kind have you got?"

"Oatmeal. I made a batch yesterday morning."

"I've never cared much for hot oatmeal as a breakfast food, but it's sure good in cookies."

Betsy smiled and hurried over to the stove. As soon as she put the water on to boil, she placed a tray of cookies on the table and took two cups down from the cupboard.

A short time later she joined him at the table, and Bristle Face, who'd been put on the floor, lay under the table, snoring.

For the next half hour, Pastor William and Betsy discussed the storm, how they could offer aid to those who might be flooded out of their homes, and how good it was to know that many people from their church would be willing to help out.

Finally Pastor William pushed his chair away from the table and stood. "Thank you for the tea and cookies. I should get back to the church and see what I can do to help out. If things keep going as they are, probably several families will be in need of shelter by nightfall."

Betsy followed him across the room, where he slipped into his jacket and headed for the door. "As soon as I finish mending the shirts I promised to have done by the end of the day, I'll come over to the church and see what I can do to help."

He smiled and took a step toward her. "Thank you, Betsy. I appreciate that."

Betsy's mouth went dry. The strange sensation that came over her whenever Pastor William looked at her was unnerving. Even more unsettling was the urge she had to hurl herself into his arms and declare the love she felt for him. The old Betsy might have considered such a bold move, but now she would never dream of being so audacious.

"Maybe I'll see you a little later then." He turned and walked out the door.

For the next several days, rain continued to pelt the earth. William spent every waking moment ministering to someone in need either at the church, where many had come to take refuge, or at homes where some who were ill were able to remain. When the rain finally stopped, a group of men began working on the breaks that had occurred in several places along the canal. Despite Mrs. Bevens's insistence that William's place was in town, he'd offered his assistance wherever he was needed at the canal.

As William settled himself at the kitchen table for his devotions one morning, he was overcome with a sense of gratitude and amazement as he reflected on how well the community had rallied to help one another during this unforeseen disaster.

He thought about Betsy Nelson and how each day she had spent several hours at the church, helping cook and serve meals for those who'd taken shelter there. At home, Betsy washed and mended clothes free of charge. She'd also taken Sarah Turner and her children into her home, because the first floor of their lock tender's house had been badly flooded. Since the boats weren't running and many of the locks were broken, including the one in Walnutport, Sarah's husband, Sam, spent his days helping with repairs on the canal breaks. At night, he slept on the one of the canalers' boats so he would be close at hand when the work began each morning.

Leaning back in his chair, William laced his fingers behind his head and closed his eyes. A vision of Betsy came to mind. He'd spent most of the night thinking about

Betsy, in spite of trying not to. She seemed to be everything he wanted in a wife—if he was looking for one. She was talented, helpful, selfless, and kind. And she made some of the best-tasting oatmeal cookies he'd ever eaten.

"What's that silly grin you're wearing all about?" Mrs. Bevens placed a cup of coffee in front of him and tipped her head. "I would think as tired as you must be from working so hard this past week you'd be grumpier than an old bear."

His eyes snapped open, and he looked up at her sullen face. "On the contrary, I find helping others to be quite rewarding—even exhilarating."

"Humph! You'll wear yourself out if you're not careful, and I doubt your hard work will be appreciated."

He ran his fingers along the edge of his Bible. "Proverbs 19:22 says, 'The desire of a man is his kindness.' It's my desire to be kind and helpful to others because I care about them, not so they will show their appreciation."

Mrs. Bevens shrugged and moved over to the sink, and William went back to reading the Bible.

When a knock sounded on the back door, Mrs. Bevens hurried to answer it. She returned to the kitchen with Mike Cooper at her side. "I'm sorry to bother you, Pastor," he said, "but there's been an accident at the canal, and you're needed right away."

"An accident?" William jumped up, nearly knocking over his chair.

Mrs. Bevens pursed her lips. "Shouldn't the doctor be

called for something like that?"

"Dr. McGrath has already been notified, and he's on his way." Mike's eyes were huge, and his lips compressed. "I'm thinking poor Sam Turner may have more need of a preacher right now than he does a doctor."

Chapter 23

William was relieved to see that Mike had brought along two horses. They would get them to the canal quicker than by taking the time to hitch up a wagon or trudging on foot through the murky floodwaters. After slipping his Bible into the saddlebag while offering up a prayer for Sam, he mounted his horse and followed Mike to the other side of town.

A short time later, they arrived at the Walnutport lock, which was where Mike said the accident had occurred. Dr. McGrath's rig was parked outside the lock tender's house, and several boatmen stood near the front door, wearing anxious expressions.

"The doc's got Sam inside on a table. Guess it's about

the only piece of furniture that ain't covered in water," Bill Bellini said, shaking his head. "It don't look good for Sam. No, it don't look good a'tall."

"Can you tell me exactly what happened?" William asked after he and Mike had dismounted and tied their horses to the hitching rail.

Bill nodded grimly. "A boat broke loose from where it was tied, and then it floated over to the lock and got jammed. Sam and several others were workin' hard at tryin' to get it free."

"That's right," another burly man spoke up. "Me, Slim, and Amos was tryin' to help Sam when things went sour." He grimaced and pulled his fingers through the ends of his wiry beard. "Sam was standin' on top of the lock, and his foot must have slipped, 'cause from what I could tell, he tumbled straight into the water. Next thing we knew, the boat shifted, and Sam was smashed between it and the lock." The boatman paused and gulped in a quick breath. "It took all three of us to get him out, but I ain't sure it did much good, 'cause that poor fellow's in real bad shape."

William reached into his saddlebag and pulled out his Bible before following Mike into the house. "May God's will be done," he whispered.

"Are you sure you wouldn't like another cup of tea?" Betsy asked Sarah as the two of them sat at her kitchen table, doing some mending while Sarah's three little ones took their naps.

Sarah looked up and smiled. "I've already had three cups, and if I have one more, I might float right out the door."

Betsy chuckled. She enjoyed Sarah's company and, during the time Sarah and the children had been staying with her, the two of them had gotten better acquainted. Betsy had come to realize that she and Sarah could be good friends, and she hoped they could spend more time together even after Sarah and her children were able to return home. *Of course,* she reasoned, *Sarah keeps awful busy caring for her little ones and helping Sam bring the canal boats through the lock. She probably doesn't have a lot of free time on her hands.*

A knock at the back door drove Betsy's musing aside, and she excused herself to answer it.

When she opened the door, she was surprised to see Pastor William standing there with a pained expression on his face. "Is. . .is Sarah here? I need to speak with her right away."

Betsy nodded. "Would you like to come in and join us for a cup of tea?"

He shook his head. "There's no time for tea."

Betsy grimaced. She had a sinking feeling that something terrible had happened and it involved Sarah's husband. "Please come in. You'll find Sarah in the kitchen."

Pastor William took a few steps forward and halted. He leaned close to Betsy's ear. "Sarah's going to need you at her side when she hears my news."

Not since the day Papa died had Betsy seen their pastor looking so glum, and with a sense of dread, she led the way to the kitchen.

Sarah looked up from her mending as soon as they entered the room and smiled. "Pastor William, it's nice to see you." Her smile quickly faded. "You look upset. Is something wrong?"

He moved quickly across the room and sat in the chair beside Sarah. Betsy took the seat on the other side of her. "There's been an accident at the lock." The pastor placed one hand on Sarah's shoulder.

"Is. . .is it Sam?" Sarah's lower lip quivered, and her eyes opened wide.

"Yes, Sarah."

"Wh–what happened?"

"One of the boats that had been tied near your home broke loose and got stuck in the lock. Sam and a couple of other men tried to get the boat out, and. . ." He paused and glanced over at Betsy as though seeking her help.

Betsy reached for Sarah's hand to offer support. She dreaded Pastor William's next words.

"There's no easy way to tell you this, but Sam—he fell into the water, and his body was smashed between the boat and the lock."

Sarah gasped and covered her mouth with her hand. "Is he. . .dead?"

He nodded soberly. "He died soon after I arrived."

The color drained from Sarah's face, and she slumped over. Betsy grabbed one arm, and Pastor William grabbed the other as they helped her over to the sofa in the living room.

Several minutes passed before Sarah was composed enough to speak again, and when she did, her first words came out in a squeak. "Was. . .was there time for you to pray with Sam?"

"Yes. I read him the twenty-third Psalm."

"Sam didn't always believe in God," Sarah said tearfully. "But two years ago he started attending the services Pastor Nelson held along the canal. One day he prayed and asked God to forgive his sins." Her voice broke on a sob. "He was a changed man after that and attended church nearly every Sunday."

Betsy was at a loss for words. All she could do was cling to her friend's hand and murmur, "I'm sorry, Sarah. I'm so sorry."

The next several weeks went by in a blur. Pastor William conducted the funeral for Sam Turner, helped finish up the canal repairs, and assisted Sarah and her family as they moved back to the lock tender's house. Betsy pleaded with Sarah not to go, insisting that she and the children could stay with her as long as they wanted. But Sarah was adamant about leaving. "I must support my children," she'd said over a cup of coffee one morning. "I'm responsible for the Walnutport lock now, and I've got to do whatever it takes to provide for my children's needs."

Betsy couldn't argue with that, but she did have some concerns about Sarah's ability to run the lock by herself. Sam's mother, Maria, who had been living in Easton with her older son since her husband's death two years ago, had agreed to move back to Walnutport to help care for Sarah's children. That relieved Betsy's mind some, and she was sure that many in the community would help the Turner family in any way they could.

Betsy had clothes to wash for some of the boatmen who were back to work hauling coal up and down the canal. Tomorrow morning she planned to go over to the church and practice some songs for Sunday morning's service. After that she hoped to visit Sarah and her children and take them a basket of food for their evening meal.

Reaching into the cupboard underneath the sink, Betsy retrieved a washtub and a bar of lye soap. Kelly had been trying to get her to buy some of the pure white floating soap they sold in their store, but Betsy preferred the homemade kind, believing it got the clothes cleaner. Besides, she had gone through a lot of soap since she'd started taking in washing, and the lye soap she made was cheaper than the store-bought kind.

She opened the back door and set the tub on the porch. Then she returned to the kitchen to get the kettle of water she had heated on the stove. Once that was dumped into the washtub and she'd added the bar of soap and stirred it around, she dropped three shirts in to let them soak. Then she went back inside to fetch her washboard.

When she returned a few minutes later, she was surprised to see Bart Jarmon, one of the canalers, standing on the porch. Bart was a tall, burly man with a thick crop of kinky black hair and a wooly beard that matched. As far as Betsy knew, Bart had never been married, and since he wasn't a churchgoer and had quite a foul mouth, it came as no surprise to her that he had no wife.

"I'm sorry, Bart," she said politely, "but your shirts won't be done until later today. When you dropped them off on Monday, I thought I told you they wouldn't be ready until late afternoon on Thursday."

He shuffled his boots across the wooden porch slats and grinned at her in a disconcerting way. "Figured I'd come by early, just in case."

Betsy motioned to the washtub on the other end of the porch. "As you can see, I've just begun my washing for the day."

Bart pulled his beefy fingers through the ends of his beard. "That's okay. I can wait."

Wait? Bart had to be joking. It would take Betsy awhile to get the shirts washed and rinsed, and then it would be a few more hours until they were sufficiently dried. When she told him that, he merely shrugged and plopped down on the top porch step with a grunt.

"Aren't you boating today?" Betsy asked, hoping the reminder of work might persuade the man to leave.

He shook his head. "Gotta hole in my boat that needs fixin', so I'm takin' a couple days off."

"Well then, shouldn't you be down at the canal, working on the boat?"

"Nope. Got Abe Wilson, my helper, doin' that."

"I see." Betsy shifted restlessly. Should she go about her washing and ignore Bart, or should she insist that he leave? Maybe it would be best to get on with the clothes washing. She moved to the other side of the porch, knelt in front of the washtub, and reached in to pick up the first shirt.

She'd only been scrubbing a few minutes when she felt a strong hand touch her shoulder. Turning, she was shocked to see Bart staring at her in a most peculiar way. "What's wrong? Why are you looking at me like that?"

His lips curved into a wide smile, revealing a set of badly stained teeth. "I was just wonderin' how come a purty lady like you ain't married."

Before Betsy could think of a sensible reply, Bart dropped to his knees beside her. "If you was my wife, you wouldn't have to wash for anyone but me, and I'd be the only one earnin' a living."

"I assure you, I'm getting along fine by myself." She

wrung out the first shirt, set it aside, and picked up the second one.

With no warning, Bart leaned closer, grabbed Betsy's cheeks between his calloused hands, and kissed her squarely on the mouth.

She jerked back, reeling from the shock of his kiss and feeling as though it was her mouth that needed a good washing instead of Bart's shirts. "How dare you take such liberties!" She plucked the rest of his shirts from the water, grabbed the one she'd set aside, and threw them at him.

As Betsy stood on shaky legs, she shook her finger in his face. "Don't come back here anymore, Bart Jarmon, because even if I were starving to death, I would never do business with you again!"

Chapter 24

William placed his sermon notes on the pulpit and pulled his watch from the pocket of his trousers. He was supposed to meet Betsy here at ten o'clock so they could go over some songs for the service tomorrow; it was already ten fifteen, and she hadn't shown up.

Had she slept in this morning and been too tired to come? William smiled as he thought about how tirelessly Betsy had worked to help those who'd been without homes or jobs during the previous weeks of flooding. Betsy had shared her home, her food, and her time, and he'd never heard her complain.

He gripped the edge of the pulpit, as the truth slammed

into him with such force he feared he might topple over. He didn't know when or how it had happened, but he'd fallen hopelessly in love with Betsy. He'd foolishly lowered his defenses and allowed his heart to open up to this sweet, caring woman with the voice of an angel.

William whirled around to face the wooden cross that hung between the stained glass windows behind him then folded his hands and squeezed his eyes shut. *Heavenly Father, Betsy has given me no indication that she's anything like Beatrice, yet I'm afraid to trust again. I believe Betsy cares for me, but does she love me? Do I dare let her know how I feel and risk possible rejection? Oh Lord, please show me what to do.*

A door slammed shut, and when William heard the shuffle of feet, it ended his prayer. He turned and was surprised to see Ben Hanson enter the sanctuary, wearing a dour expression. Had something happened? Could there have been another accident on the canal?

He stepped off the platform and moved quickly toward the deacon. "What is it, Ben? You look upset."

The older man clenched his fists, as he held his body rigid. "I am upset, and I need your advice."

William motioned to the closest pew. "Let's have a seat, and you can tell me what's wrong."

Ben nodded as he sank to the pew. "Actually, it's my wife who's the most upset. And when Freda's upset, it upsets me."

William took the seat beside him. "What's the problem?"

Ben folded his arms. "Freda was heading over to see Betsy yesterday morning, and she was about to enter the backyard when she caught sight of Betsy kissing one of the canalers."

William's mouth dropped open, and a muscle on the side of his neck went into a spasm. Surely this couldn't be true. He couldn't imagine Betsy kissing any of the rugged boatmen who often used foul language and rarely came to church.

"I can see by your look of surprise that you're as shocked as I was to learn of this news." Ben slowly shook his head. "Kissing a man in broad daylight doesn't seem like something Betsy would do, but if Freda says she saw it, then it must be true."

William cleared his throat. "I'm sure there must be some logical explanation." *There has to be. Betsy can't be in love with someone else.*

"What kind of explanation could there be?"

"I don't know."

"Freda doesn't think we should continue to allow Betsy to rent our house if she's going to carry on like that with the boatmen."

William lifted his hand. "I can't believe you would evict Betsy when you haven't heard her side of the story. Besides, it's not our place to judge her. Only God has that right."

"I told Freda the same thing, but she says...." Ben paused

and clasped William's shoulder. "Will you speak with Betsy about this, Pastor?"

"I suppose I could." William stood, hoping Ben would take the hint and leave. If Betsy were to show up soon, he didn't think it would be good for Ben to be here when he confronted her about what Freda had seen.

"I think Freda was hoping it would be you Betsy would fall for, not one of the canalers like Bart, who's so rough around the edges." Ben shuffled his feet a couple of times and stared at the floor.

William grimaced as confusion swirled in his head like the raging canal floodwaters. If what Freda said she saw was true, then maybe the reason Betsy hadn't shown up at the church this morning was because she was too embarrassed by her actions to face the pastor.

"I'd best be getting back home to Freda. She'll be anxious to hear how my meeting went with you." Ben shuffled up the aisle, calling over his shoulder, "As soon as you've spoken to Betsy, let me know what she said!"

For the next several minutes William stood there, feeling too stunned and confused to know what to do. He needed to speak with Betsy, but how should he broach the subject of Freda's accusation? Should he simply march up to Betsy, tell her that Freda had seen her kissing one of the boatmen, and then demand an explanation? Or should he try to get Betsy to tell him what had happened yesterday morning of her own accord?

He pulled his pocket watch out of his trousers for the second time and noted that it was now ten thirty. She was obviously not coming. Maybe he should go over to her place and tell her that he was concerned because she hadn't shown up to practice the songs as they'd planned.

William started up the aisle and had just reached the foyer, when the front door opened. Betsy stepped inside, her cheeks flushed, and several strands of hair that had come loose from her bun were swirling around her neck.

"I'm sorry I'm late," she said with a huff. "I had a little problem with Bristle Face this morning, and it took me awhile to tend to the matter."

He felt immediate concern. "Bristle Face? What's happened to the dog?"

"It seems there was a skunk prowling around our house last night, and the dog must have gotten in its path." She shook her head. "I spent several hours trying to get that putrid smell out of Bristle Face's hair, but the poor animal still reeks, and I'm afraid he'll have to stay outside for a while."

William chuckled. He could just picture that little dog sitting in a tub of water, covered with lye soap and tomato juice.

"Shall we see about selecting some songs and practicing them now?" Betsy moved toward the sanctuary.

William halted, leaning against the doorjamb that separated the foyer from the sanctuary. "I. . .uh. . .need to discuss something with you first."

As Betsy followed Pastor William into the other room, a feeling of dread came over her. He looked so solemn, and the tone he had used when he'd said they needed to discuss something made her wonder if she'd done something wrong. Was he unhappy with the way she'd been playing the organ? She did tend to play a bit loudly, and maybe he thought the music was too lively.

When they reached the front of the sanctuary, he motioned to the first pew. "Please, have a seat."

She smoothed the wrinkles in her long, gray skirt and sat.

Pastor William took a seat on the same pew but left enough space between them to accommodate two people. He sat there several seconds, staring at his folded hands.

Unable to stand the suspense, Betsy turned to face him. "Is something wrong?"

His serious expression sent shivers up her spine. "It has come to my attention. . . ." He paused and cleared his throat. "Someone said that. . . ." He looked away as though unable to meet her gaze.

"If this is about my organ playing, I'll try to tone it down some."

"No, no, it's not about that. I. . .uh. . .someone said that they had seen you the other morning on your back porch with a man."

Betsy nodded. "I did laundry yesterday, and several of the boatmen came by in the afternoon to pick up their clean clothes."

He stood and moved to stand in front of the communion table. "It was one of the canalers this person saw you with, and you were. . .uh. . .kissing him."

Betsy's mouth felt so dry she could barely swallow. Someone must have witnessed what had happened between her and Bart.

"Is it true, Betsy? Were you kissing a man on your porch?"

Her face heated up. "Bart kissed me, but I did nothing to encourage it. I threw his wet shirts at him and said I never wanted to do business with him again."

At first, Pastor William looked relieved, but then he frowned. "If I wasn't a minister of God, I would march down to the canal, wait for Bart's boat to come through, climb aboard, and punch him in the nose."

Betsy swallowed around the laughter bubbling in her throat. Pastor William was jealous, and he wanted to defend her reputation. What a glorious thought! What a glorious day!

Chapter 25

Pastor William continued to stare at Betsy in a most peculiar way, and a shiver started low on her spine and fluttered up her neck. "Are—are you upset because Bart kissed me?" she squeaked.

His ears turned pink, and the blush spread quickly to his cheeks. "I. . .I don't want to think about any man kissing you—unless it's me."

"Pastor William," Betsy murmured, feeling more flustered by the moment.

"I–I'm sorry. I shouldn't have said that. It's just that I. . ." His voice trailed off, and his gaze fell to the floor.

She left her seat and took a step forward. "You what?

What were you going to say?"

Slowly he lifted his head until their gazes locked. "As hard as I've fought against it, I find that I'm hopelessly in love with you, Betsy."

"You—you are?"

He nodded. "I was jilted at the altar about a year ago, and the pain and shame of it left me full of mistrust. I'd convinced myself that I could never love or trust another woman, but getting to know you has changed my mind."

Betsy swallowed hard and blinked against stinging tears that threatened to spill over. No matter what happened in the future, this special moment would be imprinted on her heart forever.

"I love you, too," she said in a voice barely above a whisper.

"What did you say?"

"I love you, too, Pastor William."

"I was hoping you would say that." He chuckled. "But don't you think it's time you started calling me William?"

She nodded slowly.

"You know what I think we should do?" he asked, reaching for her hand.

Her hand fit so well in his. It was as if they'd touched like this before, if only in her dreams. "What do you think we should do?"

"I think we should practice our songs for tomorrow and then go over to the Hansons' and have a little talk with Freda. She needs to know the truth about what happened between you and Bart, so she doesn't spread any ugly rumors."

"I suppose that would be a good idea. And then I want to pay a call on Sarah and her children. I've made a big batch of pork float and thought I would take it there for supper."

He smacked his lips. "That sounds good. Maybe I'll accompany you there, and we can share the meal with them."

Betsy smiled. "I'm sure they would appreciate a visit from their pastor, and I would enjoy the company on the trip over there as well."

"That's good to hear, because the two of us have much to talk about."

As Betsy prepared for church the following morning, she burst out singing. " 'Praise God, from whom all blessings flow. Praise Him, all creatures here below. Praise Him above, ye heavenly host. Praise Father, Son, and Holy Ghost.' "

In all her thirty-one years, she had never felt so deliriously happy. She loved William, and he loved her. After a suitable time of courtship, he might ask her to marry him. Hearing his declaration of love had seemed too good to be true, and Betsy felt like pinching herself to be sure she wasn't dreaming.

"William is all I've ever wanted in a man," she murmured

to her reflection in the mirror. "He's kindhearted, gentle, handsome, even tempered, and next to Papa, he's the finest preacher I've ever heard."

Betsy reflected on how William had handled things when they'd gone to see Freda and Ben Hanson. He'd said there had been a misunderstanding and that what Freda had actually seen was Bart kissing Betsy, not the other way around. Betsy had then explained her reaction to Bart. Freda had expressed sorrow for jumping to conclusions and explained that she'd walked away after she'd seen them kissing, so she hadn't witnessed whatever had followed.

After Betsy and William had left the Hansons' home, they'd gone to Betsy's to get the pork float she'd made and then headed in Betsy's buckboard to the lock tender's house to see Sarah and her family. They had used that time to get better acquainted. When William had asked if he could court Betsy, they'd discussed various things they might do on a date. Since winter would arrive in a few months and the weather was turning colder, picnics were out of the question.

"But we can go for buggy rides, take long walks, and go out to supper at one of the restaurants in town," William had said as he held Betsy's hand.

"Come winter, we can go ice skating, sledding, or sleigh riding," Betsy had happily added.

By the time they'd reached Sarah's house, Betsy had been so excited she could hardly contain herself. She wanted to shout to her friend and to all the world that she and William were in love and that he'd asked to court her. But she'd held herself in check, knowing she could share the news with Sarah some other time when they were alone and she wouldn't embarrass William.

Betsy pinched her cheeks one more time, grabbed her shawl and Bible from the end of her bed, and hurried out of the room.

"You're going to do what?"

William pushed his chair away from the table and stood. He didn't care for the shrill tone of his housekeeper's voice, and he wasn't going to stay here and listen to one of her insistent lectures. "I'm going to court Betsy Nelson." He grabbed his Bible from the kitchen counter and started for the back door.

Mrs. Bevens jumped up and positioned herself between him and the door. "Where are you going?"

"To church, and I don't want to be late."

"But. . .but we need to talk about this."

"What's there to talk about?"

She planted her hands on her hips and scowled at him. "I can't believe you actually want to court that woman."

"Her name is Betsy, and I love her."

Mrs. Bevens's normally pale cheeks turned bright pink.

"She's not right for you, William."

"I think she is."

"There's been a conspiracy at church to get the two of you together, and I think Betsy is in on it. Why, I wouldn't be surprised if every encounter you've had with Betsy wasn't set up by her or one of her cohorts. I'm sure she's only after you for your money."

William bit back a chuckle. This conversation was bordering on ridiculous. "What money are you talking about, Mrs. Bevens? I'm a poor preacher now. Have you forgotten that?"

She shook her head. "Need I remind you that your family is quite well off. Some day when your father is gone, everything will be yours."

"I have a brother, in case you've forgotten. I'm sure my parents will see that Robert gets half of their estate after they've passed on." William grunted. "Besides, I'm sure Betsy isn't interested in riches or prestige, and when the time is right, I'm going to ask her to be my wife." Before Mrs. Bevens had the chance to comment, William rushed out the door.

Chapter 26

Betsy shivered against the cold as she stepped out the back door and placed Bristle Face's dish of food on the porch. It wouldn't be long until parts of the canal would have to be drained. Then all the boatmen would look for other jobs during the frigid winter months. Some would find work in the city of Easton, and others would stay near the canal to cut ice or find other jobs that would keep them busy until the spring thaw allowed them to boat again. Betsy wouldn't have as many customers to sew and wash clothes for, but she didn't mind. Hopefully she and William would be able to spend more time together, too.

Sunday after church, he had suggested that the two of

them have supper together on Friday evening. That was only a day away now, and she could hardly wait.

A blast of wind whipped against Betsy's skirt, and she pushed her thoughts aside. "Here, Bristle Face! Come get your breakfast!" she called, scanning the yard to see where the terrier might be.

When Betsy saw no sign of the little dog, she clapped her hands and called for him again. A few minutes later, the terrier stuck his head out of a bush where he had obviously been sleeping. He barked, dashed across the yard, leaped onto the porch, and skidded over to his bowl.

"Slow down," she said with a chuckle. "You can't be that hungry."

Betsy was tempted to stay and watch the dog eat, but the frigid wind drove her back to the warmth of her kitchen. Once inside she poured herself a cup of tea and was about to take a seat at the table, when she heard a knock at the front door. *I wonder who that could be.*

When Betsy opened the door, she was surprised to see Mrs. Bevens standing on the porch, wrapped in a heavy shawl and shivering badly. "I n–need to speak w–with you."

"Of course. Please come inside where it's warmer."

Mrs. Bevens nodded curtly and stepped into the hallway.

"If you'd like to go into the kitchen, we can have a cup of tea."

"That will be fine."

When they entered the cozy room, Mrs. Bevens took

a seat at the table and Betsy went to the cupboard to get another cup and saucer. She filled the cup with hot tea and placed it in front of Mrs. Bevens. "What brings you by on such a chilly morning?"

"I'm here about William."

Betsy smiled and slipped into the chair opposite the woman. "That was a fine sermon he preached on Sunday morning, wasn't it?"

Mrs. Bevens shrugged, then she picked up her cup and took a sip of tea. "I have known William for most of his life."

Betsy nodded. "I understand you used to be his nanny."

Mrs. Bevens squinted as her lips compressed. "I've been widowed for several years and never had any children of my own, but William is like a son to me." She paused and flicked her tongue across her lower lip. "So as his housekeeper and previous nanny, I feel it's my duty to care for him."

"I understand."

Mrs. Bevens shook her head. "No, I don't think you do. I don't believe you have any conception of what William needs or what makes him happy."

Betsy's face heated up. "I haven't known William nearly as long as you, but we are getting better acquainted, and—"

"I hope you have no designs on him because it wouldn't be right for William to marry someone beneath his social standing."

Betsy's mouth dropped open, and she set her cup down

so quickly that some of the tea spilled out and splashed onto the saucer.

Mrs. Bevens leaned forward slightly and stared hard at Betsy. "If and when William decides to take a wife, he will choose a woman who comes from the same background as himself. Someone like you, who lacks all the necessary social graces, would not make a good wife for the Reverend William Covington III." Mrs. Bevens drew in a deep breath and released it with a huff. "The only reason William has shown any interest in you is because he's become bored with this little hick town and needs some form of entertainment."

Betsy blinked as though coming out of a trance. She could hardly believe the things Mrs. Bevens had said to her. Surely they couldn't be true. The William she'd come to know and love couldn't possibly care about money, prestige, or social graces. "William doesn't seem bored," she said in his defense. "He's done well in his ministry here in Walnutport, and the way he reacts to those in his congregation seems genuine to me."

Mrs. Bevens took a long, slow drink of tea, and when she set her cup down again, her lips curved into a crooked smile. "I agreed to come here as William's housekeeper as a favor to his mother. She asked me to care for her son and keep an eye on him. She wanted to be sure that no one would ever hurt her boy again."

"You mean the way Beatrice did?" Betsy asked.

"You know about his fiancée?"

Betsy nodded. "I understand that she left him standing at the altar."

"That's right, and I'm here to see that it never happens again."

"I assure you, I'm not like Beatrice. I would never hurt William in such a way."

Mrs. Bevens pushed her chair away from the table and stood. "I plan to see that you never do."

Betsy stood, too. "What does that mean?"

"It means that if you do not stop seeing William, I will tell him that you're only interested in him because of his money and that you're looking for a way to climb the ladder of success by marrying into a prestigious family such as his."

"But that's not true." Betsy was close to tears, and she gripped the back of her chair tightly, hoping to keep her emotions in check. "I love William, and I think he knows me well enough to realize that I'm not after his family's money."

Mrs. Bevens tapped her toe against the hardwood floor. "There's something else you should know."

"What's that?"

"Even if William did choose to accept a commoner such as yourself, his family never could. Would you want to be the one responsible for coming between William and his parents?" She pursed her lips. "Don't make him choose between you and them. If you really love William, prove it by stepping aside so he can find someone who is worthy of being his wife. Someone he would not be ashamed to take home to meet his family. Someone his parents would readily accept."

Before Betsy could say anything more, Mrs. Bevens turned on her heel and marched out of the room. Betsy heard the front door slam shut. Resting her head on the table, she gave in to her tears.

When Betsy climbed out of bed the following morning, she had made a decision. She couldn't come between William and his family, no matter how much she loved him. The best thing for her to do was return to New York and her position with the Salvation Army, which she probably should have done right after her father died. If she'd left Walnutport sooner, she wouldn't have fallen in love with William and wouldn't be facing this problem.

Betsy's gaze came to rest on the Bible lying on the small table beside her bed. "I love William and would like to be his helper in the ministry," she murmured, thinking of how God had created Eve as Adam's helpmate. "But I will not come between the man I love and his family, so I have no choice but to remain an old maid and serve God without a husband."

She hurried to the desk across the room. Opening the top drawer, she removed a piece of paper and a pencil, then she took a seat in front of the desk. *I can't leave Walnutport without telling William good-bye.* Tears coursed down Betsy's cheeks, and she sniffed as she reached up to swipe them away. *I'll write him a note and leave it on the pulpit at church, for I could never say to his face all that's on my heart.*

Chapter 27

As William stepped into the church on Friday morning, he was overcome with a sense of joy. Tonight he and Betsy would be going on their first official date. He would escort her to the Walnutport Hotel dining room for supper, and tomorrow after they practiced some songs for Sunday, he hoped they could go for a buggy ride along the canal. Maybe by Christmas he would feel ready to ask Betsy to marry him.

Whistling one of his favorite hymns, William made his way to the front of the sanctuary and onto the platform. When he stepped up to the pulpit to place his sermon notes there, he was surprised to see an envelope with his name on it. He quickly tore it open and read the note inside.

Dear William,

After much prayer and consideration, I have come to realize that you and I are not meant to be together. I won't be going to dinner with you this evening, as there's no point in us beginning a courtship that could only end in disaster. I'm returning to New York and my job with the Salvation Army. By the time you read this note, I'll be gone.

You're a wonderful preacher, and the Walnutport Community Church is fortunate to have you as its pastor. I wish you well, and I pray that someday you'll fall in love with the right woman who might assist with your ministry in the proper way.

Most sincerely and with deep regret,

Betsy

William stood for several seconds, letting Betsy's words sink into his brain. "*Not meant to be together. . . Returning to New York. . .*" It made no sense. Betsy was nothing like Beatrice. Or was she?

"What a fool I've been to allow myself to fall in love again. I never should have trusted my heart—or Betsy Nelson. She was obviously toying with my affections."

William's hands shook as he crumpled the note and jammed it into his jacket pocket. "*You're a wonderful preacher. Walnutport Community Church is fortunate to have you.*" He slammed his hand down on the pulpit, scattering his sermon notes to the floor. He bent to pick them up then slowly, deliberately ripped them in two.

"I'll never be able to preach this message on forgiveness," he said with a groan. "I may never be able to preach another sermon again."

He crammed the pieces that were left of his message into his other pocket, bolted off the platform, and rushed out of the church.

As he sprinted through the tall grass growing between the church and the parsonage, his thoughts ran amuck. *Why would Betsy say she loved me and then decide we can't be together? I'm sure it's not about money or prestige. Is she afraid I might ask her to marry me? Does she have reservations about being a pastor's wife?* He clenched his fists so tightly that his nails dug into his palms. *Dear God,* he prayed, *help me understand this. Show me what to do.*

Inside the parsonage William found Mrs. Bevens sitting in the living room with a piece of needlepoint in her hands. "William," she said, smiling up at him, "I thought you were going to the church to work on your sermon for Sunday."

He dropped into the chair across from her and let his head fall forward into his open palms. "I was, but something happened to change all that. I think I'll be getting out of the ministry altogether."

"Leaving this town behind is a good idea, but don't you think you should try to seek a pastoral position in another church—one that has a larger congregation?"

He lifted his head and stared at her. "I don't care about having a larger congregation, Mrs. Bevens."

"But if you had more people attending your church, they could pay you more."

"I'm not worried about money either." He grimaced. "After reading the note I just found on the pulpit, I'm wondering if God might want me to leave the ministry."

"Note? What note?"

"From Betsy. She's left Walnutport and is going back to New York."

Mrs. Bevens released a noisy sigh. "That's good news."

"What did you say?"

"I said, 'That's good news.'"

"How can you say such a thing? I told you the other day that I'm in love with Betsy and had planned to ask her to marry me when the time was right."

Mrs. Bevens gave a quick nod. "And I said Betsy's not the woman for you."

William thought back to the conversation he'd had with Mrs. Bevens the other day, remembering how adamant she had been, saying Betsy was interested in his family's money and that she thought there had been a conspiracy at church to get the two of them together. Could she have expressed those things to Betsy? Might that be the reason for Betsy's change of heart?

He reached into his pocket and withdrew her crumpled

note, lifting it in the air. "Do you know anything about this, Mrs. Bevens?"

She pursed her lips and resumed her needlework. "How would I know anything about that note?"

"Have you spoken with Betsy lately?"

"We did have a brief conversation yesterday morning," Mrs. Bevens replied with a lift of her chin.

"What about?"

"Oh, just womanly things."

"What kind of *womanly* things?"

She released an undignified grunt and set her sewing aside. "If you must know, I spoke with her about your future."

"What about my future?"

"I told Betsy that she's not right for you and explained that your family would never accept someone as common as her."

"You did what?"

Mrs. Bevens tipped her head and looked at him like he was a little boy who'd done something wrong. "I was trying to protect you from getting hurt again—trying to keep you from making the biggest mistake of your life."

"Loving her is not a mistake." He stood. "Betsy is a sweet, caring, beautiful woman, and she would make any man a wonderful wife."

"Any of the boatmen or townsmen perhaps, but she's not right for you."

William paced between the fireplace and sofa. "How can you say that? How can you know what kind of woman I need?" He stopped pacing long enough to draw in a deep breath. "I love Betsy, and she loves me. At least that's what she told me before you stuck your nose in where it doesn't belong."

"I am only concerned for your welfare, William."

His head began to pound as the realization set in as to why Betsy had written the note. Mrs. Bevens had convinced her that she wasn't good enough for him and that his family would never accept her. It wasn't true—none of it. William didn't need a woman with a fine upbringing, and even if his parents chose not to welcome Betsy into their prestigious family circle, he didn't care. He loved her, and they were meant to be together. He was sure God had brought Betsy into his life, and he needed to bring her back, even if he had to travel all the way to New York, get down on his knees, and beg her to return to Walnutport.

Betsy had decided the best way to get out of town would be to flag down one of the canal boats heading to Easton and ask for a ride. That way she wouldn't have to worry about renting a carriage or asking someone to drive her there. So with her suitcase in one hand and Bristle Face's leash in the other hand, Betsy trudged determinedly toward the canal.

It obviously wouldn't work for her to take the dog along, but perhaps she could leave him with Sarah, whose children would probably enjoy having a dog of their own. She would miss the little fellow but was sure he would eventually adjust to his new surroundings. She would miss her friends in Walnutport, too—most of all, William.

As Betsy neared the lock tender's house, tears clouded her vision. *I was so sure things would work out for William and me, but maybe this is all for the best. He will go on with his life and find someone else to love, and I'll go back to my work at the Salvation Army.*

She'd found satisfaction in her duties there, but that had been before she met William. Even if she worked around the clock, she would never forget the love she felt for the special man she was leaving behind in Walnutport.

By the time Betsy reached Sarah's front door, she was so worked up she could barely speak. When Sarah's mother-in-law, Maria, answered her knock, it was all Betsy could do to ask for Sarah.

"She's in the kitchen, bakin' bread," Maria said, nodding in that direction. "Why don't you go in and surprise her?"

Betsy glanced down at Bristle Face. "Is there a place where I can tie the dog?"

"Bring him inside. He can play upstairs with the kids."

"Are you sure it's all right?"

"Is the critter housebroke?"

Betsy nodded.

433

"Then he's more than welcome to come in." Maria smiled and stepped aside.

Betsy set her suitcase inside the door and unhooked Bristle Face's leash. The dog let out a quick bark and darted up the stairs as though he knew exactly where the children were playing.

Maria went to the living room, and Betsy headed for the kitchen. She found Sarah bent over the stove.

"Hello, Sarah. How are you?"

Sarah closed the oven door and whirled around. "Betsy, this is a surprise. I didn't expect to see you today."

"I. . .uh. . .came to ask you a favor."

"What is it?"

"I'm moving back to New York, and I need a home for Bristle Face."

Sarah's eyebrows drew together. "You're leaving Walnutport?"

Betsy nodded.

"But why? I thought you liked it here. Walnutport's your home, and you've become an important part of our lives." Sarah took a step toward Betsy. "I was even hoping that you and Pastor William might—"

Betsy held up one hand. "There's no chance of anything happening between me and William."

Before Sarah could respond, a blaring horn sounded in the distance. "That's a conch shell blowing out there, so I must open the lock for the boat that's coming through."

Betsy grabbed her suitcase and hurried out the door behind Sarah, thinking this might be her chance to secure a ride. Sure enough, Amos McGregor's boat was lining up at the lock, and he was heading in the direction of Easton.

Betsy waited until the boat was safely through, then she rushed to the edge of the canal and called out to him. "Mr. McGregor, could you give me a ride to Easton?"

At first he tipped his head and looked at her strangely, but then he finally nodded. "Let me drop the gangplank for you, and you can come on board."

Betsy glanced over at Sarah, who had just closed the lock. "What about my dog? Will you keep Bristle Face?"

Sarah gave a quick nod. "Of course I will, but I really wish you weren't going."

A lump lodged in Betsy's throat, and she swallowed hard, trying to dislodge it. "It's better that I go. Better for everyone." She gave Sarah a hug, lifted the edge of her skirt, and hurried up the gangplank.

Amos hollered at his young mule driver to get the mules going again, and the boat moved forward. They'd only gone a short way when someone called Betsy's name. She shielded her eyes from the glaring sun and spotted William running down the towpath, waving his hands. "Stop the boat!"

Betsy looked over at Amos. "Please, keep going."

Amos nodded and signaled his mule driver to continue walking.

William cupped his hands around his mouth. "I need

you to stop the boat, Mr. McGregor! This is an emergency!"

Betsy's heart pounded so hard she could feel the rhythm of it inside her head. Why had William come here? Maybe it wasn't to try and stop her from going to New York. There could actually be an emergency. Perhaps something had happened to someone in Amos's family. "You'd better stop, Mr. McGregor," she said.

"Hold up them mules!" Amos shouted to his driver, then he dropped the gangplank.

William rushed on board and hurried over to Betsy. "I went by your place, and when I saw your buckboard, I figured you might have come down here, hoping to get a ride on one of the boats." He reached up to wipe the sweat from his brow. "Thank the Lord I'm not too late."

"Too late? Too late for what, Preacher?" Amos asked before Betsy could say a word.

"Too late to stop this woman from leaving." William picked up Betsy's suitcase and took hold of her hand.

"Wh–what are you doing?" she stammered.

"I'm taking you back to Walnutport where you belong."

She stared up at him as tears dribbled onto her cheeks. "Didn't you get my note?"

He nodded. "I also talked to my housekeeper, and I know about the things she told you yesterday."

"Then you must realize why I have to leave."

He leaned closer until his warm breath tickled her nose. "I love you, Betsy, and I don't give a wit about your station in life or my parents' money. If they accept you, I'll be happy and they'll be blessed, but if they choose not to accept you, then it's their loss."

"Oh William, I can't stand the thought of coming between you and your family."

"I don't think you have to worry about that. I'm sure once Mother and Father meet you they'll see how wonderful you are and will come to love you as much as I do." William grinned. "Well, maybe not quite that much." He dropped to one knee. "Betsy Nelson, I know we haven't had even one official date, but I've come to know you pretty well, and I think you would make a fine preacher's wife. So, after a suitable time of courtship, would you consider marrying me?"

Betsy stood with her mouth hanging open, too stunned to say a word.

Amos nudged her with his elbow. "I can't keep my boat stopped here all day, missy. Would ya answer the preacher's question so I can get on up to Easton with my load?"

Tears coursed down Betsy's cheeks as she smiled at William. "When the time is right, I would be most honored to become your wife."

Epilogue

Two months later

$\mathcal{Y}$ ou're the most beautiful bride I've ever laid eyes on," Kelly said as she brushed Betsy's long hair away from her face and secured it at the back of her head with a white satin bow.

Betsy smiled as she studied her reflection in the mirror they had set up in the classroom where she taught her Sunday school girls. She felt honored to be wearing the same satin gown William's mother had worn on her wedding day, so that was her "something borrowed." The pearls that graced Betsy's neck were brand new—a wedding present from her handsome groom. And for "something blue," she had chosen to carry a lacy white handkerchief with her father's initials, HN, embroidered in blue thread. The hankie had belonged to her mother, so even though neither of Betsy's parents could share in this special day, it gave her a sense of comfort to know she carried something that reminded her of them both.

"I can hardly believe this is happening," Betsy murmured. "I feel like a princess from a fairy tale."

Kelly gave Betsy a hug. "You deserve to be happy, and I'm glad you didn't make William wait until next Christmas to make you his bride."

"I'm almost thirty-two," Betsy said, puckering her lips. "I don't want to be old and gray before we start our family. So when William suggested we be married on Christmas Eve, I could hardly say no."

Sarah chuckled as she stepped into the room. "I heard that remark, and you're not old, Betsy Nelson, soon-to-be Mrs. William Covington III."

Betsy reached one hand out to Sarah and the other one to Kelly, her two dearest friends. "William and I love each other so much, and neither of us could stand the thought of waiting a whole year to be married."

"It's wonderful that William's family could be here for the wedding," Kelly said, giving Betsy's hand a gentle squeeze.

Betsy nodded. "And to think I was worried that they might not accept me."

Sarah squeezed Betsy's other hand. "The real miracle is

that Mrs. Bevens has found a personal relationship with the Lord and no longer objects to the wedding." She wiggled her eyebrows. "Since William's housekeeper will soon be out of a job, I have to wonder if she might not end up marrying Rev. Carter from Parryville, who became a widower last year."

"That's right," Kelly agreed. "I saw Mrs. Bevens in the sanctuary earlier, putting the finishing touches on the decorations, and I couldn't help but notice the glances she and Rev. Carter kept exchanging."

"No one could be any happier than I am on this special Christmas Eve," Betsy murmured with a dreamy sigh. She took one last look at herself in the mirror and then turned toward the door. "Shall we go, ladies? I don't want to keep my groom waiting."

As Betsy walked down the aisle behind her friends, her throat constricted. The sanctuary was beautiful with glowing candlelight, boughs of holly mixed with evergreens, and red velvet bows decorating each pew.

Her gaze came to rest on William, looking ever so handsome as he stood at the front of the church beside his brother, Richard, and Mike Cooper. He was dressed in a black suit with a red bow tie, and he gazed at Betsy as though she were the most beautiful woman in the world. She felt blessed, and her heart swelled with joy. *Oh, I wish Papa and Mama were here to share this special moment with us.*

William's aunt Clara, who had volunteered to play the organ, switched from the traditional bridal march to the soft strains of "The First Noel." Betsy smiled through a film of tears. *That was Papa's favorite Christmas carol. Maybe he and Mama are looking down from heaven right now and can see how happy I am.*

"I love you, Papa," Betsy whispered. She stepped up to her groom and took hold of his hand. "I'm so glad I returned to Walnutport so I could meet you, Pastor William."

Recipe for Betsy's Pork Float

Hunk of salt pork
2 large onions, cut up
6 large potatoes, diced
1 (14.5 ounce) can diced tomatoes
1 (14.5 ounce) can crushed corn
Biscuit dough

Cut salt pork into small pieces and fry in a pan to get the grease out. Brown and set aside. Fry onions in pork fat. Set aside. In large pot, combine potatoes, tomatoes, and crushed corn. Cook until potatoes are tender. Add browned salt pork and onion; season with salt and pepper to taste. Bring to a boil. Make dough as you would for biscuits, and spoon into pork stew to make dumplings. Keep covered and boil slowly for about 10 minutes or until dumplings are done.

Discussion Questions for Betsy's Return

1. When Betsy received the news that her father was ill and had to retire from preaching, she decided to give up a job she enjoyed and return home to care for him. Despite the fact that Betsy liked her job, she loved her father more. Have you ever made a sacrifice to care for someone in your family? How did it make you feel?

2. When William was asked to interview for the position of pastor at the small church in Walnutport, PA, his well-to-do, rather snobbish parents were very upset. They wanted William to have a bigger church where he could make more money, and they hoped he would live closer to them. However, William cared nothing about wealth or prestige. His greatest desire was to minister to others. Why do you think some people put so much emphasis on money and prestige?

3. When Betsy discovered that another preacher was coming to take her father's place, she was sad and a bit resentful. Even so, she was willing to help out at the church when the new minister came. Sometimes, when a minister whom we especially like leaves the church, it's hard to accept the new preacher who takes over for him. What are some ways we can make the transition easier when a minister is replaced?

4. William's greatest concern when he took over the church in Walnutport was that he wouldn't be able to fill the shoes of the previous pastor, Rev. Nelson, who had lovingly served the small canal community for many years. What are some ways we can help a new pastor feel accepted and welcomed in his new church?

5. Since William was single, several women in the church decided he should have a wife, so they decided to play matchmaker. Do you think this helped or hindered Betsy and William's relationship?

6. Sometimes rumors get started because someone sees or hears something and misinterprets it. This happened to Betsy when someone saw a man trying to kiss her. What's the best way to handle rumors? Is there ever a time when the pastor should be told when one church member sees another church member doing something they feel is wrong?

7. William struggled with the pain of having been left at the altar. The woman he'd planned to marry backed out of the wedding because she didn't want to be a preacher's wife. What are some ways you might help your minister's wife feel like part of the church family?

8. Due to the fact that William had been jilted by his fi-ancée, he was leery of starting a relationship with Betsy, fearing that she might hurt him, too. What would you tell someone who has been hurt in a relationship so they don't close themselves off from love again?

Sarah's
CHOICE

BRIDES *of* LEHIGH CANAL

BOOK THREE

DEDICATION/ACKNOWLEDGMENTS

To my husband, Richard. Thanks for all the interesting things you've shared with me about playing on the towpath and swimming in the Lehigh Canal when you were a boy.

The Lord seeth not as man seeth;
for man looketh on the outward appearance,
but the Lord looketh on the heart.
1 SAMUEL 16:7

Chapter 1

Walnutport, Pennsylvania—Summer 1898

*W*o–o–o–o! *Wo–o–o–o!* The low moan of a conch shell drifted through the open window in Sarah Turner's kitchen.

Leaving a pan of bacon cooking on the coal-burning stove, she peered out the window. Although she saw no sign of the canal boat, the sound of its conch shell could be heard for a mile and signaled the boat would be approaching the lock soon.

"A boat's coming. Would you mind finishing the bacon while I go out to open the lockgate?" Sarah asked her mother-in-law, who stood at the counter, cracking eggs into a ceramic bowl.

"Sure, I can do that," Maria said with a weary-looking

nod. A chunk of her nearly gray hair had fallen loose from the back of her bun, and her dark eyes looked dull and puffy.

Sarah's heart went out to Maria, who looked more tired than usual. Sarah feared that caring for the children was too much for her mother-in-law—especially since she'd begun having trouble with her vision.

Wo–o–o–o! Wo–o–o–o! Wo–o–o–o! The sound of the conch shell drew closer.

Sarah hurried across the room. She was almost to the door when her eight-year-old son, Sam Jr., raced up to her, bright-eyed and smiling from ear to ear.

"Can I help raise the lock, Mama?" he asked.

Sarah shook her head. "Sorry, Sammy, but you're not strong enough for that."

"Am so strong enough! I ain't no weaklin', Mama." When the boy pulled his shoulders straight back and puffed out his chest, a lock of sandy blond hair fell across his forehead.

"Of course you're not a weakling, but raising and lowering the lock is hard work, even for me."

His blue eyes darkened as he tipped his head and looked up at her with furrowed brows. "How come ya always treat me like a baby?"

Sarah blew out an exasperated breath. "I don't treat you like a baby. I just know that you're not strong enough to raise and lower the lock. Now if you really want to help, run back to the parlor and keep an eye on your little sister and brother for me."

"Okay." Sammy thrust his hands in his pockets, turned, and shuffled out of the room.

With a shake of her head and a silent prayer for guidance, Sarah hurried outside.

As the flat-roofed wooden boat approached, she cranked open the upper wicket gates to fill the lock. Once it was filled with water, she lowered the upper head gate, and the boat was drawn into the stone walls of the lock. Then the upper head gates were raised and the upper wicket gates were closed, so that no more water could enter the lock. Next, the lower wicket gates were opened and the water rushed out of the lock. Following that, the lower gates were opened, and the boat was drawn out and into the lower level of the canal. Finally, Sarah opened the main gate to let the boat out and on its way.

As the boat moved on down the canal, Sarah headed back to the house, arms aching and forehead beaded with perspiration. This was hard work—too hard for a twenty-seven-year-old woman like her—and definitely too hard for a young boy. But she had no other choice. When her husband, Sam, died nearly a year ago, she'd taken over his job of tending the lock in order to provide for her three children.

She shuddered, thinking of the accident that had taken

Sam. A boat had broken loose from where it was tied and floated to the lock, where it had jammed. Sam and several others had been trying to free the boat. While Sam was standing on top of the lock, his foot slipped, and he'd tumbled into the water. The boat shifted, and Sam's body had been crushed between the boat and the lock.

Lock tending could be dangerous work, and Sarah had to remind herself every day to be very careful in all that she did during the process of letting the boats in and out.

Sarah was grateful that Sam's mother lived with them and had helped to care for the children ever since Sam died. But with Maria's health failing, Sarah couldn't help but worry.

She thought about her own mother, who'd died of pneumonia a few months ago. Papa had given up canaling and sold his boat soon after that. He'd moved to Easton and taken a job at one of the factories where he'd previously worked during the winter. Sarah missed seeing both of her parents, but she understood Papa's need for a change.

Sarah leaned wearily against the side of the lock tender's shed and sighed. "Oh, Sam, I miss you so much. How I wish you were still here." Tears slipped from her eyes. How many more things would change in her life? How much longer would Maria be able to help out? Could she and the children make it on their own if Maria moved back to Easton where she used to live with Sam's brother, Roger?

Sarah knew that's where Maria belonged, but could she convince her of that?

"I hereby bequest to my grandson, Elias Brooks, my canal boat, with all the supplies and mules that go with it."

Twenty-eight-year-old Elias looked over at his parents to gauge their reaction to the reading of his grandfather's will. Mother, with her light brown hair pinned tightly in a bun, sat with a stoic expression on her face.

Father frowned, making his smooth, nearly bald head stand out in contrast to the deep wrinkles in his forehead. "It won't be easy to sell that stupid boat," he said, glancing at Elias and then quickly looking away. "With the canal era winding down, I doubt the old man's boat will be worth much at all."

"How can you talk about your own father like that?" Elias's twenty-five-year-old sister, Carolyn, spoke up. "Grandpa was much more than an old man. He was your father, and a wonderful grandfather to me and Elias."

A muscle on the side of Father's neck quivered. "That man was never much of a father to me. Always thought about that ridiculous boat and how much money he could make haulin' coal up the canal from Mauch Chunk to Easton."

"It was Grandpa's money that allowed you to get the

453

schooling you needed to run your newspaper," Elias dared to say.

Father slammed his fist on the table where they sat in Clifford Moore's law office. "How dare you speak to me like that!"

"Sorry," Elias mumbled, "but I think it's disrespectful to talk about Grandpa in such a way. He did his best by you, and—"

"His best?" Father's face flamed. "If he'd done his best, he would never have bought that boat. He'd have stayed here in Easton and helped me run the newspaper, which is where he belonged."

Mr. Moore cleared his throat a couple of times. "Can we get back to the reading of Andrew's will?"

"You mean there's more?" The question came from Mother, who'd begun twiddling her thumbs, a gesture Elias knew indicated she was becoming quite agitated.

Mr. Moore looked at Elias. "Your grandfather also left a note saying he wanted you to have his Bible. I believe it's somewhere on the boat."

Elias nodded. He looked forward to reading Grandpa's Bible and searching for all the places he'd underlined in it. During the times Elias had spent with Grandpa when he was a boy, he'd enjoyed hearing Grandpa's deep voice as he read passages of scripture each evening before bed. It was largely due to Grandpa's godly influence that, at the age of sixteen, Elias had come to know the Lord personally. He'd been trying to live a Christian life ever since, which was why he couldn't let any of the things Father said today rile him.

Elias stared out the window as he thought about the summers during his teen years that he'd spent aboard his grandfather's boat. Father hadn't wanted Elias to go, but Mother had convinced him, saying she thought it'd be a good experience for the boy. Elias had enjoyed those days on the water, helping with various chores as Grandpa hauled load after load of coal on the Lehigh Navigation System. Grandpa hadn't expected anything from Elias except a good day's work, and he'd always offered his acceptance and praise. Not like Father, full of unreasonable demands, and critical of everything Elias said or did.

"I'll see that an ad is run in tomorrow's newspaper," Father said, bringing Elias's thoughts to a halt. "If we're lucky, someone who's still determined to haul that dirty coal up the canal might see the ad and buy the old man's boat."

Elias gripped the arm of his chair and grimaced. Grandpa deserved more respect, especially from his only son. But then, Father had never had any respect for Grandpa; at least not as far as Elias could tell.

Carolyn, her blue eyes flashing, spoke up again. "Please stop referring to Grandpa as an 'old man.'"

"I agree with Carolyn, and there's no reason for you to advertise Grandpa's boat in your newspaper either," Elias said, summoning up his courage.

Father folded his arms and glared at Elias. "Oh, and why's that?"

"Because the boat's mine, and it. . .well, it's not for sale."

Father's dark eyebrows shot up. "What?"

"Grandpa wanted me to have the boat, or he wouldn't have willed it to me." Elias loosened his collar, which suddenly felt much too tight. He wasn't used to standing up to his father like this. "If Grandpa wanted me to have his boat, then he must have wanted me to continue hauling coal with it."

The wrinkles in Father's forehead deepened. "Wh–what are you saying?" he sputtered.

"I'm saying that I'm going to quit my job at the newspaper and captain Grandpa's boat."

Mother gasped. "Elias, you can't mean that!"

He nodded. "I certainly do."

Father's thin lips compressed so tightly that the ends of his handlebar mustache twitched up and down. "That would be a very foolish thing to do."

"I don't think it's foolish," Carolyn put in. "In fact, I think—"

Father's gaze swung to Carolyn, and he glared at her. "Nobody cares what you think, so keep your opinion to yourself!"

She blinked a couple of times, pushed a wayward strand

of honey-blond hair into the tight bun she wore, and sat back in her chair with a sigh.

"Perhaps your grandfather didn't mean for you to actually captain his boat," Mother spoke up. "Maybe he left it to you so you could sell the boat and use the money for something else."

Elias's face heated, and he became keenly aware that his left cheek, partially covered by the red mark he'd been born with, felt like it was on fire. "I think Grandpa did mean for me to captain his boat. Maybe to you and Father it would be foolish for me to do so, but I feel a strong need to fulfill Grandpa's wishes."

Father's piercing blue eyes darkened like a storm cloud. "You take that boat out, and there will be no job waiting for you at my newspaper when the canal closes! Is that understood?"

Mother gasped again. "Aaron, you can't mean that!"

"Yes, Myrtle, I most certainly do." Father turned to look at Elias. "Well, what's it going to be? Are you working for me or not?"

A sense of determination welled in Elias's soul as he made his final decision. Rising from his chair, he looked his father in the eye and said, "I'm going to captain Grandpa's boat, and there's nothing you can do to stop me."

Chapter 2

I'm not moving back to Easton," Maria said with a shake of her head. "You need me to care for the kids and help with things here."

Sarah dropped to a seat on the high-backed sofa beside her mother-in-law and reached for her hand. "I'm concerned because you haven't been feeling well for some time, and now that your eyesight's failing, you need to be where you can get the best medical care."

Maria's forehead puckered. "Are you sayin' that Dr. McGrath isn't giving me good care?"

"I'm not saying that at all, but there's a hospital in Easton, and doctors who specialize in—"

"I'm not leaving you to raise three kids alone, so this discussion's over." Maria rose from the sofa and shuffled across the room. When she bumped the rocking chair, she swayed unsteadily, nearly hitting her head on the fireplace mantle.

"Are you all right?" Sarah rushed to take Maria's arm.

Maria brushed Sarah's hand aside. "I'm fine. Just lost my balance for a minute, that's all." She shuffled on and disappeared into the kitchen.

Sarah groaned. "Oh, Sam, I wish you were still the lock tender and I could just be here taking care of your mother and our kids."

Elias drew in a deep breath to help settle his nerves. He and Ned Guthrie, the fifty-year-old man who'd been Grandpa's helper for the last several years, were heading up the Lehigh Navigation System in Grandpa's old boat. Ever since they'd left Easton, Elias had been a ball of nerves. He'd found a twelve-year-old boy, Bobby Harrison from Easton, to drive the mules, but Bobby didn't have a lot of experience around mules. Between that concern, and the fact that Elias hadn't ridden on Grandpa's canal boat for nearly ten years, he wondered if he'd be able to comply with Grandpa's wishes and actually run the boat himself. Well, he couldn't quit now and return to Easton, where Father would only say "I told you so."

Elias glanced at Ned, who stood at the bow of the boat, hollering at Bobby to keep the lines steady. The rusty canaler with a scruffy-looking brown beard might be a bit rough around the edges, but he'd been working the canal a good many years and had plenty of experience in all aspects of it.

It's a good thing, too, Elias thought, *because I can't remember much of what Grandpa taught me.*

As Elias's boat drew closer to the lock at Walnutport, Ned lifted the conch shell to his lips and blew so that the lock tender would know they were coming. When they approached the lock a short time later, he blew on it again. *Wo–o–o–o! Wo–o–o–o!*

Elias was surprised when a young woman with dark hair pulled into a loose bun at the back of her head, came out of the large stone house next to the canal and cranked open the lockgate. The last time he'd come through here with Grandpa, it had been an older man who'd opened the Walnutport lock. This petite woman didn't look strong enough to be doing such hard work. But maybe she was stronger than she appeared. Maybe her husband was sick or had business in town, and she was taking over for him today. Elias figured it wasn't his business to worry about whoever was tending the lock. As long it opened and his boat made it through, that's all that mattered.

Elias directed his gaze to Bobby, waiting off to one side with the mules. The boy had been working hard and trying his best, despite Ned's constant nagging.

Once the lock tender had opened the gates and Elias's boat had made it through, Ned called to Bobby, "Get the team movin'!"

The mules' ears twitched as they moved slowly forward.

Ned turned to Elias and smiled. "Can ya believe how easily that little lady handled the gates for us?"

Elias shook his head. "I was surprised to see a woman doing the job of a man."

"That was Sarah Turner," Ned said. "Her husband, Sam, died nearly a year ago, when he fell and got himself smashed between the lock and one of the boats. Sarah's been actin' as lock tender ever since, and with her havin' three kids to look after, I'm sure it ain't no easy task."

"No, I suppose not."

When another conch shell blew behind them, Elias glanced over his shoulder and saw Sarah Turner run out of her house to open the gate again. "She must be exhausted by the end of each day," he remarked.

Ned tugged on his beard, sprinkled with a bit of gray. "Only day off she gets is Sundays, when the canal closes down."

Elias knew the reason for that, and it made good sense to him. Besides the fact that Sunday was the Lord's Day, the rugged, hardworking canalers needed a day of rest, and he was sure that the lady lock tender needed one, too.

As they continued on their way, Elias found himself beginning to relax. He felt more at peace than he had in a very long time.

"I think I'm going to enjoy running this boat up and down the canal," he said to Ned, who'd pulled a piece of chewing tobacco from his shirt pocket.

"Are ya sure ya won't miss workin' in the office at your daddy's newspaper business?"

"I don't think so," Elias said with a shake of his head. "Running a newspaper is nothing like this—especially one in a busy town like Easton." The truth was, having his father scrutinize everything he did had made Elias feel insecure and inferior, like he could never measure up. He'd tried for a good many years to make Father proud, but all Father ever did was find fault. Well, maybe after Elias proved he could run this canal boat, Father would finally take notice and say a few kind words about Elias's accomplishment. Then again, by taking over Grandpa's boat, Elias may have ruined all chances of him and Father ever making peace.

Chapter 3

"What's wrong with the mules? Why aren't they moving?" Elias called over to his young driver.

"Don't know!" Bobby pushed a lock of sandy brown hair away from his face and grunted. "They was movin' just fine a few minutes ago." He motioned to Daisy and then Dolly. "All of a sudden, they both just stopped dead in their tracks."

"That's 'cause there's a huge puddle in the middle of the towpath," Ned said as he joined Elias at the bow of the boat. "Mules hate water, and Dolly and Daisy ain't no exception. They'll do anything to avoid walkin' through water—even a puddle."

"Oh yeah, that's right." Elias thumped the side of his head. He glanced over his shoulder. Another boat was coming up behind them. "What shall we do to get the mules moving?" he asked Ned.

"Gotta take 'em around the water." Ned leaned over the bow of the boat and shouted to Bobby, "Lead the mules around the puddle! Take 'em through the tall grass!"

"Haw!" Bobby shouted at the mules.

"Not *haw*!" Ned bellowed. "*Haw* means to the left. *Gee* means to the right!" He looked at Elias and groaned. "Ya should've hired a driver with more experience."

"Bobby was the only boy I could find on such short notice," Elias said. "Besides, the poor kid's folks are in need of money, and I thought I could help by giving him a job."

"Humph!" Ned snorted. "Then he'd better be a quick learner, or it'll take us a week instead of a few days to get up the canal to Mauch Chunk!"

Ignoring Ned's tirade, Elias turned his attention back to the mules. "Lead them to the right, Bobby. Lead them to the right!"

"Gee!" Bobby yelled.

When the mules didn't budge, he grabbed hold of their bridles and had just started moving them toward the thick grass when a deep voice hollered from behind Elias's boat, "Get outa my way; my boat's comin' through!"

"We can't do nothin' about movin' the boat to one side until that stupid boy gets them mules walkin' again," Ned muttered, shaking his head. He cupped his hands around his mouth and hollered at the other boat captain, "Just hold your boat back a minute, Bart, and we'll let ya pass!"

Elias was tempted to climb out of the boat and swim to shore so he could see if he might be able to help Bobby get Dolly and Daisy moving faster, but he quickly dismissed that dumb idea. It would be foolish to get his clothes wet for no good reason, because Bobby seemed to be managing okay. It was just taking much longer than Elias would have liked; especially with the burly, dark-haired fellow in the boat behind them, waving his hands and hollering, "Get that boat outa my way!"

If I'm gong to make it as a canal boat captain, I'll need to pay closer attention to things, Elias told himself. *And I'll have to try harder to remember more of what Grandpa taught me about running this boat.*

Sarah had just let another boat through the lock when she spotted her sister, Kelly, walking along the towpath next to the canal with her two children: Marcus, who was three, and Anna, who'd recently turned four.

As usual, Kelly's dark hair hung down her back in long, gentle waves. With the exception of Sundays, Kelly rarely wore her hair up in a bun.

"It's good to see you," Sarah said when Kelly and the

children joined her on the section of towpath that ran along the front of the lock tender's house.

Kelly smiled. "It's good to see you, too. Except for our time together on Sundays, we don't get to see you as much as we'd like."

"I know. There's not much chance for me to get away." Sarah motioned to the lockgate. "With boats coming through at all hours, I'm needed here every day but Sunday."

"I'm sorry you have to work so hard." Kelly gave Sarah a hug. "I wish there was more I could do to help, but with two young ones to care for, helping Mike run the store, and trying to squeeze in time for painting, I don't have much free time on my hands these days."

"You can't sell any of your artwork if you don't take the time to paint."

"That's true, and I do love to paint. Have ever since I was a girl and could hold a piece of homemade charcoal in my hands." Kelly smiled. "I'm ever so grateful that Mike added on to the store so I could have my own little gallery where I can paint and sell my work."

Sarah nodded. "So what brings you over here today?"

"Things have been kind of slow at the store this morning, so I decided to take the kids outside for some fresh air and a walk." She glanced down at Marcus, who was now down on his knees inspecting a beetle. Anna stood beside him, her face lifted to the sun. "I thought maybe they could play with your kids awhile."

"Sammy's at school, of course, but Willis and Helen were playing on the porch awhile ago, when I was doing our laundry in the metal washtub," Sarah said. "When the last boat came through the lock, I sent them inside."

Kelly gave Sarah's shoulder a tender squeeze. "Are things going okay? Are you managing to keep up?"

"Everything's about the same, but there's always so much to do. Between tending the lock, washing clothes, and making bread to sell to the boatmen, I hardly have any time to spend with my kids." Sarah sighed deeply. "Seems like they're always trying to get my attention, and there's just not enough of me to go around."

"What about Maria? Isn't she keeping the kids occupied during the day?"

"Maria's not doing well. Her vision problem seems to be getting worse, and she's always so tired. It's all she can do to keep the house clean and help cook our meals, much less keep an eye on my two youngest all day."

Kelly's mouth formed an O. "Are you saying that Willis and Helen have been fending for themselves when you're out here tending the lock?"

"Maria does what she can to keep them occupied, but she's not up to caring for them the way I would if I could be with them all the time."

"Say, I have an idea," Kelly said. "Why don't I take Willis

and Helen home with me for the rest of the day? That way they can play with Marcus and Anna. It'll give Maria a break, and you won't have to worry about them while you bake bread and tend the lock."

"Are you sure you don't mind? I mean, how are you going to help Mike in the store if you have four kids to keep an eye on all day?"

"I told you, things have been slow at the store today. Besides, Willis is old enough to keep the other three entertained if Mike needs me for anything. Since our house is connected to the store, if there's a problem, Willis can come and get me."

Sarah hesitated, but finally nodded. "You're right, Willis is always thinking up something to keep Helen entertained, and it would be a big help if Maria didn't have to be responsible for the kids today."

"Let's go inside and get them now," Kelly said. "Then the five of us will be on our way."

When Sarah, Kelly, and Kelly's children entered the house, Sarah was surprised to see her six-year-old son and four-year-old daughter sitting in the middle of the kitchen floor with a bag of flour between them. They'd scooped some of it onto the floor, some into a baking pan, and a good deal of it was in Helen's dark hair.

"What in the world are you two doing?" Sarah asked, squatting down beside them.

"We're makin' bread." Helen smiled up at Sarah, and swiped a floury hand across her turned-up nose. "It was Willis's idea."

"Where's your grandma?" Sarah asked. Surely Maria wouldn't have let the kids make a mess like this if she'd known what they were doing.

"Grandma's in there." Willis pointed to the door leading to their small, but cozy, parlor. Sarah noticed then that he had some flour in his light brown hair as well. So much for Willis keeping Helen entertained.

"I'll clean up this mess while you talk to Maria," Kelly offered.

"Thanks, I appreciate that." Sarah rose to her feet and hurried from the room.

When she entered the parlor she gasped. There lay Maria, facedown on the floor!

Chapter 4

"Well, wouldn't ya just know it?" Ned shouted from where he'd been stirring a pot of bean soup sitting on the small, coal-burning cookstove in the middle of the boat. For some reason, Ned preferred cooking on it rather than the slightly larger stove that was below in the galley.

Elias, not wanting to take his eyes off the waterway ahead, glanced quickly over his shoulder. "What's wrong, Ned?"

"We're outa bread. Shouldn't have ate any at breakfast, I guess."

"That's okay. We can do without bread for lunch."

"Maybe so, but we'll need it tomorrow, and the next day, too."

"We can stop at one of the stores between here and Easton and pick up a loaf of bread."

"Stoppin' at a store would take too long. We'd end up lookin' at other things we don't really need, and there's no time for lollygaggin' today." Ned pulled a hunk of chewing tobacco from his shirt pocket and popped into his mouth. "Already spent too much time up in Mauch Chunk, waitin' on the other boats that was ahead of us. When that noisy, sooty train showed up, it took a load of coal before we even got up to the loadin' chute."

"You're right, it did take a long time to get our coal." Elias hoped it wouldn't be that way every time they went to Mauch Chunk, but if it was, they'd just have to deal with it.

"Guess we could always see if that lady lock tender in Walnutport has any bread we could buy," Ned suggested. "She often sells bread to the boatmen who come through her lock."

"Sure, we can do that."

They traveled in silence for a while, interrupted only by the sound of the water lapping against the boat and an occasional undignified grunt from Ned as he stirred the soup on the stove.

"Here's a cup of soup for ya, boss," Ned said, stepping up to Elias a short time later.

Elias took the warm cup in his hands. "Thanks."

"Got any idea what you'll do once the railroad takes over haulin' all the coal in these here parts?" Ned asked, leaning against the side of the boat.

"I'm not sure. To be honest, I haven't really thought about it that much."

"Well you'd better think about it, 'cause it's bound to happen sooner or later."

"I guess I'll deal with that when it comes. I'm just taking one day at a time right now."

"If the time comes that you can't boat any longer, will ya go back to work at your daddy's newspaper office?"

Elias shook his head. "That will never happen. My father's not even speaking to me right now."

"How come?"

"He thinks I was foolish for leaving the newspaper and taking over Grandpa's boat. The way he talks about the poor man, you'd never know Grandpa was his father." Elias frowned. "Father said if I left Easton to captain Grandpa's boat I'd never work for him again."

Ned leaned his head over the boat and spit out his wad of tobacco. "Aw, I'm sure he didn't mean it. Probably just said that, hopin' you'd change your mind. If you was to leave the canal and return to Easton, he'd probably welcome ya back with open arms."

"I'm not so sure about that." Elias shrugged. "But I'm not going to worry about it either. I'm just going to do the job Grandpa wanted me to do."

"Guess that's the best way to deal with things all right." Ned pointed up ahead. "Looks like Walnutport's comin' into view. You'd best get out the conch shell and let the lock tender know that you're needin' to come through."

"Maria! Maria, can you hear me?" Sarah's heart pounded as she knelt on the floor beside her pale-faced mother-in-law.

Kelly entered the room just then and gasped. "Oh my! Is. . .is she dead?"

"No, thank goodness. I can see by the rise and fall of her chest that she's breathing." Sarah cradled Maria's head in her hands. "I think we should get Dr. McGrath."

Kelly stood. "I'll run into town and see if he's at his office. If he's there, I'll ask if he can come look at Maria right away."

Just then, Maria's eyes fluttered open, but she stared at Sarah with a blank expression. "Wh–what's going on? What am I doin' on the floor?"

"Kelly and I were outside visiting, and when I came into the parlor, I found you lying here."

"What happened, Maria? Did you get dizzy and pass out?" Kelly questioned.

"I. . .uh. . .was heading upstairs to do some cleaning, and all of a sudden everything looked real blurry. Guess I must have tripped on the braided throw rug. Then I lost my balance, and. . ." She rubbed her forehead. "I must've hit my head, and then everything went dark."

"Let's get you over to the sofa so you can rest," Sarah said. "Then Kelly's going into town to get the doctor."

"There's no need for that." Maria pushed herself to a sitting position. "Once I get my bearings, I'll be fine."

"You're not fine, Maria. You fell and hit your head. Now I insist that you lie down awhile," Sarah said.

"Oh, all right."

Sarah took hold of Maria's left arm, and Kelly took her right arm; then they guided her to the sofa. They'd no more than gotten her settled when a knock sounded on the door.

"I'll see who that is." Kelly hurried from the room.

When she returned, young Pastor William and his wife, Betsy, were with her.

"We were taking a walk along the towpath and thought we'd stop in to visit and see how things are going here." Betsy smiled at Sarah, but her bright eyes and cheerful expression quickly turned to a look of concern when she saw Maria on the sofa. "What's wrong? Is Maria sick?"

Sarah quickly explained what had happened. "Maria's vision seems to be getting worse, but she refuses to see Dr. McGrath," she said, hoping Pastor William or Betsy might intervene. "I've suggested that Maria move back to Easton to live with her son, but she's flatly refused."

"Sarah's right." Pastor William moved over to the sofa and took Maria's hand. "The last time I was here, you were having trouble seeing, and I think you ought to see the doctor today and tell him what's happened," he said in his usual gentle tone.

Maria shook her head stubbornly. "I'll be fine; I just need to rest awhile."

"When Dr. McGrath examined Maria's eyes a few weeks ago, he said her vision's getting worse," Sarah said.

Betsy's pale blond hair, which she'd worn down, swished across her shoulder as she knelt on the floor in front of where Maria sat. "If you moved back to Easton, you'd have access to a hospital and many good doctors, and you'd be cared for in your son's house and wouldn't have the responsibility for caring for Sarah's three active children."

Tears welled in Maria's eyes. "I. . .I love those kids, and I couldn't move away and leave Sarah alone with no one to watch them. Who would take care of things while she's outside tending the lock?"

"I'll manage somehow," Sarah said with a catch in her voice.

"Maybe I can come over to help out when things aren't real busy at the store," Kelly volunteered.

"Better yet, I can come over here to help out." Betsy looked at Maria. "Would you be willing to move back to Easton if I did that?"

Before Maria could reply, the low moan of a conch shell floated through the door that Kelly had left open.

Sarah stood. "A boat's coming through, and I need to go out and open the lock. We'll have to finish this discussion when I come back."

Chapter 5

*A*s soon as Sarah ran out the front door, she realized there was more than one boat waiting to come through the lock. In fact, there were three.

"Oh great," she moaned. "It'll take me forever to get back inside."

Lifting the edge of her long gray skirt, she hurried to open the first set of gates. Once the boat was completely in, she closed the gates and opened the wickets in the lower set of gates so that water flowed out of the lock, allowing the boat to drop slowly. Then the next set of gates was opened, allowing the mules to pull the boat on down the canal.

As the second boat came through the lock, Sarah's face contorted. The captain of the boat was Bart Jarmon, a tall burly man with thick black hair and a full, wooly-looking beard to match. Bart's foul mouth and overbearing ways were bad enough to deal with, but ever since Sam had died, Bart had often made suggestive remarks whenever he saw Sarah. Once, he'd even been so bold as to suggest that the two of them should get hitched, saying she could quit her job as lock tender and spend her days on his boat, cooking, cleaning, and washing his dirty clothes.

This canal would have to freeze over solid in the middle of summer before I'd ever consider marrying someone like Bart. Sarah gritted her teeth. *And what kind of stepfather would he make for my kids?*

She thought about the time, before Betsy married Pastor William, when Bart had gone to Betsy's place to pick up some clothes she'd washed for him. She could still see the look of disgust on Betsy's face when she'd later confided that after Bart had boldly kissed her, she'd thrown his wet shirt at him and told him never to come back.

Bart would be a lot wetter than he was then if he tried something like that with me, Sarah thought. *I'd push him into the muddy canal if he even looked like he was going to kiss me!*

Much to Sarah's relief, Bart wasn't steering the boat. His helper, Clem Smith, an elderly man with several missing teeth, was at the tiller. Sarah figured Bart was probably below on his bunk, sleeping off the effects from the whiskey he'd likely had the night before.

Sarah exchanged only a few words with Clem and kept

her mind on the business at hand. She knew how dangerous it could be for a lock tender who didn't pay close attention to what they were doing. Some lock tenders had gotten knocked over when they tried to get the pin in the wicket with one hand while they cranked with the other. If Sarah said more than a few words to any of the boatmen, it was usually after she'd finished the dangerous details of opening and closing the lock.

After Bart's boat passed through the lock, the next one came in, steered by Elias Brooks, the new boatman Sarah had met on his last trip through.

"My helper said you might have some bread to sell," Elias called to her.

She gave a quick nod. "There's some in the house."

"I'd like to buy a couple of loaves if you have any to spare." Elias pulled his fingers through his thick reddish-blond hair, cut just below his ears.

Sarah noticed for the first time that he had a large red blotch on his left cheek. No doubt, he'd been born with it.

She pulled her gaze quickly away for fear that he would think she'd been staring at him. "I'll get the bread as soon as your boat goes through. If you have time, you can tie up to one of the posts along the bank."

Elias looked at Ned, as though seeking his approval. Ned turned his hands palms up. "Guess we'll have to 'cause we do need the bread."

"That's what we'll do," Elias said with a nod.

Sarah did her job, and after Elias's boat made it through the lock, he maneuvered the boat toward the bank, while she hurried to the house to get the bread.

When she stepped inside, she stuck her head into the parlor. Maria was still on the sofa, and Kelly and Betsy sat in the chairs across from her.

"Where's Pastor William?" Sarah asked.

"He went to get Dr. McGrath," Betsy replied.

Sarah had been so busy with the boats that she hadn't seen the pastor leave her house.

"I need to take some bread to one of the boatmen," she said. "I'll be back as soon as I can."

Kelly smiled. "No problem. Take your time."

Sarah rushed into the kitchen, grabbed two loaves of bread, and ran out the door. She was halfway up the wooden plank leading to Elias's boat when her foot caught on a loose board, and one of the loaves flew out of her hands. She lunged for it, and gasped when it plopped into the canal.

Elias raced down the ramp and grabbed Sarah's arm. "Are you okay?"

Sarah's face heated as she nodded slowly. She felt like a clumsy fool. "I—I'm so sorry, but I dropped one of your loaves of bread into the canal."

Quack! Quack! Quack! A pair of mallard ducks landed on the water and quickly converged on the bread.

"Well, at least it won't go to waste," Elias said with a chuckle.

Sarah handed him the one good loaf. "I'll go back to the house and get you another."

"I'll walk with you," Elias said. "That way you won't have to come back out here again."

"At least not until another boat comes," Sarah muttered. This had not been a good way to begin her day.

Elias waited on the porch while Sarah went into the house. When she entered the kitchen to get another loaf of bread, Bristle Face, the scruffy-looking terrier Betsy had given them several months ago, ran in front of her, and she nearly lost her balance.

Sarah looked at Willis, who sat at the kitchen table with Helen and their cousins. "Would you please hold on to the dog until I've gone back outside?"

"Sure, Mama."

Sarah stuck her head into the parlor again. "Is everything okay in here?"

"Maria's sleeping," Betsy whispered. "Are you done outside?"

"Not yet. I accidentally dropped a loaf of bread into the canal and had to get a new one."

"Is there anything I can do to help?" Kelly asked.

"I think everything's under control. Elias Brooks is waiting outside for his bread, and he was very nice about the bread I dropped. I'll just be a few more minutes."

Sarah hurried outside, and found Elias sitting on the porch step, talking with his young mule driver, as well as Sammy, who'd just gotten home from school.

"Do you get to do much fishing in the canal?" Elias asked Sammy.

Sammy shook his head. "Used to fish some when Papa was alive." He glanced up at Sarah. "Mama's too busy for fishin', and she won't let me fish alone."

"Sure wish I had time to go fishin'." Bobby stared at the canal with a wistful expression. "But I guess that's never gonna happen 'cause I'm too busy leadin' the mules."

"Maybe some Sunday we can do some fishing," Elias said.

Bobby's eyes lit up, and so did Sammy's. "Ya mean it?" Bobby asked.

Elias nodded. "Sure thing."

"Can I fish with ya?" Sammy asked.

"If we're anywhere near here on a Sunday, we'd be happy to have you join us. That is, if your mother doesn't mind." Elias looked up at Sarah, as if to gauge her response.

"I—I don't know." Sarah leaned on the porch railing. She became edgy any time her children got too close to the water. After Sam had been killed, she'd been more nervous than ever.

Sammy tugged on the edge of Sarah's apron. "Please,

Mama. Can I go fishin' with Bobby and the nice man?"

Not wishing to create a scene or embarrass Sammy, Sarah patted the top of his head and said, "We'll have to wait and see how it goes." Secretly, she hoped that Elias never stopped anywhere near Walnutport on a Sunday.

Chapter 6

As Sarah, followed by Sammy, approached their front door, Pastor William showed up with the doctor.

"I'm so glad you're here, Dr. McGrath. As you know, Maria hasn't been feeling well for some time. Earlier today, she fell and hit her head because she couldn't see where she was going." Sarah drew in a quick breath. "I'm really worried about her, and we've been trying to talk her into moving to Easton to live with her son, Roger, but she refuses to go."

Dr. McGrath nodded his nearly bald head. "Pastor William has already filled me in. So let's go inside, and after I've examined Maria, I'll see if I can convince her to move."

"I appreciate that."

As Dr. McGrath and Pastor William headed for the parlor, Sarah ushered Sammy into the kitchen where the other children were playing.

"Is. . .is Grandma gonna die, Mama?" Sammy's chin trembled, and his blue eyes widened.

"No, son, but she's losing her eyesight, and it's not good for her to be here anymore. She needs to be in Easton where she can get help for her eyes and have someone to take care of her."

"I'll take care of her, and I'll keep an eye on Helen and Willis, too. I can quit school and stay home so I can help with whatever you need to have done."

Sarah gave Sammy's shoulder a gentle squeeze. "It's nice of you to volunteer, but you're still a little boy. Taking care of Grandma would be a full-time job, not to mention your busy little brother and sister." She tweaked the end of his nose. "Besides, you need to go to school so you can learn to read and write. You need to get an education so you can get a good-paying job when you grow up—something that will get you away from the canal."

Deep wrinkles etched his small forehead. "But I like the canal. Just wish I could go fishin' whenever I wanted to."

"Maybe your uncle Mike will take you fishing sometime, but you're never to go near the water when you're alone. Is that clear?"

He nodded. "That nice man with the red blotch on his face said he'd take me fishin' some Sunday. Can I go with him, Mama? Can I, please?"

"We go to church on Sundays; you know that."

"How 'bout after church? That canaler said some Sunday afternoon, so he must've meant after church."

"We'll see, Sammy. In the meantime, I want you to go in the kitchen." Sarah opened the door. "Now, shoo."

"Here you go," Elias said, handing the bread he'd bought to Ned. "This should last us for a few days, don't you think?"

Ned grunted. "I s'pose it will, but after all the time you spent gabbin' to the lock tender, we'll be even later gettin' to Easton with our load of coal."

"We'll get there when we get there."

Ned glanced over his shoulder. "Sure is a shame a purty lady like Sarah has to work so hard to provide for her kids."

Elias nodded. "Here on the canal, a lot of men and women work hard for a living."

"Which is why I can't figure out how come a smart, school-learned man like yourself would wanna run this here boat."

"I've told you before. . . I'm honoring my grandfather's wishes." Elias motioned to the trees bordering the towpath along the canal. "Besides, I enjoy it here on the water. It's peaceful, and the folks who live along here are down-to-earth, not phony."

"It ain't always so peaceful," Ned said with a shake of his head. "When some liquored-up canaler starts spoutin' off at some other fella, things can get real loud and ugly 'round here. Not to mention some of the brawls that take place when someone loses his temper 'cause they're tryin' to beat some other boat through the lock." Ned cupped his hands around his mouth and turned away from Elias. "Hey, mule boy," he called to Bobby, "quit draggin' your feet and get them mules movin' faster! We ain't got all day, ya know!"

Elias's jaw clenched as he ground his teeth together. Why did Ned think he needed to shout orders at Bobby like that? This was Elias's boat, and he was the only one who should be giving orders.

Of course, he reasoned, *the boy was walking kind of slow and probably did need a bit of prodding. It just could have been done in a nicer tone.*

"I don't think you need to holler at Bobby like that," Elias told Ned. "A little kindness goes a long way, you know."

Ned slapped the side of his pant leg and snorted real loud. "A little kindness might go a long way if you're tryin' to court some purty woman, but ya need to let your mule driver know who's boss from the get-go, or he'll slow ya down. And that'll cost ya more money than he's worth."

"I'll take your advice under consideration."

When Sarah stepped into the parlor, she stood off to one

side with the others as Dr. McGrath examined Maria. When he was done, he took Maria's hand and said, "Your eyes have gotten much worse, and as I've said before, without proper treatment it's only a matter of time before you'll be completely blind. I do think you'd be better off in Easton, where you can be seen by a specialist."

Maria opened her mouth as if to respond, but Sarah cut her off. "I'm going to send Roger a letter tomorrow morning and ask him to come get you."

Betsy stepped forward. "And you don't need to worry about anything here, because we'll see that Sarah gets all the help she needs."

Tears welled in Maria's eyes as she slowly nodded. "I'll go, but I don't have to like it."

Sarah knew she and the children would miss Maria, but it was for the best. She just wished she didn't have to rely on Betsy and Kelly for help, because they both had busy lives of their own. If only there was some other kind of work she could do to support her children. She just didn't know what it could be.

Chapter 7

One week later, Roger came to escort Maria to Easton.

As Sarah helped Maria pack her bags, she was filled with a deep sense of sadness. It was hard to let Maria go. The dear woman had lived with them after Sarah and Sam came back to the canal when Sammy was still a little guy. Then when Sam's father died, Maria had gone to live with Roger and his wife in Easton, but she'd returned to the canal to help Sarah after Sam was killed. Sarah had become dependent on Maria, and the children were attached to her, too.

"I wish I didn't have to go," Maria said. "I wish my eyes weren't failing me."

Sarah took a seat on the bed beside Maria and slipped her arm around Maria's waist. "I wish that, too, and we're going to miss you very much, but moving to Easton is the best thing for you right now."

Maria sighed. "I know."

A knock sounded on the bedroom door. "Are you ready, Mom? We need to get a move on if we're going to catch our train to Easton," Roger called through the closed door.

"Come in," Sarah said. She closed Maria's reticule and set it on the floor.

"Is everything ready?" Roger asked as he entered the room.

"Yes, her trunk is packed, and so is her smaller reticule." Sarah swallowed past the lump in her throat. Roger, though a bit taller and a few years older than Sam, looked so much like him. Roger had the same blond hair and blue eyes as his brother, only Roger sported a handlebar mustache, and Sam had always been clean-shaven. Roger worked at Glendon Iron Works, not far from Easton, and his wife, Mary, who was home all day, would be the one responsible for taking care of Maria. Sarah found comfort in knowing that Maria would have good care in Easton.

Sarah picked up the reticule, and Roger lifted Maria's trunk. Then they all went downstairs. The children, who'd been eating breakfast in the kitchen, gathered around Maria near the door.

"Sure wish you didn't hafta go," Sammy said, his voice quivering as he struggled not to cry.

Maria patted the top of his head. "Maybe you can come

to Easton to visit me sometime."

"That ain't never gonna happen," Sammy said with a shake of his head. "Mama has to be here all the time so she can open the lock."

"Maybe you can visit us sometime this winter when the canal's closed," Roger suggested.

Sarah bit her lip to keep from saying what was on her mind. With her limited funds, she didn't see any way that they'd ever be able to afford a trip to Easton. She wasn't about to tell Sammy that, though. No point in upsetting him any more than he already was.

"Well, it's time to go," Roger said. "If we don't head out now, we will miss our train."

Maria bent to give each of the children a hug, then she turned to Sarah and said, "Take care. I'll be praying for you."

Sarah hugged Maria. "I'll be praying for you, too."

When Betsy arrived at Sarah's, she found Sarah outside, letting a boat through the lock. "Oh no," she muttered. "I should have gotten here sooner. I'm sure the children are in the house by themselves, and poor Sarah must be worried about them."

Betsy hurried to the house, where she found Sarah's children sitting at the kitchen table, coloring a picture. "I thought you would have left for school by now," she said to Sammy.

He shook his head. "Since there was no one here to watch Willis and Helen, Mama said I should stay until you got here, 'cause someone has to keep an eye on 'em."

"I'm so sorry. I should have been here sooner." Betsy pulled out a chair and took a seat beside Sammy. "Now that I'm here, you can go to school."

His nose crinkled as he frowned. "I'd rather stay here so I can teach Bristle Face some new tricks. I wanna teach him to play dead and roll over."

"You can do that after you get home from school."

His eyes brightened. "Since Bristle Face used to be your dog, do ya wanna help me teach him some tricks?"

"I probably won't be here when you get home from school," Betsy said. "Your aunt Kelly will be taking over for me later this afternoon so I can practice the songs I'll be playing this Sunday at church." She smiled at the children. "If your mother's willing, I'd like to have you all over to our house for lunch after church lets out."

"Oh, Mama will be willing," Sammy said. "Now that Grandma's gone, Mama will be stuck with all the cookin' whether she likes it or not."

Betsy suppressed a smile. Children could be so honest about things. She looked forward to the day that she and William would have children of their own. Of course, they'd only been married since Christmas of last year, so most folks would say they still had plenty of time. Betsy didn't see it that way, though. She was thirty-three and wanted some children before she was too old to enjoy them.

She pointed to Sammy's lunch pail sitting on the counter. "You'd better head to school now, Sammy, or you'll really be late."

He grunted as he pushed his chair aside and stood. "Okay. I'll see ya tomorrow, Betsy."

"Hey, mule boy, get a move on!" Ned shouted from the bow of the boat. "How come you're draggin' your feet again?"

"I ain't feelin' so well," Bobby called in return. "Think I might throw up."

Ned flapped his hand, like he was shooing away a pesky fly. "Aw, quit your bellyachin' and get a move on now!"

Elias frowned as he stepped up to Ned. "Stop yelling at the boy. If he's sick, then we can't make him work."

Ned's forehead wrinkled, and he popped a piece of chewing tobacco in his mouth. "If that boy don't keep walkin', we'll never get this load of coal back to Easton."

"But if he's sick. . ."

"He ain't sick. He's just lazy, that's all."

Elias shook his head. "I don't think he's lazy. I think. . ."

493

"What in tarnation is that boy doin'?" Ned leaned over the boat and shook his fist. "What are ya doin' there in the bushes?"

Bobby, who was now crouched behind a clump of bushes, rose slowly to his feet as he clutched his stomach. "Just lost my breakfast, and I feel kinda weak."

"That's it, we're stopping!" Elias grabbed the tiller and turned the boat into the bank.

"What are we stoppin' for?" Ned grumbled. "We'll never get to Easton if we stop here."

"Bobby's too sick to lead the mules," Elias said. "He needs to lie on his bunk and rest, because if he keeps walking, he'll probably keel over."

Ned grunted. "What are you plannin' to do? Are ya goin' to leave the boat here until the boy feels well enough to walk?"

"No, I'll lead the mules, and you can steer the boat."

Ned's bushy eyebrows shot straight up. "Are you kiddin' me?"

"No, I'm certainly not. If we want to keep going, then it's the only thing we can do."

Ned spit his wad of chewing tobacco into the canal. "That's great. Just great! I doubt that you can lead the mules any better than the kid."

Elias set his lips in a firm line. He'd show Ned how well he could lead the mules.

Chapter 8

*T*he next morning as Sarah was about to join her children for breakfast, she heard the familiar moaning of a conch shell.

"Oh no," she said with a groan. "Another boat's coming through." She'd begun working at five thirty and had already opened the lock to six boats.

The conch shell blew again, and Sarah knew that even though Betsy hadn't arrived yet, she really must go.

"Sammy, keep an eye on your sister and brother," she instructed.

"Okay, Mama."

"And don't any of you leave the house," she said as she hurried out the door.

Sarah's fingers felt stiff and cold as she struggled to put

the pin in the wicket.

Suddenly, before Sarah realized what had happened, she was jerked backward and fell on her back. A stab of pain shot through her ribs. She was sure they must be broken. She tried to sit up, but the pain was so intense, all she could do was lie there and moan.

Elias had been walking the towpath since yesterday morning, and he was beginning to have an appreciation for how hard young Bobby worked. The boy was feeling somewhat better today, but was still too weak to walk. So Elias had decided to lead the mules again, as he was determined to see that Bobby got the rest he needed.

As Elias approached the Walnutport lock, he was shocked when he saw Sarah Turner get knocked to the ground.

"We need to stop!" he hollered at Ned.

"What for?" Ned leaned over the boat and glared at Elias. "I thought we was supposed to be goin' through the lock."

"The lock tender's been hurt!" Elias pointed to where Sarah lay on the ground. "I'm going over there to check on her." He secured the mules' lead rope to a nearby post and dashed over to where Sarah lay.

"What happened? Are you hurt?" he asked, squatting down beside her.

"I. . .I was pulling the pin from the wicket and ended up flat on my back." She curled her fingers into the palms of her hands tightly, obviously trying not to cry. "I think I may have broken my ribs."

"Let me help you into the house, and then I'll go into town and get the doctor," he said.

She shook her head. "I can't go in the house. Someone has to let your boat through the lock."

"I'll have Ned secure my boat, and then he can tend to the lock if any other boats should come through."

"Oh no, I couldn't expect him to do that. I need to—" She flinched as she tried to stand.

"You're in no shape to be working right now. I'm taking you into the house." Gently, Elias slipped his arm around Sarah's waist, and then he walked her slowly toward the house. They were almost there when Betsy Covington, the preacher's wife whom he'd met at Cooper's store the last time he'd stopped, showed up. When she looked at Sarah, her face registered immediate concern.

"Sarah, what happened?"

Sarah explained what had happened to her, and then Elias told Betsy that Ned was going to take care of the lock while he went to fetch the doctor.

"That's so nice of you," Betsy said. "Let's get Sarah inside so she can lie down."

They stepped into the house, and Elias helped Sarah into the parlor and over to the sofa. "I'm going out to tell Ned what he needs to do, and then I'll head to the doctor's office." He paused and looked at Betsy. "I'm not that familiar with Walnutport yet. Where is the doctor's office anyway?"

"It's on Main Street, next to the barber shop."

"Thanks." Elias turned and hurried out the door.

When he stepped outside, he found Ned standing by the post where he'd tied the mules.

"Sarah may have broken some ribs, so you're going to have to act as lock tender while I get the doctor," Elias said.

Ned's bushy eyebrows furrowed. "You've gotta be kidding!"

"You told me once that you'd worked as a lock tender for a while."

Ned shrugged. "So?"

"So I'm sure you know exactly what to do."

Ned motioned to the boat, which he'd tied up. "What about our load? How are we gonna get that delivered to Easton if we waste time hangin' around here?"

Elias's spine stiffened. "Helping someone in need is not a waste of time. And for your information, I'm wasting time right now, standing here arguing with you when I should be on my way to the doctor's office."

Ned grunted. "You're a do-gooder, just like your grand-pappy was."

Elias smiled. He saw being compared to his grandfather as a compliment. "Are you going to tend the lock or not?" he asked Ned.

Ned released a noisy grunt. "I'll do whatever you say, but only because you're the boss."

Chapter 9

When Elias returned with Dr. McGrath, Pastor William was at the house. "How's Sarah doing?" he asked Betsy, who sat at the kitchen table with the children.

"I fixed her some tea, and she's resting on the sofa, but every time another conch shell blows, she gets upset and says it's not right for someone else to be doing her job." Betsy rose from her seat and came to stand beside him. "I'm really concerned about her. She pushes herself too hard and is doing the work of a man when I'm sure she'd rather be taking care of her children."

"Sarah needs to provide for them," Pastor William said. "And she's been doing a good job of it, wouldn't you say?"

Betsy nodded. "But now that she's been hurt, she may not be able to work at all."

"Ned's helping out," Elias interjected.

"That's true, but he can't tend the lock indefinitely," Betsy said.

Pastor William slipped his arm around Betsy's waist. "Let's wait and see what the doctor says. In the meantime, the best thing we can do for Sarah is to pray."

"Well, your ribs don't appear to be broken," Dr. McGrath said as he examined Sarah. "However, they are severely bruised. I'll give you some liniment to put on them, but you'll need to rest for the next few days to give your ribs a chance to heal so you don't injure them any further."

Sarah shook her head. "I can't lie around here and rest. I need to tend the lock."

"I'll be right back."

When Dr. McGrath left the parlor, Sarah leaned her head against the arm of the sofa and listened to the wood crackling in the fireplace. If not for the pain in her ribs it would have felt nice to lie here and relax.

A few minutes later, the doctor returned with Betsy, Pastor William, and Elias.

"The doctor told us that he wants you to rest, and I think I have an answer to your problem," Elias said as he approached the sofa.

Sarah tipped her head. "What's that?"

"My mule driver's sick right now, but if I can find someone to fill in for him, then I'll leave Ned here to tend the lock and I'll head to Easton with my load of coal. By the time I get back, you may feel up to tending the lock again."

"I'll lead the mules for you," Sammy said, rushing into the room.

Sarah shook her head vigorously. "Absolutely not! I won't have any child of mine walking the towpath for hours on end."

"We'll go slow and easy," Elias said. "And I'll make sure to keep a close eye on the boy."

Sammy took a seat on the sofa beside Sarah and clutched her hand. "Please, Mama. I know I can do it. It'll make me happy to do somethin' helpful while you're here gettin' better."

Sarah looked up at Pastor William, whose deep blue eyes wore a look of concern. "Will you please tell my son what a bad idea that is?"

"I can do it, Mama," Sammy said before the pastor could respond. "I'm good with animals, and I've walked the mules a bit when some of the boats have stopped at Uncle Mike's store."

Sarah frowned. "What were you doing walking the mules?"

"Wanted to see what it was like, so one of the mule drivers let me try it awhile." Sammy puffed out his chest. "Leadin' the mules wasn't hard a'tall. Fact is, I kinda liked it."

Sarah shook her head again. "I said no, and that's final."

"But, Mama..."

Holding her sides, Sarah gritted her teeth and pulled herself off the sofa. "I'm not seriously hurt, and there's no need for Ned to stay and tend the lock."

Betsy rushed forward and took Sarah's arm. "You heard what the doctor said. You're not up to working yet."

Pastor William nodded. "My wife is right. You need to spend a few days resting so your ribs can heal." He turned to Elias. "If your offer's still open to leave Ned here to tend the lock, then I'll head back to town and see if I can find a mule driver for you."

Elias nodded. "My offer's still open. I'll go explain the situation to Ned, and then I'll move my boat over to Cooper's store, because I need to get some supplies."

"Want me to lead the mules so ya can get the boat over to the store?" Sammy asked.

Sarah held up her hand. "No! You need to go to school."

"But I'm already late, Mama. Can't I stay home today and help out around here?"

"Betsy came here to help. Now I want you to head for school right now."

Sammy frowned. "Don't see why ya hafta treat me like a baby all the time. Don't see why ya don't want my help."

"It's not that I don't want your help. I just don't think you should miss any school." She motioned to the kitchen. "Now go get the lunch I made for you earlier and be on your way."

With shoulders hunched and head down, Sammy shuffled out the door.

Pastor William gave Betsy's shoulder a squeeze. "I'm off to see if I can round up a mule driver for Elias, and then there are a few members from our congregation I need to call on. I'll see you at home this evening."

Betsy smiled. "Have a good day."

Elias looked over at Sarah. "When I go to the store for supplies, I'll ask Mike Cooper if it'll be okay for Ned to bed down in his stable when he's done working for the day. But he'll be back over here early tomorrow morning, ready to tend the lock."

Sarah managed a weak smile. "Thank you, I appreciate that."

After Elias and William left, Betsy turned to Sarah and said, "I'm going out to the kitchen to check on the children, and then I'll make us a pot of hot tea. While I'm doing that, why don't you lie down and rest?"

Sarah heaved a sigh. "Oh, alright. I can see with you all ganging up on me that I really have no other choice."

"I still don't see why I have to hang around here playin' lock tender while you head to Easton," Ned said after Elias had instructed him to lead the mules so he could pull the boat over to Cooper's store.

"I told you already. Sarah's ribs are badly bruised, and the doctor wants her to rest."

"But how are you gonna manage on the boat without me, and who are you gonna get to lead the mules?"

"I've seen a few other canalers manage their boats alone, so I'll get by somehow." Elias pointed in the direction of town. "The pastor's gone looking for someone to lead the mules, and as soon as he shows up, I'll be on my way."

Ned folded his arms and spat on the ground. "This is somethin' like your grandpappy would've done, and all I've gotta say is, sometimes a body can be too nice!"

Elias shook his head. "There's no such thing as being too nice. It's a Christian's duty to—"

"Now don't start preachin' to me. I had enough of that when I was workin' for your grandpappy."

"I'm not preaching. I'm only saying—"

"Don't care about a Christian's duty. I ain't no Christian, so my only duty is to work hard and try to earn a decent living."

Elias was tempted to argue, but he knew it would fall on deaf ears. He figured the best way to witness to Ned was through his actions. Maybe if he saw Christianity put into practice often enough, he'd realize he was missing something and would eventually seek the Lord.

"I'm getting back on the boat now," Elias said. "So it might be a good idea for you to get the mules heading down the towpath in the direction of the store before another boat comes along needing to get through the lock."

Ned grunted. "Whatever you say, boss."

Elias boarded the boat and took hold of the tiller. When they arrived in front of the store, he lowered the wooden plank and stepped onto the grassy bank. "You'd better get back to the lock now," he told Ned. "I hear a conch shell blowing in the distance, so it won't be long until the lock needs to be raised."

Ned opened his mouth like he might argue, but then he snapped it shut and ambled down the towpath in the direction of Sarah's house.

Elias hurried into the store, rounded up the supplies he needed, and was about to pay for them when Sammy entered the store.

"What are you doing here?" Elias asked. "I thought you'd gone to school."

Sammy shook his head. "Went home to ask Mama one more time if I could lead your mules." He gave Elias a lopsided grin. "She finally gave in and said I could go."

Elias rubbed his chin as he studied the boy. "Are you sure about that?"

Sammy nodded. "Guess we'd better get goin', huh, mister. . . What's your name, anyway?"

"It's Elias. Elias Brooks." Elias looked at Mike Cooper, who stood behind the counter, boxing up his supplies. "If Pastor William comes by with someone to lead my mules, would you tell him I've already found a mule driver and that we're on our way to Easton?"

Mike's mustache twitched, and his forehead wrinkled as he studied Sammy. "Are you sure your mama said you could go with Elias?"

Sammy bobbed his head. "And I'm ready to go now!"

Mike looked back at Elias. "I personally think Sammy's too young to be leading the mules, but if Sarah said it was okay then I guess I have no say in it."

"Will you give Pastor William my message?" Elias asked.

Mike nodded. "I'll be sure to tell him."

Elias paid Mike, scooped up the box, and headed out the door behind Sammy. He hoped he wasn't making a mistake by taking the boy along, but the eager look on Sammy's face gave him the confidence to believe that everything would go just fine on the trip to Easton.

Chapter 10

Sarah yawned and pulled herself to a sitting position. She had no idea how long she'd been sleeping, but the shadows on her bedroom wall told her it must be late afternoon. She rose slowly from the bed and ambled over to the window facing the canal. A boat was going through the locks. She'd been sleeping so hard she hadn't even heard the captain blow his conch shell. As much as she hated to admit it, having Ned here to tend the lock was a comfort. It would have been difficult, maybe even impossible for her to carry out her duties, hurting the way she did.

Sarah's stomach growled, reminding her that she hadn't eaten anything since noon. It was probably getting close to supper, and the children would no doubt be hungry. She really should go downstairs and help get their supper going so Betsy could go home and fix something to eat for her and Pastor William.

Sarah moved over to the dresser and peered at herself in the oval looking glass. She'd taken her hair down when she'd come upstairs to rest, and it was a tangled mess. She squinted at her reflection as she pulled her comb through the ends of her hair. The dark circles lying beneath her eyes seemed more pronounced than usual.

Many days, the first boat would come through the lock as early as five in the morning, and the last boat might not arrive until nine thirty at night. The only day Sarah got to sleep in was Sunday. Even then, she was up early so she and the children could go to church. Sometimes Kelly would take Sarah's children to her house after church so Sarah could rest. She didn't know what she would do without the help of her sister, as well as her dear friend Betsy. Even near-strangers like Elias had offered help. She still couldn't believe that he'd headed to Easton without anyone on the boat to help him. He'd obviously been successful in finding someone to lead his mules.

Sarah's stomach rumbled again, pulling her thoughts aside. Moving slowly, she left the room and made her way carefully down the winding stairs.

When she entered the kitchen, she found Betsy standing in front of the stove, stirring a kettle of stew. The tantalizing aroma made Sarah's mouth water.

"Did you have a good nap?" Betsy asked, turning to look at Sarah.

Sarah nodded. "I slept longer than I thought I would."

"I'm glad you did. You needed the rest." Betsy motioned to the table, where a gas lantern had been lit. "If you'd like to take a seat, I'll fix you a cup of tea, and we can visit while I finish making supper."

"Don't you want my help?"

"I can manage. Besides, you're supposed to rest."

Sarah pulled out a chair and winced as she sat down. "I can't believe I fell asleep like I did. I haven't slept that hard in ages."

"With the long hours you've been working, you need all the rest you can get." Betsy placed a pot of tea on the table and a cup for Sarah.

"Where are the kids?" Sarah asked as she poured herself some tea.

"Helen and Willis are playing a game in the parlor, but Sammy's not home from school yet."

Sarah frowned. "That's strange. He's always here way before it's time to start supper."

"Maybe he stopped by one of his friend's houses on the way home," Betsy said. "Or maybe the teacher kept him after school."

Sarah's frown deepened. "I hope not. Sammy's always had a mind of his own. I hope he didn't say or do anything to get in trouble with his teacher today." She rose from her seat and glanced out the kitchen window at the darkening sky. It looked like it might rain. "Maybe I should walk over to the schoolhouse and see if he's there. It'll be better than sitting here worrying about him."

"If anyone's going to the schoolhouse, it'll be me," Betsy said with a shake of her head. "The stew's simmering and should be okay, and when I get back, I'll fix some of that dough dab bread you often make to go with it. In the meantime, why don't you go into the parlor and watch the children play?"

"Are you sure you don't mind going after Sammy? If it rains you could get awfully wet."

Betsy smiled. "It wouldn't be the first time I got caught in a downpour, and a little water won't hurt me."

"Oh, all right," Sarah finally agreed. She just hoped Sammy wasn't in trouble with his teacher.

A few drops of water splattered Elias's arm, and he realized that it had started to rain. "Oh great, this is not what I need." He glanced at the towpath to see how Sammy was doing. The poor little fellow was limping and must have developed a blister from walking all day. Either that or he'd managed to get a rock in his boot. The boy had never complained even once, and had kept moving at a pretty good pace. The little bit Sammy had been taught about leading mules had obviously stuck, for Dolly and Daisy behaved as well for Sammy as they had for Bobby.

I still can't believe Sammy's mother agreed to let him go with me, Elias thought. *She'd seemed so dead set against it at first. Guess after she thought things through, she decided that Sammy was up to the task.*

Elias's stomach growled noisily. *I'd better fix us something to eat,* he decided. *If it keeps raining like this, I may as well stop for the night.*

"Hold up the mules!" Elias called to Sammy. "You can tie them to that tree over there, and then be ready to tie off the boat when I throw you the rope."

Sammy did as he was told, and then Elias steered the boat close to shore and set the wooden plank in place.

"What are we stoppin' for?" Sammy asked. "Did I do somethin' wrong?"

"No, not at all. You've done real well today. We need to eat supper, and since it's raining, I thought this would be a good time to stop." He pointed to Sammy's right foot. "I noticed you were limping. Do you have a blister on your foot?"

Sammy nodded. "I think so. Maybe tomorrow I'll walk in my bare feet."

Elias shook his head. "That's not a good idea. You might come across some poisonous snake on the path. Come aboard now. I've got some ointment on the boat for cuts, so I'll put some of that on your blister and then wrap it real good."

"That's nice of you, Mr. Brooks. You're a good man, just like my papa was."

Elias smiled. "You know, I'd like it if you'd leave out the 'Mr. Brooks' part, and just call me Elias."

Sammy grinned up at him. "You're a nice man, Elias."

As Betsy left the schoolhouse, a feeling of concern welled in her chest. Mabel Clark, the teacher, had been cleaning the blackboards when Betsy arrived, and when asked about Sammy, she'd explained that the boy hadn't been at school.

So, if he didn't go to school, where did he go when he left Sarah's house this morning? Betsy asked herself. *Did he decide to go fishing in the canal, or could he have gone into the woods to play? I need to go home and talk to William about this,* she decided. *Sure don't want to go back and tell Sarah her son is missing. At least not until we've looked for him.*

Betsy hurried her steps, and when she entered the parsonage, she was relieved to find William sitting at his desk, studying his sermon for Sunday.

"Sammy Turner's missing," she said, touching William's shoulder. "I need your help finding him."

William's forehead creased. "Did you look at the schoolhouse?"

"I did, but Mabel said Sammy never came to school, and I know for a fact that he hasn't been home all day."

William pushed his chair aside and stood. "That's not good. You're right; we need to look for him."

For the next hour, Betsy and William went up and down the streets of Walnutport, searching for Sammy and asking everyone they met if they'd seen any sign of the boy. No one had, and Betsy's concerns turned to fear. "What if he went fishing and fell in the canal?" she asked William. "What if he—"

William held up his hand. "Let's not think the worst. We need to keep looking."

"Where else shall we look?"

"I think we should check at Cooper's store. Sammy might have gone there to play with his cousins."

"Do you think he'd do that without asking his mother?"

William shrugged. "I'm not a father yet, so I'm no expert on children, but I wouldn't be surprised by anything Sammy might do. He's always been a challenge for Sarah, and his curiosity has sometimes gotten him in trouble."

"That's true, but if he'd gone to the store to play with his cousins, wouldn't Kelly or Mike have let Sarah know?"

William turned his hands palms up. "Not if they thought he'd gotten his mother's permission to come over."

"But surely they know Sarah would never allow Sammy to skip school so he could play."

"Maybe he found something else to do during school hours and then went over to the Coopers' later in the day."

"Well, it's worth checking anyway," Betsy said. "Should we walk or go back home and get our horse and buckboard?"

"We may as well walk, because we're at the end of town now, and it would take too much time to get the horse hitched to the buckboard."

"You've got a point." Betsy clasped William's arm, and they hurried toward the store, which had been built close to the canal, and was only a short distance from the lock tender's house.

When it came into view, Betsy noticed several children playing in the side yard near the Coopers' house, which was connected to the back of their store. She didn't, however, see Sammy among the children there.

"Should we check at the house or the store?" she asked William.

"Let's start with the store, because I'm sure it's still open."

When they entered the store, they found Mike behind the counter, waiting on Patrick O'Grady, the town's able-bodied blacksmith. Patrick, who was in his early thirties and still single, had wavy red hair and pale blue eyes—obvious traits from his Irish heritage. When they stepped up to the counter, he turned and gave them a nod. "I talked to

Gus Stevens at the livery stable, and he said you gave a fine sermon last Sunday, Preacher," Patrick said with a smile. "Gus said it got him to thinkin' that he oughta spend less time worryin' and more time prayin'."

"I'm glad Gus took something away from the sermon," William said. "I deliberated for a while on what I should preach last Sunday, but that was the sermon the Lord laid on my heart." His brows furrowed above his finely chiseled nose. "We'd like to have you join us in church sometime, Patrick."

"Maybe someday; we'll see," Patrick mumbled.

Betsy cleared her throat and nudged William's arm. "Did you want to ask Mike about Sammy, or should I?"

William's face turned red. "Oh, sorry. I forgot for a minute what we came here for. That happens to me sometimes when I'm talking about the Lord's work."

"What can I help you with?" Mike asked after he'd handed Patrick his purchases.

"Sammy's missing," Betsy said before William could even open his mouth. "His teacher said he didn't go to school today, and William and I have looked all over town for him."

"He's probably sitting along the bank of the canal someplace with his fishin' pole," Patrick called over his shoulder as he headed out the door. "That's what I used to do when I was his age." The door clicked shut behind Patrick.

"Sammy's not missing," Mike said. "I know exactly where he is."

A sense of relief flooded Betsy's soul. "Where?"

"He's walking the towpath, leading Elias's mules."

William's jaw dropped, and Betsy sucked in her breath. "Are—are you sure about that?"

Mike gave a nod. "Elias and Sammy were in the store earlier, and Sammy told Elias that his mother gave her permission for him to lead the mules."

Betsy clutched William's arm. "Sarah did not give Sammy permission to go with Elias. She told him in no uncertain terms that he couldn't go."

"I can't believe Sammy would lie to Elias like that," William said.

"We've got to go after him." Betsy's voice raised a notch. "We've got to bring him back to Sarah!"

"When they left here it was still early," Mike said. "They could be halfway to Easton by now. Elias seems like a very nice man. I'm sure Sammy will be fine with him."

Betsy glared at Mike. "Are you suggesting that we just let the boy walk to and from Easton, leading two mules who could easily trample him to death?"

"I'm well-acquainted with Elias's mules. He put them up in my stable when he docked his boat here for the night a week or so ago." Mike shook his head. "They were two of the most docile mules I've ever met, so I'm sure they won't harm Sammy in any way."

"Humph!" Betsy folded her arms. "Mules can kick and

bite, even the very tame ones. Why I remember once when I was girl, one of the young mule drivers ended up with a broken leg because a mule kicked him."

"I think we need to go over to Sarah's and tell her where Sammy is," William said. "After that, we'll decide what we should do about the situation."

Betsy nodded and drew in a deep breath. She dreaded telling Sarah what had happened to Sammy.

Chapter 11

Since the rain hadn't let up, Elias decided to stay put for the night, because he didn't want Sammy to get soaked. Even though most of the canal boats ran as many as eighteen hours a day, Elias felt that walking the mules that many hours was out of the question for such a young boy. Sammy looked so tired, Elias was afraid the boy might drop. And with a sore foot, asking him to walk any farther tonight would be just plain stupid.

"Let's go down below," Elias told the boy. "I'll cut a loaf of bread and heat us some bean soup."

Sammy nodded eagerly. "I am kinda hungry. Fact is, I think I could eat the whole loaf of bread."

Elias smiled and led the way to the galley, furnished with the barest of essentials. A small kitchen table was covered with oilcloth, and four stools were stored under the table when not in use. A black, coal-burning stove sat off to one side, and a kerosene lamp had been placed in a bracket on the wall over the table.

Elias set a pan of water on the stove to boil and then added some soaked navy beans, diced carrots, a cut-up onion, a hunk of salt pork, and just enough salt and pepper to season the soup. While it cooked, he cut some bread. Then after a short prayer, he and Sammy each had a piece.

"Have you ever been on a canal boat before?" Elias asked the boy.

Sammy nodded. "I was on my Grandpa McGregor's boat a few times, but of course, Mama wouldn't let me ride very far with him. Said she didn't want me gettin' used to the idea of canalin'."

"Why's that?"

"Mama's always said that she hates the canal. Says it took my papa, and that it's given her nothin' but misery."

"Does your grandpa still have his boat?" Elias asked, feeling the need for a change of subject.

Sammy shook his head. "He sold it and moved to Easton after Grandma died."

"That's too bad."

Sammy leaned his elbows on the table and stared at Elias. "Can I ask ya a question?"

"Sure."

"I've been wonderin' about that red mark on your face. Did ya burn yourself or somethin'?"

Elias shook his head. "I was born with it."

"Does it hurt?"

"No, not at all."

"Can I touch it?"

In all Elias's twenty-eight years, he'd had lots of people ask about the birthmark, stare at him curiously, and even make fun of him, but he'd never had anyone ask if he could touch it. "I. . .uh. . .guess it'd be okay," he said.

Sammy leaned over and placed his hand on Elias's cheek. "It feels like skin—same as any other."

A smile tugged at the corners of Elias's mouth. "Yes, Sammy, it's just a different color from the rest of my skin."

Sammy nodded and leaned back in his chair, lacing his fingers behind his head. "Can I ask ya another question?"

"Sure."

"My other grandma used to live with us, but she's goin' blind and had to move to Easton awhile back. I was wonderin' if we could stop and see her there."

Elias shook his head. "I'm sorry, Sammy, but I don't know where your grandma lives. Even if I did, I couldn't leave my boat and mules unattended to take you there." He gave Sammy's shoulder a squeeze. "Maybe you'll get to Easton to see her some other time."

Sammy stared down at his plate and mumbled, "I sure hope so."

Elias pushed the loaf of bread toward Sammy. "Would you like another piece?"

"Think I'd better wait for the soup. Wouldn't wanna eat up all your bread."

"That's okay. There's plenty." Elias cut Sammy another piece of bread; then he went to the small cabin where he slept and got out his accordion.

"Ever heard one of these?" he asked the boy.

"Nope, but the preacher's wife plays the zither and the organ."

"Well, this is called an accordion. It has keys and bellows, sort of like an organ." Elias slipped the straps over his shoulders. "Now here's a song just for you, Sammy. It's called 'Go Along Mule.'"

Elias began to play and sing: *"I've got a mule, she's such a fool; she never pays me no heed. I'll build a fire beneath her tail, and then she'll show me some speed."*

Sammy laughed and joined Elias as they sang the song together.

What a joy it was for Elias to spend time with this easygoing young lad. It made him long to be a father.

But that's just an impossible dream, Elias thought as he touched the red mark on his face. *Surely no decent woman would want someone as ugly as me.*

"Mama, I'm hungry." Willis, who sat at the table beside Sarah as she drank a cup of tea, tugged on her sleeve. "Is it time for supper yet?"

Sarah glanced at the windup clock sitting on the counter across the room. It was time for supper, but she didn't want to eat until Sammy got home. She couldn't figure out why he wasn't here yet. Even if he'd been kept after school, he should have been home by now.

Willis gave Sarah's sleeve another tug. "Mama, I'm hungry."

"We'll eat supper as soon as Betsy gets back here with Sammy." Sarah rose from her chair. "Would you like a piece of jelly bread to tide you over?"

Willis bobbed his head and then pointed to his little sister, who was sitting on the floor, petting Bristle Face. "I think Helen would like one, too."

Sarah winced when she picked up a knife to butter the bread. Even a simple movement caused her ribs to ache.

She'd just given the children some bread spread with jelly and a glass of milk when the back door swung open and Ned stepped in. "If supper's ready, I can eat real quick and get back outside, 'cause the last canaler who went through said there were three more boats comin' up the canal behind him.

"Let me check on the stew." Sarah lifted the lid on the kettle and poked a potato with a fork. "It seems to be done enough, so as soon you wash up I'll dish you and the kids a bowl and then you can eat."

"I already washed in the canal."

"Oh, I see. Well, have a seat then, and I'll get you some stew."

"What about you? Ain't you gonna eat with us?"

She shook her head. "I'll wait until Sammy gets home."

"Didn't realize he wasn't here." Ned pulled his fingers down the length of his bristly face. "Where'd the boy go?"

She shrugged. "I don't know. I think he may have been kept after school."

Ned grunted as he took a seat at the table. "Can't tell ya how many times I was kept after school when I was a boy. 'Course, I only had a few years of learnin' before I started workin' for my pappy." He reached for a piece of bread and slathered it with some of the strawberry jelly Maria had made before her eyesight had gotten so bad. "I was eight years old when I started leadin' the mules that pulled Pappy's boat."

Sarah cringed. She wouldn't even think of taking Sammy out of school so he could walk the rutted towpath for hours on end, the way she and Kelly had done when they were girls. "Didn't you go to school at all after you began walking the mules?" she questioned.

"Went durin' the colder months when the canal was

shut down, but by the time I was twelve, I'd begun cuttin' ice with Pappy during the winter. Then in the spring when the boats started up again, I'd quit school and start walkin' the mules." Ned puffed out his chest. "Got pretty good at it, too, I might add."

Sarah was glad she and Kelly had been allowed to attend school during the winter months. Mama had taught them some on the boat before bedtime, too, so at least they'd gotten a fairly good education.

Turning her thoughts aside, Sarah ladled some stew into three bowls and set them on the table. She was about to tell the children to bow their heads for prayer when the back door opened. Betsy and Pastor William stepped in. The solemn look on Betsy's face sent a chill up Sarah's spine.

"What's wrong?" she asked fearfully. "Didn't you find Sammy?"

Pastor William shook his head. "No, but we know where he is."

"Wh–where is he?"

"He's with Elias—leading his mules."

Sarah gasped and grabbed the back of a chair for support. "But how can that be? This morning I specifically told him that he couldn't lead those mules, and Elias heard me say it, too." She looked at Pastor William. "When Elias's boat disappeared, I thought you must have found a mule driver for him in town."

He shook his head. "I couldn't find anyone, and when I went to the place where Elias had tied up his boat, he was gone. So I figured he must have found someone on his own."

White-hot anger boiled inside Sarah, and she clenched her fists in frustration, until her nails dug into her palms. "How could that man have taken my son when he knew I didn't want Sammy to go?"

Betsy shook her head. "That's not how it happened, Sarah. William and I just spoke to Mike, and he heard what Sammy said to Elias at the store this morning."

Sarah's eyebrows squeezed together. "What are you talking about? I sent Sammy to school, and Elias was going to wait until Pastor William found someone to lead his mules. How could Mike have heard Sammy talking to Elias at the store?"

Betsy explained about the conversation that had taken place between Elias and Sammy. "Apparently, Sammy never went to school. Instead, he convinced Elias that you'd changed your mind and had given your permission for Sammy to go with him."

Sarah stomped her foot, and winced when a jolt of pain shot through her ribs. "I never changed my mind, and I can't imagine that Sammy would lie and say that I had."

"So what are you sayin'?" Ned spoke up. "Are you sayin' that the storekeeper was lyin'?"

"I'm not saying that at all. What I think is that Elias was

so desperate for someone to lead his mules that he talked Sammy into going with him. Who knows, maybe he even told Sammy that he'd spoken with me again, and that I'd said it was all right for him to go."

Ned shook his head. "Elias would never do nothin' like that. He's a good man—and an honest one, to boot."

Sarah clasped Pastor William's arm. "Would you go after my boy and bring him home?"

Pastor William slowly shook his head. "They left hours ago, Sarah. They're probably halfway to Easton by now. I think the best thing we can do is trust God to take care of Sammy and wait for him to come home."

Sarah blinked back tears that were stinging her eyes and sank into a chair at the table with a moan.

"Not to worry," Ned said. "Elias will take good care of your boy."

Sarah couldn't even speak around the lump in her throat. She was worried sick and didn't know Elias well enough to have any confidence that he'd take proper care of her boy. Besides, there were so many things that could happen while he was leading the mules. He could get kicked or bitten by one of those stubborn beasts. He could collapse from the exhaustion of walking too many hours. She remembered how when she was a girl working for her father, she'd once seen a young boy get dragged by his mule right over one of the lockgates. It was a frightening thing to watch, and it was a miracle the boy hadn't drowned in the canal.

"I think what we all need to do is hold hands and offer a prayer for Elias and Sammy," Pastor William suggested.

"You can count me out of the prayer," Ned said. "I ain't into all that religious stuff!"

Pastor William gave Ned's shoulder a squeeze. "The Lord never makes a man do anything against his will, so if you're not comfortable with praying you can just sit and listen. How's that sound?"

Ned gave a nod. "Suits me just fine."

Pastor William joined hands with Sarah and Betsy. "Heavenly Father," he prayed, "please be with Elias and Sammy wherever they are right now. Give them a safe trip to Easton and back, and let them know that You are right there with them. Be with Sarah and her children here, and give her a sense of peace, knowing that You'll watch over her son and bring him safely back home. Amen."

Sarah sniffed as tears rolled down her hot cheeks, wishing once again that there might be some way to get her children away from the canal.

Chapter 12

*A*fter spending a night on the canal near Kimmet's Lock, about fourteen miles from Walnutport, Elias was able to make his coal delivery to Easton by late afternoon the following day. They'd headed out as soon as the boat was unloaded and had gone as far as the Catasauqua Lock and then spent that night. They'd gotten an early start this morning, and if all went well, they should be back at Walnutport before noon.

It had rained off and on yesterday, and even though the sun was out now, the towpath was quite muddy. Elias hoped it wouldn't slow them down too much. He alternated between looking up ahead as he steered the boat and keeping an eye on Sammy as he led the mules.

He frowned when he realized that Sammy's trousers

were caked with mud. He wished he could wash the boy's clothes before he dropped him off at home, but if he took time for that, they'd be even later getting back to Walnutport. Besides, the sun wasn't warm enough to dry the clothes.

As they continued to travel, Elias reflected on the time he'd spent with Sammy and realized he was going to miss the boy when he returned him to his family. Last night, they'd visited during supper again, and afterward, Elias had played the accordion while they sang. Just before they'd gone to bed, Elias had told Sammy that when they got back to Walnutport, he would pay him for walking the mules. Sammy had smiled and said he planned to use the money to buy his mother a birthday present, because this coming Sunday was her birthday.

That boy is sure thoughtful, Elias thought. *Most kids Sammy's age only think of themselves. He must love his mother very much.*

"Get up there! Haw! Haw!"

Elias jerked his head to the left and grimaced when he saw Sammy slipping and sliding along the muddy towpath, as he struggled to keep the mules moving. They balked whenever they came to a puddle, and Sammy had to lead them around it, no matter how small the puddle of water was. At the rate they were going, it would be late in the day before they made it back to Walnutport.

Elias cupped his hands around his mouth. "Are you doing okay, Sammy? Do you need to stop for a while?"

"I'm fine. Just need to show these stubborn mules who's boss." Sammy tipped his head back and began to sing, "*I've got a mule, she's such a fool, she never pays me no heed. I'll build a fire under her tail, and then she'll show me some speed.*"

Elias chuckled. The boy had determination, as well as a sense of humor—exactly what was needed here on the canal.

When Betsy showed up at Sarah's much later than usual that morning, Sarah noticed right away that she looked pale and seemed kind of shaky.

"What's wrong?" Sarah asked. "Has something happened?"

Betsy shook her head. "I'm just feeling a bit queasy this morning. I think I might be coming down with the flu. If that's the case, then I probably shouldn't be here today. I wouldn't want to expose you and the children, but at the same time I don't want to leave you alone all day when I know you're still hurting."

"I'm feeling better now, so if you're not well, then you need to go home and rest."

Betsy hesitated a minute. "I. . .I don't suppose Sammy's come home yet."

Sarah slowly shook her head. "I'm trying not to worry, but it isn't easy."

"I'm sure it's not, but you need to keep trusting the Lord."

Betsy offered Sarah a smile. "When Sammy does get home, send him over to the parsonage to let me know. That way I can spread the word to those who've been praying for him."

"I will, and if you're not feeling up to watching my kids when I start working again, let me know, and I'll see if Kelly's available for a few hours to help out."

"I'm sure I'll be fine in a day or so." Betsy placed both hands against her stomach. "It could even be something I ate last night that didn't agree with me." She turned and started down the stairs, calling over her shoulder, "See you soon, Sarah."

When Sarah returned to the kitchen she discovered that Willis and Helen had gotten out some of her pots and pans and had them strewn all over the kitchen floor.

"Pick those up and put them away!" Sarah shouted.

Willis blinked his eyes rapidly, and Helen started to howl.

Sarah's head began to pound. Everything seemed to bother her more since Sammy had taken off with Elias. If she only knew whether he was safe or not. If he'd just come home to her now.

"I'll tell you what," she said to the children in a much softer tone. "If you two will put the pots and pans away I'll take you for a walk to Aunt Kelly and Uncle Mike's store."

"Can we have a peppermint stick?" Willis wanted to know.

Sarah nodded. "If you do as I say and pick up the pots and pans."

Willis went to work immediately, and even Helen put a few of the pans back in the cupboard. When they were done, Sarah got their jackets and led them out the door.

As they walked the towpath, Sarah felt a cool morning breeze blowing through the canal that ran north and south.

She glanced at the hills surrounding Walnutport and noticed how green they were. Spring was definitely here, and it wouldn't be long before the flowers she'd planted near the house would be in full bloom.

"Look, Mama...a quack, quack." Helen pointed to a pair of mallard ducks floating gracefully on the canal.

"And look over there," Willis said, pointing to a bushy-tailed squirrel running through the grassy area on one side of the towpath.

Before Sarah could respond, Willis darted through the grass, giving the poor squirrel a merry chase. Helen tried to join him, but Sarah took hold of her hand.

"Leave that squirrel alone, Willis," Sarah scolded. "If we don't keep walking, we'll never get to the store."

Willis halted the chase and joined Sarah and Helen on the path again.

When they entered the store, the children went immediately to the candy counter, which was their favorite place.

"What can I do for the two of you?" Mike asked as he stepped out from behind the counter where he waited on customers.

"Candy! Candy!" Helen shouted. She hopped up and down on her toes, while Willis pressed his nose against the glass and peered at the candy.

Mike looked at Sarah and chuckled. "These two seem pretty eager today. Did you say they could have some candy?"

"Yes, I did," Sarah replied. "I said they could have a peppermint stick."

"Alright, then." Mike opened the back of the candy counter and pulled out the glass jar full of peppermint sticks. Then he came around, knelt beside the children, and handed them each one. "Anna and Marcus are in the house," he said. "Why don't the two of you go over there and play awhile?"

The children didn't have to be asked twice. They each took a lick from their peppermint sticks and scurried through the door leading to Mike and Kelly's house.

Sarah pulled some money from her apron pocket and handed it to Mike.

"What's that for?" he asked.

"The kids' peppermint sticks."

He shook his head. "No way; the candy's my treat."

She smiled. "Thank you." Her kids were fortunate to have such a nice uncle, and Sarah was glad that Kelly had found such a considerate husband.

"How are your ribs feeling?" Mike asked.

"They don't hurt quite so much, but I'd feel a lot better if Sammy would come home."

"I'm sure he'll be here soon. Elias has probably been taking his time so he doesn't wear Sammy out."

"Humph! Sammy's too young and inexperienced to be leading a pair of unpredictable mules. He shouldn't have gone with Elias at all!"

"You're right, but I'm sure he'll be fine."

"Is Kelly in the house or her studio?" Sarah asked, changing the subject. If she kept talking about Sammy she'd get all worked up.

"She's in her studio, painting. Why don't you visit with her awhile? I'm sure she'd be glad to see you."

"Okay." Sarah started in the direction of the adjoining art studio, when she heard the familiar moaning of a conch shell. She moved quickly to the front window. "Maybe that's Elias and Sammy." She stepped outside and waited until the boat came around the bend, but when it came into her line of vision, she realized it was traveling toward Easton, so it couldn't be them.

She was just about to step back into the store, when Patrick O'Grady, the town's blacksmith, showed up.

"Top of the mornin', Sarah," he said, tipping the straw hat he wore over his curly red hair. "How are you doin' this fine spring day?"

"I've been better," she mumbled.

"I heard about the fall you took a few days ago and have been wonderin' how you were doin'. Fact is, I'd planned to come by your place yesterday, but I got so busy in my shop that I couldn't get away."

"I'm doing some better, and my ribs aren't quite so sore."

"That's good to hear." He grinned, and the deep dimples in his cheeks seemed to be winking at her. "Say, I was wondering. Would you and your youngsters be interested in goin' on a picnic with me this Sunday? Thought maybe we could start out in the morning and do some fishin' in the canal before we eat."

Sarah's fingers tightened around the edge of her jacket. "Well, uh. . .we always go to church on Sundays."

"Oh yeah, that's right. Well, how about we get together later in the day?"

"Maybe some other time—when my ribs are feeling better, and my boy Sammy's back home."

"Where'd he go?"

Sarah explained about Sammy's unexpected trip with Elias and ended it by saying, "So I don't feel that I can go anywhere until my boy's home safe and sound."

"When I was in here the other day I heard the preacher and his wife say they'd been lookin' for Sammy. But I figured the boy had probably just gone off fishin' somewhere." Patrick's nose wrinkled as he gave an undignified snort.

"What in the world was that boatman thinking? He had no right to take off with a kid as young as Sammy."

"I've been thinking the very same thing."

Another conch shell blew, and a few minutes later a boat came into view. Sarah's heart gave a lurch. It was Elias's boat, and there was Sammy, leading the mules.

As the boat pulled up to a wooden post near the store, Sarah lifted the edge of her skirt and raced through the tall grass, ready to give both Elias and Sammy a piece of her mind.

Chapter 13

*O*h, I'm so glad you're back." Sarah pulled Sammy close and hugged him tightly. "I was worried sick about you."

When Sammy looked up at her, his eyes shone brightly. "I did real good leadin' the mules; Elias said so." He patted the pocket in his trousers. "He paid me for helpin' him, too."

Sarah looked up at Elias and shook her finger, the way she often did when one of her children had done something wrong. "What were you thinking, taking off with my boy like that—and without even getting my permission?"

Elias's face turned red, matching the birthmark on his cheek. "But I. . .I thought—that is, I mean, Sammy said you'd given him your permission."

Sarah shook her head. "I told him no. You were right there when I said it, too."

"I realize that, but Sammy said you'd changed your mind, and. . ."

Sarah turned back to Sammy. "Did you lie to Elias and tell him I said it was okay for you to lead his mules?"

Sammy nodded slowly and dropped his gaze to the ground. "I wanted to earn some money so I could—"

"There's no excuse for lying; I've taught you better than that." Sarah's hands shook as she held them firmly at her sides. "You disobeyed me, and then lied to Elias, and now you'll need to be punished." She pointed to the store. "Go inside and wait for me. I'll be in soon, and then we'll be heading for home."

Sammy's eyes filled with tears. "I'm sorry, Mama. Sure didn't mean to upset ya, but I—"

"Just go into the store; we'll talk about this later. Oh, and please tell Uncle Mike to ask one of his customers from town to let Pastor William and Betsy know that you've come home."

"I can let them know," Elias spoke up. "I have to go into town to check on Bobby, my mule driver, so it'll be right on my way."

"Okay, thanks," Sarah mumbled.

Sammy started to walk away but turned back and looked up at Elias. "Thanks for all the things ya taught me. I had a real good time."

Elias smiled and nodded. "I had a good time with you, too."

Sammy turned and sprinted to the store.

"I'm really sorry about this," Elias said. "If I'd had any idea that Sammy—"

"Sammy's only a boy. You shouldn't have taken his word. You should have checked with me first."

He nodded. "You're right. In fact, I take the full blame, so please don't be too hard on Sammy."

Irritation welled in Sarah's soul. "Don't tell me how to raise my son. Sammy lied, and he needs a reminder not to do it again."

"You're right, of course. I only meant that it wasn't solely his fault, and I hope you'll take that into consideration."

"I'll consider all that needs to be considered. Now, if you'll excuse me, I need to get my kids and go home." She started to move away, but Elias touched her arm, and she whirled around to face him. "What?"

"How are your ribs? Are they better?"

"They're not fully healed, but I'm sure I can manage to do my work again now."

"Why not give yourself another day or so to heal? I'll be staying here until Monday morning, so Ned may as well continue opening the lock for the rest of the day, and since Sunday's a day of rest it'll give us all a chance to renew."

Sarah considered Elias's suggestion. He really did seem to care about her predicament. "That's fine," she said with a nod. "If I don't have to worry about the lock for the rest of the day it'll give me some time to care for my kids. From the looks of Sammy's trousers and shirt, I'd say he and his clothes both need a good washing."

"We had some rain on the way to Easton, which made the towpath quite muddy."

"Oh, I know all about the muddy towpath. I traipsed through more mud than I care to think about when I was a girl leading my papa's mules."

Elias quirked an eyebrow. "I didn't realize you'd ever been a mule driver. I thought maybe you'd grown up in the lock tender's house."

"No, my husband's folks tended the lock before he took it over, and then after he died, it became my job." Sarah frowned. "I hated walking the towpath when I was a girl, so when I turned eighteen, I ran away with Sam, and we got married. We both worked in Phillipsburg, New Jersey, for a time, before returning here to Walnutport." Sarah didn't know why she was telling Elias all this. She barely knew the man, and it was really none of his business, and yet he seemed so easy to talk to and seemed to be interested in what she was saying. "I'd better go," she murmured. "Thanks for bringing Sammy home safe." Sarah turned and hurried toward the store.

Elias, still feeling bad about taking Sammy without checking with Sarah first, headed over to the lock to see Ned. He found him sitting on a rock close to the canal, with a fishing pole in his hand.

"I saw your boat pull in," Ned said when Elias took a seat on the ground next to him. "Sure took ya long enough to get up to Easton and back here again."

"Since Sammy's not an experienced mule driver, I didn't want to push him too hard. We also had some rainy weather to deal with."

Ned grunted. "I heard you'd taken the kid along. His mama wasn't too happy about that, ya know. In fact, I had to hear about it several times."

"Yes, I'm sure. I've apologized to Sarah for taking Sammy's word and not checking with her first." Elias frowned. "I still don't understand why he lied to me."

Ned spit a wad of chewing tobacco into the canal. "Lyin's what kids do best." He snorted. " 'Course I'm sure someone as good as you has never told a lie in his life."

"I'm not perfect, and I think everyone's lied at some time or another. The Bible says in Romans 3:23, 'For all have sinned, and come short of the glory of God.'"

Ned spat again. "Don't start preachin' to me, now. I ain't in the mood."

"I wasn't preaching. I was just saying that everyone has sinned, which means that most people have told a lie or two."

"Yeah, whatever."

Elias decided it was time for a change in conversation. "I see you're making good use of your time when you're not bringing a boat through the lock," he said, motioning to the fishing pole in Ned's hand.

"Yep. Thought I might catch me a mess of fish for supper tonight. 'Course I'd figured on offerin' them to Sarah, since she's been feedin' me while you've been gone. Now that you're back, and since Sarah's feelin' better, I'd better quit fishin' so we can be on our way to Mauch Chunk."

Elias shook his head. "I've decided to stay here for the rest of today and Sunday, of course. We'll head out on Monday morning."

Ned's bushy eyebrows lifted high on his forehead. "And waste the rest of a perfectly good day? Are ya crazy, man?"

"No, I'm not crazy, and need I remind you that you're working for me, not the other way around? So I'd appreciate it if you just accepted my decision without grumbling about it."

"But why would ya wanna hang around here all day when you've got a load of coal to pick up?"

"So you can continue opening the lock. I think Sarah needs an extra day or so to allow her ribs to heal sufficiently. If we stay here until Monday, it'll give me a chance to visit the church in Walnutport, too."

Ned squinted his beady eyes, and his thin lips compressed. "Guess if you wanna go to church, that's your decision, but don't look for me to tag along."

Elias shrugged. "That's entirely up to you." He pulled himself to his feet. "We'll eat on the boat tonight, so if you catch any fish, we can have them for supper."

"Mike Cooper loaned me this fishin' pole, since mine was on your boat. Why don't ya go over to his store and see if he's got another pole you can use? That way we'll have twice as many fish for supper."

"It's tempting, but I need to go over to the boardinghouse where we left Bobby with his aunt Martha and see if he's feeling better and will be ready to lead the mules on Monday morning. You haven't heard anything about how the boy's doing, have you?"

Ned shook his head. "Been too busy here to check on him."

"Okay. After I inquire about Bobby, I need to stop by the preacher's house and let him and his wife know that Sammy made it home okay. I'll either see you back here or at the boat."

"Sure thing, boss. Whatever you say."

Elias shook his head as he walked away. He hoped that someday Ned might be won to the Lord, but he wouldn't push. He'd just allow things to come naturally and let the Lord lead.

Chapter 14

*O*n Sunday morning as Sarah sat on one of the wooden pews in church with her children, she was surprised to see Elias enter the sanctuary and take a seat in the pew across from her. As the first song, "We Have an Anchor," was announced, everyone stood. Sammy slipped quickly past Sarah and darted across the aisle to stand beside Elias.

Sarah gritted her teeth. She wasn't one bit happy about this but didn't make a move to bring him back to her pew because she figured he might balk. She sure didn't want to create a scene during church.

Sammy was a spirited child with a mind of his own. He obviously preferred to sit with Elias instead of her.

Maybe he's still angry about the paddling I gave him for lying yesterday, Sarah thought. *I don't think he realized that it*

545

hurt me more than it did him. But he needed to learn that lying is not acceptable.

From past experience, Sarah knew that a strong lecture or even some extra chores, wouldn't have been enough to get Sammy's attention and help him remember not to tell more lies.

Sarah focused her thoughts back to the song. The words were fitting for this group of people who lived along the canal. She needed the reminder that even when the storms of life threatened to overtake her, Jesus was the anchor she could count on.

When the song ended, everyone sat down. Then Pastor William moved over to stand beside Betsy at the organ. They sang a duet, "Tell It to Jesus."

Sarah leaned against the back of her pew and closed her eyes as she took the words of the song to heart.

"Are you weary, are you heavy-hearted? Tell it to Jesus; tell it to Jesus. Are you grieving over joys departed? Tell it to Jesus alone."

Sarah was indeed, weary. She'd been weary ever since Sam's passing. Even on Sundays, her only day of rest, she was sometimes so tired she could hardly keep her eyes open. She was also grieving over joys departed because it seemed like she and Sam had only had a few short years of real happiness in their marriage.

When she'd first run away and married him, it had been

to get away from the canal and her father's harsh ways. Then, after they'd moved to New Jersey and taken jobs, Sam had started drinking and had lost his job. Eventually, he'd walked out on Sarah and little Sammy. It wasn't until Sarah moved back to the canal to live with her folks that Sam had finally come to his senses and begged her to give him a second chance.

They'd moved into his folks' house, and Sam had tended the lock with his dad while Sarah helped Sam's mother bake bread to sell to the boatmen. After Sam's father died, Maria moved to Easton to live with Roger. Sam took over the lock tender's responsibilities, and Sarah started doing laundry for the boatmen to help with their finances.

Soon after that, Sam began attending church and had made a sincere commitment to the Lord. From that point on, they'd had the kind of marriage God intended for a husband and wife. During the short time before Sam's death, he'd been a loving husband and father. If only he hadn't been snatched away. If things could have stayed the way they were. Then Sarah wouldn't be faced with the responsibility of raising three children on her own, while trying to make a living doing something she'd rather not do.

"Now if you'll turn in your Bibles to First Peter, we'll be reading from chapter five, verse seven," Pastor William announced.

Sarah's eyes snapped open. She'd been so consumed with

her thoughts that she hadn't even realized Betsy and Pastor William had finished their song.

She opened her Bible and found the scripture passage in 1 Peter. As Pastor William read the verse, she followed along: *"Casting all your care upon him; for he careth for you."*

Sarah needed that reminder. She knew she should read a few verses of scripture every day if she was going to make it through the storms of life. The Bible was full of wisdom, and she was reminded of Psalm 119:105 that said God's Word was a lamp unto her feet and a light unto her path.

Elias glanced at Sammy, sitting so close to him that their arms touched, and he smiled. During the short time he and the boy had spent together on the trip to and from Easton, they'd established a bond. Elias didn't know if it was because Sammy missed his father and needed a man in his life, or if it was because he, wishing to be a father, had bonded with the boy. In any case, it appeared Sammy liked being with Elias, or he wouldn't have left his seat and come over here to sit beside him.

I wonder how his mother feels about that. Elias glanced across the aisle at Sarah, who seemed to be listening intently to the pastor's message. He wondered if Sammy had been able to buy his mother a birthday present, like he'd wanted to do. He also wondered if Sammy had been punished for lying. No doubt he had, since Sarah had been so upset about it. Even though Elias didn't know Sarah very well, she seemed like a good mother who loved her children and wanted the best for them. Sometimes that included discipline—or as Elias's mother used to say when he was a boy: *"I'm punishing you for your own good, and someday you'll thank me for it."*

Elias wasn't sure he'd ever felt thankful for the spankings he'd gotten, but he knew that reasonable discipline was necessary in order to teach children right from wrong.

He glanced around the room at the group who'd come to worship the Lord this fine spring morning. Being in church with these simple folk who didn't put on airs like some of the people in his church back home gave him a sense of belonging. He saw sincerity on their faces, not pride or holier-than-thou expressions. Maybe it was because the people who attended the Walnutport Community Church were hardworking, plain folks, who didn't put on airs or judge a man by how much money he made or how powerful he'd become. *"A man's life is judged not on the things he has but on the things he does,"* Elias's grandfather used to say.

Elias turned his attention to the Bible in his hands, and the words on the page blurred as tears clouded his vision. Grandpa had been a good man with a heart for people, and Elias missed him.

If only Father could be as caring and understanding as

Grandpa used to be, Elias thought ruefully. He'd never understood how the son of such an endearing man could turn out so cold and unfeeling. If not for the religious upbringing Elias's mother had given him, along with the godly influence of his grandfather, Elias might never have found a personal relationship with the Lord.

"And now, let us stand for our closing hymn, 'Rescue the Perishing.'"

Elias pushed his thoughts aside, realizing that the pastor's sermon had ended, and their young song leader now stood behind the pulpit, while the pastor made his way to the back of the room to greet everyone at the close of the service.

When the song ended, Sammy looked up at Elias and said, "I'm glad you're here today. I didn't think I'd get to see ya before ya headed up the canal to Mauch Chunk."

Elias smiled. "I decided to hang around Walnutport so I could visit the church here."

Sammy grinned. "Sure glad ya did."

"Is everything all right between you and your mother?" Elias asked.

Sammy bobbed his head. "'Course she paddled my backside for tellin' ya she said it was okay for me to lead your mules." He clasped Elias's hand. "It was worth the paddlin' to be able to spend those two days with ya, though."

Elias ruffled the boy's thick blond hair. "I'm glad we could be together, but it wasn't right to lie."

"I know, and I won't do it again."

"That's good to hear."

"Can we talk about somethin' else now?"

"Of course."

"Know what I think?"

"What's that?"

"I think you oughta bring your accordion to church sometime."

Elias smiled. "Maybe I'll talk to the pastor about that."

Sarah and her two youngest children stepped up to Elias, and she touched Sammy's shoulder. "Would you please take Willis and Helen outside and wait for me? I'd like to speak to Elias for a minute."

Sammy hesitated, but when Elias gave his shoulder a squeeze, the boy finally nodded.

Sarah waited until the children had left the church; then she moved closer to Elias. "I'm sorry for my harsh words yesterday. I was very upset when I discovered that Sammy had taken off with you, and I needed someone to blame."

Elias nodded. "I understand, and you were right—I shouldn't have taken Sammy's word. I should have checked with you first."

"There's one more thing I wanted to say," she said, lowering her voice.

"What's that?"

"I'd appreciate it if you didn't encourage my boy to take

551

an interest in working on the canal. I don't want him getting any ideas about becoming a mule driver or even a boatman when he grows up."

Elias's forehead wrinkled. "I'd never try to influence Sammy in any way. And as far as him becoming a boatman, with the way things are going, by the time he grows up, the canal boats might not even be running."

"You're probably right, and I really appreciate your understanding."

Sarah moved away, and she stopped at the back of the church to talk to Pastor William and his wife.

Elias's heart clenched, realizing how difficult it must be for her raising three children alone and not wanting her oldest boy to look to the canal for work.

As Elias moved toward the back of the church, he was greeted by the storekeeper's wife, Kelly, whom he'd only met briefly the first time he'd stopped at their store.

"It's nice to see you in church today," she said with a friendly smile. "We hope you'll join us whenever you're in the area."

"Yes, I plan to do that. I enjoyed the service."

"I spoke to my sister, Sarah, before the service began, and she said she's feeling up to taking care of the lock again. So I assume you'll be heading on up the canal in the morning?"

He gave a nod. "I didn't realize Sarah was your sister."

"Yep. She's my older sister by a few years, and we're very close."

"And speaking of her," Kelly continued, "Betsy Nelson and I have planned a surprise picnic in honor of Sarah's birthday this afternoon. You and your helper are more than welcome to join us if you have no other plans."

"I have no plans, and I'd like to come, but I'm not sure about Ned. He's not very social, but I will check with him and see."

"Great. The picnic's going to be on the grassy area outside our store. We'll start eating around one, or as soon as everyone we've invited gets there."

"That sounds fine. It'll give me time to speak with Ned, and then I'll be over to join you." Elias started to move away, but halted and turned to face her again. "Is there anything I can bring?"

She shook her head. "Just a hearty appetite. There's always lots of good food at one of our picnics."

"All right then. I'll see you around one."

Elias moved over to where the pastor and his wife stood, greeting people near the door, and waited his turn. After he'd spoken to Betsy and told her how much he'd enjoyed the music, he shook Pastor William's hand. "I enjoyed the service. The music and sermon were both uplifting."

"This is a hand-clapping congregation." Pastor William smiled. "It took me awhile to adjust to that when I first came to pastor the church, but now I can't imagine being anywhere but here with these warm, friendly folks."

"I know what you mean," Elias said. "The services in the church where I grew up are very formal. No one would dare to shout *amen* or clap their hands."

"Starting next week, after the morning service, I'll be holding regular services along the canal near the lock tender's house. Now I have to say that those services really bring out the people's enthusiasm."

"I assume the services along the canal are for the benefit of the boatmen who might not feel comfortable inside a church?"

The pastor nodded. "My wife's father used to hold services along the canal, and I continued the tradition at Betsy's suggestion." He smiled. "Many a boatman's been won to the Lord after attending one of our canal services."

Maybe there's some hope for Ned, Elias thought. "Perhaps I can talk my helper into attending one of your canal services with me when we're in the area again."

"That would be nice. I'm sure if nothing else he'd enjoy hearing my wife play her zither. Some of the boatmen who play instruments often join in, too."

"I play the accordion," Elias said. "Do you think folks would enjoy hearing that?"

"Oh, definitely. That would be a nice addition to our services, so do bring it if you come, and even here at the church, we'd enjoy hearing you play sometime."

Elias smiled. Not only was there some hope for Ned, but now he'd have the chance to play his accordion in praise to the Lord. He could hardly wait for the next time he was in Walnutport on a Sunday. Maybe he'd plan their trips in such a way that he could be here most every Sunday.

Chapter 15

*A*s Patrick O'Grady stood near Sarah, watching her open the birthday presents some folks had brought to the picnic, he found himself hoping she would like the box of chocolates he'd bought for her and that she'd eventually agree to become his wife. Patrick had never admitted it to anyone, but he'd been interested in Sarah when they were children. From the first day Sarah had come into Pop's blacksmith shop with her daddy, Patrick had been intrigued—not only by her pretty face, but by her determination and spirited ways.

When Sarah became a teenager, he'd found her even more appealing, but she hadn't returned his interest, choosing instead to run off with Sam Turner, who was even more spirited than Sarah. Patrick always wondered if Sarah had chosen Sam over him because Sam was determined to get away from the canal, while Patrick was content to stay and take over his father's blacksmith shop.

He'd known from the comments Sarah had made that she would have done most anything to get away from the canal. Yet here she was, not only living along the canal, but doing the job of a man.

If she married me, Patrick thought as he gazed at Sarah's pretty face, *she wouldn't have to work anymore, and I'd have a wife to come home to at night, not to mention someone who'd be there to clean the house and put decent meals on the table.*

He glanced over at Sarah's oldest boy, Sammy, and grimaced. The only drawback to marrying Sarah would be in having to help her raise those three children—and one of them thought he was too big for his britches.

Oh well, I'll worry about that when the time comes. The first thing I need to do is win Sarah's heart. Maybe I should consider going to church so I can see her more often, and then she might see me in a different light.

Tears sprang to Sarah's eyes as she was handed several gifts. Just the picnic in honor of her birthday was surprise enough, and she'd certainly never expected so many people would come and give her birthday presents. She'd already opened a box filled with sweet-smelling soaps from Betsy and Pastor

William, as well as a journal that Sammy's schoolteacher had given her.

"This one's from us," Kelly said, handing Sarah a large, flat package.

The first thing Sarah saw when she tore off the wrapping paper was some pale blue material.

"It's for a new dress," Kelly explained. "I know you don't have time to sew, but I thought I'd take the material to Doris Brown from church, who has recently begun doing some sewing for others, and then she can make the dress for you."

"I appreciate that." Sarah only had one Sunday dress, so it would be nice to have another.

"The gift that's under the material is just from me," Kelly said.

Sarah lifted the material and a sob rose in her throat as she gazed at a beautiful painting of her three children playing in the grassy area in front of her house. Behind them, several ducks floated on the canal.

"This is so nice," Sarah murmured. "Thank you, Kelly."

"You're welcome."

"Open mine next," Sammy said, pushing a paper sack in Sarah's direction.

She opened the sack and withdrew a calico sunbonnet with dark blue trim.

"Your old bonnet's lookin' pretty shabby," Sammy said,

"so I bought ya a new one with the money I earned leadin' Elias's mules."

"Thank you, son, I appreciate that." Sarah pulled Sammy close and gave him a hug. It touched her to know that even though she'd disciplined him yesterday, he'd spent his hard-earned money on a gift for her.

"I have a present for you, too." Patrick handed her a small rectangular box wrapped in fancy red paper.

Sarah pulled the paper away and lifted the lid on the box. She smiled when she saw the box of chocolates inside. Candy, especially fancy chocolates, was a luxury—something she never bought for herself, so this was a real treat.

"They each have a different filling," Patrick said, looking rather pleased with himself.

She smiled. "Thank you. I appreciate the gift and will enjoy every bite."

Willis tugged on Sarah's sleeve. "Ain't ya gonna give us any of them chocolates, Mama?"

She tweaked his nose. "If you're a good boy, I'll be happy to share."

He grinned as he bobbed his head. "I'll be good as gold; I promise."

Everyone chuckled, and then Mike stepped forward and said, "Now it's time to eat the birthday cake, but before we do that, there's a song that I know from a reliable source"— he smiled at Kelly—"was a special favorite of your mama's.

We'd like to sing it for you, Sarah." He motioned to Elias, who stood nearby. "When I talked to Elias after church, I found out that he plays the accordion, so I asked him to accompany us as we sing 'What a Friend We Have in Jesus.'"

Elias played a few introductory notes, and then everyone began to sing: *"What a friend we have in Jesus, all our sins and griefs to bear! What a privilege to carry everything to God in prayer!"*

Sarah's eyes clouded with tears, and she blinked a couple of times to keep them from spilling over. It was wonderful to know that she had so many caring friends.

"Thank you, everyone," she said when the singing ended and she could trust her voice. "This has been a very special birthday."

"Why don't we sing a few more hymns now?" Ben Hanson, one of their church deacons, suggested.

Pastor William looked over at Elias. "Would you be willing to accompany us?"

Elias nodded. "I know most of the traditional hymns, so I'd be happy to play along."

For the next hour, everyone sat on the grass and sang a variety of hymns. The singing probably would have continued for another hour or so, but the sky had darkened, and it began to rain.

In short order, all the leftover dishes, as well as Sarah's presents, were gathered up, and everyone started for home.

"Thanks for making my day so special," Sarah said, giving Kelly a hug.

"You're very welcome."

As the raindrops increased, Sarah urged her children to hurry home.

"Aw, do we hafta go now?" Sammy frowned. "I wanna visit with Elias awhile."

"I'd like to visit with you, too," Elias said, "but we'll see each other again—maybe the next time I come through the lock."

"Okay." Sammy turned and started running toward home, singing loudly as he went: *"I've got a mule, she's such a fool, she never pays me no heed. I'll build a fire beneath her tail, and then she'll show me some speed!"*

Sarah clenched her teeth. It was nice to see Sammy so happy, but she didn't want him singing or even thinking about things related to the canal, fearful that he might want to drop out of school and become a mule driver. Sarah didn't know what she'd do if that happened. She really did need to find some way to get her children away from the canal.

Chapter 16

*I*t had been two weeks since Sarah's surprise birthday picnic, and every time Sarah looked at the picture Kelly had drawn of her children, which she'd hung in the parlor, she thanked God for the privilege of being their mother. Even though she didn't get to spend nearly as much time as she'd like with them, she enjoyed every free moment they could be together.

This morning, as she slipped her new bonnet onto her head, she appreciated once again the thoughtfulness of her oldest boy. He was a lot like his father—headstrong, determined, and much too outspoken, but he had a tender spirit and wanted to please.

School would be out for the summer in just a few weeks, and Sarah knew that Sammy would do his best to help wherever he could. Of course there were many things he couldn't do well, especially cooking. However, with Betsy's help, most of their meals were taken care of, and for that, Sarah felt grateful. Betsy was also good with Sarah's children, often finding fun things for them to do and keeping a close eye on them whenever they went outside to play. What a shame that Betsy didn't have any children of her own.

Sarah glanced at the jars of jelly stacked in her pantry and thought of Maria. She'd gotten a letter from Roger's wife yesterday, letting her know how Maria was doing. She'd been seeing a specialist in Easton but was told there wasn't much that could be done. Her eyes were getting progressively worse. Sarah was glad Maria was where she could be looked after. She'd done well by the children for many months, but now it was her turn to be the one who was cared for.

Sarah pulled her thoughts aside and looked at her children, who still sat at the kitchen table, eating their breakfast. "I'm going outside to hang out the wash. Sammy, as soon as you're done eating, you need to get ready for school."

"Okay, Mama."

Sarah picked up her laundry basket and opened the door. As she stepped outside, a blast of muggy, warm air hit her full in the face. If it was this warm in late May, she could only imagine how hot it would be by the middle of summer.

Sarah set the wicker basket under the clothesline and had just hung the first towel in place when she heard a conch shell blowing in the distance. She knew it would be several minutes before the boat showed up so she hurried to hang a few more pieces of laundry.

When the boat finally appeared, she left the clothes and hurried to the lock. The boat's captain, Lars Olsen, gave her a friendly wave. "Got any bread today, Sarah? I could use a loaf or two."

"I have some in the house. I'll get it for you as soon as your boat's gone through the lock."

"All right then. I'll tie up on the other side after we've passed through."

Sarah pulled the pin out of the wicket, being careful not to let it slip. She didn't want to fall again and reinjure her ribs—or worse yet, end up with a more serious injury.

Once Lars's boat was through, Sarah dashed into the house and got two loaves of bread. She frowned when she saw that the children were still at the table.

"Hurry up, Sammy. You're going to be late for school if you don't get a move on."

His nose wrinkled. "Wish I didn't hafta go. Wish I could stay home and do some fishin' in the canal."

"If and when you're allowed to go fishing, it'll probably be during the summer when you're out of school, and it will definitely have to be with an adult."

"Elias said he might take me fishin' sometime, and he's an adult."

"We'll have to wait and see how it goes. Elias isn't usually here long enough to do any fishing."

"If he's here on a Sunday he could."

She thumped his shoulder lightly. "Maybe so, but right now you need to get ready for school, and I need to get this bread out to Lars."

Sarah hurried out the door and over to where Lars had docked his boat.

"Thanks, Sarah," he said when she handed him the loaf of bread. He gave her the money he owed and stepped back onto his boat. "I'll see you again on my way back from Mauch Chunk."

Sarah put the money in her apron pocket and returned to her job of hanging out the wash. She'd only been working a few minutes when Sammy came out the door with his lunch pail.

"I'm headin' to school now, Mama."

"Okay, have a good day."

He waved and hurried off in the direction of the schoolhouse.

A few minutes later, Betsy showed up, wearing a smile that stretched ear to ear.

"You're looking mighty chipper on this hot humid morning," Sarah said, wiping the perspiration from her forehead.

"Actually, I'm not feeling that chipper, but I am deliriously happy," Betsy said, stepping up to Sarah.

"How come?"

"I went to see Dr. McGrath yesterday, and what I've suspected for the last few weeks is true."

"What's that?"

Betsy's smile widened. "I'm in a family way. The baby should be born sometime in December."

Sarah dropped Sammy's wet trousers into the basket and gave Betsy a hug. "I'm so happy for you. I was just thinking this morning that you'd make a good mother."

Betsy sighed. "Oh, I hope so. I didn't always have a fondness for children, but that all changed during the time I spent helping at the orphanage in New York. I've had a desire ever since to have children of my own."

"I'm sure you and William will make good parents. He seems to have a way with kids, too."

"Yes, he does, and he was so happy when we learned that I'm expecting. In fact, he can't quit talking about it, and has already begun thinking of names for the baby."

Sarah chuckled. "Sam did that when I was pregnant with Sammy. When we couldn't make a decision, we finally decided to call the baby Sam Jr. if it was a boy."

"William said that if our baby's a boy he doesn't want to name it after himself. He said William Covington IV would be a bit too much."

Sarah smiled. "You could always call him Willy."

"Oh sure, and then with your Willis and our Willy, everyone would be confused."

"Well, maybe it'll be a girl, and then you can call her Betsy."

"No way. One Betsy in the family's enough. If it's a girl, I think we might name her Rebekah. I've always liked that name, and we can call her Becky for short."

"So how are you?" Sarah asked. "You said you're not feeling chipper. Does that mean you're not feeling well?"

Betsy nodded slowly. "My stomach's been real queasy, especially in the mornings, which I realize now is because I'm pregnant. I also tire easily."

"Maybe you should be at home resting instead of coming over here to help me every day." Sarah slipped her arm around Betsy's waist. "I don't want you to feel obligated to help just because you said you would. Things have changed, and your health and the health of your baby should come first."

"But you need someone's help here. Taking care of the lock, watching the children, baking bread, and keeping house—it's all too much for one person to do alone."

"I'll manage somehow. Sammy will be out of school soon, and he'll help me as much as he can."

Betsy bent down and picked up one of Helen's little gingham dresses. "Let's just wait and see how I feel in the days ahead, okay?"

Sarah nodded. "But I want you to promise that if you need to quit you'll say so."

"I promise."

As Patrick approached the lock tender's house, he spotted Sarah and Betsy standing near the clothesline, and his heartbeat picked up speed. Sarah's long dark hair hung down her back in gentle waves, and the floppy sunbonnet her son had given her was perched on her head. Despite the fact that she wore a faded yellow dress that was obviously well-worn, he thought she looked beautiful. He wished Betsy wasn't here so he could talk to Sarah in private, but he hoped that once he approached them Betsy would go inside.

"Top of the morning to you," Patrick said, stepping between the two women and smiling at Sarah. "Sure is a nice day, wouldn't ya say?"

She gave a nod. "I just wish it wasn't so warm and muggy."

"It's that, all right." He gave Betsy a slight nod. "Did ya come to help Sarah again today?"

"Yes, I sure did, and I'd better get inside and see how the children are doing. It was nice seeing you, Patrick." Betsy turned and headed for the house.

"Came to see if you have any bread," Patrick said, moving closer to Sarah.

"Yes, I made some last night. I'll go get a loaf from the kitchen." Sarah turned toward the house.

"I'll go with you." Patrick hurried along beside her. "I also came by to see if there's anything you'd like me to do while I'm here."

"That's kind of you, but I can't think of anything right now."

Sarah opened the door to the house, and as they stepped into the kitchen, Patrick was greeted by a yappy little dog.

Woof! Woof! Woof! The wiry terrier bared its teeth and snapped at Patrick's pant leg.

"Bristle Face, no!" Sarah pointed to the braided throw rug in front of the sink. "Go lie down!"

The dog slunk off to the rug, growling all the way.

"Sorry about that. I don't know what's wrong with him this morning. He's usually friendly to everyone and rarely ever growls."

"He don't like everyone, Mama," Willis said as he and his little sister entered the room. "Some folks he don't like a'tall—same as me. I don't like everyone neither."

Patrick gritted his teeth. *That boy is sure rude. I bet all three of Sarah's kids are probably too much for her to handle. I think what they need is a father who can teach them some manners.*

Sarah shook her finger at Willis. "That's not a nice way to talk, son. You shouldn't dislike anyone."

"Sorry," Willis mumbled.

Sarah turned to face Patrick. "How many loaves of bread did you want?"

"Just one for now. When I run out, I'll be back for more." Patrick looked over at the children, wishing they'd go back to wherever they'd been before he came into the house with Sarah. "What'd you two have for breakfast this morning?" he asked when he noticed a blob of something stuck to Helen's dress.

"We had mush," Willis answered.

"We had mush," Helen echoed.

Patrick wrinkled his nose. "I've never cared much for mush, unless it's covered in maple syrup."

"We can't afford maple syrup," Sarah said. "We use melted brown sugar instead."

"Maybe I'll bring you some maple syrup sometime."

"There's no need for that. My kids are fine using brown sugar." Sarah handed Patrick a loaf of bread. "Here you go."

Patrick paid Sarah. "Thanks a lot. I'm sure it's real tasty bread."

"I hope you'll excuse me, but I need to get the rest of my laundry hung out, and then I have some other chores to do when I'm not letting boats through the lock."

Patrick was tempted to hang around while Sarah did her chores but figured she might not appreciate it. Besides, he had some things of his own to get done at the blacksmith shop. So he picked up the bread and headed for the door. "I'll see you soon, Sarah," he called over his shoulder.

"Sure will be glad when we get to Walnutport," Ned said, joining Elias at the bow of the boat. "I'm just about outa chewin' tobacco, and I'm hopin' you'll stop at Cooper's store so I can get some more."

Elias frowned. "Chewing's a nasty habit, Ned. You should give it up and spend your money on something more constructive."

"Can't think of nothin' I'd rather spend my money on. Unless maybe it's for a bottle of whiskey."

"Whiskey's a tool of the devil. It'll take you down, sure thing."

Ned shrugged his shoulders. "It's my life, and I'll go down any way I choose."

"I know it's your life, but the Bible says—"

"Don't care what the Bible says and don't need ya preachin' to me neither."

"I didn't mean it as preaching, I just wanted you to—"

"Whoa! Whoa there!" Bobby shouted.

"What's wrong?" Elias turned his attention to the towpath. "Oh no, one of the mules is down." He steered the boat toward shore.

"Daisy stepped in a rut, and I think her leg's broken," Bobby said, eyes wide with obvious concern. "I can see the bone stickin' out."

"Now that's just great," Ned mumbled. "The last thing we need is a dead mule."

"She's not dead," Elias said. "Bobby said he thinks she's broken her leg."

Ned slowly shook his head. "We can't fix her leg."

Daisy kept braying and trying to get up. Elias wished there was something he could do to help the poor mule.

"Look, boss, the critter has to be put out of her misery. Now I'm goin' below to get my gun."

Elias stood there in stunned silence. With only one mule, they'd never get to Mauch Chunk for another load of coal. They'd have to stop in Walnutport for sure now and see if they could find another mule.

Chapter 17

*T*hat afternoon, Elias's boat limped into Walnutport with only one mule pulling for all she was worth. While Elias and Ned went to speak with Mike Cooper about getting another mule, Bobby stayed outside to keep an eye on the boat and feed and water Dolly.

Entering Cooper's store, Elias spotted Mike behind the counter, waiting on Bart Jarmon, a burly boatman. Elias held back and waited until Bart had exited the store, then he stepped up to the counter.

"It's good to see you again," Mike said. "What can I help you with?"

"I need a new mule and was hoping you might know where I can find one."

Mike's eyebrows rose. "What do you need a mule for? I

thought you had two good ones."

"I did, but one of them stepped in a hole and broke her leg. Ned had to put her down."

"Sorry to hear that." Mike fingered his mustache. "Let's see now. . . . I think Patrick O'Grady, the town's blacksmith, traded some of his work for a mule awhile back."

"Maybe I'll head over there."

Elias found Ned at the back of the store, no doubt in search of his chewing tobacco. "Mike says the blacksmith has a mule he might be willing to sell, so I'm going over to his shop and see if he's there."

Ned gave a nod. "Sure, go right ahead. I'll get what I'm needin' here and wait for ya at the boat."

"Hopefully I won't be too long." Elias turned and headed out the door.

Patrick had just finished putting new shoes on the doctor's horse when that fancy-talking boatman with the red blotch on his face showed up.

"I lost one of my mules, and Mike Cooper mentioned that you might have one I could buy," Elias said, stepping up to Patrick.

Patrick nodded. "I do have a mule. Somebody who couldn't pay for my services gave her to me a few weeks ago.

Not sure what I'm gonna do with her, though. So if you're interested you can have her for fifty dollars."

Elias scratched the side of his head. "Guess that's a fair enough price."

"I think so, since a lot of mules go for as much as seventy-five dollars."

"Has your mule ever pulled a canal boat?"

"Sure thing. Least that's what her owner said when he gave her to me."

"Okay, good." Elias reached into his pants pocket and pulled out the money, which he handed to Patrick. "Guess I'd better get the mule and be on my way, because I want to make a quick stop to see Sammy Turner."

Patrick's eyebrows lifted. "Sarah's son?"

"Uh-huh. The boy led my mules while my helper, Ned, was tending the lock for Sarah after she fell and hurt her ribs."

"I heard about that. Ever since Sarah's husband died, she's been real protective of her kids. I was surprised she'd allow Sammy to go with you."

Elias leaned against Patrick's workbench. "Well, she didn't exactly say he could go. Sammy took off without her permission."

"I'm sure she was upset about that."

"She was at first, but Sarah seems to be an understanding woman, and after I apologized and explained everything,

575

she was quite nice about it."

Patrick studied Elias several seconds. From the look he saw on Elias's face when he'd mentioned Sarah's name it made him wonder if the man might be interested in her.

"I've known Sarah since we were kids," Patrick said. "I'd have to say that she and I are good friends."

"I see." Elias turned toward the door of Patrick's shop. "Well, I'd best get that mule."

"Sure, of course." As Patrick led the way to the stall where he'd put the mule, he wondered if the boatman was using Sammy to get close to Sarah. *Well, if he is, I'd better move fast.*

"I see ya got yourself a new mule," Ned said when Elias returned to the boat.

Elias ground his teeth together. "Yes, and I've already discovered that she's got a mind of her own. The stubborn animal balked every step of the way."

"Did Patrick say the mule was used to pullin' a boat?"

Elias nodded. "But I guess that doesn't mean she can't be stubborn."

"Well, hopefully she'll do better once she's harnessed up. Since Dolly's the lead mule, I'm sure she'll show this new one who's boss. What's the mule's name, anyway?"

"I don't know. Guess we could call her Wilma, since she's so willful."

Ned scratched the mule behind her ears. "All right then, Wilma, let's get you harnessed and ready to go."

"Before we head out, I want to go over to the lock tender's house and see Sammy," Elias said.

Ned frowned. "For cryin' out loud! We've lost enough time already! If you get involved talkin' to that kid, we'll never get to Mauch Chunk."

Irritation welled in Elias. It seemed like Ned was forever telling him what to do. "I won't be over there that long. I just want to see how Sammy's doing, and then we can get through the lock and be on our way."

"You sure it's Sammy you're wantin' to see and not his purty mama?"

Elias shook his head. "I'm only interested in Sarah's son."

"Whatever you say. After all, I'm just a dumb helper, and you're the educated boss."

Choosing to ignore Ned's snide remark, Elias turned Wilma over to his outspoken helper and walked away.

When he arrived at Sarah's, her three children were playing with their dog on the grassy area along the side of the house. As soon as Sammy spotted Elias, he raced right over to him. "Sure is good to see ya again! Can ya stay awhile and visit?"

Elias shook his head. "I'm afraid not. I just wanted to

stop and say hello and see how you're doing."

Sammy grinned up at him. "I'm fine, but I'll be doin' even better after school's out for the summer."

"When will that be?"

"Tomorrow's our last day."

"I'll bet you're looking forward to being home all summer."

"Sure am." Sammy tipped his head and shielded his eyes from the glare of the sun. "Can we still go fishin' sometime?"

"I'm planning on it. Thought maybe we could go when I'm in the area on a Sunday again. It'll be after church, of course."

"That sounds good, but I'll have to ask Mama first." Sammy's forehead creased. "Sure wouldn't wanna upset her the way I did when I led the mules for ya."

"No, we surely wouldn't want to do that." Elias glanced at the house. "Where is your mother, Sammy? Is she inside?"

Sammy nodded. "She's bakin' more bread to sell to the boatmen."

Elias was tempted to knock on the door and say hello to Sarah, but when he glanced over his shoulder and saw Ned and Bobby waiting at the boat, he changed his mind. "I'd better get going," he told Sammy, "but I'll see you again soon, I promise."

Chapter 18

*T*wo weeks later, Pastor William showed up at Sarah's, explaining that Betsy wasn't feeling well and didn't think she could help Sarah today.

"I'm sorry to hear that. Has her morning sickness gotten worse?" Sarah asked.

He nodded. "She's very tired, too, and the doctor recommended that she stay home and rest."

"That's probably what she needs to do then."

"I'd stay and help you today, but I think I need to be at home in case Betsy needs me for anything."

"You're right; your place is with her. Since Sammy's out of school now, I think with his help we can manage."

"Are you sure? Maybe I can find one of the ladies from church who'd be willing to fill in for Betsy."

"No, that's okay. We'll be fine."

"All right then. I'll be on my way." Pastor William smiled and went out the door.

Sarah sighed, wondering how things would really go with just Sammy's help today. Maybe she should have taken Pastor William up on his offer to find someone else.

For the past two weeks, Elias's boat had been moving up and down the canal at a snail's pace, thanks to the contrite mule he'd bought from Patrick O'Grady. The stubborn critter kept nipping at Dolly, tried to kick Bobby a couple of times, and stopped right in her tracks whenever she didn't like something she saw. Elias had hoped to stop in Walnutport so he could go to church there, and hopefully take Sammy fishing, but so far it hadn't worked out for him to be in that area on a Sunday. If Wilma didn't start acting right he might have to sell her and invest in another mule—one that would cooperate so they could make better time.

On the brighter side, Elias had gotten word from his sister, Carolyn, who was a teacher in Easton. She'd surprised him by saying that she wanted to spend her summer break on his boat, and that she'd be glad to do the cooking, cleaning, and laundry for Elias and his helpers. That meant

Ned could take over for Elias at the tiller more often, giving Elias a break.

Today, when Elias stopped in Easton to deliver his load of coal, he would pick up Carolyn. Of course, Carolyn's letter had mentioned that Mother and Father weren't too happy about her joining him for the summer. However, Carolyn had a mind of her own, so probably nothing their parents said had made much difference to her.

"You'd better quit daydreamin' and watch where you're steerin' the boat," Ned said, nudging Elias's arm. "If you're not careful you'll run us aground."

"I was just thinking about my sister, who'll be joining us soon."

Ned snorted. "Just what we need—some hoity-toity woman on the boat tellin' us what to do."

"Carolyn's not hoity-toity. She's pleasant, smart, and I think she's a pretty good cook."

"You sayin' I'm a bad cook? Is that what you're sayin', boss?"

"I'm not saying that at all." Elias bumped Ned's arm this time. "Just think, if you don't have to cook you'll have more time for other things. Maybe you can get that stubborn Wilma trained to pull a little better, and then we'll be able to travel faster, which means we'll make more money."

Ned puckered his lips. "You mean *you'll* make more money, don'tcha? You're the captain of this boat, not me."

Elias merely shrugged. At least Ned hadn't called him *the boss* again.

As Sarah's day progressed, things went from bad to worse. She'd been trying to bake bread all day, but between the boats coming through the lock, and the children vying for her attention, by midafternoon she still had not made any bread. This wasn't good, because she only had a few loaves left, and if any of the boatmen stopped and bought bread today she'd be out.

Wo–o–o–o! Wo–o–o–o! Wo–o–o–o! Wo–o–o–o! The moaning of a conch shell, and then another, alerted her that two boats were coming. Maybe after they'd passed through the lock, she'd have time to make some bread.

"I've got to go! Keep an eye on your sister and brother," Sarah called to Sammy as she raced out the door.

Sarah let the first boat through, and then the second.

Wo–o–o–o! Wo–o–o–o! Another boat rounded the bend.

She'd just begun to raise the lock again, when Sammy raced out the door wearing a panicked expression. "Helen's gone! I can't find her anywhere!"

Chapter 19

Sarah quickly let the boat through the lock and dashed into the house behind Sammy. "Where'd you last see your sister?" she panted.

He shrugged. "I ain't really sure."

"What do you mean? Weren't you watching her like I told you to do?"

"I was, but you know how Helen is, Mama. She moves around all over the place. I can't be watchin' her and Willis at the same time."

"You can if you keep them in the same room with you." Sarah cupped her hands around her mouth. "Helen! Where are you?"

"She ain't in here, Mama," Willis said when Sarah stepped into the kitchen. "She ain't anywhere in the house."

"How do you know?"

" 'Cause Sammy and I went lookin'."

"That's right," Sammy put in. "We looked everywhere down here and upstairs, too."

"Did you see her go outside?"

Sammy shook his head. "But she mighta snuck out when we wasn't lookin'."

Sarah's mouth went dry, and her heart began to pound. If Helen went outside by herself, she could have fallen in the canal. *Oh dear Lord, please let her be all right.*

She drew in a deep breath and tried to think. "Where's Bristle Face? He usually follows Helen wherever she goes."

Sammy turned his hands palms up. "Beats me. Haven't seen him for quite a spell neither."

Another conch shell blew, and Sarah groaned. She needed to let the boat through the lock, but she needed to find Helen more than anything. Oh, how she wished Betsy was here to help her right now.

"Sammy, run down to the store and get Uncle Mike. Tell him that Helen's missing, and that I've gone looking for her. Ask if he can leave the store long enough to come and let the boat through the lock."

"I can do it, Mama. I can let the boat through the lock," Sammy said.

Sarah shook her head. "No, you can't. It's too hard for

you, and you might get hurt. Just do as I said and go get Uncle Mike."

Sammy had just started across the room, when the door swung open and Kelly stepped in with Helen and Bristle Face. "Are you missing someone here?" she asked, looking at Sarah.

Sarah's breath caught in her throat, and she bent down and swept Helen into her arms. "Oh, I was so worried. Where were these two?" she asked, looking at Kelly.

"Came over to our store. Helen said she was takin' Bristle Face for a walk, and I figured she'd wandered off without your permission."

Sarah nodded, feeling such relief. "I thought we could get along okay with just Sammy's help today, but apparently I was wrong."

"What do you mean? Where's Betsy?" Kelly asked.

"She's not feeling well, so she stayed home today."

Wo–o–o–o! Wo–o–o–o!

"The boat's getting closer; I've got to go. Can you stay and watch the kids while I open the lock?" Sarah asked her sister.

Kelly nodded. "Of course; and as soon as you're done, I'll take your kids to stay at my place for the rest of the day."

"Thank you," Sarah said with a nod. It might not be the best situation, since Kelly had her hands full watching her own two children, plus helping Mike in the store, but at least Sarah would be able to get some baking done when she wasn't busy opening the lock.

"How are you feeling?" William asked Betsy the following morning when he stepped into the kitchen.

She leaned against the cupboard and heaved a sigh. "About the same. I had no idea being pregnant could make a person feel so sick and tired."

"Dr. McGrath said that it's different with everyone." William gave Betsy a hug. "You're just one of the unfortunate women who feels sicker than some. I'm sure it'll get better, but in the meantime, I want you to rest as much as possible and drink that ginger tea the doctor suggested."

"But I didn't go to Sarah's yesterday to help out, and I really should go there today."

"No, you need to stay home and rest."

"I'm worried about Sarah. How's she going to manage with just Sammy's help? He's only a little boy."

William slipped his arms around Betsy and kissed the top of her head. "You let me worry about that. As soon as I've had some breakfast, I'm going out to look for someone to help Sarah."

Sarah had just finished the breakfast dishes when a knock sounded on the door.

Woof! Woof! Bristle Face, who'd been sleeping on the braided throw rug in front of the stove, leaped up and raced to the door.

Sarah gently pushed the dog aside and opened the door. She was surprised to see Pastor William there with Ruby Miller, one of the older women who attended their church.

"Good morning, Sarah," he said with a cheerful smile. "I knew it must have been hard for you yesterday, so I brought Ruby to help you today."

Sarah wasn't sure if the elderly woman could keep up with three lively children, but she smiled at Ruby and said, "I appreciate you coming."

Ruby gave a nod. "I'm sure the children and I will get along well."

Sarah turned to Pastor William. "Give Betsy my love and tell her to keep getting lots of rest."

"I will." He nodded at Ruby. "I'll be back to get you this evening."

Pastor William had just gone out the door when a conch shell sounded, followed by another and another. "The children have already had their breakfast," Sarah told Ruby, "but if you could see that the kitchen gets cleaned up and make sure the children get dressed while I'm letting those boats through the lock, I'd appreciate it."

"No problem." Ruby waved a hand. "You go ahead and take care of business. By the time you come back, the kitchen will be clean as a whistle."

When Sarah stepped outside, she saw three boats waiting in line to go through the lock. She was glad to have some help in the house today, because if the boats kept coming like this all day, she'd have her hands full just opening and closing the lock.

After the boats had gone through, Sarah turned toward the house. She was almost to the door when another conch shell sounded. By the time she'd let that boat through another boat was coming.

It was nearly noon by the time Sarah had a break and could return to the house. When she stepped into the kitchen she expected to see Ruby fixing lunch. What she saw instead caused her to gasp.

Helen sat on the kitchen floor with an open bag of flour in front of her. Some had spilled onto the floor, but most of it was in her hair, on her dress, and all over her arms and legs.

"Oh no—not the flour again," Sarah moaned.

Willis sat at the kitchen table eating a piece of bread that he'd smeared with strawberry jam, but there was no sign of Sammy or Ruby.

Sarah placed her hand on Willis's head. "Where's Sammy?"

"He took Bristle Face out for a walk."

"Where's Ruby?"

"She's in the parlor takin' a nap."

Sarah frowned. So much for the help she thought she was getting today. She'd have been better off with no help at all!

She cleaned up Helen and the floury mess, then hurried into the parlor. Sure enough, Ruby was sprawled out on the sofa, her eyes shut, her mouth hanging slightly open.

Sarah bent down and gently shook the woman's shoulders.

Ruby's eyes snapped open. "Oh, Sarah, it's you! Guess I must have dozed off."

Sarah didn't bother to tell Ruby about the mess she'd found in the kitchen. Instead, she helped the exhausted-looking woman to her feet. "It's noon. If you feel rested enough would you please fix the children some lunch?"

Ruby yawned noisily. "Of course." She ambled into the kitchen just as another conch shell blew.

Sarah could only hope that by the time she returned to the house, the children's lunch would be made and Sammy would be back from walking the dog.

Chapter 20

When Sarah awoke the following morning, she had a pounding headache. Oh, how she wished she could stay in bed and sleep all day. But duty called, and already, at just a few minutes after five, a conch shell was blowing.

Sarah hurried to get dressed and tiptoed down the stairs so she wouldn't wake the children. Amazingly enough, the blowing of the conch shells didn't usually wake them, but if Sarah moved about the house too loudly, they were wide awake.

The conch shell blew again, and Sarah stepped outside just in time to see Bart Jarmon's boat approach the lock. Bart was not her favorite person—especially not this early in the morning when she hadn't even had a cup of coffee yet. She hoped he wouldn't make any rude remarks, like he'd often done in the past. He'd have never done that when Sam was alive, because Bart, along with all the other canalers, respected Sam and knew better than to smart off to him the way some of them did to Sarah.

As Sarah prepared to open the lock she prayed that God would give her the right words, should Bart say anything crude. She was relieved when his only remark was, "It's already gettin' warm. Looks like it's gonna be another hot one today."

Sarah nodded and called, "Summer's here. There's no doubt about it."

"Yep."

She stood silently while the water level rose and was relieved when Bart's boat was on its way. She hurried back to the house to start breakfast.

By the time Sarah had some bacon and eggs cooking, the children were up.

"Somethin' sure smells good, Mama," Willis said. "I'm hungry!"

Sarah smiled. "If the three of you will take a seat at the table, I'll dish up your breakfast."

The children clambered onto their chairs with eager expressions.

"Sure don't understand why I haven't seen Elias lately," Sammy said. "Makes me wonder if he'll ever take me fishin'."

"The last time he came through the lock, he was having trouble with his new mule," Sarah said, placing a platter of eggs and bacon on the table. "Maybe the mule's still acting up, and that's slowing him down."

Sammy's forehead creased. "If I was leadin' his mules, bet I could make that stubborn mule go faster."

Sarah frowned. "Don't get any ideas about leading Elias's mules, because that's not going to happen ever again."

"But Mama, I could make us some extra money."

Sarah shook her head. "We don't need extra money that bad, and I won't have any of my children walking the dusty towpath from sunup to sunset." She placed an egg and a hunk of bacon on Sammy's plate. "Now please stop talking and eat your breakfast."

Sarah dished up an egg and some bacon for Helen and Willis, as well as some for herself. She'd just started eating when a knock sounded on the door. "That must be Ruby," she told the children. "You need to help her out today and not make any messes."

Sarah hurried to the door, and when she opened it she was surprised to see Hortence Andrews, one of the young, single women from church, standing on the porch. "I'm here to help out," she said. "Pastor William came by my house last night and said that Ruby didn't feel up to coming anymore, so I'll be helping you from now on."

Sarah heaved a sigh of relief. Surely things would go better today with someone younger and more energetic overseeing the children.

"I'm anxious to introduce you to the storekeeper and his wife," Elias told his sister as his boat approached Cooper's store. "They're good Christian people, and I think you'll like them as much as I do."

Carolyn smiled, and her blue eyes twinkled as the sunlight brought out the golden color of her shiny blond hair, which she'd worn in a loose bun. "I'm sure if you like them, then I will, too."

"Elias likes everyone," Ned said with a grunt. "Never met anyone, 'cept for his grandpa, who was as agreeable as him."

Elias's face heated. "I'm only trying to be a good Christian."

Ned folded his arms. "Humph! I've known a lot of nice folks who weren't Christians, and I've known some who called themselves Christians but acted as disagreeable as that stupid, stubborn mule you bought from the blacksmith."

Elias made no comment. He wasn't looking for an argument with Ned this morning.

When they docked at the store, Ned put down the gangplank and Elias helped Carolyn off the boat. "Are you coming into the store with us?" he called over his shoulder to Ned.

"Nope, not today. I'm gonna sit right here and have myself a smoke."

Carolyn wrinkled her nose but said nothing.

Elias grimaced. He wished Ned would give up his nasty habits.

"You can unhitch the mules and tie them to a tree so they can rest awhile," Elias told Bobby. He handed the boy a quarter. "Then you can go into the store and get yourself some candy or something cold to drink."

Bobby's eyes lit up. "With a whole quarter I can buy both!"

Elias smiled and patted the boy's shoulder. "You work hard and deserve a special treat."

When they entered the store, Elias led Carolyn over to the counter and introduced her to Mike.

"It's nice to meet you," Mike said, shaking Carolyn's hand. "Elias mentioned that you'd be joining him on the boat for the summer."

Carolyn smiled. "I've been looking forward to it."

Elias glanced around. "Where's your wife? I'd like her to meet Carolyn, too."

Mike motioned to the adjoining room. "She's in her art gallery working on a new painting."

"I'd like to see it," Carolyn said. "Would she mind if I went in?"

Mike shook his head. "Not at all. Kelly never minds when someone watches her paint."

Elias led the way to Kelly's little studio. They found her standing in front of a wooden easel painting a picture of a beautiful rainbow hovering over the canal.

Kelly smiled as they approached her. "It's nice to see you again, Elias."

"It's good to see you, too." He motioned to Carolyn. "This is my sister, Carolyn."

Kelly wiped her hands on her apron and extended one hand to Carolyn. "It's real nice to meet you."

"It's good to meet you as well." Carolyn moved closer to Kelly's easel. "That's a beautiful picture you're painting. Will it be for sale?"

Kelly nodded. "Just about everything I paint is for sale. Unless it's something I've made as a gift for someone, that is."

Carolyn glanced around the room, where several framed pictures were on display. "Sometime before I go back to Easton at the end of summer I'd like to buy one of your paintings. It will make a nice gift for our mother's birthday in September."

"If you see something you like now, I'd be happy to hold it for you," Kelly said.

"Hmm. . ." Carolyn tapped her chin. "How about the picture you're working on? I think I'd like that one."

"But it's not done. How can you be sure that's the one you want?"

"I can already see that it's going to be beautiful, so if you'll hold it for me, I'll pick it up before I leave the canal near the end of August."

Elias stood off to one side as the women talked more about Kelly's artwork. It was obvious that Carolyn liked Kelly, and he was sure Carolyn would like Kelly's sister equally well. Elias certainly did.

While Carolyn and Kelly continued to visit, Elias went back to the store and bought a few things they were running low on. He'd just finished shopping when Carolyn joined him at the front counter.

"Think I've got everything you'll need for cooking our meals, but is there anything specific you need or want?" Elias asked her.

She shook her head. "I can't think of anything right now."

"All right then. Let's walk over to the lock tender's house so you can meet Kelly's sister and her children. I'd also like to buy some of Sarah's bread."

Carolyn smiled. "That sounds nice. I've been looking forward to meeting these people you've written me so much about."

When Elias and Carolyn arrived at Sarah's house, Sammy, who'd been walking his dog on the towpath, rushed up to Elias and grabbed hold of his hand. "It's sure good to see ya! Did ya come to take me fishin'?"

"Not today, but maybe this Sunday, if we're back from Mauch Chunk by then."

"I don't think you'll be goin' to Mauch Chunk today," Sammy said with a shake of his head.

"How come?"

"There's a break in the canal, just on the other side of our lock. Mama thinks it was caused by some of the muskrats around here."

"Oh great. That's just one more thing to slow us down. Is the break being fixed?" he asked.

Sammy shrugged. "Beats me."

"Is your mother in the house?"

Sammy nodded. "She's bakin' some bread."

Elias turned to Carolyn. "Let's find out what Sarah knows about the break in the canal."

Sammy led the way, and when they stepped into the house, the delicious aroma of freshly baked bread overwhelmed Elias's senses, causing his mouth to water.

"Mama's in the kitchen, so follow me," Sammy said.

When they entered the kitchen, Sarah turned from the counter where she was working some bread dough and smiled. "It's nice to see you, Elias. Did you come to buy some bread?"

"I did, and I also wanted you to meet my sister." He motioned to Carolyn. "Carolyn's a schoolteacher in Easton, and since she's off for the summer, she decided to join me on the boat for the next few months."

Sarah wiped her floury hands on a dish towel and shook hands with Carolyn. "It's nice to meet you."

Carolyn smiled. "It's delightful to meet you as well. Elias has told me some nice things about you and your family."

Elias's cheeks warmed. He hoped Sarah wouldn't get the wrong idea.

"Well, I can't imagine that he'd have much to tell," Sarah said with a slight nod of her head. "I mean, our life here on the canal isn't all that interesting. It's pretty much the same old thing from day to day."

"You must keep very busy tending the lock," Carolyn said. "That seems like a difficult job to me."

"It's not easy." Sarah glanced toward the door leading to the parlor. "One of the young women from church has been helping me, so that takes some of the inside responsibilities off my shoulders at least."

"I understand that the canal has a break in it right now," Elias said.

Sarah sighed. "I'm afraid so. Some of the men from town are coming down to the canal to fix it today, but you may be stuck here several hours or even overnight before you're able to move on up the canal."

"That's fine with me," Sammy spoke up. "It'll give me a

chance to spend time with Elias, and he can finally take me fishin'."

"Maybe Elias has other things to do," Sarah said.

"I'd better offer my help on the canal repairs today, but I'd like to take Sammy and Willis both fishing after church on Sunday afternoon, if that's okay with you," Elias said.

"Well..."

"Maybe we could all go," Carolyn spoke up. "We could pack a picnic lunch and make a day of it." She smiled at Sarah. "While Elias and the boys are fishing, you and I can visit and get better acquainted."

"That sounds like fun," Sammy said excitedly. "Can we do that, Mama? Can we, please?"

Elias held his breath as he waited for Sarah's answer and was relieved when she nodded and said, "A picnic lunch does sound like fun. I'll bring some fried chicken, biscuits, some dill pickles, as well as either a cake or some cookies for dessert."

"I'm not much of a baker, but I'd be happy to fix a pot of beans to take along," Carolyn was quick to say.

"And I'll go back over to Mike's store and get several bottles of soda pop for us to drink." Elias thumped Sammy's shoulder. "Why don't you come with me? You can pick out whatever flavors you all like. Maybe we ought to buy a few pieces of candy for you, Willis, and Helen, too."

A wide smile spread across Sammy's face. "Oh boy, I can hardly wait!"

Chapter 21

On Sunday morning, Elias and Carolyn headed to church in Walnutport. The canal repairs had been completed on Saturday evening, and Elias was glad he would be able to resume his trip to Mauch Chunk on Monday morning. He was equally glad for this chance to spend more time in Walnutport. He was looking forward to fishing with Sammy, Willis, and Bobby after church, and also to the picnic lunch they would share with Sarah and her children. He knew this would give Carolyn a chance to get better acquainted with Sarah, and even though he'd never admit it, he was looking forward to spending more time with Sarah, too. She was not only pretty, but kindhearted. She was also a good mother to her children. If it was only possible that she could ever be interested in someone like him.

"You're sure quiet this morning," Carolyn said as they walked side by side. "Is something bothering you?"

He shook his head. "Just thinking is all."

"What are you thinking about?"

"Nothing much. Just thinking about going fishing with Sarah's boys and Bobby."

Carolyn smiled. "You always did like to fish, so I'm sure you'll have a good time. Sammy seemed awfully excited about it yesterday."

"Yes, he did, and I would have taken him fishing right then if I hadn't felt obligated to help the men fix the break in the canal."

"That was important, and I'm sure your help was appreciated."

As they approached the church, Carolyn put her hand in the crook of Elias's arm. "I'm also looking forward to today. Not only going to church, but the picnic with Sarah and her family afterward. Sarah seems so nice, and if we had the chance to spend much time together, I'm sure we could become good friends."

He nodded. "I think you could, too."

When they entered the church, they were greeted by Pastor William, who stood inside the front door.

"Elias, it's good to see you again," the pastor said with a warm smile and a hearty handshake.

"It's good to see you as well." Elias motioned to Carolyn.

601

"This is my sister, Carolyn. She's going to be riding on the boat with me this summer."

Pastor William shook Carolyn's hand. "It's nice to meet you. I'm sure that being on a canal boat will be an interesting experience for you."

She smiled and nodded. "No doubt, and I'm looking forward to enjoying the scenery along the canal when I'm not busy cooking and cleaning for my brother and his helpers."

"Speaking of your helpers," Pastor William said, looking at Elias, "I take it you didn't have any luck getting Ned or Bobby to come to church with you."

Elias shook his head. "Bobby's so tired after walking the mules all week, he just wants to sleep on Sunday mornings. Sometimes he doesn't wake up until noon. And Ned. . .well, that man is more stubborn than the contrary mule I bought awhile back."

"Maybe he'll decide to join us for one of the services I'll be holding along the canal this summer."

"That would be nice, but I'm not holding my breath."

"God can work a miracle in anyone's life," the pastor said. "I'm just hoping my wife, Betsy, will feel well enough to accompany the singing with her zither during our canal services."

"Is your wife ill?" Carolyn asked.

Pastor William shook his head. "Betsy's expecting a baby,

and so far she's had a lot of morning sickness and fatigue."

"That's too bad," Carolyn said. "I hope she'll feel better soon."

"Yes, we're hoping that, too." The pastor motioned to the doors leading to the sanctuary, where the beautiful strains coming from the organ drifted into the foyer. "Betsy's here today, and she'll be playing during our service, but after church is over, she'll need to go home and rest."

"Betsy plays and sings beautifully," Elias told Carolyn.

"You do a pretty fine job of playing that accordion of yours, too." Pastor William thumped Elias on the back. "You should have brought it to the service with you today. You could have either accompanied Betsy or played us a special."

Elias's face heated. "I forgot about bringing it with me, and I'm not sure I'd feel comfortable playing a special by myself."

"Well the next time you're in the area, please bring the accordion and plan to play along with Betsy during our congregational songs."

Elias gave a nod. "Yes, I'll do that."

As Carolyn stood beside Elias, singing the opening hymn in church, her spirits soared. Not only was the song uplifting and lively, but the joy she saw on the people's faces gave her a sense that all was right with the world.

This congregation, made up of many of the townspeople, as well as a few of the canalers and their families, were a friendly bunch who didn't put on airs. The people Carolyn had met before the service had made her feel right at home; not like a stranger visiting their church for the first time.

She glanced at Betsy playing the organ with such enthusiasm. The sincere smile on her face seemed to light up the room.

Carolyn turned her attention to young Sammy Turner. It was so touching when Sammy had entered the sanctuary with his family and plunked down on the pew beside Elias. It was even more touching when Elias smiled and put his arm around the boy's shoulders.

My brother would make a good father, Carolyn thought. *I hope he gets married someday and has a houseful of children.*

Tears pricked the back of her eyes as she thought about her desire to be a wife and mother, but she'd never even had a serious boyfriend. She knew it wasn't because she was unattractive. She'd been told by many people that her shiny blond hair and dazzling blue eyes made her stand out in a crowd. Mother always said Carolyn was holding out for the right man, but the truth was, no man had ever shown her more than a passing interest. It made her wonder if there might be something irritating about her personality that turned men away. Maybe she was too fussy about things, or perhaps she spoke too often when she should have been listening. Whatever the reason, Carolyn had made up her mind that she'd probably spend the rest of her life an old maid schoolteacher, living in a big city with too many people and not enough fresh air.

It was a shame, because she felt relaxed and comfortable here in Walnutport and wished she could live in a small town like this instead of the bustling, ever-growing city of Easton. She knew that wasn't possible, though, because her job was in Easton, and from what Elias had told her, they already had a schoolteacher in Walnutport.

I guess I'll have to enjoy my time on the canal this summer and quit longing for the impossible, she decided. *I just hope I don't disappoint Elias when he finds out that I'm not the world's best cook.*

Soon after church was over, Sarah and her family, along with Elias and Carolyn, headed to a grassy spot near the canal, where they shared the picnic lunch Sarah had made. It was amazing how comfortable she felt with Elias and his sister, and she looked forward to getting to know them both better in the coming weeks.

"Can we go fishin' now?" Sammy asked Elias after he'd finished eating his chicken.

"For goodness' sake, let Elias finish his meal before you start pestering him," Sarah scolded. "We haven't even had our dessert."

"It's all right." Elias wiped his hands on the cloth napkin Sarah had given each of them, and set his plate aside. "We can have our dessert after we've fished awhile."

"Yippee!" Sammy leaped to his feet and grabbed his and Willis's fishing poles. "Let's go find us a good spot to sit and fish!"

Bobby, who had slept all morning on the boat and then joined them for the picnic, seemed eager to fish, too.

While Elias and the boys headed down the towpath looking for the right spot to fish, Sarah and Carolyn cleared away the dishes, and Helen kept herself entertained by trying to teach Bristle Face to roll over.

"This is such a pleasant way to spend a Sunday afternoon," Carolyn said as she leaned back, resting her elbows on the grass.

Sarah nodded. "Since Sundays are my only day off, I always enjoy every minute. Spending time with family and friends is one of the best ways I know to relax."

"Sunday is Elias's only day off as well. I could see by his expression during lunch that he not only was relaxed, but he also thoroughly enjoyed your fine cooking."

"I'm sure he'll enjoy the cooking you do for him on the boat this summer."

Carolyn shrugged. "The meals I fix might be better than what he's used to having, but they'll pale in comparison to the wonderful fried chicken and biscuits you served us today." She sighed. "My cooking abilities get me by, and I can make most basic meals, but I've never gotten the hang of baking bread or making cakes, cookies, and pies."

"Baking's really not that hard," Sarah said. "It just takes patience and lots of practice. Maybe when you're in the area for a while sometime, you can help me make some of the bread I sell to the boatmen."

Carolyn sucked in her bottom lip. "I'm afraid if the boatmen tasted any baked goods I had made, they'd never buy bread again."

Sarah chuckled. "I'm sure you're not that bad at baking."

"You'd be surprised. Once, when I was still living at home with our folks, I forgot about the cookies I'd put in the oven, and by the time I remembered to check them, they'd turned into little lumps of charcoal. The kitchen was filled with smoke, and the smell of burned cookies lingered for nearly a week. No one in the family wanted me to bake anything after that."

Sarah patted Carolyn's arm. "As I said, I'd be happy to give you a lesson."

"Maybe I'll take you up on that. . .if we're ever in the area long enough, and if you're not too busy with other things."

"Now that Hortence Andrews is coming over every day

to help out, I have a little more time for baking and other things when I'm not letting boats through the canal. So I'm sure I could find the time."

Carolyn pointed to where Elias and the boys sat on some boulders near the canal, a little distance away. "I think my brother's having just as much fun fishing as your two boys are."

Sarah shielded her eyes from the glare of the sun as she studied Elias holding his fishing pole with one hand, while his other hand rested on Sammy's shoulder.

Sarah smiled. It was good for her boys to enjoy the company of a man. Since Sam died, they didn't get to do many fun things, and Sammy had taken such a liking to Elias, looking up to him almost like he was his father.

Elias seems like such a nice man. If only he wasn't a boatman, Sarah thought with regret.

Chapter 22

*A*s Patrick walked along the dusty towpath in the direction of Sarah's house, he kicked at every stone in his way. He'd heard that Sarah and her children had gone on a picnic with Elias and his sister on Sunday afternoon, and that worried him. He'd also heard from one of the boatmen who'd seen them on Sunday that Elias had taken a special interest in Sarah's son Sammy and taken him fishing. Patrick was even more convinced that Elias was using the boy to get close to Sarah.

"I can't let that happen," Patrick mumbled. "I lost Sarah to Sam Turner when we were teenagers, and I'm not gonna lose her to some canaler who has nothing to offer but fancy words and a dingy boat full of dirty coal."

By the time Patrick got to Sarah's house, he was so

worked up that he had to stop and take in a few deep breaths. It wouldn't be good to let his Irish temper take over. He had more self-control than that. He'd convinced himself that the best thing he could do was try to win Sarah's heart by being nice and offering to help her with anything she needed.

Patrick was about to knock on Sarah's front door, when it swung open suddenly and that shaggy terrier of hers leaped out at him, barking and showing its teeth.

"Come back here, Bristle Face!" Sammy shouted as he grabbed the dog's collar. "And quit that yappety-yapping!"

The dog's barking changed to a low growl, as though he was warning Patrick not to come any closer.

Patrick cleared his throat a couple of times. "Uh. . .is your mama in the house?"

Sammy gave a nod. "She and Hortence are fixin' some sandwiches for our lunch."

At the mention of food, Patrick's stomach growled. He'd shoed several horses this morning and had only taken time for a quick cup of coffee and a stale piece of bread. Maybe if he played it right, Sarah would invite him to join them for lunch.

"I suppose ya wanna come in," Sammy said, crinkling his freckled nose as he squinted up at Patrick.

"Yes, I sure would."

"Well, go on in the kitchen then. I'm takin' Bristle Face out for a walk, but I'll be back in time for lunch." The boy hurried away, and Patrick stepped into the house.

He found Sarah and Hortence in the kitchen, with their backs toward him as they worked at the counter. Willis and Helen sat at the table, staring at Sarah's back with anxious expressions. He thought they looked like a couple of baby birds waiting to be fed.

"Oh my, you startled me, Patrick!" Sarah said when Patrick cleared his throat to announce his presence. "I didn't hear you knock on the door."

"I didn't knock. I ran into Sammy when he was coming out the door to take his dog for a walk, and he said you were in here and that I should come in."

"Oh, I see. Well, what can I do for you? Are you in need of more bread?"

He gave a nod. "I just have a few pieces left, and what I do have has gotten stale."

"I only have a few loaves right now," Sarah said, "but I can sell you one of those if you think that'll be enough."

"One should do me fine." Patrick glanced at the pieces of bread Sarah had been buttering. "What kind of sandwiches are you making?"

"Some will be just jelly for the kids," Hortence spoke up before Sarah could respond. She smiled at Patrick. "And we'll make a few sandwiches with leftover chicken."

Patrick's stomach rumbled and he licked his lips. "Umm... I haven't had a chicken sandwich in a long time."

"If you haven't had lunch yet, you're welcome to join us," Sarah said.

Patrick nodded eagerly. "I haven't eaten anything since early this morning, so I appreciate the invite."

Sarah motioned to the table. "Take a seat. We'll have these sandwiches made in no time, and then we can eat."

Patrick pulled out a chair and took a seat beside Willis. "I heard you went fishing the other day," he said, hoping to win the boy over.

Willis bobbed his head. "Didn't catch nothin', but we sure had fun. Elias told me and Sammy lots of funny stories 'bout when he was boy."

"I have some funny stories to tell from my childhood. Would you like to hear one of 'em?" Patrick asked.

Willis shrugged. "I guess so."

"Well, once when I was helpin' my pa shoe an ornery mule, the crazy critter grabbed hold of Pop's shirtsleeve and bit a hole right through it."

Willis frowned. "Don't see what's so funny 'bout that. If a mule woulda made a hole in my shirt, I'da been real mad."

"My pa did get mad, but it was funny to see that old mule holding a piece of Pop's shirt between its teeth while she shook her head from side to side."

"I'll bet that did look pretty funny," Hortence spoke up as she placed a platter of sandwiches on the table. "If I'd been there, I'm sure I would have laughed." She gave Patrick a wide smile and plunked down in the chair on the other side of him. "I think we're ready to eat. We just need to wait for Sammy to get back from walking the dog."

"Here he is now," Sarah said as Sammy stepped into the room. "Go to the sink and wash your hands, son."

"Okay, Mama." Sammy cast Patrick a quick glance, then ambled across the room to the sink, where, using both hands, he pulled the handle of the pump several times for some fresh water. When he returned and took a seat across from Patrick, Sarah set a pitcher of milk on the table, and then she seated herself next to Helen.

"Close your eyes, kids; I'm going to pray," Sarah said sweetly.

Patrick, not being the religious type, never prayed when he ate a meal, but out of respect for Sarah, he bowed his head.

"Dear Lord," she prayed in a sincere tone, "we thank You for this food we're about to eat. Bless it, and use it to strengthen our bodies. Amen."

Everyone dug in, and Patrick savored his first bite of the chicken sandwich. How nice it would be to have a wife waiting for him at home each evening with a tasty meal on the table.

He leaned closer to Sarah. "Say, I was wondering if you'd like to—"

Wo–o–o–o! Wo–o–o–o! The moaning of a conch shell floated through the kitchen window.

"I'd better go get ready for that boat," Sarah said, pushing her chair away from the table.

Patrick jumped up. "Would you like me to help you open the lock?"

She shook her head. "Thanks anyway, but I can manage. Just have a seat and enjoy your lunch. I'll be back soon."

Sarah hurried out the door so quickly that Patrick couldn't even formulate a response. He sat back down and took another bite of his sandwich.

"Do you like it?" Hortence asked. "Is there enough butter on your bread?"

"It's just fine. Very tasty, in fact."

She smiled at him. "Maybe you'd like to come over to my house for supper sometime. Mother likes it when we have guests."

A trickle of sweat ran down Patrick's forehead. Was Hortence making a play for him? The look he saw on her face did appear kind of desperate, and the fact that she was nearly thirty years old and still not married made him wonder if she might be looking for a husband. Well, if she had him in mind, she could forget it. The only woman he wanted was Sarah.

After Elias had picked up a load of coal at Mauch Chunk on

Monday afternoon, he'd been surprised at the way Wilma, their stubborn mule, had cooperated with Bobby. Not only was she walking faster, but she was no longer picking on Dolly. Maybe she'd finally come to know her place and had decided to cooperate. Maybe things would go better for them now, and they wouldn't lose so much time.

"Are you planning to stop in Walnutport today?" Carolyn asked as she joined Elias at the bow of the boat.

He shook his head. "Thanks to that break in the canal and several days of dealing with a contrary mule, I've already lost too much time. So I think it's best if we keep heading straight for Easton."

"I suppose you're right." Carolyn sighed. "I enjoyed being with Sarah so much the other day and was hoping I might have the chance to visit with her again."

"I'm sure there will other times for visiting," Elias said. "I plan to stop in Walnutport whenever I can for church, and since Sarah doesn't work on Sundays, she'll have more time to visit then, anyway."

"I don't know how Sarah manages her job. It seems like such hard work."

Elias nodded. "I don't think it's the kind of work a woman should do, but Sarah seems to manage okay."

"Mind if I ask you a personal question?"

"What's that?"

"I was wondering if you might be interested in Sarah."

His eyebrows shot up. "What would make you think that?"

"I couldn't help but notice the smile on your face when we were with Sarah and her children on Sunday. You seemed very content."

"I did enjoy being with them, but Sarah's just a friend and will never be anything more."

"How do you know?"

"Because I'm sure that a pretty woman like her would never be interested in someone like me."

"What's that supposed to mean?"

He touched the side of his face. "Who would want a man with an ugly birthmark?"

"You're too sensitive about that." Carolyn placed her hand on his arm. "Mother's told you this before, and I'm going to say it again now. When the right woman comes along, she won't even notice that red mark on your face. What really counts is what's in a person's heart, not his outward appearance."

Elias shrugged. "I wish that were true, but I grew up hearing the jeers and taunts from others about my ugly red mark, and no woman has ever shown me more than a passing interest. I've come to accept the fact that true love will probably never happen for me."

"That's ridiculous. If you'd just relax and let your charming and sensitive personality shine through, you could win any woman's heart."

"Ya can't be charmin' or sensitive and be a boatman," Ned said, stepping up to them. "A boatman's gotta be tough as nails."

"Like you?" Elias asked with a grin.

Ned lifted his bearded chin. "Yep, just like me."

Elias rolled his eyes, and Carolyn snickered quietly. Then she tapped Elias on the shoulder and said, "I'm going below to make some soup for lunch. Should I bring you up a cup when it's ready?"

"That'd be fine. Ned can take over steering the boat while I eat lunch, and then I'll take over leading the mules so Bobby can come aboard and eat."

"Okay." Carolyn turned and hurried away.

Ned looked at Elias and frowned. "When do I get to eat?"

"You can either eat before I do, or wait until Bobby is done."

"Guess I'll go first. I work better when my belly's full."

"I would have suggested that we tie the boat up for a while and all eat together," Elias said, "but we've lost enough time these last few weeks."

"That's for sure." Ned leaned over the boat and spit a wad of chewing tobacco into the canal. "You never shoulda bought that stupid mule from the blacksmith in Walnutport."

"If you'll recall, there were no other mules available,"

Elias reminded. "And as I'm sure you must have noticed, Wilma seems to be behaving herself much better now."

"Yeah, I guess." Ned spat another hunk of tobacco into the water. "At least for now, she is."

"I think she just needed to get used to walking with Dolly and learn what she's supposed to do."

Ned opened his mouth like he was about to respond, when a bloodcurdling scream from below caused them both to jump. Elias turned the tiller over to Ned and raced down the stairs.

Chapter 23

W hat's wrong?" Elias called as he rushed into the galley.

Carolyn turned from the stove and held up her left hand. "I burned myself on the stove," she said tearfully. "It hurts so bad I can barely stand the pain."

Elias stepped closer and examined her hand. Several ugly blisters had already formed, and all of her fingers looked red and swollen. "We'd better stop in Walnutport, after all," he said. "I think you need to be seen by a doctor. In the meantime, you'd better take a seat at the table and put your hand in some cold water to help with the pain."

"I'm so sorry about this." Carolyn's chin trembled and her eyes filled with tears.

Elias shook his head. "You have nothing to be sorry for. It was an accident, plain and simple."

619

"But if you stop in Walnutport so I can see the doctor, you'll be losing more time, which is exactly what you didn't want to do."

"Your needs come before my schedule, so stop worrying about it and take a seat at the table."

She sighed deeply and did as he asked. When he set a pan of cold water in front of her, she plunged her hand in and gasped. "It still hurts, Elias. It hurts so much!"

"I'm sure it does, but you'd better keep it there until we reach Walnutport."

Elias turned and hurried back to the main deck. He knew it was important for Carolyn to see the doctor, and right now it didn't matter how long it took to make his coal delivery.

By the time Sarah got around to eating her lunch, the children had finished and gone over to Mike and Kelly's to play with their cousins. When she stepped into the kitchen, she was surprised to see that Patrick was still there, sitting at the table with Hortence and drinking coffee.

"I didn't realize you were still here," Sarah said to Patrick. "I figured by now you'd be back working in your blacksmith shop."

He shook his head. "I was waiting for you. I wanted to ask if you—"

Wo–o–o–o! Wo–o–o–o! "It sounds like another boat's coming through." Sarah groaned. "At this rate, I'll never get to eat my sandwich."

"I wish you'd let me help you outside," Patrick said. "We could get the job done twice as fast with the two of us working."

Sarah flapped her hand. "Tending the lock is my responsibility, and it really doesn't take that long. The problem today has been that too many boats have come through in such a short time." She started for the door, but turned back. "Please don't let me keep you from whatever work you might have in your shop."

"Guess you're right. I really oughta get back. I'll be by to see you again in a few days." He stood and moved toward the door, and she hurried out behind him.

Just as Sarah approached the lock gate, she spotted Elias's boat, which was almost at the lock. "I have a few loaves of bread left if you want any today," she called.

He shook his head. "Not this time, but we do need to stop. Carolyn burned her hand real bad, and she needs to see the doctor."

"Oh no! I'm sorry to hear that."

When Elias's boat had gone through the lock, she pointed to a post on the other side of it. "You can tie up here, if you like."

"Thanks."

Elias had no more than docked his boat when another boat came through. As much as Sarah wanted to see how badly Carolyn had been burned, she knew she had a job to do.

"When you get done at the doctor's, stop by and let me know how Carolyn's doing," she called to Elias.

"All right, we will."

Sarah whispered a prayer on behalf of Elias's sister and hurried to do her job.

"I really don't think it's necessary for me to stay here in Walnutport," Carolyn said as she and Elias left the doctor's office later. "I can stay on the boat with you and change my own bandage every day."

Elias shook his head. "That's not a good idea. What if infection sets in? If you don't want to stay in Walnutport, then when we get to Easton, I should drop you off at Mother and Father's."

"No way! Father didn't want me to join you on the boat, so if he knew about my hand, he'd give me a hard time and probably blame you for it, saying that the conditions on your boat are crude and unsafe." She cringed at the remembrance of her father's earlier words. "And Mother would hover around me all day and treat me as if I'm a little girl. I think the best thing we can do is go over to the boardinghouse Dr. McGrath recommended and see if they have room for me to stay there."

"I suppose we could do that, but I think I might have a better idea."

"What's that?"

"We could see if Sarah would be willing to let you stay at her place. I heard that Sarah's mother-in-law used to live with her, so I'm sure she has the room."

"I don't know if that's such a good idea. Sarah has enough on her hands, tending the lock and taking care of her three children. She doesn't need me to look after."

"I'm not suggesting that she look after you, because I'm sure you can manage to look after yourself," Elias said. "What I was thinking was that I'd be willing to pay Sarah for your room and board, and since I'm sure she could use the extra money..."

"Ah, I see now. You're concerned about Sarah and are looking for some way to help her out."

His face turned red as he slowly nodded. "She has a lot of responsibility on her shoulders. I also know that she doesn't make a lot of money tending the lock, and I'm sure that selling bread to the boatmen doesn't bring in much either."

"I understand your concerns, but what if Sarah would rather not have a near-stranger staying with her?"

Elias shrugged. "Well, we won't know until we ask, and if

she says no, then you can rest on the boat while I head over to the boardinghouse and see about getting you a room."

Carolyn contemplated the idea and finally nodded. If she had her preference, it would be to stay with Sarah.

Chapter 24

I can't thank you enough for letting me stay here with you," Carolyn told Sarah several days later as they cleared the dishes from the breakfast table. She lifted her left hand, still wrapped in a gauze bandage. "The salve and herbs Dr. McGrath gave me for the burn are working quite well, and I've enjoyed being here with you and the children."

Sarah smiled as she pushed a wayward strand of hair away from her face. "We've enjoyed having you here and will miss you when you join Elias again."

Carolyn set the dirty plates in the sink. "I hope things are going okay for him. From all that he's told me, it seems as if he's had nothing but trouble since he took over our grandfather's boat. If Father knew about everything that had gone wrong, he'd say to Elias, 'I told you so, son.'"

"A lot of things can go wrong for the boatmen, as well as those who live and work along the canal." Sarah slowly shook her head. "I can't begin to tell you about all the accidents that have occurred over the past few years, just along the stretch of canal that runs by Walnutport."

"I understand that your husband was killed in an accident involving the canal."

Sarah blinked against unwanted tears. She always felt weepy when she thought about Sam's untimely death. "He was crushed between a boat and the lock," she murmured. "I'm just grateful Sam found the Lord before he died, because I have the assurance that he's in heaven now and someday we'll be reunited."

"As Christians, we do have that consolation," Carolyn agreed. "It makes me wonder how those who haven't had a personal relationship with Christ deal with death and other tragedies that occur in their lives."

Sarah stared out the window, watching a pair of geese floating on the canal. "Several of the boatmen have come to know the Lord after attending one of the services Pastor William holds along the canal, but there are many others who are still deeply rooted in their sinful way of life."

Carolyn nodded. "I think Elias's helper is one of those. From what I've seen, Ned has several nasty habits, and he sometimes uses foul language and even takes the Lord's name in vain. It makes me wonder why Elias puts up with him and his crude ways."

"I understand that Ned used to work for your grandfather, so maybe Elias feels a sense of responsibility toward Ned."

"I believe you're right about that. I also think Elias believes that in time Ned will see his need to change and give his heart to the Lord."

"With Elias setting the example of Christianity, maybe Ned will become a Christian someday." Sarah took a sack of flour down from the cupboard. "Would you like me to teach you my secret for making light and airy bread?"

"Yes, I would. I'd like to learn how to make the dough dab bread you fixed to go with the stew we had for supper last night, too."

Sarah slipped her apron over her head. "I'd be happy to teach you to make dough dab. Hopefully, the boats coming through the lock today will be far enough apart that we'll have time to get lots of baking done."

"With your baking skills, I'm wondering. . . Have you ever considered opening a bakery?"

"The idea has crossed my mind," Sarah replied, "but I'm sure the rent on a building in town would be expensive, so I doubt that I'd ever be able to afford it."

"Well, it's always nice to have a goal and something to plan for."

"Yes, and if I owned my own bakery I could give up lock tending."

The sound of giggling coming from the parlor could be heard, and Sarah smiled. "Since Hortence has been coming to help out, she keeps my kids well entertained, which helps me get more done. Before, even when Maria was here to help, the kids always seemed to be competing for my attention."

"It's good that she's such a big help with the children."

A knock sounded on the door, interrupting their conversation. "I'll get that!" Hortence called from the other room over Bristle Face's frantic barking.

A few seconds later, she entered the kitchen with Patrick at her side and Bristle Face nipping at his heels.

"Stop it, Bristle Face," Sarah scolded. "Sammy, come get your dog!"

Sammy rushed into the room and swept Bristle Face into his arms. "Sorry, Mama. He got away from me when Hortence went to answer the door."

"Just make sure you keep that stupid mutt away from me," Patrick said roughly. "I'm gettin' sick of him yappin' and snappin' every time I come around."

Sammy's eyes narrowed. "Bristle Face ain't stupid, and he only barks at people he don't like."

Sarah frowned. "That'll be enough, Sammy. Just take the dog outside for a walk."

"He was outside awhile ago, so I don't think he's gotta go again."

Sarah pointed to the door. "Just do as I said."

Sammy ambled out the door mumbling under his breath.

Sarah turned to Patrick and smiled. "Sorry about that. I don't know why Bristle Face is so testy around you."

"You heard what the boy said. The dog doesn't like me, though I can't figure out why. I've never done nothin' to make him mad."

"Some dogs are temperamental," Carolyn spoke up. "They pick out certain people to bark at for no particular reason."

Patrick swung his gaze from Sarah to Carolyn. "Don't think I've met you before. Are you new to the area?"

Sarah introduced Carolyn to Patrick and explained that she was Elias's sister. Then she told Carolyn that Patrick was the town's blacksmith.

Carolyn smiled and explained why she was staying with Sarah.

"It's nice of Sarah to take you in." He glanced back at Sarah and grinned. " 'Course she's always been kind to others."

Sarah felt the heat of a blush creep up her neck and cascade over her cheeks. "It's a Christian's duty to help others, and with Carolyn staying here, the two of us have become good friends."

Carolyn nodded. "Sarah's going to teach me the secret of making good bread."

Patrick smacked his lips. "Well, you've got a good teacher,

'cause nobody bakes bread any tastier than Sarah's."

Sarah's cheeks grew hotter. "I don't think my bread's anything special."

"You're wrong about that; your bread's the best I've ever had." Patrick took a step closer to Sarah. "I was wonderin' if I could talk to you alone for a few minutes."

"I guess so." Sarah motioned to the door. "Should we go outside?"

"Sure, that'd be fine."

"I'll be right back," Sarah said to Carolyn. "You can fix yourself a cup of tea while I'm gone if you like."

"I might just do that." Carolyn smiled at Patrick. "It was nice meeting you."

"Same here," Patrick said as he went out the door.

Sarah stepped out behind him. "What was it you wanted to talk to me about?"

Patrick cleared his throat a few times and glanced around as though he was afraid someone might hear their conversation, which Sarah thought was silly. Sammy was way down the towpath with Bristle Face, and no one else was around.

"I...uh...was wondering if you'd go on a picnic with me this Sunday," he said in a near whisper.

Sarah shook her head. "I've told you before, Patrick. We always go to church on Sundays."

"I know that," he said with an exasperated groan. "I was

talkin' about after church."

"I won't be free in the afternoon because Pastor William will be holding another preaching service along the canal after the service in town. He plans to baptize several people in the canal."

"Are you gettin' baptized, Sarah?"

"No, I've already been baptized."

"Then there's no need for you to go."

"Yes, there is. I know several of the folks who are getting baptized, so I want to attend the service to offer my support and approval."

"I see." Patrick pursed his lips as he tapped his foot. "It makes it kinda hard for us to court when you have to be here to let boats through the lock six days a week, and then on Sundays you always seem to have other plans."

Sarah's mouth fell open. "You—you think we're courting?"

He shrugged. "I guess not officially, but I'd like for us to be. Fact is, I've cared for you ever since we were kids, and—"

She held up her hand. "You're a nice man, Patrick, but I really can't think about being courted by anyone right now."

"How come?"

"I have a job to do, three kids to raise, and as you mentioned, very little free time."

"Then why don't we skip the courtin' part and just get married?"

"Wh–what?"

"I said why don't we—"

"I heard what you said. I'm just shocked that you said it."

"But I've been interested in you since we were kids. Fact is, if you hadn't run off with Sam when you did, I'd planned to court you."

Sarah leaned against the porch railing, feeling the need for some support. She'd had no idea Patrick felt that way about her when they were children. Although in the last few months, she'd suspected he was interested in her now. But the thought of marrying him hadn't even entered her mind.

Wo—o—o—o! Wo—o—o—o! The sound of a conch shell pulled Sarah's thoughts aside. "A boat's coming. I'll need to get the lock opened, so I'm afraid I can't talk any longer."

She started to move away, but he reached out and touched her arm. "Would you at least think about what I said and let me know when you have an answer?"

She gave a brief nod and hurried off to open the lock.

"Sure am glad we're not far from Walnutport," Ned said, joining Elias at the bow of the boat. "I'm out of chewin' tobacco again and need to stop at the store."

Elias shook his head slowly as he rolled his eyes. He wished Ned would give up that nasty habit, but he'd been doing it for a good many years, so it wasn't likely he'd give it up now. Some things, no matter how much he wanted them, just weren't meant to be.

"Does that shake of your head mean we're not stoppin' at Walnutport?" Ned asked, bumping Elias's arm.

"Of course we're stopping. I want to check on Carolyn. I was shaking my head because I can't understand why you think you need that awful chewing tobacco."

Ned merely shrugged in reply; then he leaned over the boat and hollered at Bobby, "Get them mules movin' faster! When they start laggin' like that, you need to take control!"

Bobby swatted Wilma's rump, and the next thing Elias knew the crazy mule let out a loud bray and kicked her left foot back. Bobby screamed and crumpled to the ground.

Chapter 25

"My leg hurts!" Bobby wailed. "I've never had anything hurt so much!"

As soon as Elias looked at Bobby's twisted leg he knew it was broken. White-hot anger boiled in his chest. That stupid mule the blacksmith sold him had caused nothing but trouble, and now his young mule driver had been put out of commission because of the stubborn, temperamental critter.

"I'm real sorry," Bobby said, tears streaming down his face. "I shoulda never slapped that ornery mule on the rump."

Elias scooped the boy into his arms and carried him onto the boat. "It wasn't your fault. You were only doing what Ned told you to do."

"I know, but I shoulda realized Wilma was still fidgety

and might decide to pull somethin' on me."

"It's okay." Elias carried Bobby down to his cabin and laid him carefully on the bunk. "We're almost to Walnutport, and as soon as we arrive we'll take you to see Dr. McGrath."

"B–but who's gonna lead the mules?"

"I will, and Ned can steer the boat."

Elias splinted the boy's leg with two pieces of wood and then tied a strip of cloth around it. "Now just lie here and try to relax. We'll be in Walnutport soon."

The first thing Elias did when they arrived in Walnutport was to take Bobby to see Dr. McGrath. While the doctor took care of Bobby's leg, Elias went to tell Bobby's aunt Martha what had happened. After he returned to the doctor's office and picked up Bobby, he took him to the boardinghouse so his aunt could care for him, then he returned to the boat where he'd left Ned.

"How's the kid?" Ned asked. "Did ya get him to the doctor okay?"

Elias nodded. "His leg's broken pretty bad, and he'll have to be off it for a good many weeks."

"Figured as much." Ned grunted. "Now you'll need to find another mule driver somewhere."

"You're right, and another mule, too." Elias frowned.

"I've had it with that animal! In fact, I'm taking her right back to the blacksmith!"

Ned's forehead wrinkled. "What if Patrick don't want the critter back?"

Elias shrugged. "I won't know until I go over there and ask. Are you coming or staying?"

"Think I'll come along. If Patrick gives you a problem about the mule, I wouldn't wanna miss out on a fight between you two."

Elias shook his head. "There won't be any fighting. I'm just going to take the mule back and ask Patrick to refund my money."

Ned let out a low whistle. "This I've gotta see."

Patrick had just finished repairing the wheel on a wagon owned by one of the farmers in the area, when Elias showed up. His helper, Ned, was with him, leading the mule Patrick had sold Elias several weeks ago.

"What can I do for you?" Patrick asked.

"I'm here to return your mule."

Patrick shook his head. "She ain't my mule. You paid for the critter, fair and square, so she's your mule now."

"She's not working out for me," Elias said. "She's been nothing but trouble since the day I got her."

"That's not my problem. Maybe you just need to work harder with her. . .get her trained."

"We've been working with her, and as far as I'm concerned, she's not trainable. The stupid animal kicked my mule driver this morning and broke his leg."

Patrick ground his teeth together. "If I'd have known the fool mule would do somethin' like that, I'd never have sold her to you."

"Then you'll take her back?"

Patrick shook his head. "Don't know what I'd do with her if I did."

"You could sell her to someone else," Ned spoke up. "Someone who has the time and patience to work with her."

Patrick contemplated things a few seconds then finally nodded. "Tell ya what I'll do. I'll take the mule and give you back half your money."

Elias's eyebrows furrowed. "Why only half?"

"You've used her awhile, so she's worth less to me now."

A muscle on the side of Elias's neck quivered. "That's not fair. The mule's worth what I paid, and—"

"Take it or leave it."

"We'll take it," Ned cut in. He handed the mule's rope to Patrick. "Any idea where we can find another mule?"

Patrick scratched the side of his head. "Let's see now. I believe Slim Collier has a couple of mules he uses on his farm, but I doubt he'd be willing to part with either of 'em."

Elias frowned. "Do you know of any other mules I might buy?"

"I think maybe Gus over at the livery stable has one now."

"Guess I'll head over to his place and see." Elias hesitated a minute and then held out his hand. "What about the money you owe me for returning your mule?"

Patrick reached into his pants pocket and pulled out twenty-five dollars. It irked him that he had to take the mule back, but he didn't want the fancy boatman going around town blabbing to everyone that Patrick O'Grady was unfair in his business dealings. So he'd take the dumb mule and hopefully make a profit when he found someone else willing to buy the critter.

"Isn't that Elias's boat tied up over there by Mike and Kelly's store?" Sarah asked Carolyn as the two women hung clean clothes on the line.

Carolyn shielded her eyes from the glare of the sun. "I believe it is. I don't see any sign of Elias or his helpers, though."

"Maybe they're in the store. If you'd like to walk over there and see, I'll finish hanging the last of these towels."

"I'll wait until we're done," Carolyn said. "That way if a boat comes through and you need to open the lock, I'll be able to finish hanging the laundry for you."

Sarah smiled. Carolyn was such a thoughtful person. "I appreciate your help, and I'm going to miss you when you join Elias on his boat again."

Carolyn smiled, too. "I'll miss you as well. These last two weeks have been fun, even though I was in a lot of pain the first few days." She glanced at her hand, almost completely healed from the burns.

"They've been fun for me, too. Between you and Hortence, I've had more help than I know what to do with."

Carolyn chuckled. "I can't believe you said that. No one as busy as you can ever have too much help."

"I guess that's true." Sarah glanced at the towpath and saw Elias heading their way, while Ned, leading a mule, turned in the direction of Elias's boat. "Here comes your brother now," she said, pointing in that direction.

Carolyn squinted. "I don't see Bobby though, and I wonder if Ned's leading the mule because they took it to the blacksmith to have it shod."

Sarah shrugged. "I don't know, but that looks like a different mule to me."

A few minutes later, Elias joined them under the clothesline. "Hello, ladies."

"Hello, Elias," Sarah said.

"It's good to see you." Carolyn stepped forward and gave him a hug.

"It's good to see you, too. How's your hand?"

"Much better. Dr. McGrath said as long as I keep it clean and continue to put the ointment on, I should be fine."

"That's good to hear, because I really need you on the boat again."

"How come? Hasn't Ned been feeding you well enough?"

"We've managed okay until this morning."

"What happened?" Sarah asked.

"That troublesome mule I bought from the blacksmith kicked Bobby and broke his leg." Elias groaned. "I returned the mule to Patrick and got half my money back; then I bought another mule from the man who runs the livery stable. This creature seems to have a more agreeable temperament, so hopefully she'll work out better than the last one. My big concern is that I have no one to lead the mules." He scuffed the toe of his boot and looked at Sarah. "I don't suppose you'd consider letting Sammy come to work for me until he goes back to school at the end of summer?"

Her spine stiffened, and she glared at him. "How can you even ask me that? After my reaction when Sammy ran off to lead your mules before, you ought to know how I feel about it."

"I understand your concerns, but I'll take good care of him and make sure—"

"Absolutely not! None of my kids will ever work on this canal!" Sarah turned and tromped into the house.

Chapter 26

*A*s Elias's boat headed toward Mauch Chunk, with Ned steering and Elias leading the mules, he fumed with every step he took. He didn't like having to lead the mules when he should have been on the boat. Well, at least the new mule he'd bought was more cooperative than the last one, and since Elias had no one else to lead the mules, he had no choice but to take over that responsibility. If he could only have had Sammy working for him, it would have helped a lot, but that wasn't to be.

Elias knew he'd upset Sarah by asking if Sammy could work for him and wished he hadn't brought it up. He figured he'd ruined whatever chances he may have had with Sarah— if he'd ever had any chance at all. He'd seen the way she couldn't make eye contact with him most of the time. She probably couldn't stand to look at the ugly red mark on his face.

As they drew closer to Mauch Chunk, Elias spotted a young, red-haired boy running after a chicken along the edge of the towpath.

"What are you doing with that chicken?" Elias called.

The boy screeched to a halt and turned to face Elias, his eyes wide with fear. "I. . .uh. . ."

"Is it your chicken?"

"No, sir. I was tryin' to catch it so my ma would have somethin' to fix us for supper tonight. Somethin' besides beans."

Elias studied the boy a few seconds. He was barefooted, wore a pair of tattered trousers and a faded blue shirt, and looked to be about ten years old.

"What's your name and where do you live?" Elias asked.

The boy stared at the ground and dragged his big toe through the dirt. "My name's Frank. Me and my two sisters live in a shack with our ma."

"Near Mauch Chunk?"

"Yeah."

"What about your father? Is he a canaler?"

Frank shook his head. "Pa used to work at the coal mines in Mauch Chunk, but now he's dead. Ma washes clothes for the boatmen sometimes, but she don't make much and can't hardly feed us no more."

Elias's heart clenched. There were so many poor people living along the canal. He wished he could help them all.

"How would you like to come to work for me?"

"Doin' what?"

Elias motioned to his mules. "Leading them while they pull my boat."

Frank's pale eyebrows shot up. "Really?"

"That's right. The mule driver I had has a broken leg, so I need someone to take over the job for the rest of the summer."

"I'd like to earn some money to help my ma, but I've never led a mule before."

"I'll teach you."

"That'd be great." Frank nodded enthusiastically. "I'll have to run home and tell Ma first, though."

"I'll tell you what," Elias said. "I'll get my load of coal in Mauch Chunk and meet up with you here in a couple of hours."

Frank offered Elias a toothless grin. "Sounds good to me."

Elias reached into his pants pocket and pulled out a five dollar bill. "Give this to your mother, so she can buy something to eat. And no more stealing chickens," he added as he handed the money to Frank.

"Wow! Thanks, mister."

"My name's Elias Brooks, but you can just call me Elias."

"Okay. See you soon, Elias!" Frank waved and hurried away.

Elias hoped he hadn't made a mistake. For all he knew, Frank might not even be the boy's real name. For that matter, he might never see the boy again. Well, if that was the case, then so be it. Elias had done what he felt was right, and he'd just wait and see if Frank was waiting for him when he came back.

As Patrick headed for Cooper's store, he struggled with the urge to stop over at the lock tender's house and talk to Sarah. After he'd blurted out the way he felt about her the other day and suggested that they get married, he wasn't sure if he should give her some time to think about things or keep trying to pursue her. One thing he knew was that he'd never get anywhere with Sarah if he couldn't spend more time with her so he could show her what a good husband he'd make. Since Sunday was her only day off and she spent part of it in church, he'd come to the conclusion that he needed to attend church, too. Maybe Sarah wouldn't mind if he sat beside her during the service.

Of course, he reasoned, *that will mean sitting beside those kids of hers, and one in particular doesn't like me very much.*

Patrick leaned over, picked up a flat rock, and tossed it

into the canal, the way he'd done many times when he was a boy. There had to be some way for him to win Sammy over.

When he entered the store a few minutes later, his gaze came to rest on the glass-topped counter full of candy. Ah, that might be just what he needed!

He studied the variety of candy—gumdrops, lemon drops, horehound drops, licorice ropes, peppermint sticks, and several kinds of lollipops. *Hmm. . .which one should I choose?*

"Can I help you with something?" Mike asked, positioning himself on the other side of the counter.

"I'm lookin' to buy some candy, but I'm not sure what kind. Have you got any suggestions?"

"Guess that all depends on what kind you like."

Patrick shook his head. "It ain't for me. It's for Sarah's kids, but I was hopin' to get the kind that Sammy likes best."

"Oh, that's easy then. I know exactly what my nephew likes." Mike picked up the jar of lollipops. "Sammy likes cherry—although he'll eat most any kind except orange. His little sister likes orange, though. I think Willis does, too."

"All right then, I'll take two orange lollipops and one cherry." Patrick smiled. He could hardly wait to see the kids' expressions when he gave them the candy on Sunday after church.

As Elias led the mules down the towpath coming out of Mauch Chunk, he looked for Frank, but saw no sign of the boy. *He's probably not coming,* Elias told himself. *Either his mother said no, or he took off with the money I gave him and never said a word to his mother about working for me.* He flicked at a fly that kept buzzing his head. *Guess that's what I get for being so nice, but I couldn't help feeling sorry for the boy.*

"Hey, mister—I mean, Elias. I've been watchin' for you!"

When Frank stepped out of the bushes, Elias jumped, causing both mules to bray and nearly run into his back.

"Sorry. Didn't mean to scare ya." Frank looked up at Elias and squinted his blue eyes. "If ya haven't changed your mind about me leadin' your mules, I'm ready to go." He lifted the small satchel he held in his hands. "Don't have many clothes, but Ma said I'd need another pair of trousers to wear, and I've also got an old pair of my pa's boots, 'cause she said I might need 'em if my feet get too sore from walkin' the towpath."

"Does that mean your mother's okay with you working for me the rest of this summer?"

"Yeah, sure. Said I could work clear up to the time the canal closes for the winter."

"What about school? Won't you need to quit so you can return to school in the fall?"

Frank shook his head. "Don't need no schoolin'. Pa didn't have much, and he got by."

Elias was tempted to argue with the boy but figured he'd wait until summer was nearing an end and then bring up the subject again.

"So what should I do to make the mules go?" Frank asked.

"If you walk along with me for a while, I'll teach you all you need to know about leading the mules." Elias gave the boy's shoulder a gentle squeeze.

"What are their names?"

"The lead mule is Dolly. She's been with me since the beginning of the season. I just got the other mule and haven't named her yet, so if you have any ideas, I'm open to suggestions."

"How 'bout Jenny?"

Elias considered that a few seconds and finally nodded. "Jenny sounds like a good name to me."

They walked together for a time; then Elias handed the lead rope to Frank, staying close to the boy to be sure both mules cooperated.

When they reached Walnutport sometime later, Carolyn leaned over the edge of the boat and called to Elias, "Can we spend the night in Walnutport and go to church tomorrow morning?"

"I don't think so," he shouted in return.

"Why not?"

"I just hadn't planned on stopping, that's all." Elias wasn't about to tell Carolyn that the reason he didn't want to stop was because he was sure Sarah was angry with him for asking if Sammy could lead his mules again. He especially didn't want to talk about it in front of young Frank, who was staring up at him with a curious expression.

"I'd really like to spend the night in Walnutport," Carolyn persisted. "I miss Sarah and was hoping for the chance to visit with her."

The pleading look on his sister's face made Elias alter his decision. "Oh, all right. We'll spend the night in Walnutport and go to church there in the morning." *I just hope Sarah won't give me a cool reception.*

Chapter 27

On Sunday morning when Sarah entered the church with her children, she was surprised to see Patrick standing in the foyer talking to Pastor William. While she'd seen him in Sunday school a few times when they were children, she couldn't remember him ever coming to church since he'd become a man.

Sammy, Willis, and Helen gathered with a group of other children to visit, so Sarah headed over to say hello to Patrick.

"It's nice to see you here today," she said, joining him and the pastor.

"Figured it was the only way I'd get to—" Patrick halted his words, his face turning a light shade of red. "Uh. . .what I mean to say is, I figured it was about time I exposed myself to some religion." He looked over at Pastor William and grinned. "Sure don't want to end up like some of them rusty old canalers who only speak the Lord's name when they're mad about somethin'."

Pastor William's brows furrowed. "It's a shame to hear the way some of those men talk, and I'm hoping some of the services I'll be holding down at the canal will reach several of them for the Lord. Maybe some will seek Him this afternoon during the baptismal service we'll be having down there."

"I think I might like to attend that service," Patrick was quick to say.

"Are you planning to be baptized?" Sarah questioned.

Patrick shook his head. "Uh, no. Don't think I'm ready for anything like that."

"Well, let me know when you're ready to talk more about it." Pastor William glanced across the room. "I see Deacon Simms motioning to me, so if you two will excuse me, I'd better see what he wants."

When the pastor walked away, Patrick moved closer to Sarah. "Would you mind if I sit with you during church?"

Sarah hesitated but finally nodded. She didn't want people to get the wrong idea and think she and Patrick were courting, but she didn't want to discourage Patrick from coming to church again either.

Probably the best way for me to handle this, she decided,

is to put Helen on one side of me and Willis on the other. That will mean Patrick will have to sit beside Sammy.

As Patrick sat on a blanket with Sarah and her children, sharing a picnic lunch after church, he was grateful that she'd invited him to join them. Not only was the fried chicken she'd prepared delicious, but he was finally getting a chance to visit with her. Of course, that was only when one of her kids wasn't blabbering about something he thought was unimportant. He couldn't believe that three little kids would have so much to talk about. Truth was, he wished they'd go off somewhere by themselves and play so he could talk to Sarah without any interruptions.

Just then, Patrick remembered the lollipops in his pocket. As soon as the kids were done eating their meal, he pulled the candy out and handed a red lollipop to Helen and the two orange ones to Willis and Sammy. "Here you go. . .a special treat from me," he said with a smile.

"Thanks!" Willis removed the wrapper and swiped his tongue over the lollipop.

Helen did the same. "Yum. . .good!"

Patrick looked over at Sammy and was rewarded with a scowl. "I hate orange. Ugh, it makes me sick!"

A wave of heat shot up the back of Patrick's neck. He

remembered now that Mike had said Sammy liked cherry but didn't care for orange.

"Sorry about that. I really meant for the red one to be yours." Patrick looked over at Helen. "Would you trade your lollipop with your brother's?"

"No way!" Sammy shouted before Helen could respond. "I ain't eatin' that after she's licked on it!"

"I'll tell you what," Patrick said, "I'll buy you another lollipop the next time I go to the store."

"Don't bother," Sammy muttered. "Oh look, there's Elias." He pointed across the way, scrambled to his feet, and dashed off.

"Oh look, there's Sarah," Carolyn said to Elias as they finished their picnic lunch. "I'd go over and talk to her, but it looks like she's kind of busy right now."

Elias glanced to the left and winced, feeling as if he'd been punched in the stomach. Sarah sat on a blanket next to Patrick. He knew he had no right to feel jealous, because he certainly had no claim on Sarah. But he couldn't help the urge he felt to go over there and tell Patrick to stay away from Sarah.

Carolyn rose to her feet. "I think I'll go talk to Sarah's sister, Kelly, awhile. She's sitting on the grass near the lock, sketching a picture. I'd like to see what it is."

Carolyn had just walked away when Sammy ran up to Elias and gave him a hug. "I'm glad you're here today! Why don't ya come over and sit on the blanket with us?"

"I don't think that's such a good idea," Elias said.

"Why not?"

"Your mother's visiting with Patrick, and I don't want to interrupt."

"I don't think she'd care." Sammy frowned. "Besides, if you go over, maybe Patrick will leave."

"I doubt that, but I'm curious. Why would you want Patrick to leave?"

Sammy wrinkled his nose. "He hangs around Mama all the time, and he says mean things to our dog."

Elias wasn't sure how to respond. It was clear that Sammy didn't care much for Patrick. The truth was, neither did he. One thing was clear: If Sarah was getting serious about Patrick, then Sammy might have to accept that fact whether he liked it or not.

Elias was about to suggest that he and Sammy go down to his boat so Sammy could meet Frank, who'd stayed on the boat with Ned, but Pastor William had just made the announcement that the baptismal service was about to begin.

"I'd better get ready to play along with the songs," Elias said, slipping the straps of his accordion over his arms and rising to his feet.

"Can I stand beside ya?" Sammy asked.

"Sure, that'd be just fine."

The pastor opened the service by leading the people in several lively songs. Elias enjoyed accompanying on his accordion, just as he'd done during church today, and Betsy, who'd apparently felt well enough to come, played along with her zither.

When the singing ended, Pastor William opened his Bible. "Proverbs 16:9 says, 'A man's heart deviseth his way: but the Lord directeth his steps.'" He smiled and stretched out his hands, as though encompassing the crowd. "Some folks think they know what's best, and they wander through life never asking God for direction. Some folks think they can do whatever they choose, and believe they don't need God at all."

Pastor William moved closer to the crowd. "In 1 Samuel 16:7, it says, 'The Lord seeth not as a man seeth; for man looketh on the outward appearance, but the Lord looketh on the heart.' We should all ask ourselves what the Lord sees when He looks on our hearts. Are we clean before the Lord, or does He see our sin—ugly and black?"

A hush fell over the crowd. No doubt everyone was taking to heart what the pastor had said.

"Before I begin baptizing, I want to invite any who haven't yet done so to confess their sins and accept Christ as their personal Savior."

To Elias's surprise, Ned, who'd obviously left the boat, stepped forward, lifted his gaze to the sky, and said, "Oh Lord, if You can care for a man as vile as me, then let it be so. I know I'm a sinner, and I ask You to forgive my sins and make me a new man."

Pastor William asked Ned to kneel before him, and then he placed his hands on Ned's head and prayed for him. Then he guided the tearful canaler through a prayer of repentance. Following the prayer, the pastor explained that those who were about to be baptized would be following Christ's example, and that the act of baptism was an outward public showing of an inward faith. Finally, Ned and several others followed Pastor William into the canal, where he baptized each of them.

When Ned came out of the water, he wore a huge grin. "I'm now a clean vessel for my Master's use," he said, stretching his arms open wide. "I'm a changed man. My thoughts are different, and from this moment on, my actions will be different. I'm going to give up chewing tobacco, smoking cigarettes, swearing, and drinking. I'm going to try and live the way a Christian should."

Pastor William smiled, and then he reminded those who had been baptized that the Lord was stronger than the devil. "Remember, too," he said, "no matter what troubles come your way, never give up."

Elias pondered those words and realized that he needed

to take them to heart. With all the troubles he'd had since he took over his grandfather's boat, he'd been on the verge of giving up several times. From now on, he was going to trust the Lord and take one day at a time.

Chapter 28

On Monday morning, as Elias headed his boat in the direction of Easton, he was pleased to see how well Frank was doing with the mules. The boy had caught on quickly and didn't complain about a thing. With the exception of Sarah giving Elias the cold shoulder on Sunday while she became friendlier toward the blacksmith, things were looking up for Elias. He was quite sure that she was still angry with him for asking if Sammy could lead his mules.

"Hey, Ned," Bart Jarmon called as they passed his boat, going in the opposite direction, "I hear ya went for a dip in the canal yesterday."

Ned leaned over the boat and waved at Bart. "Found the Lord and got myself baptized, that's what I did!"

Bart leaned his head back and roared. "So you've done

got religion now, huh?"

"That's right. I'm a new man in Christ, and I've given up chewin', cussin', smokin', and drinkin'. From now on, I'll be totin' a Bible everywhere I go."

Bart put his hands around his neck and coughed, like he was gagging. "Well, you'd better stay far away from me then, 'cause I sure don't want none of that holier-than-thou religious stuff rubbin' off on me."

"You'd be surprised how good you'd feel if ya confessed your sins and got right with God," Ned shouted in return.

Bart shook his head vigorously. "No thanks! I'm happy just the way I am."

As Bart's boat went past, Elias turned to Ned and said, "You handled that well, my friend. There was a day when I don't think you would have responded so nicely."

"That's true. I'd of shouted a few cuss words and waited until I saw Bart again, and then I'd have knocked his block clean off. Now I know it's best just to turn the other cheek."

Elias smiled. It was good to see such a positive change in Ned. Elias knew that his grandfather would have been pleased to see his old friend and helper witnessing to one of the other canalers.

Elias motioned to the tiller. "Would you mind steering the boat awhile? Carolyn's going to be washing some clothes soon, and I should go down there and see what I have that needs to be washed."

"Sure, boss, I'll do whatever ya ask."

"Thanks, I appreciate that." Elias thumped Ned on the back. "I shouldn't be gone too long."

When Elias went below, he found Carolyn in the galley, fumbling around in one of the cabinets.

"What are you looking for?" Elias asked.

"I thought I had two bars of that soap that floats, but there's only one in here now."

Elias frowned. "That's strange. Do you think you can get by with just the one until we stop at Cooper's store again?"

"I'm sure I can manage."

"How's your hand feeling?"

"Just fine."

"Are you sure you're up to washing clothes?"

She held up her hand. "It's almost as good as new, and it certainly won't hurt for me to get it wet."

"All right then. I'll go to my room and see what I have that needs to be washed."

"Ned gave me some of his clothes already, and Frank just had one shirt he said I could wash."

"I know. That poor boy and his family have been practically destitute since his father died. When Frank quits working for me at the end of the season I plan to see that he goes home with some money he can give his mother to help with expenses."

"You're a good man, Elias. I'm pleased to call you my brother."

He grinned. "I'm pleased to have you for a sister."

When Elias entered his cabin, he gathered up his dirty clothes, and then opened the drawer where he kept the pocket watch his grandfather had given him for his birthday several years ago.

"Now that's sure strange," he murmured when he saw that the watch wasn't there. *I wonder if I put it someplace else and forgot. Well, I don't have time to look for it right now, so hopefully I'll find it later on.*

"I'm going out to the garden to pull some carrots," Sarah told Hortence after they'd washed the breakfast dishes. "I want to do it before more boats come through."

"That's fine. I'll get started washing some clothes while you're in the garden."

"Thanks. Since the kids are playing upstairs in their rooms, the two of us should be able to get a lot done." Sarah smiled and hurried out the door.

When she stepped into the garden, she gasped. Not only were all of her cucumbers missing, but someone had taken most of her carrots. Everything had looked fine yesterday. This had to have happened sometime during the night or early this morning.

Sarah wondered if one of the mule drivers had come

along and stolen the vegetables. It had happened before to several others who had gardens near the towpath.

She bent down and pulled six of the carrots that were still left, then turned toward the house. She was almost to the door when Kelly showed up.

"I haven't talked to you since Sunday, so I decided to come over and let you know that someone broke into our store and stole several things."

Sarah frowned. "I'm sorry to hear that. When did it happen?"

"We think it must have occurred either while we were in church, during the baptismal service, or sometime during the night."

Sarah pointed to her garden. "I wonder if it was the same person who stole from my garden."

Kelly folded her arms and tapped her foot. "It's always a concern when someone steals, especially when we don't know who it is, or if and when they might steal again."

"I know." Sarah frowned as she slowly shook her head. "Taking some things from my garden's a minor thing, but breaking into your store and stealing things is robbery. I hope that whoever did it will be caught and punished."

Chapter 29

A few weeks later, Elias decided to stop at Cooper's store to buy some more soap that floated, as well as several other items they were nearly out of. While he did the shopping, Ned and Frank waited on the boat, and Carolyn headed over to the lock tender's house to visit Sarah.

"It's nice to see you," Mike said when Elias entered the store. "How are things going?"

"Fairly well. I've got a new mule driver, and he's working out pretty good."

"Glad to hear it. I know Bobby was disappointed when he broke his leg and had to quit leading the mules."

"How's Bobby doing?" Elias asked. "I didn't get to see him the last time I was in Walnutport."

"He's getting along okay, but according to his aunt

Martha, he's bored and doesn't like to sit around."

"Guess that's how it is with most kids."

"Yeah. My two never sit still." Mike chuckled. "From the looks of their rumpled bedsheets, I think they must keep moving even when they're sleeping."

Elias smiled. "How are things going here at the store? Is your business doing well?"

"It won't be if we keep getting broken into."

Elias's eyebrows shot up. "You had a break-in?"

Mike nodded. "It happened on the Sunday we were at the baptismal service. Whoever did it stole some groceries, as well as two of Kelly's paintings." Mike frowned. "The same day, Sarah had some vegetables taken from her garden, so we're thinking it might have been done by the same person who broke into our store."

"That's a shame. Any idea who might have done it?"

Mike drew in a quick breath and released it with a groan. "Here on the canal, we have so many poor folks, not to mention the rugged canalers who don't seem to have a conscience at all. It could have been most anyone, really."

"You're probably right."

"I'm always glad when any of the boatmen find the Lord, because then they give up their sinful lifestyle."

"I know I've seen a big change in my helper, Ned. He's not only given up his bad habits, but now he's begun witnessing to some of the other boatmen."

"That's good. Maybe if one of them's responsible for breaking into my store, they'll repent and won't do it again. And who knows. . .they might even make restitution." Mike shrugged. "I figure it was either done by one of the boatmen or maybe some desperate kid."

Elias thought about Carolyn's missing bar of soap and the pocket watch he hadn't been able to find, and wondered if Frank could be responsible. Might the boy have also stolen from Sarah's garden and broken into Mike's store? He did have an opportunity to do those things while Elias, Carolyn, and Ned were at the baptismal service that Sunday. He hated to think the boy would do such a thing, but knowing how poor Frank's family was, there was a chance that he might be the one. Elias debated about whether he should confront Frank and decided to wait for the right time to mention that things had been taken and then see if the boy acted guilty or owned up to it.

"It's so good to see you again," Sarah said, giving Carolyn a hug.

"It's good to see you, too. I've really missed our long talks."

"Same here. How's your hand feeling? Are the burns completely healed?"

Carolyn nodded. "I can't believe how well the salve

worked that Dr. McGrath gave me."

"I'm glad. I know how miserable you were at first."

"Oh look, here comes that handsome blacksmith," Carolyn said, motioning to the kitchen window.

Sarah gulped. She hoped he wasn't coming to ask if she'd considered his marriage proposal. She wasn't ready to deal with that yet, and certainly not in front of Carolyn.

She hurried to the front door and opened it before Patrick had a chance to knock.

"Hello, Sarah. How are you?" he asked with a friendly grin.

"I'm fine. How are you?"

"Doin' all right." He shifted his weight from one foot to the other. "I need more bread. . .if you have some, that is."

"Yes, I do. If you'll wait right here, I'll get it for you." Sarah shut the door and hurried into the kitchen, leaving Patrick alone on the porch.

When she returned a few minutes later, she handed him the bread and said, "It's fresh. I just baked it this morning."

"I'm sure it'll be real good." Patrick moved a bit closer. "I. . .uh. . .was wondering if—"

"I'm sorry. I can't visit with you right now because I have company inside."

"Who is it?"

"Elias's sister, Carolyn."

Patrick crooked an eyebrow. "Is Elias in there, too?"

"No, just Carolyn."

"That's good." Patrick's face flamed. "I mean, it's good you have some free time to visit with her."

"I don't get much free time for visiting, but traffic on the canal has been slower than usual today."

"Guess you may as well get used to it, because it probably won't be long and there won't be any boats hauling coal on the canal. The trains seem to be taking over more of that business all the time."

Sarah didn't need the reminder. Hardly a day went by that she didn't think about the future of the canal, which made her wonder how much longer she'd be able to support her children. If she could just save up enough money to open her own bakery, as Carolyn had suggested, all her problems would be solved.

"If you married me, you wouldn't have to work so hard or worry about the future of the canal." He leaned closer. "What do you say, Sarah? Have you given it some thought?"

"I have thought about it, but I don't have an answer for you yet."

"When do you think you will?"

"I. . .I don't know. I'll need to pray about it some more and discuss it with my kids, of course."

"Oh." Patrick's brows furrowed. "Guess if it's left up to them, you'll say no 'cause I don't think any of 'em likes me too well."

"They need to get to know you better." Sarah glanced toward the house, wishing Patrick would go so she could continue her visit with Carolyn.

As if by divine intervention, the door opened, and Carolyn stepped out. "I'm sorry to interrupt, but Willis asked if he could take the dog out for a walk. Since Hortence is busy cleaning upstairs, I told him I'd have to ask you."

"I have no objection," Sarah said, "as long as he doesn't go far and stays right on the towpath."

"All right, I'll tell him." Carolyn smiled at Patrick. "I'm sure you'll enjoy that bread you're holding. Sarah's an excellent baker."

"Yeah, I know." Patrick stood for a moment, then mumbled, "Guess I'd better go."

"Good-bye, Patrick."

"See you at church on Sunday," he called as he headed in the direction of town.

When Patrick was a safe distance away, Sarah turned to Carolyn and said, "He asked me to marry him awhile back and wondered if I had an answer for him yet."

Carolyn's eyes widened. "What'd you tell him?"

"I said I'd need to think about it, pray about it, and discuss it with my kids."

"And have you?"

"I've thought about it, and prayed about it, but I haven't

mentioned it to any of the kids."

"How come?"

"They don't like Patrick so well. . .especially Sammy, so I'm worried about how they might respond."

"Are you in love with Patrick?"

Sarah shook her head. "No, but I don't dislike him either."

"He seems to be a nice man, and he's very good-looking." Carolyn's cheeks turned pink. "Of course, that's just my opinion, although I don't know him very well."

Sarah sighed. "You're right, Patrick's good-looking and nice enough, but he's not—"

The front door swung open, and a yapping Bristle Face raced out the door with Willis on his heels. "Come back here you bad dog!" he shouted.

Bristle Face picked up speed, barking and growling as he ran along the edge of the canal. Sarah figured if the dog wasn't careful he might end up going for an unexpected swim.

In the next minute, Willis darted past Sarah, leaped for the dog, and landed with a splash in the canal!

"Help! Help! I can't swim!"

Chapter 30

Elias had left the store and was almost to the lock tender's house, when he heard a splash and someone hollering for help. That's when he spotted Willis, kicking, screaming, and gasping for air.

With his heart pounding like a blacksmith's anvil, Elias dropped his packages to the ground and raced down the towpath. "I'll get him!" he shouted to Sarah, who looked like she was about to jump into the canal.

Elias pulled off his boots, leaped into the water, and swam over to Willis. In one quick movement, he pulled the boy to his side. Using his free arm to swim, he brought Willis safely to shore.

With arms outstretched, Sarah dropped to her knees, reached for Willis, and pulled him to her chest. "Oh, thank the Lord you're all right!" Tears coursed down her cheeks, and then she and Willis both began to sob.

Instinctively, Elias squatted beside Sarah, wrapped his arms around her and Willis, and held them tightly. They sat like that for several minutes, until Elias felt someone touch his shoulder. He looked up and saw Carolyn smiling down at him.

"Thank God you came along when you did," she murmured. "You saved the boy's life."

Sarah pulled slowly away and nodded, apparently unable to speak.

Willis reached out to Elias and gave him another hug. "If ya hadn't jumped in the canal and grabbed holda me, I mighta died like my papa did."

The floodgates opened, and Sarah started sobbing again. Elias, unsure of what more he could do to calm Sarah down, looked up at Carolyn, hoping she could help.

"It's all right," Carolyn said, patting Sarah's shoulder. "Willis is safe now, and he seems to be fine."

When Sarah's sobbing finally subsided, Carolyn suggested they go inside. "Willis needs to get out of his wet clothes," she said.

"You're right." Sarah stood and took hold of Willis's hand. Then with a murmured, "Thank you, Elias," she hurried with her son toward the house.

Carolyn touched Elias's soggy shirtsleeve. "You'd better

get back to the boat and change your wet clothes, too."

He gave a nod. "Although they'd probably dry on their own if I stayed out here in the hot sun awhile longer."

"I'll go inside and check on Sarah," Carolyn said. "Then I'll meet you on the boat."

Elias headed down the towpath to get the packages he'd dropped. He hoped Sarah would be okay. She'd looked so pale and shaken, and he wished there'd been more he could do. Well, at least he'd broken the ice with her, and he was glad she was speaking to him again.

After Sarah got Willis changed into some dry clothes, she went to her room and checked her appearance in the looking glass. She was shocked by the red blotches on her face, and the swollen look around her red-rimmed eyes made her appear as if she'd been crying for hours. She'd had a hard time getting control of her emotions and had continued to cry even while changing Willis's clothes. What if Elias hadn't come along when he did? She wasn't a strong swimmer, and Willis might have drowned if she'd jumped in and tried to save him. She would have done it, though. She would do whatever she could in order to save any of her children.

She thought about how secure she'd felt when Elias had

put his arms around her and Willis. Even though she hadn't known Elias very long, she was strangely attracted to him.

Sarah gripped the edge of her dresser. *I can never give in to those feelings. I can never fall in love with a man who works on the canal.*

Thanks to the canal, she had lost her husband. She couldn't let it take one of her children, too. She had to do something to get them away from the canal. Would marrying Patrick be the answer for her and the children?

Wo–o–o–o! Wo–o–o–o! The sound of a conch shell drove Sarah's thoughts aside. She'd have to think about their future later on. Right now, she had to get that stupid lock opened so another boat could come through.

Sarah dipped her hands into the washbasin she kept on her dresser, splashed some water on her face, and dried it with a towel. Then she hurried from the room and quickly made her way down the winding stairs.

She stopped in the parlor to check on the children, but they weren't there. She found them in the kitchen with Hortence and Carolyn, having cookies and milk.

"There's a boat coming," Carolyn said.

Sarah nodded. "I heard the conch shell blowing." She moved toward the door, calling over her shoulder, "Hortence, don't let any of my kids leave the house!"

"I won't," Hortence replied. "I'll keep them right here with me."

When Sarah stepped out the door, Carolyn followed. "I need to get back to Elias's boat so we can be on our way, but I wanted to make sure you were okay," she said, slipping her around Sarah's waist.

"I'll never be okay as long as we're living near the canal. I need to find a better way of life for my kids." Sarah hurried toward the lock before Carolyn could respond.

When Carolyn returned to the boat, she found Elias in the galley, putting away the things he'd purchased at the store.

"How are Sarah and Willis doing?" he asked.

"Willis is fine. He and his sister and brother are sitting at Sarah's table eating cookies and drinking milk. It's Sarah I'm worried about. She was very upset when Willis fell in the canal."

Elias nodded. "I didn't know what to do or say to help calm her down."

"You saved her son's life, and she's very grateful."

He pulled his fingers through the back of his hair. "Yeah, but she still seemed upset when she went to the house."

"Of course she was. It was a shock when Willis fell in the canal. When Sarah came downstairs after helping the boy change his clothes, her face was red, and her eyes were swollen. I'm sure she did more crying after she went upstairs." The chair squeaked when Carolyn pulled it out and took a seat at the small table. "There's something else I think you should know."

"What's that?"

"The blacksmith asked Sarah to marry him, and I believe she's thinking about it."

Elias's forehead wrinkled, but then he shrugged. "If she loves him, then I wish them the best."

"But she doesn't love him. She's only considering his offer because she wants to get her children away from the canal."

"Guess that makes sense."

She shook her head. "No, it doesn't. I don't think Sarah should marry someone she doesn't love."

"Patrick seems like a nice-enough guy. Maybe she'll learn to love him."

Carolyn tapped her fingers along the edge of the table. "Maybe you should ask Sarah to marry you."

Elias's eyebrows shot up. "You're kidding, right?"

"No, I'm not. You love Sarah—I know you do. I can see the look of longing on your face when you talk about her, and there's a gentleness in your voice when you say her name."

"Okay, you're right; I do love Sarah. It's strange, though, because I haven't known her that long, but I began to have feelings for her soon after we met." He leaned against the cupboard and folded his arms. "I care about Sarah's children, too, and if I thought there was any chance at all that Sarah could love me in return, I might ask her to marry me. However..."

"You won't know if you don't ask. Why don't you go over there and talk to Sarah?"

"Now?"

"Yes, right now."

"I can't do that, Carolyn. We need to get moving up the canal."

She pursed her lips. "If you don't ask her now, it may be too late. She might accept Patrick's proposal."

Elias blinked a couple of times. "You think so?"

"I do."

"But what if she turns me down?" He touched the left side of his face. "What if she thinks I'm a fool for asking, when we've only known each other since the beginning of spring? What if she doesn't want to marry a man who looks like me?"

"You're too sensitive about the way you look, Elias. I've told you before that it's what's in a person's heart that counts." She placed her hand on his arm. "You really need to tell Sarah how you feel about her. If you don't, you'll always wonder if she could love you or not."

Elias drew in a deep breath and nodded slowly. "All right then, but I'd better do it quickly, before I lose my nerve."

Chapter 31

Sarah had just let a boat through the lock, and was about to enter the house, when Elias showed up. "How's Willis doing?" he asked.

"He's fine. Still a little shook up after falling into the canal."

"That's understandable." He leaned against the porch railing. "What about you, Sarah? Are you okay?"

She shrugged. "I'm doing as well as can be expected."

"I know it must have been frightening for you when Willis fell in, and I'm sure if I hadn't been there, you would have rescued him."

"I'm not a good swimmer, but I would have done my best. There have been so many accidents on this canal involving children, as well as adults. It scares me to think that one of my kids might get hurt or drown because I'm not able to be with them all the time." Sarah grimaced. "If I didn't have to be out here tending the lock, I could be a better mother to my kids."

Elias dipped his head, as though unable to look her in the eye. "I. . .uh. . .think I know a way that you could be with your children more."

"Oh?"

"You could marry me."

Sarah opened her eyes wide and sucked in her breath. "I appreciate your concern, but I could never marry a man like you."

Elias's face flamed, and without another word, he whirled around and raced back to his boat.

"It was a stupid thing to do," Elias mumbled as he hurried toward his boat. "I should never have listened to Carolyn. I should have expected Sarah would respond that way. I will never open myself up to another woman!"

When Elias stepped onto the boat, Ned frowned and narrowed his eyes. "It's about time ya got back. Are we ever gonna get this boat goin'?"

"Don't start snapping at me," Elias shot back. "Need I remind you that I'm the captain of this boat?"

"Sorry, boss," Ned mumbled. "Guess I overstepped my bounds."

Elias, feeling more frustrated by the minute, leaned over the side of the boat and shouted at Frank: "Get those mules moving now; I'm ready to go!"

Ned hurried to pull up the gangplank, and soon the boat was moving toward the lock.

"Take over the tiller, would you, Ned?" Elias stepped aside. "I need to go below for a few minutes."

"Sure thing, boss." Ned took Elias's place, and Elias hurried below, unable to bear the thought of seeing Sarah again.

He found Carolyn in the galley, peeling potatoes and carrots. "How'd it go with Sarah?" she asked with a hopeful expression.

"She said she would never marry a man like me." He touched the side of his face. "I told you she was bothered by my birthmark, and I guess I can't really blame her. Who'd want to be seen with a man who bears an ugly red blotch on his face?"

Carolyn stopped peeling and turned to face Elias. "I'm sure Sarah's not bothered by your birthmark."

"Yes, she is. She was looking right at the mark on my face when she said she could never marry a man like me."

"Are you sure about that? Did you ask her what she meant by that?"

"There was no point in asking when I already knew."

"Maybe you should go back there and ask—just to be sure you didn't misunderstand."

He shook his head determinedly. "We need to get going. We've lost enough time in Walnutport as it is. Ned's steering the boat into the lock right now."

"But what if Sarah marries Patrick?"

He shrugged. "What Sarah does is none of my business. As far as I'm concerned, I never want to see her again!"

Chapter 32

I want to stop and see Sarah," Carolyn said to Elias as they approached the Walnutport Lock several weeks later.

"What for?"

"Since you'll be dropping me off in Easton so I can get things ready for the new school year, this will be my last opportunity to say good-bye to Sarah. Besides, I need to go into Cooper's store and get that painting Kelly's been holding for me. It's the one of the rainbow that I want to give Mother for her birthday next month."

"Okay, but I don't want to spend a lot of time here. After Ned takes us through the lock, we'll dock near Cooper's store and I'll go inside to get the picture while you go over to Sarah's." He rubbed his chin. "Probably should pick up a few supplies I'm needing, too."

"Wouldn't you like to see Sarah?"

Elias shook his head. "Right now, I'm going below, just like I've done whenever we've gone through the Walnutport lock these last several weeks."

Carolyn placed her hand on his arm. "I wish you'd reconsider and see Sarah with me."

"I'm not going, and I'd appreciate it if you didn't keep asking."

"Okay," Carolyn mumbled. "Would you tell the Coopers I said good-bye?"

"Sure." Elias turned and tromped down the stairs. When he entered his cabin, his nose twitched at the musty odor. He ought to be getting used to it by now, but the lingering smell still bothered him.

He dropped to his knees and reached under his bunk for the tin can where he kept his money, but felt nothing. "Now, that's sure strange," he muttered.

He flattened his body closer to the floor and peered under the bunk, feeling around with his hands. The can was missing!

Elias's heartbeat picked up speed. Despite further searching, he still hadn't found his pocket watch, and now his money was missing, too. Someone had obviously been in his cabin and taken these things. The question was, who?

When Elias was sure the boat had gone through the lock, he went up to the main deck, finally ready to confront

Frank about his missing things.

"Pull the boat over near Cooper's store," Elias told Ned. "Carolyn's getting off so she can visit Sarah, and I've got some business with Frank."

"Sounds good. Think I'll go into the store and get some root beer," Ned said. "Will you be doing some shopping there today?"

"I'd planned to, but since I can't find my money. . ."

Ned's bushy eyebrows shot up. "You lost your money?"

"I'll explain things later." Elias moved over to where Carolyn stood near the bow of the boat. "Would you have some money I could borrow for the supplies I need? I seem to have misplaced my can of money." He didn't want to frighten Carolyn by telling her he thought his things had been stolen.

"I'd be happy to loan you some money." Carolyn went below and returned a few minutes later with an envelope. "Here you go," she said, handing it to Elias. "Take as much as you need."

"Thanks."

"Do you need me to help you look for your money?" she asked.

"That's all right. I'm sure it'll turn up." *It had better turn up*, he thought grimly.

"Okay." She lifted the edge of her gingham dress and stepped onto the gangplank Ned had set in place. "I shouldn't be at Sarah's too long, and I'll meet you back here when I'm done."

As soon as Carolyn left, Elias hurried off the boat. "I need to speak to you," he said, joining Frank, where he stood several feet off the towpath, feeding the mules.

"Sure, what's up?" the boy asked.

"Several weeks ago, Cooper's store was robbed. Do you know anything about that?"

Frank shook his head. "Just heard some talk about it, that's all."

Elias rested his arm against a nearby tree. "The same day the store got robbed, I discovered that my pocket watch was also missing. Then a short time ago, I went to my cabin to get my money, but the can I keep it in is missing, too. Would you know anything about that?"

"No, sir. I've never seen your pocket watch, and I don't know nothin' about your money neither."

"There were some things taken from Sarah's garden the same day as the store was robbed. Would you know anything about that?"

The boy's face colored, and he hung his head. "I...I did snitch some of her carrots 'cause I was hungry, but that's all I ever took." He lifted his head and looked at Elias with a sober expression. "Maybe you oughta ask Ned about your missin' things. He's on the boat most of the time, so he's had more of a chance to sneak into your cabin and take stuff than I have."

Elias debated what to do. Ned had changed since his conversion, and even before that, as far as Elias knew, Ned had never stolen anything from him or his grandfather. Elias wondered how Ned would respond if he questioned him about this.

He placed his hand on Frank's shoulder. "I'm going to trust that what you've told me is true, but from now on, if you're hungry or need something, I want you to tell me."

"Okay."

"And no more taking things from Sarah's or anyone else's garden. Is that clear?"

"Yes, sir."

"Good boy." Elias turned and headed for Cooper's store.

When Hortence let Carolyn into Sarah's house, she informed her that Sarah was upstairs in her room.

"Is she taking a nap?" Carolyn questioned.

"I don't think so. She said she was going up there to look for something in her trunk." Hortence motioned to the stairs. "Why don't you go on up? I'm sure she'll be glad to see you."

Carolyn hurried up the stairs. When she saw that Sarah's door was shut, she rapped lightly on it.

"Come in," Sarah called.

Carolyn entered the room and found Sarah standing in front of her looking glass, wearing a beautiful, ivory-colored dress with a high neckline and puffed sleeves.

"What a pretty dress," Carolyn murmured. "You look lovely in it."

Sarah whirled around. "Oh, Carolyn, it's so good to see you." She moved quickly across the room and gave Carolyn a hug.

"I'm heading back to Easton to get ready for the new school year," Carolyn said. "I asked Elias to stop in Walnutport so I could come here and say good-bye."

"I'm sorry you have to go. Do you think you might be back next summer?"

"I don't know. I guess it all depends on whether Elias still has his boat."

"Why wouldn't he have it? Is he thinking about selling it?"

"I'm not sure; he hasn't said anything about that. But even if I don't come to Walnutport again, maybe you can visit me in Easton sometime."

Sarah shook her head. "As long as I'm stuck here on the canal, I won't be able to visit anywhere."

"Maybe this winter, when the canal's closed."

"We'll have to wait and see how it goes."

Carolyn had a hunch the reason for Sarah's hesitation

was because of her financial situation. She probably didn't have the money to make the trip to Easton by train, and with the canal closing down during the winter, catching a ride on one of the boats was out of the question. Even hiring a driver to take them by horse and carriage would be costly.

Carolyn was tempted to offer to pay Sarah and the children's way to Easton, but didn't want to offend her, so she changed the subject.

"Now about that beautiful dress you're wearing. . . Please don't tell me it's a wedding dress and that you've decided to marry Patrick O'Grady."

"It is a wedding dress, but not for a marriage to Patrick." Sarah shook her head. "I still haven't made a decision on that. I think I'm going to wait until the end of boating season to make any decisions about my future."

"That's probably a wise decision. You wouldn't want to make a mistake about something you'll have to live with for the rest of your life."

Tears welled in Sarah's eyes as her fingers traced the edge of the collar on her dress. "If Sam were still alive, today would have been our tenth wedding anniversary." She sniffed. "I thought it might make me feel closer to him if I tried the dress on today, but it's only made me feel weepy."

"I'm sure you still miss him."

Sarah nodded. "Some days more than others, but as time

goes on, the pain lessens."

Carolyn stared out Sarah's bedroom window at the puffy white clouds floating past. She wanted to talk to Sarah about Elias but wasn't sure how to begin.

"Where are your thoughts taking you?" Sarah asked. "You look like you're someplace else right now."

"I. . .uh. . .was thinking about my brother."

"How's Elias doing? His boat has come through the lock several times in the last few weeks, but I haven't seen him even once, and I—well, I've really missed him."

"He's been staying below in his cabin, while Ned steers the boat."

"All the time?"

"No, just when he goes through the Walnutport lock."

"What's the reason for that?"

Carolyn drew in a quick breath. "He's been avoiding you."

"Is it because I turned down his unexpected marriage proposal?"

"Yes. No. Well, that's only part of the reason."

Sarah tipped her head. "I don't understand."

"Elias was deeply hurt when you said you could never marry a man like him. He thinks you turned him down because of his birthmark—because it's ugly, and you can't bear to look at it."

Sarah shook her head. "That's not true. I've never minded Elias's birthmark. The reason I said I could never

687

marry a man like him is because he's a boatman." Sarah took a seat on the edge of her bed and motioned for Carolyn to do the same.

"From the time I was a young girl, I vowed never to marry a canaler," Sarah continued.

"Why's that?"

"I'd seen how hard Mama worked on Papa's boat, with little or no appreciation, and both my sister and I were expected to lead Papa's mules, walking long hours every day with no pay at all. Papa kept all the money we should have earned." Sarah released a lingering sigh. "I ran away with Sam, and we got married just so we could both get away from the canal. Then later, when we ended up coming back to Walnutport and he began tending the lock, I was faced with a different problem."

"What problem was that?"

"Fear. I became fearful that something bad would happen to my husband or one of my kids because we lived so close to the canal. Sure enough, the canal took Sam, and if not for Elias, it might have taken Willis, too." Tears welled in Sarah's eyes as she slowly shook her head. "So you see why I could never marry a boatman or anyone else who works on the canal."

"I'm glad you explained all this. Now I just have one more question to ask before I go."

"What's that?"

"Do you care for my brother?"

Sarah nodded. "Yes, I do. Even though I haven't known him very long, his kindness and gentle spirit have touched my heart deeply. If Elias wasn't a boatman, I would have accepted his proposal."

Carolyn took hold of Sarah's hand and gave her fingers a gentle squeeze. "Thanks for sharing from your heart. It gives me a better understanding of things." She rose from the bed. "I don't want to keep Elias waiting, so I'd better go. I'll write to you when I get to Easton, and I hope you'll write to me."

"Yes, I will."

Carolyn gave Sarah one final hug; then she hurried out the door. She needed to speak with Elias right away.

Chapter 33

"Can I talk to you a minute?" Elias asked Ned, when he found him sitting on a rock near the canal with his fishing line cast into the water.

"Yeah, sure. What's up?"

Elias lowered himself to the ground beside Ned. "I know you're aware of the break-in that occurred at Cooper's store several weeks back."

"Uh-huh."

"And you knew that someone had also taken some things from Sarah's garden that day."

Ned nodded. "That's nothin' new around here, though. People steal stray chickens and snitch things from the gardens along the towpath all the time." He offered Elias a sheepish grin. "Not that it's right, of course."

"No, it's certainly not, and neither is stealing from me."

Ned's bushy eyebrows furrowed. "What are ya talkin' about?"

"My pocket watch came up missing around the same time as Cooper's store got robbed, and now my money's also missing."

"Maybe you misplaced them."

Elias shook his head. "No. I've been keeping the money in a tin can underneath my bunk, and it's not there."

"Do ya think Frank might have taken it? I mean, the kid's family is poor as a church mouse."

"I asked the boy about it before I went to Cooper's store."

"What'd he say?"

"He said he hadn't stolen anything from me."

"And ya believe him?"

Elias shrugged. "I've no reason not to believe him."

"Have ya looked in the boy's cabin?"

"Yes, I did that right after I spoke to him, but there was no sign of my watch or the money. I've looked pretty much everywhere on the boat—everywhere except for your quarters, that is."

Ned's forehead wrinkled deeply. "I hope ya don't think I had anything to do with it." His face turned red as he pulled his fishing line in with a jerk. "Before I became a Christian, I had lots of bad habits, but other than a few vegetables and

691

chickens I took when I was a kid, I've never stolen anything in my life!"

Elias placed his hand on Ned's shoulder. "Calm down. You're getting yourself worked up for nothing. I wasn't accusing you of taking my things. I was just going to ask if you knew anything about it."

Ned shrugged Elias's hand away. "If I knew anything, don'tcha think I'd woulda told ya about it right away?"

Elias's face heated. "Well, I hope that you would."

"Did ya have anything missin' before ya hired Frank to lead the mules?"

"No, but—"

Ned clapped his hands. "There ya go! He's the one who done it, and I don't care what he says."

Elias drew in a deep breath and released it with a groan. "Since I have no proof that he stole anything, I suppose I'll have to take him at his word."

"Take who at his word?" Carolyn asked, touching Elias's shoulder.

He whirled around. "Oh, I didn't realize you were back."

She gave a nod. "I just got here and heard you talking about taking someone at his word."

"I was talking about Frank."

"What about him?"

Elias told Carolyn about the conversation he'd had with Frank.

"He accused me of it just now," Ned spoke up.

Elias shook his head. "I did not accuse you. I just—"

"It makes no never mind. The money's gone, and I think Frank took it." Ned rose to his feet. "The fish ain't bitin' today. Think I'll wait for you on the boat."

When Ned left, Carolyn took a seat on the rock where he'd been sitting. "Do you think Frank was telling the truth about not taking your things?" she asked Elias.

He shrugged. "I've got no proof that he did, so unless and until I do, I'll have to give him the benefit of the doubt." Elias started to rise, but she placed her hand on his arm.

"There's something I need to tell you."

"What's that?"

"It's about what Sarah told me while I was at her house, saying good-bye."

He frowned. "I'm not interested in anything she has to say."

"I think you will be when you hear what it is."

"I doubt it."

"Elias, please let me tell you what she said."

He folded his arms and stared straight ahead. "Go ahead, if you must."

"When I told Sarah how upset you were over her saying she could never marry a man like you, she said—"

"You discussed my feelings with Sarah?" Elias's jaw clenched so tightly that his teeth ached.

"Well, yes, and—"

"How could you, Carolyn? How could you even think of talking to Sarah about my reaction to her rejection of me?"

"Since you were so upset about it, I thought she had the right to know."

He shook his head. "Sarah doesn't care how I feel."

"Yes, she does, and she wasn't referring to the red mark on your face when she said she could never marry a man like you."

"What was she referring to?"

"She was talking about the fact that you're a boatman."

"You mean she'd be ashamed to be married to a boatman?"

"Not ashamed. Fearful."

"Of what?"

"That the canal might take you or one of her children the way it did her husband. She's also afraid that if she married a boatman, one of her children might be forced to become a mule driver, the way she and her sister were when they were girls."

Elias slapped his hand against his pant leg. "That's ridiculous! I'd never force Sarah's children or any children we might have of our own to lead my mules."

"That's good to hear. Why don't you tell Sarah that?"

He shook his head. "If she's fearful of the canal and

doesn't want to be married to a boatman, then I doubt she'd change her mind about marrying me."

"She might if she knew how much you loved her and if you gave her your word that you'd never make any of the children lead your mules."

Elias sat silently, mulling things over.

"If you don't do something soon, it might be too late."

"What's that supposed to mean?"

"Patrick's still after Sarah to marry him, and she plans to give him her answer by the time the canal closes for the winter."

"That's a few months away."

"Yes, but she might make her decision sooner, and if she chooses him, it'll be too late for the two of you."

"She'd probably be better off with Patrick than me."

"Why do you say that?"

"He's handsome and doesn't work on the canal."

"But if she doesn't love him. . ."

"It doesn't matter. Sarah won't marry me as long as I'm a boatman." Elias jumped up. "We need to get back on the boat. It's time we headed for Easton."

"Did you get the painting and tell the Coopers good-bye for me?"

"Yes, and I'm sure Mother will be very happy with her birthday present."

Carolyn sighed. "I wish we didn't have to go. I wish

we could stay right here and enjoy the sunshine and warm breeze blowing off the water."

"Well, we can't. I need to get to Easton, and so do you."

Chapter 34

*T*hroughout the month of September, Elias avoided Sarah. He'd been thinking about the things Carolyn had told him but wasn't sure what, if anything, he should do. If Sarah wouldn't marry him because he was a boatman, then even if he spoke to her about marriage again, she wouldn't change her mind. Yet if he didn't speak to her about it, she might end up marrying the blacksmith. Still, if Sarah wasn't going to give Patrick an answer until the canal closed for the winter, Elias had some time to decide what he should do.

Carolyn had also mentioned that she'd suggested to Sarah the idea of opening a bakery in town, but Sarah had said she didn't have the money for that. Elias felt bad that Sarah had to work so hard and struggle financially. If she married Patrick, she wouldn't have to worry about either of those things anymore.

"Ya look like you're a million miles from here," Ned said, joining Elias at the bow of the boat. "Whatcha thinkin' about anyway?"

"Nothing much." *Nothing I wish to talk about.*

Ned tipped his head back and sniffed the air. "Fall's definitely here. Can ya smell the musty odor from the leaves that have fallen on the ground?"

Elias gave a quick nod.

"Won't be long, and the canal will be closin' down for the season. Got any idea what you'll do durin' the winter months?"

"I haven't figured that out yet."

"Well, you'd better figure somethin' out soon, 'cause both of the boardin' houses in town fill up real quick with the boatmen who've got no homes of their own, and word has it that one of the boardin' houses might be up for sale, so that one could be gone by winter."

"I hear that some of the canalers live on their boats during the winter months."

"Yep, that's true. Think ya might do that?"

Elias shrugged. "Right now my plan is to stop at Cooper's store as soon as we get to Walnutport so I can pick up some supplies. Then we'll push on and get our load of coal picked up in Mauch Chunk before the end of the day."

"Ya still want me to steer the boat when we head into the lock at Walnutport?"

"Yes, I'll stay below until we get through, and then, unless you need something from the store, you can stay on the boat and keep an eye on things while I go in."

"Don't need a thing this time." Ned clicked his tongue noisily as he shook his head. "Sure don't make sense to me the way ya hide out below every time we go through that lock. Ya don't do it at the other locks we go through."

Elias gripped the tiller until his fingers ached. He wished Ned would stop plying him with questions—especially questions he'd rather not answer.

When Elias entered Cooper's store, he found Mike sweeping up some broken glass near the front window.

"What happened?" Elias asked.

Mike frowned. "Sometime during the night, someone broke into the store again. This time, they took even more items than before."

"That's a shame. Do you think it was done by the same person who broke in the other time?"

"I'm not sure, but I wouldn't be surprised."

"Several weeks ago someone stole something from me, too."

"Really? What'd they steal?"

"A can of money I had hidden in my cabin."

"Did they leave any clues?"

Elias shook his head.

"Well, they left one here." Mike reached under the front counter and produced a faded piece of blue material. "I found this stuck to a chunk of the glass that was still in the store window. I'm guessin' it came off the thief's shirt when he crawled through the window."

Elias pursed his lips. "Hmm. . . There's nothing unusual about the color of the material. I suppose it could belong to most anyone."

"But here's something interesting. Look at this." Mike pointed to a blotch of blood on the material. "Whoever came in through the window must have cut his arm on the broken glass."

Elias studied the material. "That's definitely a clue—or at least it would be if we knew who in the area had a cut on his arm." Whew! At least he knew for sure that it hadn't been Frank or Ned. They were definitely not here last night, and neither of them had a cut on their arm. "Have you looked around outside for any clues? It rained yesterday, so maybe the thief left some footprints."

"No, I haven't looked. Let's go see."

Elias followed Mike out the door. Sure enough, a pair of large footprints led to the window of the store.

"So we know it was a man," Mike said as they returned to the store. "Only trouble is there are a lot of men in the area with big feet."

"Have you notified the sheriff?"

"Not yet. I was going to do that as soon as Kelly had time to mind the store for me so I could go to town."

Elias was about to say that he would tell the sheriff, when the door opened and burly Bart Jarmon stepped in.

"Came to get a few supplies I didn't realize I still needed," he said, looking at Mike.

"That's fine," Mike replied. "Look around the store and get whatever you need."

Bart headed down one of the aisles and returned a few minutes later with several items, which he placed on the counter.

"That'll be ten dollars," Mike said after he'd added up Bart's purchases.

Bart reached into his pants pocket. As he fumbled, trying to get his money, a gold pocket watch fell out and landed on the floor.

Elias gasped. It was his missing watch—the one Grandpa had given him.

"Where'd you get that?" he asked Bart.

Bart's face colored as he bent to pick it up. "Found it. Can't remember where, though."

"Can I take a look at it?"

"What for?"

"I had a pocket watch like that, but it's missing."

Bart quickly stuck the watch back in his pocket. "What are ya sayin'? Are ya accusin' me of takin' your watch?" He squinted his beady eyes and glared at Elias.

Mike moved closer to Bart and pointed to the bandage sticking out from under the man's rolled-up shirtsleeve. Elias hadn't noticed it until now.

"What happened to your arm?" Mike asked.

The crimson color in Bart's face darkened, and rivulets of sweat beaded up on his forehead. "I...uh...cut myself on a piece of metal."

Mike looked over at Elias, then back at Bart. "Someone broke into my store last night, and I'm sure whoever did it cut their arm on the broken glass in the front window. You wouldn't know anything about that, would you?"

Bart's eyes narrowed as he shook his head. "And you've got no proof that I do."

"Maybe we ought to take a look around your boat," Elias spoke up. "Just to be sure you're telling the truth."

"I think that's an excellent idea," Mike agreed.

Bart shifted nervously and pulled his fingers through the sides of his dark, bushy hair. "There's no need for that—no need a'tall."

"Why's that, Bart?" Mike questioned.

Bart started edging toward the door, but Mike moved quickly to block it. Elias, his heart hammering in his chest, jumped in front of the door, too.

Bart scowled at them. "Get outa my way! Ya can't keep me here, ya know!"

Mike planted his hands on his hips and stared at Bart. "Then tell us what you know about the break-in here at my store."

Bart put up his fists like he was ready for a fight, but Mike didn't back down.

Elias had never been one for violence and didn't know what he'd do if Bart started swinging. He sure couldn't let Mike, who was several inches shorter and weighed a lot less than Bart, do battle with the brute alone. On the other hand, Elias wasn't sure how successful he and Mike would be, even if they both took Bart on. A man like Bart, whose breath smelled of liquor, might be a lot stronger than the two of them put together.

"All right, I'm the one," Bart blurted, staring at Mike with a look of defiance. "I broke into your store twice and woulda done it again if I'd run outa money." His gaze swung to Elias. "And yes, I came aboard your boat when you were docked here so you could attend one of them Bible-thumpin' preacher's meetings, and I stole your pocket watch and a bar of that white soap that floats. Then later, when you was docked near one of the stores in Mauch Chunk, I took the can of money."

White-hot anger welled in Elias's chest, and he had to take a couple of deep breaths to calm down. "Why, Bart?

What made you do such a terrible thing?"

"I'd like to know that myself," Mike put in.

Bart took a step back and leaned against the counter. "Things have been bad for me lately, and I was afraid I might lose my boat."

"How come? What's happened?" Mike wanted to know.

"I spent most of my money on liquor and gambling, and if I hadn't done somethin' quick, I'da been headed for the poorhouse."

"Stealing other people's property is not the answer," Elias said. " 'Thou shalt not steal' is one of God's commandments."

Bart slammed his left fist into his right hand. "I don't give a hoot nor a holler 'bout God's commandments! I live by my own rules. Have ever since I was a boy and my old man ran off and left me, Ma, and my three sisters alone to fend for ourselves."

"I understand you've had a hard life," Mike said, "but stealing's against the law, and now you'll have to go with us to see the sheriff."

Bart shook his head vigorously. "Uh-uh, no way! I'd rather die than go to jail." Bart lowered his head and barreled right between Mike and Elias, nearly knocking them off their feet. He jerked open the front door and dashed outside.

As soon as Mike and Elias regained their balance, they ran out the door after him.

Elias could see Bart up ahead, racing down the path in

the opposite direction of town.

A wagon pulled by two horses came out of nowhere. When Bart ran in front of it, the horses spooked and reared up. One of the horses struck Bart in the head, and he fell to the ground.

By the time Mike and Elias caught up to the scene of the accident, the driver of the wagon was on his knees beside Bart, shaking his head.

"He ran in front of me before I even knew what had happened," the man said, looking at Mike.

Blood oozed from Bart's head, and he didn't appear to be breathing.

Elias knelt down and felt for a pulse, but there was none. He looked up at Mike and slowly shook his head. "Bart's dead, and what a tragedy. Life is so short, and to waste it the way he did is a real shame."

"Yes," Mike agreed, "and now Bart's life is over, and he'll never have a chance to make restitution for what he did. Bart's last words to us were that he'd rather die than go to jail. It's sad to say, but the poor lost soul got his wish."

As Elias and his crew headed up the canal toward Mauch Chunk, he kept thinking about Bart and everything that had transpired after he'd been killed. Mike had gone to town to get the sheriff, as well as the undertaker, while Ned and Elias had searched Bart's boat for evidence. They'd not only found several items that had been taken from Mike's store, but also Elias's can, with what was left of his money. Of course, Elias had retrieved his watch from Bart's pocket before he'd boarded the man's boat.

"I'm going down to my cabin to put my money away," Elias told Ned. "Would you take over the tiller for me?"

"Sure thing, boss." Ned offered Elias a wide grin. "Sure am glad ya got some of your money back."

"So am I, but I wish it could have been under better circumstances."

Ned nodded solemnly. "Yeah, it's too bad about Bart. Wish he coulda found the Lord and turned his life around before he died."

"There are too many like Bart in our world," Elias said. "That's why we, who are Christians, should take every opportunity to witness to others about the Lord—not only through our words, but by our deeds."

"Yep, you're right, and that's just what I'm aimin' to do."

Elias thumped Ned's back. "I'm going below now, but I shouldn't be long."

When Elias entered his cabin, he decided that he needed to find a better hiding place for his money than under his bunk. He thought about putting it inside one of the small cabinets in the room, but figured that'd be one of the first places someone would look.

He glanced around, taking in every detail of the small, dimly lit cabin. Finally, his gaze came to rest on the old trunk sitting at the foot of his bunk. It had been Grandpa's trunk, where he'd kept his clothes and possibly a few other things. Elias had been meaning to go through it but just hadn't taken the time.

Maybe I could hide my money at the bottom of the trunk, he thought. *If someone should open it, they'll think it's just a trunk full of clothes.*

Elias knelt on the floor and opened the lid of the trunk; then he reached inside and removed a stack of clothes— shirts, trousers, and Grandpa's old straw hat.

He spotted something black and reached inside again. When he pulled it out, he realized it was Grandpa's Bible.

A lump formed in his throat. Many an evening when Elias and Grandpa had been on the boat together, Grandpa had shared several passages from the Bible.

Elias slid his fingers along the edge of the leather cover; then he opened the Bible to a place where a piece of paper stuck out. He quickly discovered that it was a letter that had been written to him:

Dear Elias,

After I'm gone, my boat will belong to you. It's yours to do with as you choose. I love this old boat, and it's given me many good years, but I know it won't be long before the canal era comes to a close. So if you decide not to captain the boat yourself, you're free to sell it, and then you can use the money to buy whatever you like.

Tears welled in Elias's eyes as he stared at the letter. *If Grandpa really meant what he said, then I have a decision to make. Should I keep the boat going for as long as I can, or sell it and find something else to do?*

Chapter 35

"How come we haven't seen Elias in so long?" Sammy asked Sarah one morning in early October.

"I'll bet he comes by when you're in school." Willis poked Sammy's arm with his bony elbow. "Besides, he don't stop to say hi to us no more, anyhow." He looked at Sarah. "Is Elias mad at you, Mama?"

Sarah blinked. "Now what made you ask such a question?"

"'Cause once I heard Uncle Mike say that Ned told him Elias hides out on his boat when he comes through the lock so he don't have to see you."

Sarah cringed. For some time, ever since she'd turned down Elias's marriage proposal, Ned had been the one steering the boat whenever it came through her lock. *Maybe Elias is still*

709

upset with me for turning down his marriage proposal. I hope
Carolyn explained my reasons to him. I hope he understands.

Willis tugged on Sarah's sleeve. "Is Elias ever comin' to
see us again? Is he, huh?"

"I don't know, son." She pointed to his bowl of mush.
"Hurry now and finish your breakfast. Hortence will be here
any minute, and I'd like us to have the dishes cleared away
before she arrives."

"I hope Elias is at church this Sunday," Sammy said. "I
sure do miss him."

I miss him, too, Sarah thought with regret. Her gaze came
to rest on the letter she'd placed on the counter. It was from
Carolyn and had arrived yesterday at Mike's store, which
also served as the local post office. Carolyn had told Sarah
some interesting things about Easton and mentioned how
things were going with the students in her class. But she'd
made no mention of Elias at all.

Willis nudged Sarah's arm. "Sure hope that mean
blacksmith's not at church this time. I don't like it when he
sits on the pew between us, Mama."

"Patrick is not mean. He's a nice man, and you shouldn't
talk about him that way," Sarah said with a shake of her
head.

"He's mean to Bristle Face," Helen spoke up. "I seen him
kick at our dog once when you wasn't lookin'."

Sarah flinched. Even after all these months of Patrick

coming around, the children—and the dog—still didn't care for him. She hadn't given him an answer to his proposal yet, and with the children feeling the way they did, she didn't know what to do. Would things be better for them if she married Patrick? Would the children learn to accept him as their stepfather?

Sarah took a sip of her tea and contemplated things further. *If I don't marry Patrick, how will I get my family away from the canal?*

She didn't have near enough money saved up in order to open her own bakery and she might never have enough. With winter coming, the only money she'd make would be from the bread she planned to sell in Mike and Kelly's store. As far as she could tell, her family's future looked hopeless. Maybe her only choice was to marry Patrick.

A knock sounded on the door, and a few seconds later, Hortence entered the kitchen.

"You don't have to knock every time you come over," Sarah said, smiling at Hortence. "You're like one of the family now."

Hortence smiled in return. "I realize that, but as Mother always says, 'You don't want to ever forget your manners.'" She motioned to the table. "I see you're still eating breakfast. I must be early this morning."

Sarah shook her head. "You're not early. We've just spent more time visiting than usual."

"We was talkin' about Patrick and how much he hates our dog," Willis said.

"Before that it was Elias we was talkin' about," Sammy added.

Hortence pulled out an empty chair at the table and sat down. "Speaking of Elias, did you know that he sold his boat and left the canal?"

Sarah's mouth opened wide. "He did?"

"That's right. Mother heard it from Mavis Jennings, and Mavis said she heard it from Freda Miller."

"Where'd Elias go?" A sense of sadness settled over Sarah like a heavy blanket of fog. "Did he move back to Easton?"

Hortence shrugged. "I'm not sure. I just know he's gone."

Sammy jumped up, nearly knocking over his glass of milk. "That's not fair! If Elias sold his boat and went away, we'll never see him again!" Tears welled in his eyes, and he started pacing.

"Calm down, Sammy. You're getting yourself all worked up." The truth was, Sarah felt pretty worked up herself, but she couldn't let the children or Hortence know that. Oh, how she wished things could have worked out for her and Elias, but under the circumstances, it was probably for the best that he was gone. If he'd stayed any longer, she might have weakened and changed her mind about marrying him. For her children's sake, she couldn't allow that to happen—not with him being a boatman.

Sammy stopped pacing and stomped his foot. "Wish I knew where Elias was. If I did, I'd go after him!"

Sarah reached out and pulled him to her side. "Elias must have had a reason for leaving. We need to accept his decision."

"Maybe he went back to Easton to work in his father's newspaper office," Hortence said. "Hauling coal up the canal means long, hard days, and he probably got tired of it."

Sammy cast Sarah an imploring look. "Can we go to Easton and see if he's there? Can we ask him to come back here, Mama?"

Sarah blinked against the tears clouding her vision. "No, son. We need to let him go."

"But I love Elias, and was hopin' he'd be our new papa someday."

Sarah's heart felt as if it would break in two. "It's not meant to be. Someday, if it's God's will, I might get married again."

At that moment, Sarah made a decision. As soon as she saw Patrick again she would give her answer to his proposal.

As Patrick headed for Sarah's place, he thought about what he was going to say to her. He'd given Sarah several months to make up her mind, and he was tired of waiting. Well, she'd better give him an answer today, or he might tell her to forget it. Sarah wasn't the only fish in the canal, and if she didn't want him, he was sure he could find someone who did.

He stepped onto her porch and rapped on the door. When it opened, Willis stood there with that scruffy terrier, who immediately began to bark and growl.

"Can I speak to your mama?" Patrick asked the boy, making sure he was talking loud enough to be heard.

"I guess so. She's in the house."

"Could you ask her to come outside? I'd like to speak to her in private."

Pulling the dog with him, Willis disappeared into the kitchen.

A few minutes later, Sarah showed up. "Good morning, Patrick. I was just thinking about you."

He smiled. "You were?"

"Yes, and I think we should talk."

He nodded. "That's why I'm here. I have something I need to say to you."

"What's that?"

He motioned to a grassy spot near the canal. "Can we go over there and talk?"

"Sure." Sarah followed him across the grass, and they took seats on a couple of boulders.

"What'd you want to say?" Sarah asked.

He moistened his lips with the tip of his tongue. "Well, I've been thinkin' about my marriage proposal."

"I've been thinking about it, too, and I've reached a decision."

"Before you tell me what you've decided, there's something I need to say first."

"What's that?"

"If you agree to marry me, then it'll have to be on one condition."

"What condition?"

"You'll have to get rid of that yappy dog."

Sarah's face blanched. "That's not going to happen, Patrick."

"You mean you won't get rid of the dog?"

"No, and I'm not going to marry you."

"Because the dog doesn't like me? Is that the reason?"

"Of course not."

"Then it's the kids, isn't it? I'm sure they don't like me either."

Sarah nibbled on her bottom lip. "The thing is. . .my kids loved their papa, and I don't think they're ready for me to get married again. Especially not to someone—"

"If the kids weren't in the picture, then would you marry me?"

Sarah scowled at him. "I'd never abandon my kids for any man!"

His face heated. "I'm not askin' you to leave your kids. I just wondered if things were different, and you didn't have any kids, would you have said yes to my proposal?"

Sarah slowly shook her head. "I don't think so, Patrick. You're a nice man, but you're not a committed Christian, and—"

"I've been goin' to church almost every Sunday for the past few months. Doesn't that show you something?"

"I know you've been in church, and I'm glad you have, but attending church doesn't make a person a Christian. You have to make a commitment to the Lord, and ask Him to forgive your sins and invite Him into your heart."

"I've been listening to the preacher's sermons, and givin' it some thought. Someday—maybe soon—I might be ready to take that step. Might even let the preacher baptize me in the canal next summer."

Sarah smiled. "I'm glad to hear you're considering that, but please don't do it for me. You have to want it in here." She touched her chest. "You have to want it because you know you need to seek forgiveness for your sins."

He nodded. "I realize that, but once I do become a Christian, will that change your mind about marrying me?"

"I'm sorry, Patrick, but I'm not in love with you, and without love, I'd never marry again." She touched his arm gently. "If you wait and seek God's will, I'm sure you'll find the right woman someday."

Patrick stood, trying to absorb all she'd said. He'd been hoping to get Sarah's answer, and he had. In one way, he felt disappointment. In another way, he felt relief. Maybe in time, he would find someone else, but when he went looking, he'd make sure that the woman he proposed to didn't have a yappy dog.

Chapter 36

*I*t's sure gotten quiet around here since the canal closed for the winter," Kelly said to Sarah as the two of them sat at Sarah's kitchen table, drinking a cup of tea one Saturday morning in the middle of December.

Sarah nodded and sighed. "It's good not to have to run outside all the time to let boats through the lock, but I'm worried that I won't have enough money to see us through until spring."

"But you don't have to pay Hortence for helping you now that you're here with the kids all day."

"True."

"And you get to live here, rent free."

"Uh-huh."

"Have you been saving some of the money you've

made from lock tending?"

Sarah nodded. "Yes, but I've been saving most of it in the hope that someday—"

A knock sounded on the door just then, and Sarah pushed away from the table. "I'd better see who that is."

When Sarah opened the door, her breath caught in her throat. "Elias! I. . .I thought you'd left the canal."

"I did, but I came back." He leaned against the doorjamb as though needing some support.

"We heard you sold your boat."

"That's true. I sold it to someone who doesn't have a home and wants to live on it all year."

"Oh, I see. What about Ned and your mule driver?"

"Ned's staying at the boardinghouse right now, and I sent Frank home with some money so his mother can feed her family while Frank goes to school." He motioned to the horse and buckboard secured to a nearby tree. "If you're not busy right now, I'd like to take you and the kids for a ride."

Sarah tipped her head. "Where would we go?"

"It's a surprise."

Sarah wasn't sure what to think of Elias's sudden arrival or of the fact that he wanted them to take a ride with him on this cold, snowy day, but she nodded agreeably and said, "Let's go inside and get the kids."

As soon as they entered the kitchen, the children left their seats at the table and swarmed around Elias.

"It's so good to see ya!" Sammy said, when Elias gave them all a hug. "Are ya back for good?"

"I hope so, but it'll depend on how things go." Elias looked over at Kelly and winked. At least Sarah thought it was a wink. Maybe he just had a snowflake stuck to his lashes.

"Elias wants to take us for a ride in his buckboard," Sarah said to the children. "So if you want to go, you'd better hurry and get your coats."

The children let out a whoop and raced upstairs. They were back in a few minutes, bundled up and wearing excited expressions.

Kelly rose from her seat. "I'd better get back to the store. I left the kids in Mike's charge, and if things have gotten busy, he might need my help." She smiled at Elias. "It's nice seeing you, and I hope things work out just the way you want."

Sarah got her coat, and then everyone filed out the door. While Elias helped Sarah and the kids into the buggy, Kelly headed for home.

"Where we goin'?" Willis asked, leaning over the seat back and tapping Elias's shoulder.

Elias grinned. "It's a secret, but we'll be there soon, and then you can tell me what you think."

"What we think about what?" Sarah asked.

"You'll see."

A short time later, Elias guided his horse and wagon into town and pulled up in front of a large, wooden building with two front doors facing the street.

"Here we are," he said, guiding the horse to the hitching rail.

"What are we doing at Martha's boardinghouse?" Sarah asked.

"It's not hers anymore," Elias said. "Martha moved to Easton to live near Bobby and his folks, and I bought Martha's place. Ned's staying here right now, but eventually he'll need to move."

Sarah stared at the building, then back at Elias. "Why would you buy a boardinghouse?"

"Are ya gonna live in town and let folks stay with ya?" Sammy asked.

Elias shook his head. "No, not at all." He pointed to the first door. "That one's the entrance to the newspaper office I'll soon be opening." He grinned at Sarah and then pointed to the other door. "That one's for you."

"For me?" Sarah's forehead wrinkled. "What are you talking about, Elias?"

"The downstairs is for your new bakery, and the upstairs can be your home."

"My. . .my bakery? My home?" she murmured.

He nodded. "Carolyn told me that she'd suggested the idea of a bakery to you, and that you seemed interested. She also explained that the reason you said no to my proposal wasn't because of the ugly red mark on my face, but because I was a boatman."

"That's true." She leaned closer and touched the side of his face. "Your birthmark has never bothered me. All I've ever seen when I've looked at you is your kind, gentle spirit."

Elias took both of Sarah's hands and held them in his. "Since I knew you wanted a fresh start, I used the money I got from the sale of my boat and bought this building."

Sarah sat in stunned silence. She'd never imagined that Elias would do such a thing.

"Would you say something, Sarah? Will you take the gift I'm offering?"

"Oh, Elias," she finally squeaked. "I couldn't accept such a generous gift."

"Why not?"

"It wouldn't look right for a widowed woman to accept an expensive gift from a man who's not even a family member."

"I think we could remedy that," Elias said with a twinkle in his eyes.

"Oh?"

He leaned close. So close that Sarah could feel his warm breath tickle the back of her neck. "Carolyn said you'd written and told her that you're not going to marry Patrick."

"That's correct. It wouldn't be right for me to marry a man I don't love."

Elias sat for several seconds; then he turned to her and said, "I love you, Sarah, and if you'll agree to marry me, then no one can say anything about you accepting an expensive gift from your husband."

"Yes! Yes!" Sammy shouted from the rear seat. "Say yes, Mama. Tell Elias that you'll marry him!"

Tearfully, and with a heart full of joy, Sarah nodded her head. "I love you, too, Elias, and I'm more than willing to become your wife."

Elias smiled and then looked over his shoulder at the children. "Turn your heads for a minute, please."

"How come?" Helen wanted to know.

"Because I'm going to kiss your mama."

Helen giggled and turned her head. The boys did the same. Then Elias slowly lowered his head and captured Sarah's lips in a kiss so gentle and sweet that she thought she might swoon.

Thunderous applause erupted behind them. Sarah, her cheeks growing warm, pulled slowly away from Elias and turned around. All three children wore wide smiles as they bobbed their heads in approval.

"We're gonna get a new pa!" Sammy shouted. "And we all love him so much!"

"Yes, we certainly do," Sarah said as she clasped Elias's hand.

Just then, Pastor William came running down the street,

his eyes wide, as he waved his hands.

Sarah's heart gave a lurch. Had something terrible happened?

"I knew you were going to be here showing Sarah the building you'd bought," Pastor William said, stepping up to the buggy. "So I had to come and tell you the good news."

More good news? Sarah could hardly contain herself.

"What is it?" Elias asked before Sarah could voice the question.

"The doctor's with Betsy, and she's just given birth to a baby boy!" Pastor William's smile widened. "We've decided to name him Hiram Abel Covington, after Betsy's father. Betsy thinks we should call him Abe, though. He'll probably like that better than Hiram."

Sarah smiled. "Congratulations! Tell Betsy I'll be over to see her and the baby as soon as she's had a chance to rest up."

"I will." Pastor William looked at Elias. "How's it going here?"

"She's agreed to become my wife." Elias grinned and lifted Sarah's hand. "We'll soon be running our businesses side by side."

"I'm happy it's all worked out. Congratulations to you both." Pastor William motioned to the parsonage down the street. "I'd better get home. See you all in church on Sunday!"

As Pastor William sprinted toward home, Sarah sat

staring at the side of the building that would soon be her new home and place of business. Apparently Pastor William, and perhaps even Kelly, had been in on Elias's little secret.

Sarah's heart overflowed with so much happiness that she thought it might burst. She reflected on the verse of scripture Pastor William had shared with the congregation the previous Sunday, Philippians 4:19: *"But my God shall supply all your need according to his riches in glory by Christ Jesus."* She knew with certainty that when God brought Elias Brooks into her life, He'd supplied all of her and the children's needs.

Epilogue

Six months later

*A*s Sarah worked contentedly in her bakery, a deep sense of peace welled in her soul. Not only was her new business venture working out well, but it gave her such joy knowing that her husband was happily working in his newspaper office next door. She no longer had to worry about her children living too close to the canal, nor about them growing up and being forced to work on the canal.

She grabbed a hunk of dough and began kneading it. So much had happened in the last six months. She and Elias had gotten married in the church here in Walnutport, and then Elias had taken her and the children to Easton to meet his family. Afterward, they'd gone to Roger and Mary's house to see Maria. Sarah was pleased at how well Maria was doing. Even though her sight had gotten worse, she seemed happy, and Mary was obviously taking good care of her.

Another thing that had happened after Sarah and Elias got married was that Ned had moved into the lock tender's house and taken over the responsibility of raising and lowering the lock. He seemed quite content with his new job, and often said he didn't miss riding on the boat at all.

Carolyn, too, had a new job. She'd left her old teaching position in Easton and moved to Walnutport to take over Mabel Clark's position, because Mabel had gotten married and moved to New York. Carolyn seemed happy teaching here, and of course, second-grader Sammy and Willis, who was now in the first grade, were thrilled to have Elias's sister as their new teacher.

Hortence, who'd been sure that she would always be single, had married Sam Abernathy, one of the farmers who lived in the area, and she seemed very content.

Two more surprising things had happened: Elias had made peace with his father, who was delighted when he heard that Elias had opened his own newspaper. Then there was Patrick, who'd recently given his heart to the Lord and had begun courting Carolyn.

Sarah smiled. She'd never imagined Carolyn and Patrick together, but then a year ago, she'd never dreamed that she'd be married to Elias, or that she'd be living in town, doing something she enjoyed.

"Umm. . .something smells awfully good in here," Elias said as he stepped into the bakery. "Have you got anything I can sample this morning?"

She swatted his hand playfully as he reached out to grab one of the oatmeal cookies cooling on a wire rack. "What are you doing over here? I thought you'd be hard at work in your office."

"I was, but I got hungry and knew you'd have something I could eat."

She chuckled and handed him a cookie.

"Are you happy, Mrs. Brooks?" he murmured against her ear.

"Oh yes, very much so."

Elias turned Sarah to face him and kissed the tip of her nose. "I've never been happier than I am being married to you, and I hope you have no regrets."

"None at all." Sarah leaned into his embrace and closed her eyes. She knew without a doubt that she had made the right choice. Elias was everything she could want in a husband, and what a wonderful father he was to her children. Someday, Lord willing, they might have a child or two of their own. In the meantime, she was going to enjoy every day the Lord gave her as Mrs. Elias Brooks.

Recipe for Sarah's Dough Dab

Ingredients:
4 cups flour
1 teaspoon salt
½ cup lard or shortening
5 teaspoons baking powder
Milk

Stir dry ingredients in a bowl with a spoon. Add enough milk to make a stiff dough. Roll out on a floured board and cut into round pieces. Put in a greased frying pan and fry until done. Turn as you would for a pancake. Brown on both sides, then serve as a bread substitute.

Author's Note

*T*he Lehigh Navigation System was completed in 1829, and boats began using the entire length of it by 1832. The canal era reached its peak in 1850, and continued to diminish until it came to an end in 1931. Today, visitors can still experience some of those exciting canal days at the Canal Museum in Easton, Pennsylvania. There's also a restored canal boat pulled by two mules that can be ridden at the Hugh Moore Park, which is also in Easton. The restored lock tender's house in Walnutport is another interesting place to visit, and of course, it's always fun to walk the towpath where the steady *clip-clop* of mule teams used to be heard. Whenever I'm in Pennsylvania, I always enjoy visiting various sections of the Lehigh Canal and reliving in my mind the glory of the canal era. For more information on the Lehigh Navigation System visit www.canals.org.

Discussion Questions for Sarah's Choice

1. Being a single mother was hard for Sarah, especially since she had to keep her home running and tend the lock, too. What are some things we might do to help a single mother? If you're a single mother, what are some things others have done to help you?

2. Sarah's children often competed for her attention. What happens when children don't get the attention they need? What are some things we can do to give our children and grandchildren the time and attention they deserve?

3. When Elias learned that his grandfather had passed away and left the canal boat to him, he decided to leave his job at his father's newspaper office and become a boatman. This caused a rift between Elias and his father. Is there ever a time when it's okay to go against our parent's wishes?

4. Elias felt insecure and self-conscious about his birthmark. He thought people judged him by his appearance. Why do you think some people judge others by their appearance and not by who they really are?

5. God sees what we're like on the inside, yet so often we focus on our own or other people's outward appearance.

What are some ways we can work on our self-esteem without becoming conceited or vain?

6. In *Sarah's Choice*, a misunderstanding between Sarah and Elias took place. What are some ways we can avoid misunderstandings with those we love?

7. Sarah felt trapped by having to work on the canal. Have you ever felt trapped when you were some place you didn't want to be? Sometimes God allows us to be in certain situations to help us grow emotionally or spiritually. Sometimes the very place we don't want to be is where He wants us. How can we distinguish between our wants and needs? How can we know God's will as far as where we should live and the job we should do?

8. Sarah, like many other people, had trouble accepting help from others. What are some ways we can show someone who needs our help that it's okay to let others do things for them?

9. Elias and Patrick were both good men, but to Sarah, Elias seemed more grounded. What do you think made the difference?

10. Sarah and Betsy became friends after Sarah lost her husband. How important do you think friendship is for a widow, and what can we do to make our friendships stronger?

11. What scriptures from this story spoke to your heart? How can you put them into practice in your daily routine?

About the Author

Wanda E. Brunstetter is a bestselling author who enjoys writing historical, as well as Amish-themed novels. Wanda's interest in the Lehigh Canal began when she married her husband, Richard, who grew up in Pennsylvania, near the canal. Wanda and Richard have made numerous trips to Pennsylvania, where they have several friends and relatives. They've walked the towpath, ridden on a canal boat, and toured the lock tender's house. Wanda hopes her readers will enjoy this historical series as much as she enjoyed researching and writing it.

Wanda and her husband have two grown children and six grandchildren. In her spare time, Wanda enjoys photography, ventriloquism, gardening, reading, stamping, and having fun with her family.

In addition to her novels, Wanda has written two Amish cookbooks, two Amish devotionals, several Amish children's books, as well as numerous novellas, stories, articles, poems, and puppet scripts.

Visit Wanda's Web site at www.wandabrunstetter.com and feel free to e-mail her at wanda@wandabrunstetter.com.

Other books by Wanda E. Brunstetter

Adult Fiction

The Half-Stitched Amish Quilting Club

<u>Kentucky Brothers Series</u>
The Journey
The Healing

<u>Lehigh Canal Series</u>
Kelly's Chance
Betsy's Return
Sarah's Choice

<u>Indiana Cousins Series</u>
A Cousin's Promise
A Cousin's Prayer
A Cousin's Challenge

<u>Sisters Of Holmes County Series</u>
A Sister's Secret
A Sister's Test
A Sister's Hope

<u>Brides Of Webster County Series</u>
Going Home
Dear to Me
On Her Own
Allison's Journey

<u>Daughters Of Lancaster County Series</u>
The Storekeeper's Daughter
The Quilter's Daughter
The Bishop's Daughter

<u>Brides Of Lancaster County Series</u>
A Merry Heart
Looking for a Miracle
Plain and Fancy
The Hope Chest

White Christmas Pie

Lydia's Charm

Love Finds a Home
Love Finds a Way

Children's Fiction

Rachel Yoder—Always Trouble Somewhere Series

The Wisdom of Solomon

Nonfiction

Wanda E. Brunstetter's Amish Friends Cookbook
Wanda E. Brunstetter's Amish Friends Cookbook Volume 2
The Simple Life
A Celebration of the Simple Life